50 P   Rosalyn   Sept. 1980
       Home   £3

Departures

Departures

A NOVEL BY Jane Bernstein

ALLEN LANE

ALLEN LANE
Penguin Books Ltd
536 King's Road
London SW 10 0UH

First published in the U.S.A.
by Holt, Rinehart and Winston 1979

First published in Great Britain by Allen Lane 1980
Copyright © Jane Bernstein, 1979

ISBN 0 7139 1355 X

Printed in Great Britain by
Billing & Sons Ltd
Guildford, London and Worcester

To Paul
and in memory of my sister Laura

Departures

LYDIA RAN. She didn't think about the steady motion of her legs though they carried her around and around, twenty laps to a mile, seventy laps already run. The laps flew by unnoticed but recorded by the thumb of her right hand. Independent from the rest of Lydia, the finger pushed down and advanced the number on the lap counter each time she passed the starting point. Every day she ran. Most days she ran five miles in forty minutes. When her father died, she ran ten very fast miles.

The track was narrow and lined the perimeter of the gym. The men played basketball below. Lydia always watched the game. Today she didn't see Russian Dancer, and it disturbed her. For months she'd watched him skitter across the court, feet apart, half in a squat, Russian dancer style. His sneakers made a loud complaint as he edged sideways. The man kept his long, gray hair out of his eyes with a woven headband, and his gym shorts were always freshly pressed. The man with enormous hairless thighs was playing. He wore an oval sweat stain, the exact shape of the track, from neck to waist, and his glasses, far too small for his face, looked as if they'd permanently narrowed his head where the earpieces hit. Lydia had considered running outdoors on nice days but part of the running was the basketball game, the echo of grown-up male voices yelling like kids.

She noticed the new player before the others on the team did. He wore shorts that were really boxers with the fly sewn up, and socks that swam around his ankles after only one dribble. He was tall and broad-shouldered, with glossy hair, dark and straight as an Indian's. Lydia ran, one lap like the second and third. The new player leaped high, graceful as a diver. Each time Lydia ran a lap, each time her thumb advanced the number, he was in midair, high and arched, his black hair blown back from his face.

One lap forty seconds, two laps eighty. The new player began to show up every day. Whenever Lydia looked down onto the court there he was, frozen in midair for her. She began to come earlier to the gym, change into her shorts and T-shirt and rush upstairs to the track while the team was still warming up. She wanted to catch all of the game. Lydia was afraid one day the basketball player would disappear as abruptly as he'd come.

And one day he didn't show up. Russian Dancer, Hairless Thighs, Black Beanstalk, Bandaged Knees—all the regulars were warming up, taking turns sinking the ball into the basket. From above they looked unconcerned about the absence of the new player. What Lydia didn't know was that the basketball player was running half a lap behind her on the track. In moments he closed the gap. She ran, troubled but unaware of his presence. The basketball player wasn't interested in running five miles. He wanted to limber up by racing a couple of laps, fast ones, so he wouldn't be replaced downstairs. And he, with perfect coordination and twenty-twenty vision, ran straight into Lydia, who possessed neither, causing the first four-person crash ever to take place on the McBurney YMCA track. Lydia tripped and skidded across the track, her body buttressing the fall of the other two runners. Kramer, after causing the accident, hopped off the track and waited on the platform above. He tried to apologize to Lydia, but her hip was bruised, her ankle twisted; the effort of walking twelve steps consumed all her senses. He crept up beside her and, stooping to catch her eye, gestured, mouth forming words of apology. Lydia stood on her good leg and waited for the elevator, hardly aware of him. What if the damage was permanent? Could she live without running? She hurt.

Kramer prided himself on being an honest person, and with justification too. After catching up with Lydia at a red light a few blocks from the Y, and persuading her he wasn't so hard up he had to knock her over just for the chance to say hello, he said, "I'm glad we've met, though. I like you."

"Ditto," she said, because by this time she liked him, too.

She was still limping from the injury; he shuffled close beside in an effort not to overtake her. Their dreams were revealed before the other data: name, age, place of birth. He was a filmmaker, accidentally sidetracked into being a sound editor shortly after he finished school. Now, six years later, he was struggling to get out by writing a screenplay, what he hoped was a commercial property. Someday he wanted to direct.

Lydia told Kramer merely that she was a graduate student, because she wasn't in the habit of revealing more than that. But with his encouragement, as they walked south on Seventh Avenue, she narrowed it down. Graduate student in what? Biology. Entomology, now that he asked. Actually, she was a myrmecologist, an entomologist who studies ants. Lydia couldn't bring herself to look at him. Something unexpected could happen. She might wrap her arms around him and refuse to let go. True, it had never happened, but ... Meanwhile, he wanted to know what kind of ants, so she told him. *Neivamyrmex nigrescens,* a species of army ants found in temperate climates. Why ants? he asked. Lydia laughed. This was the standard question, but never had she heard it asked with such genuine curiosity. Not why *ants,* but what about them; tell me. So she did. By the time they reached Sheridan Square, her leg was throbbing, but she felt elated. Before they left each other, he said, "I'm really glad we talked, but I have to make sure I don't get to like you too much."

Lydia didn't know there was such a thing as too much until he said, "I'm going out with another woman." Then she thought she understood, though his honesty still unnerved her.

"Ditto—substitute man," she said. She wouldn't have told him if he hadn't told her.

"But I really like you a lot. Do you want to go out Friday?" She did.

He was late on Friday, and buzzed the downstairs bell at nine, not eight. Lydia, in the hour's wait, had decided she was a forgettable woman, and, so forgotten, an awkward woman and dumb. Kramer, this strange man, had made a date but hadn't remembered, it meant so little, while she searched in the dim light for half-hidden coffee mugs. straightened the papers on her desk, looked at her teeth in the bathroom mirror. Why this? Why anything? What is too much? She buzzed back. It took him three minutes to walk the six flights, which meant he wasn't used to stairs. There was a light rap on the door. Would she remember what he looked like? She opened the door. A glimpse, a rough hello, and Lydia turned and walked toward the darkened living room. She sank into the rocker so he wouldn't sit there first, and while he stumbled through the kitchen, into the living room, she closed her eyes and was running, flushed and invigorated, one foot, another foot, white shoes, green suede markings like warpaint on the sides, her breathing hard and regular and no more connected to her body than the echoes of the basketball players. She opened her eyes, unable to believe that the tall black-haired basketball player was on her couch, that it was his voice saying, "It's dark in here. How do you see?"

"I don't need to see, I get around by feel. Reach to your left."

He said, "Much better," when he'd switched on the light. It hurt her eyes. She took off her glasses and put her hands over her face. There were red lines where the light seeped in. She spread her fingers a fraction and the red lines were replaced by pure white light, a little at a time, until her eyes could tolerate the brightness. Kramer said he liked the apartment. He asked who put up the bookshelves. She laughed, not answering. There were books from the ceiling to the floor on either side of the window. Kramer got up and ran his finger along the bindings on one row. He said, "What neatness! Are these in size order?"

"Actually they're arranged in Lydia decimal system—sort of by subject, but not always. I know where everything is, though."

"Okay, close your eyes."

Lydia kept her glasses off. That was enough. She heard the sound of a heavy volume sliding from its space. *"Big Fleas Have Little Fleas,"* he said.

"Easy. Left-hand side, third shelf from the bottom, I think. It's filed with the invertebrates. I'd know the exact slot by feel."

"Jesus Christ."

"You think it's crazy, huh?"

"Being organized is terrific, it's an asset. Every few months I make a resolution. I say, Time to clean up your act, Kramer. I devise systems too. Last time, starting with the desk drawers, I sorted everything into a Yes pile, a No pile, and a Maybe pile. I'm at it for about a half-hour when I come across this reel with the last twenty minutes of *Duck Soup* on it. Christ, that belongs to Marty Greene. It must be six months since I've seen Mart, so I call him up and we have a few beers. A week later I'm so goddamned tired of tripping on all the stuff, I shove it back in the drawers again."

"I'm not so clean," Lydia said. The rocker creak-creaked. "Just neat. I don't shower twice a day or wax floors or anything."

Kramer roamed around the little room, touching surfaces: her desk, the cabinet, the long, low table. He didn't believe she wasn't as clean as she was neat. Lydia didn't know why, but it bothered her. Maybe it was because someone else's image of her rubbing and scrubbing the apartment was as distasteful as doing it. So she held her arms straight out and let him look at her nails. They were rimmed with rusty brown, nearly black underneath. Kramer collapsed onto the couch and fidgeted with the lamp switch, giving them bursts of light and darkness.

"I'm teasing; it's not as bad as it looks. The lighter brown around the edges—now stop hiding your eyes and listen. The lighter brown is stain from silver nitrate and this darker stuff under my nails is coffee. I have a coffee grinder and I use my fingers to get at the grounds under the blades. Which reminds me, do you want some? Coffee, that is."

He said no, but would she like to take a walk? She said okay.

She heard the leaves rustle and thought the breeze outside might cool them off. They got ice cream cones on Christopher Street and the ice cream melted faster than the tongue could lap. Kramer and Lydia tried so hard to keep the drips from going farther than the fingertips that not a word was spoken for two blocks. Up the arm was bad; on the shirt was worse.

There were more dogs than people on the street: stray dogs, tied-up dogs, dogs out for their nightly constitutional. Those without dogs were inside air-conditioned restaurants and bars. The glassed-in sidewalk cafés that lined Seventh Avenue were all crowded. Lydia felt as if she and Kramer, sweating and sticky, were an attraction as they walked by, he so tall and handsome, bounding down the street, and she five foot naught, skipping to keep up. "Do you want a beer?" Kramer asked.

"Not really, but let's go inside, it's fine with me."

He didn't stop. They walked north, then west, ending up on Hudson Street, quiet and dogless.

"Can I hold your hand?" he asked.

"Sure."

A long arm reached out and her hand was captured, her fingers entwined with his.

"Fucking hot."

"Yeah."

"And humid."

"That's for sure."

"You think I'll miss ninety-degree summer evenings or dog shit on the streets or junkies or panhandlers?" He stopped, shouting at her. "You're crazy, no way, I won't—none of it, I tell you."

A foghorn blew. The long and mournful song echoed in the streets.

"You're leaving the city?"

"The sooner the better."

Lydia didn't know what to say. They'd just met, she couldn't give him a reason to stay.

"Did you ever hear how Nathaniel Weinstein changed his name? He followed Horace Greeley's advice—'Go west, young man.' Me too. Hey, remember the last scene in *Day of the Locust*?"

"Oh God."

"What's this, 'Oh God'?"

Lydia saw her father, pale white, stuck in an inner tube, flapping his hands. She and her sister had jumped up and down, Oh Daddy, please, Daddy, and he built the pool and now he had to learn to swim in it.

"L.A. is death," she said. *Driving, driving, a Los Angeles man was killed today* . . .

"To you, maybe." There was an edge to his voice. "New York is death to me."

"All right, I'm sorry. Let's not get offended."

"That 'Oh God' usually comes from someone who hasn't ventured farther west than Beaver Falls, P.a."

If he was truly offended, he would free her hand, but he didn't. They walked down to the river and shared a bench by the pier, the only blatant heterosexuals around. Kramer started talking again. Maybe he hated the city because of his professional frustrations here. He was union and made good money, but because of the union he couldn't get any work except as a sound editor. To work steadily in New York, you had to take on industrials and do ads. In L.A. there was work on features and in TV. He could avoid the union and branch out. Kramer liked to talk, and to Lydia it was wonderful listening to someone who still had dreams. She was bored with cynicism and lethargy; she was tired of people who'd never known defeat yet had given up years ago. Kramer spoke in exclamations. He liked it when she teased and prodded him.

"Here's a question for you," she said when he was through with Los Angeles for the time. "What's Mr. Winchell's first name?"

"Walter," he said. Actually, it was Walder the way he said it, and Lydia laughed.

"Walder," she said. "Marvelous. You're from Philadelphia."

"Cheltenham, and I'm amazed. Either you have a very good ear, or I'm regressing. I haven't spent more than a week there in ten years. How about you? Are you a New Yawker?"

"No. West, young man. Brentwood."

"Brentwood? That's Los Angeles."

She nodded.

"What a close-mouthed little thing! If I didn't ask you until next month, you wouldn't volunteer it, would you?"

"Probably not." Because he said next month, she felt encouraged. Lydia put an arm around Kramer.

"Do your parents still live out there?"

"Same house I grew up in."

"What does your father do—he isn't a movie mogul, is he?"

You don't spring bad news on strangers, Lydia thought. You don't say my father died last month because then you get silence, as if death were a communicable disease, highly contagious.

"He lawyers."

"Do you say *bitchin'*?"

"Sure."

"Shirr," he said, mimicking her. "Christ, you're too much. You up for a beer yet?"

Lydia said she wasn't, but it shouldn't stop him. They got up and walked toward Hudson Street. Kramer stopped into a deli and bought a six-pack. Then they went back to Lydia's apartment.

Lydia put on a dim light. Kramer lay on his back near the window, the beer can on his chest rising and falling as he breathed. He stroked the carpet. He liked the apartment, he said again. He liked the soft-cushioned rocker and the old velvet couch. He thought the mystery man had done a fine job on the shelves.

Creak-creak went the rocker as Lydia moved back and forth.

"I just can't believe you're a California girl."

"Because I'm not blond and beautiful?"

"And because you look like an immigrant's daughter."

Never was *and* used with such honesty.

"Not Russian. Russian immigrant daughters have big tits and skinny legs. You have nice legs and—brown eyes. Russian immigrant daughters have blue eyes. Los Angeles. Let's see. Are you Mexican?"

"Sí, Cisco," she said, lying.

Kramer sat up and helped himself to another beer. He didn't mind that Lydia was quiet, but he did mind that she wouldn't drink. "A sip?" he asked. "A taste?"

Midnight; the hour for dreams. Kramer revealed his master plan. He was going to start all over again in L.A. He was going out there to hustle until he got a picture to direct. Any picture. Back in film school the movies he'd written and directed won prizes, and his friends thought it was incredible luck getting a job apprenticing a sound editor when he graduated. Anything in movies was terrific when you believed in the old work-your-way-up myth. "It doesn't exist, Lydia. I'm a great sound editor now, one of the best in town, but you know what it'll get me? More jobs as a sound editor."

The pay was excellent, and he always had more work than he could handle, but it was tedious, a drudge. He spent his days and half his nights in a studio; he sat on his ass in a room. Meanwhile, the friends who went out to Hollywood were making nurse movies, stewardess movies, movies about student teachers, bikers, kung fu killers, militant black women, militant black women who rode bikes and were kung fu killers—whatever was in style. "Not the *X*-rated pornos," he said. "But the kind of movies middle-American high school kids watch at the local drive-in. They're made cheap and premier in Richmond, Virginia. If they hit New York at all, it's for a short run, second on the bill on Forty-second Street. My friend Keith's new movie is playing in Union, New Jersey, at the drive-in. It's called *Air Follies*. Stewardesses. If it makes money, he'll get to pick the next one he does. As soon as I have enough stashed away, I'm packing up."

Kramer finished four cans of beer telling Lydia stories that were filled with faces and bodies and outrageous events. She found it funny that what he liked about Los Angeles were the things she'd most wanted to escape. "Cars! Rock and roll on car radios! Sunshine in the day, movies at night! Spanish-style stucco houses! Blue-eyed blonds!" Kramer rapped himself on the chest and slapped his hand over his mouth. "One day it hit me, six years I've been in that sound studio working with a bunch of guys who talk it up about the big break. They're lifers. They'll never leave. And if I don't make my move now, I'll get fat and lazy, too."

"Risk," said Lydia, "I'm a firm believer in it."

"Are you?"

Kramer was lying on his side, stroking the carpet. "Lydia?" he said, his voice soft.

"What?"

"Do you want to neck?"

She laughed too loudly to pretend she hadn't.

"What's so funny? I don't see what's so funny."

She tried to tell him she wasn't laughing, but she was, uncontrollably, stupidly, since she did want to neck. "The word—" she finally got out.

"Neck?"

"Neck," she repeated, the laughter deep, bubbling up again. It wasn't the word, though, it was nervousness.

"What am I supposed to say? Make out? Is that what they say in Los Angeles?"

"Smooch," she said, stalling now, scared and excited.

"Spoon." Kramer took a last swallow of beer and rolled onto his back. He looked up and out the window.

Had he changed his mind so soon? "I do," she said. "Want to neck."

Kramer got onto his knees and crawled over to Lydia. She slid off the rocker, onto the floor. She was frightened. Usually she was kissed without anticipating the moment, without permission or discussion. She'd never waited so long for a kiss or wanted one so badly. Kramer knelt in front of Lydia and held his arms out. She leaned into his embrace, wanting the safety of this stranger's warmth. The smell of freshly swallowed beer was pleasant, but she could only hide her face and hold him, touching shoulders, broad and bony, neck, salty, sweating, damp. "Neck," she said.

He held her face and gently kissed her, and Lydia trembled, feeling young and inexperienced. It was wonderful. She hardly breathed. Yet when he kissed her, she held back, unable to give way completely. Sitting cross-legged kept him distant, too. She felt his hands on her shoulders and was rigid. "I can't feel you," he said. "Don't you like me?"

"I do."

Kramer let go of her and lay on his back, moon bright on his face. She crept over and rested in the crook of his arm, frightened, hungry. He stroked her face and sang "Lydia oh Lydia," softly, as he had when they'd walked home from the Y. She lay half on his chest. half on the floor. Wanting to feel his flesh, she untucked his shirt and placed her hand on his belly. He shivered, took her hand, kissed the fingers, rubbed them, said, "A hot, sticky night and such cold fingers." He was smooth and soft, very smooth. His skin was lovely. Kramer released her hand and she put it back, then let it creep upward. His chest was hairless, his rib cage sharp and bony, a plateau above the hollow of his belly. He held her close and kissed her mouth, her nose (took off her glasses), her eyes. She loved it and knew she had to say stop. It wasn't modesty or reserve, but Lydia couldn't sleep with Kramer and the question of when to tell him made her tense, unyielding. Before they necked was pushy, premature. He was friendly, sensual in an introductory way, but it was hard to believe he wanted more than friendship. She couldn't understand why he might want her for something else. Don't wait for Adonis on your doorstep, Lydia, her mother had said when she turned sixteen. Take what you can get. Lydia knew she could make waiting at bus stops fun and could liven up breakfasts with burlesque, but Kramer didn't know that. He only knew the exterior, the surface. He was warm and loving and she didn't want him to stop.

Kramer took his shirt off and helped Lydia with hers. She lifted her arms for him. The breeze from the open window tickled her bare back. Then his broad hands, his long blunt fingers. Flesh against flesh, they turned onto their sides, then twisted again, until she was lying on top of him. She was lost, kissing him. Then he stopped and she remembered. She stiffened and he felt it.

"What is it?" he said. "What's the matter?"

What word to say? Something neither crude nor euphemistic. Lydia wasn't used to thinking things out, and so was silent.

"What's the matter?"

"Actually . . ." Her voice felt loud, conversational. "Actually, I like you a lot, and I'd like to sleep with you a lot. That is, I'd like a lot to sleep with you."

"A lot."

"A lot."

"But you're engaged to a wonderful—"

"No wait—" Lydia straddled his chest. The coolness from the open window was exquisite. "The reason I didn't drink tonight is because I'm taking antibiotics—"

"Penicillin?"

She nodded. In the darkness, he may not have seen, but he didn't need to. He said, blasé, matter-of-fact, "Oh, you have the clap."

"Actually—"

"Yes?"

"Actually—"

"Yes."

"Hey, I'm really sorry."

"Yeah, well I'm sorry too, but don't feel bad or anything."

He kissed her. Lydia lay motionless, warm in his arms. "I'm glad you told me," he said.

"I couldn't not, could I?"

"It's been done."

"I should've said something earlier, but I wanted to neck."

He kissed her again.

Lydia felt miserable. Magic is fragile and she'd broken the spell. The world outside rushed into the forefront, the itch of the rug on her bare skin, the stifling heat, now breezeless, the happy birthday chorus outside.

Happy birthday, dear How-ie . . .

Kramer pulled Lydia close to him and stroked her head, hair all tangled and wiry. "Are you going to send me home?"

"Oh no," she said. "Please stay."

It was a splendid first night. There was a faint breeze from the window above the bed, sometimes moving the heavy air, more often lost in the folds of the curtains. They slept in each other's arms despite the heat.

It was so different from Lydia's nights with other men, who, strangers or not, slept large and hot on the other side of the bed, all making her aware of their strange smell, each different, each the same, waking her once, twice, or more for love, or she waking them. Other nights it was damp skin, hair sometimes, strong arms sometimes, hard and bony, one or two with fleshy bellies or backs. They all slept on the other side of the bed. They were all nice in some ways. Lydia had a sensor for callousness and cruelty and she asked for none of it and she stood for none. Still, when Carl or Robbie, Jack or Louis was there, she woke up wanting the bed to be hers alone, needing the morning without them. She often wondered why the morning sickness, and put it down to exhaustion, stickiness, the fact that she was a loner and needed her solitude. Lydia hated breakfast with a lover, horrible, forcing herself to down a half-glass of orange juice, sitting with her face red and sore from the heavy bearded ones, her legs cramped from the ones who worked her roughly. She always tried to stay at the man's house so she could dress the first moment of conscious-ness and tiptoe out, leaving four-word notes, "Good-bye, it was nice," then running when she hit the early morning air. Lydia loved rising and escaping at 6:00 A.M., so she could sail down the empty streets, with only news trucks or street cleaners for company in her freedom. With Kramer it was different. She slept entwined, the whole night wrapped in his arms. The heat meant nothing, they slept together. They kissed and stroked each other tenderly and the only time words passed be-tween them was when Kramer asked, "How much longer do we have to wait?"

Lydia had never been part of a we before, and she loved the sound of the word. "Just a week," she said.

In a drowsy voice, his hands tucked between her legs, "Here's to some wicked basketball."

He was nearly asleep when Lydia said, "Will you see me before the week's up?"

"You don't want me to?"

"Oh, I do."

In the morning, his arms were still around her and his hair shone black and thick. While he was still asleep, his lips parted, she saw small pushed-in teeth. She put her thumb on one and indeed it seemed as if the pressure of someone else's thumb had done just that. He opened his eyes and smiled. Could she matter to him? Could her presence make an imprint?

He got out of bed and stood naked and unashamed in front of the menagerie around and on top of her bureau. There were mealworms in a globe, rustling in their bed of bran, and on the floor, a five-gallon jug for brine shrimp. He was peering inside the largest terrarium: Drosophila, ant lion, Colorado potato beetle (her first love, at six). She was uneasy, and longed for him to know everything at once so she could be saved from the painful process of revealing herself bit by bit, bad with the good. She wanted history, a past to depend on.

"A centipede," he said, tapping on the glass where the terrarium was partitioned. The centipede was long, slender, and motionless except for its antennae, sensing Kramer. So was Lydia. His body was fair-skinned, his legs long and well shaped. She walked up behind him to put her hands on his back, his ass, round and verging on fullness.

"He's a beauty," said Kramer.

"You think so? Actually, he's only second best. The big one died last week."

"And that?" Pointing to a black animal, rolled into a spiral, countless legs worn like a fringe.

Lydia wished he'd stop tapping on the glass. "A millipede," she said, stroking his arms, trying to reach his hands.

"What does he eat?"

"I feed this one bananas or dog food—he likes oranges a lot. The one behind him loves cucumbers but couldn't care less about oranges."

"So bugs are really your whole life?"

"Yeah, my whole life," Lydia said, laughing.

Kramer pulled Lydia closer, her breasts against his back. "You know what Barbara Stanwyck says to Henry Fonda, don't you?

"No—"

"What a life."

2

SOMETIMES Lydia moved in ballroom steps. For every step she took forward, she took two backward. When Kramer left her on Saturday afternoon, she felt lonely and unable to work. She missed him terribly. Mimicking her Zeyde, she said, So? If you like him so much, you call him! But she didn't. Sunday was too soon. Monday she was too tired. Tuesday she spent the night with Carl. Wednesday, replaying the image of Kramer in the doorway, blue T-shirt, black hair, so beautiful, Lydia decided she'd put far too much importance on their chance collision. Still, when the buzzer rang on Wednesday, Lydia immediately thought, Kramer. Who else could be downstairs, unannounced on a Wednesday night? She didn't answer. It was a vagrant, hoping to sleep in the lobby, a thief, wanting to break in. She'd spent the day working at home and hadn't once used her voice. She was a strange, unwashed gnome, living here in darkness. The buzz came in staccato bursts. Lydia was thankful it wasn't held down, a siren in her kitchen. A half-hour later, there was a longer buzz. "La la la," Lydia said. Her voice was hoarse, but usable; her final analysis was that if on the off-chance it was for her, it would be bad news. She didn't want bad news. She'd rather wait till morning. She'd rather be out to lunch.

Later the phone rang. In a reflexive move, she picked up the receiver. It was Kramer. To excuse her passivity, or what in her own mind was passivity, she said, "Oh, I was just about to call you."

"Were you? That's nice."

Cars splashed in the streets.

"I've been out of town or I would've called sooner. I had to talk to some people at U.S. Steel."

"Oh, Pittsburgh."

"You mean, Ohhh, Pittsburgh."

Horns, voices, it was hard to hear, so Lydia said nothing, waiting instead. He waited, too. Then coughing, uncomfortable: "I just wanted to call and say hi, see how you were doing—"

"Are you in a phone booth?"

"Stick your head out the window."

"Oh Kramer, that one has no door. You must be soaked. Why don't you come upstairs?"

"Your buzzer is broken."

"Then I'll come down," she said, hanging up, scurrying around, regretting the decision. She put on a clean shirt, brushed her teeth, then tried to get the telltale toothpaste smell out of her mouth. She felt giddy like an adolescent, scared and miserable. Five minutes passed; poor Kramer, shivering in the vestibule. She was sorry she lied. It was raining and windy. She could have dried his hair, rubbed his back with a Turkish towel. Lydia ran down the stairs, all yellow in her slicker. She stopped dead still before opening the door, seeing his back, also in a yellow slicker. He turned and saw her, so she walked out, said Hi, hello, real breezy, cool, nonchalant, and went past him into the street, avoiding his eyes. Had anything ever passed between them? She chattered on about (what else?) the weather, how humid it was, how she couldn't comb her hair when it rained like this, how she had a friend in Pittsburgh, how she'd been working her ass off (in her cool green room, but she didn't say that). She told Kramer about John, her super, bizarre but attentive, and how inconvenient it was for the buzzer to be busted, and all the time she chattered, her mind was on the man who'd shared her bed on Friday. So the man who stood beside her now distracted and frightened her. Maybe he'd find out. What if she said "It feels so good" instead of "This is my first time out today." She couldn't bear looking at Kramer because she knew she was ruining everything.

At the stoplight on Seventh Avenue, Lydia ran out of nervous energy and could think of nothing else to say. Kramer was quieter than she remembered. He didn't speak until they crossed the street. Then, "Are you taking me someplace?"

Lydia hadn't thought about it.

"Do you want to go to the Peacock?"

"The Peacock," she said. "That's my favorite place." Then worrying about being a me-too girl, she set about describing the place to prove she knew it intimately: the cracked plaster and Italian Renaissance art, the whoosh as the huge brass cappuccino machine whipped milk, the lone, shuffling waitress.

They got a window seat inside the café. Kramer took the bench by the door and Lydia sat on a wobbly wrought-iron chair. They stared intently at the menus. Kramer wanted to prove things, too. Had she tasted the rum cake? Had she tasted the apple torte? Of course; had he tasted the granita di caffè? The lone, shuffling waitress, black dress, world's most tired eyes, stopped at their table. Lydia said, "Hi, how are you?" and was embarrassed, getting no reply. Both Kramer and Lydia ordered only cappuccino.

The cappuccino came and they sat in silence. Lydia skimmed off the steamed milk with her spoon. Kramer blew into his cup until it cooled. They watched the wet and angry passersby outside as if they were of interest. But Lydia didn't want to be a spectator that night and in the midst of their terrible silence, she said, "Can I come sit by you?" She was surprised hearing her words which came out entirely unplanned. Kramer nodded, pleased. He moved to the right to make room for her on the bench.

"I really like you," he said. "I missed you when I was away."

"Did you? It's just pheromones."

Kramer put his hand on her thigh, but it was motionless, the fingers hardly resting. His hand had forgotten it had caressed her a few nights before. "It must be what?" he said.

"Pheromones. Female insects secrete a sexual attractant so powerful the males pursue them for miles. I've seen it duplicated in the lab thousands of times, and I'm still amazed." Outside of school she rarely got to talk about insects, but Kramer was so receptive she went on. The most highly publicized work with pheromones had been done with gypsy moths. Had he read about that? Basically, the female moth has within her at least .01 micrograms of gyplure, a sexual attractant. If she were to secrete all .01 micrograms (a millionth of a gram) she could theoretically excite more than a billion males. But that wasn't all pheromones were used for. With *Neivamyrmex nigrescens,* probably the most extraordinary social insects, pheromones were used for all forms of communications: to guide workers in search of food and new home sites; for alarm signals when the ants were in trouble; as an aid in grooming. *Neivamyrmex* were totally blind. How did he think they knew how to identify dead ants? Pheromones the deceased gave off. And guess how an ant could tell what sex another ant was? Pheromones again. And that was only a start. One day scientists would prove conclusively how important pheromones were in human attraction as well.

Kramer said, "So my decision to run on the track that day was biochemically triggered. I was drawn, blindly. I got so close for the fatal whiff I tripped you."

"Which is why I forgave you," Lydia said. "You couldn't help yourself."

And all along he thought it was her legs.

They spent the night together, but they didn't make love. Kramer said, "Do I have to say it's your pheromones I like? Okay, I will. I like your special Lydia pheromones."

He left New York for five more days.

Falling in love was not wonderful. For the most part, Lydia found it extremely debilitating. Two weeks before, when she ran she felt she could run forever and when she sat in the lab, she could work for hours on some minute, exacting detail. Now nothing quite held her interest. Her mind wandered. She ran faster than before, but feeling like a hamster on a wheel, around, around, she ran three miles instead of five. The only difference between falling in love and being thrown over and broken-hearted, she decided, was that loving Kramer, for all the physical pain she felt, also gave her some expectation. She had moments when the pain was replaced by serenity, the serenity with ecstasy. Otherwise the symptoms were the same: restlessness, clumsiness, a tendency toward outbursts of laughter or tears.

Kramer had many friends and spread the word, telling Michael, between reels one and two of *Casablanca,* how funny and smart Lydia was, working late in the editing room to discuss his new girl friend's pheromone theory with Sam and afterward relaying to Lydia exactly what he'd said about her. Recounting experiences, admitting to Lydia that he liked her, describing her to others, freed him from anxiety. At Rosemary's with Beth he had said, "What happened was I was watching this runner, small and fast—wait till you meet her—" And to Lydia, "I told her you had beautiful legs."

But Lydia realized how few people meant anything to her after all the years she had lived in New York. Who would care if she said, "Guess what, I'm in love" or "Guess what, my father died"? It seemed exploitive. She felt, after her father's death, that mentioning it would be a ploy for sympathy. And at the time she needed an excuse. The day her mother called with news that her father had died, Lydia went to school and worked in the lab until midnight. Before she left, she looked in on the frogs. A crowd of black eyes watched her, and as if answering their request, she topped their water with the aged water set in the brown jug beside them. In the morning she found them dead, sprawled bellies up, mouths gaping. The whole pool had been poisoned by the acetone she had poured in. She cried all the way home, her sobs drowned out by the screeching and clattering of the subway, and when she got into her apartment she phoned everyone she knew to tell them what she'd done. Why the frogs? Why hadn't she cried about her own father?

The next night she had worked late again and at eleven-thirty dropped a tray of beakers. "How unlike you," Dr. Cantoni said. She thought: I ought to tell them about my father. But she never said a word.

She didn't use Kramer to excuse random smiles or long silent moods either. No one said any of those expected things: "Gee, you glow." "Wow. you look terrific," "Oh what a lovely smile." Dr. Cantoni, Lydia, Brian, and Harriet worked together, functioning as smoothly as a miniature ant colony, their intelligence used collectively, the labor they performed divided according to their physiology. Lydia, the small worker, did indeed tend the larval broods, and Dr. Cantoni was the big soldier who led the emigrating workers. Lydia liked the people she worked with. She ate lunch with Brian and Harriet every day, often sharing their conversation about movies, restaurants, the perils of living in New York. But there were limits to relationships like these, and for Lydia there had never been a middle ground between impersonal relationships and all-out devotion.

Growing up, Lydia had had no friends outside her household

until she was eleven, when a girl named Rema moved next door. Through the new girl's persistence, she became Lydia's first, and in many ways her only friend. Rema had moved to New York when she got married two years before, and though the two women hadn't seen much of each other, partly because of the husband, who disapproved of the friendship, Lydia still hoped their bond was deeper than words.

She went to dinner at their house, planning to tell them she was in love. The conversation was impersonal, the kind exchanged in waiting rooms. Then during dessert Ken said, "Why do you wear army boots? Isn't that kind of ... um ... dykey?" Rema slapped him, harder than playfully but too soft for real dismay. He left the women alone after that.

Lydia told Rema about the man she had met at the Y, not that she'd watched him for weeks, or that he'd tripped her, bruising her badly.

"What about Carl?" Rema asked.

"Wednesday I see Carl."

"I don't understand. If you're so much in love with this Kramer, how can you go on seeing someone else?"

The way Rema said "This Kramer" made her sound like Lydia's mother, and Lydia was disappointed to see that marriage had affected not only Rema's capacity for friendship, but also her memory. She'd hoped Rema would know her nature, and understand, without further explanation, that Lydia had met someone so special she was afraid of sinking, of needing his warmth and love so badly she'd become immobile without him. She knew Darwin's theory of disuse was wrong, yet she believed that as her love for Kramer deepened, her ambition, will, and independence would atrophy.

That evening sleep was impossible, so Lydia switched on the light and reached for her glasses. When her eyes adjusted, she saw the little photograph of her grandfather on the wall. He was dressed in a felt hat, and gray suit with pleated pants, just what he'd worn when she brought him in for Show and Tell in the second grade. He sang "Tumbalalaika" and seeing her classmates' reaction Lydia was ashamed of him for the first time. Zeyde knew, and loved her anyhow. He loved her through a nasty adolescence, and, as a teen-ager, when her father suddenly seemed mysterious and omnipotent, too much of a hero to be shown new shoes or dresses, Zeyde was still her friend. They played gin rummy for nickels and dimes, gossiped and fought. Only Zeyde knew that Lydia had been seriously in love with Jonas Salk.

She asked if she'd woken him. "No no no no *no*, Lydie," he said, though he sounded weak.

"Guess what, Zeyde? I'm in love."

"With a boy, maybe?"

"I see you've kept up your subscription to *Gay World*." Lydia laughed, pleased to hear him joking. He'd been depressed since his son (her father) had died. Lydia imagined him sitting in his wing chair, heels propped up on the footrest. Her Zeyde was a round, pink man, two inches taller than Lydia, one hundred pounds heavier.

"He's a nice boy, Lydia?"

"He is, really."

"Then go—and love him." Zeyde stopped to compose his words. He had an oratorical style learned from his days as a street-corner Socialist. "Go and love him and don't worry what no one says. But Lydie, run wit your eyes open, Lydie. Remember, love is taking everyting in. Love ain't being blind, Lydie. Being blind is for old men wit cataracts."

"How are you feeling, Zeyde?"

He didn't answer. Lydia saw his face, sunken eyes, Clark Gable mustache, lips puffed out, head bobbing forward, an expression meaning: Don't ask, Lydie.

"So what's your fellow's name, Lydie?"

"Kramer."

"Kramer? A Kramer is a baker. Does he bring you cookies, Lydie?"

"No."

"Flowers, maybe?"

"No one's ever brought me flowers, Zeyde."

"That's good. Flowers, Lydie, are for funerals. This is costing you good money. Go and buy your baker a glass of tea."

Lydia went back to the clinic and found out she was cured. She stopped at the Buffalo Roadhouse and had a beer in her own honor. She toasted herself, *please make him be home*, and in the evening, after juggling around weekend plans, she made room for Kramer on Saturday, the longest and freest day of the week. Shaking, she dialed his number. She was surprised how hard it was, how she hoped he wasn't home. She said Hello, hi, when he answered, and Are you doing anything Saturday? Kramer said he was sorry, but he had other commitments. Lydia was devastated. She hung up. convinced he was cruel. He only seemed nice because being beautiful he never had to struggle to get what he wanted, so it was easy being nice. The less fortunate have to be more manipulative. They work harder.

The next day they made a date for Sunday night. A movie, a pint of ice cream and two spoons, love on his bed, high up near the ceiling. When he told her with candid and childlike expressions how much he cared for her, she was convinced she was being duped, charmed into submission, *I like you too a lot.* But he was such a gentle and attentive lover. The bluntness, the awkwardness of his words made them seem real, honest. In the following four evenings they progressed from "I like you" to "I like you too much" to "I'm falling in love with you."

3

AFTER TWO WEEKS Lydia learned the code: If Kramer said he had "other commitments" it meant he had a date with Debbie, the woman he'd been seeing regularly before Lydia. "A friend in town" was not Debbie but a woman he occasionally slept with. Sometimes "the friend" was from somewhere else—one came in from Atlanta, another from Boston. When Lydia was with Kramer, these other women didn't disturb her. She could hardly blame the friends for rushing to New York to sleep with him. But when she was alone, too anxious and distracted to work, she hated Kramer for making her feel so vulnerable, and she decided again that she was being duped.

Lydia's main commitment was Carl, who she'd been seeing twice a week for half a year now. They slept together but otherwise were not intimate. Besides the fact that he taught physics and had at one time been married, Lydia didn't know much about him. It had always been this way with the men before Kramer. Carl hadn't been the one to give Lydia the clap, so relations between them deteriorated before Kramer. Not only that, the more Lydia loved Kramer, the more she disliked Carl, which was unfortunate. Lydia wished she liked Carl—it would make her feel safer loving Kramer. But after Saturday night with Kramer, Sunday night with Carl was intolerable. He was a fuss-budget, a compulsive shirt buyer who got a new shirt whenever he was bored or unhappy, the way housewives supposedly buy hats. He conditioned his hair. Before Kramer this didn't irritate her, but now, knowing Carl spent more time on his hair than she did on hers was maddening.

If they had a history it would be better. If time would pass so she could say she'd been with Kramer for six months or a year. What was two months? Two months said nothing about possession, loyalty, habit. Six months would give their love substance.

They saw each other two or three times a week now, always spending the night together. In the warmth, under covers, they were loving and told each other very private things. Otherwise they were still strangers. Each time Kramer called there was the same awkwardness ("Hi." "Hi." "What's up?" "Oh, not too much, what's up with you?" "Oh, not too much. Listen, uh, are you busy tonight?") and Lydia wondered if he forgot what they'd shared in bed ("Do you like that?" "Yes it feels good"). Each time he knocked on her door she suffered from the same shock as the first time she saw him in the doorway, blue T-shirt, hair as black and smooth as an Indian's. Believing was hard. The answer, Lydia decided, was never again to juggle dates around, to take instead what came. But despite her best intentions, Lydia wouldn't accept a date for Saturday night because Saturday night she counted on seeing Kramer. One Wednesday she said, "Am I going to see you Saturday?" He said, "I can't, I'm sorry. I have other commitments. Are you free Friday?" But Friday she had plans and said so.

Before Lydia met Kramer she could spend weeks without dates or phone calls. Sometimes she brought her blanket to the lab and worked through the night at school, napping a little at her desk to refresh herself for classes. She hardly thought about her solitude, and when she did, she didn't consider it an unnatural state. But now that she loved someone she felt lonely being by herself for a night. An ambiguous comment, a night without a phone call, these things threw her into a depression neither work nor running could break ever since she had allowed herself to love, and acknowledged her need to be loved. It was as if when Kramer was gone, he took his love with him, leaving Lydia alone with these same yearnings. Because she'd always been an independent person, Kramer's power disturbed her. Hadn't she always considered those who were hopelessly in love to be deluded, weak, to show moral flabbiness? Rema, at sixteen, had straightened her hair chemically and at night slept on a head covered with frozen orange juice cans, all for a boy named Marc.

Every day as they walked to school, Rema, between sobs, would tell how mean Marc was, how she couldn't help herself, she was hopelessly in love. After weeks of this Lydia met Marc at a party. He had acne, greasy hair, and the intelligence and sensitivity of a rock. He tried to kiss Lydia when Rema was in the bathroom. He told Lydia what Rema "let him do." He said he'd seen her naked, and she had hair on her nipples. If this was mad, passionate love, Lydia didn't want it. And for years, lukewarm relationships were enough.

Johnny Guitar was showing at the Bleecker Street and Kramer said as an homage to Godard he was obligated to see it each time it was in town. He brought Lydia a box of chocolate-covered cherries and insisted on paying for both their tickets. *Johnny Guitar* was made in 1954, so to her their date felt like an homage to the fifties.

They walked home arm in arm after the movie, Kramer very sober. When two people, like Johnny Guitar and Vienna, love each other and then split up, they can't see each other again without the bitterness taking over. Some people saw the film primarily as an allegory about McCarthyism, but to Kramer it was about the bitterness of love.

They went back to Kramer's apartment, climbed onto his bed, and made love. He was still feeling sad when the phone rang. Kramer didn't answer his phone when they made love or after making love. Lydia was always pleased when she was beside him, but faintly troubled when she called and no one answered. This time, after the tenth ring, she said, "You may as well get it."

Kramer jumped to the floor, picked up the phone and standing naked and splendid, one hand low on his hip, said hello. He sounded pleased, comfortable. More comfortable than he is with me, Lydia thought. "No, it's as good a time as any," he said after a minute.

Lydia knew. She sat up, slipped on her shirt, crawled to the end of the bed, let a leg dangle, another, felt for the back of the chair and, finding that, eased onto the seat. What a joke this bed was: six feet high and no way to get down. He thought he'd escape from roaches up there, but roaches have internal flagellates and could digest the cellulose in the posts. Where were her glasses? Remembering that her pants made a black puddle in the corner, she kicked around, caught them with her toes and began dressing. In six months, the roaches would be sharing his pillow.

Kramer said, "It's been real good. Real good."

With me, maybe? Lydia thought.

He hung up the receiver and watched Lydia zip up her pants, then pat around on his desk for her glasses. He sat in his director's chair, seeing her glasses, not stirring. "Will you come sit with me for a second?"

She perched unsteadily on his knees.

"That was Debbie."

"I could tell."

"She wants to come up here to get some of her books."

Lydia had seen a picture of Debbie dancing, chin lifted, hands in a loop above her head, kicking, toe pointed. She had large breasts and was very pretty. Lydia didn't know how to dance. "I'm leaving, don't worry," she said.

"Hey, not like that."

Lydia stood. Kramer stood and took her in his arms. Clothes against skin, it made her ache. She felt the distance between them. It wasn't just Debbie, it was all the women, real and imagined. "Do we get to bump into each other on the stairway?"

"I'm sorry about this," he said, his voice a whisper.

Lydia tried to pull away.

"Don't be angry," he said. "Please don't be upset."

"I'm neither."

"Will you kiss me, then?"

She did, but it was a cold kiss, an obligatory one. She was in a rush to leave. She didn't want to run into Debbie. "I love you," Kramer said. "I love you so fucking much, woman."

She ran home, then ran to the gym, then ran around and around the oval track. The first six laps she ached all over and only the memory of the other days assured her that after the first half-mile, she could run forever. It was Saturday afternoon, a different team downstairs. Her breathing came fast and regular, around and around, white shorts, white shirt, her thumb recording the distance she ran. The Breather and the Walker were on the track with her. Baldy was catching up, hand reaching out for her shoulder. "Huh huh huh your shoelace, your shoelace is huh huh untied huh huh." She ran on and on, passing five miles, passing six, her neck and forehead soaked, pushing on, the pain in her calf a distant echo, far in the background, and downstairs the shouts, the squeak of sneakers skidding across the floor.

Huh huh tall and black-haired, boxer shorts with a stitched-up fly. "Look, I'm really sorry."

"I'm sure you are."

"Lookit." *Kneeling beside her, hand darting out to touch, to fix the hurt.*

"It's okay."

"Look, really."

Limping into the elevator as quickly as possible. He grabbed the door and squeezed inside too. Crowded in the front part of the car, facing forward, both on an inhale. "Look," *he whispered.*

"I'd rather not."

Third floor, limping toward the locker room; women only. The towel lady put her hand up, meaning stop. He called out, his voice loud and forlorn, "Look!"

When Lydia got home it seemed as if she hadn't thought of Kramer at all, but had digested certain facts and come up quite automatically with the decision that she couldn't bear to be another commitment. She didn't want Kramer to sleep with friends that dropped into town either. Whether she had any right to ask Kramer to come to a decision himself was irrelevant. The point was she survived very nicely alone but the way things were her career would be wrecked. Once again, her theoretical beliefs had been wrong. However much she advocated polygamy, she didn't want to share Kramer with anyone.

Late the next night she sat up in bed, reached for the phone and dialed Kramer's number. Could she come over? Yes, he said, do. She threw on clothes and raced through the streets. It was two-thirty and by two-thirty-seven she was at Kramer's, breathless, too excited for any regrets. She climbed the worn old steps to his apartment and when she got up to his door he was standing in the hall in his blue bathrobe, sleepy-eyed and beautiful. He used his foot to shut the door, put his hands around her waist, and slid her shirt over her head. He kissed her breasts, peeled off her pants, kissed her thighs, then lowered her onto the floor. They made love, she knew, but when she opened her eyes at dawn, she was on the bed, and hadn't any memory of it. He opened his eyes a minute later and she said, "I love you and I can't stand it knowing you have all these other women. If you—" She searched for the right word, while he lay in bed, completely awake and on his side. She didn't want her words to sound like a threat. Just facts: "It makes me crazy and suspicious and miserable. I don't like it."

"Lydia, baby, you know I'm going away, don't you?"

She said, "Yes," but she didn't really believe him. "I'm not asking you to do anything, Kramer. I'm just telling you the way I feel. Miserable. I can't take it."

The answer took so long in coming, she wondered what she'd do, finding he had no plans to change. She shivered from the restless night, the fear. He lay on his side, inches from touching her and said, "I've been faithful for a long time now."

4

IN SEPTEMBER, Lydia returned to school. Her course work had been completed in May, and now she'd be teaching two undergraduate labs and spending the rest of her time working on her dissertation. Dr. Cantoni, her adviser, was taking his sabbatical the following fall, and it was important she finish at least the experimentation before then.

At lunch the first day back, Brian said scientists should never marry; it weakened their commitment. Lydia told him he was an ass. Yet she left school an hour earlier than usual in order to meet Kramer at the Museum of Modern Art for an early screening of *Bluebeard's Eighth Wife*. Kramer told her beforehand it would be awful, but that it was better to see the worst film Lubitsch had made than the best film of a bad director. Lydia decided Brian was right; she preferred sitting through a bad movie with Kramer to working at something she loved without him. At least the other commitments and friends from out of town (vultures, birds of prey) were no longer hovering around and Lydia felt secure. She trusted Kramer. On the way home from the Modern, he asked if she wanted to live with him. As if they were business partners, the proposition was first presented as an economy measure, a convenience. Then awkwardly, the words getting twisted in his mouth, he said for weeks he'd been wishing they lived together. Maybe it was unfair to ask since he'd be leaving the city, but he liked waking up beside her. She was cheerful in the morning. He liked, when he woke up in the middle of the night, that her body was beside his and that still asleep when he kissed her, she responded. He wanted to share things with her, chores and pleasures. And he loved her, he really did. Lydia didn't say anything until the following week. She was at Kramer's apartment and a book she needed was at her house. Annoyed she said, "Wherever we are, whatever I need is at the other place." Then, "Maybe we ought to live together. I like the pitter-patter of your little feet."

"Is that all?"

"I like you. They're your feet, after all."

"Is that all?"

"I love you and would love to have you at odd hours and for unspecial occasions. But since your cockroaches are climbing, it better be at my place."

"You don't call me up at two A.M. and come running over like you used to," Kramer said.

"Oh." She was touched and saddened that he remembered that morning. These days they met at bars and restaurants. They ran to meet each other, embraced, kissed, and got a beer ("How's it going, Big K.?" "Come closer, that's it, a kiss, a big one on my cheek." "You look luscious today." "Truly?" "I'd grab you if we weren't in public." "Grab me." "Watch, presto, the public is gone . . ."). Their affection was luxurious, not frenzied.

Kramer packed up, ready to move into Lydia's. They chose her place not because of Kramer's cockroach problem but because Lydia's apartment was only sixty-eight dollars a month. Building rumor was that the landlord had died ten years ago. Rents were never raised, complaints never answered, repairs too complicated for John were done by private contractors at the tenant's expense. No one moved. Now that the rent control era was over in New York, tenants were lifers, trapped by the cheap rent. The apartment was too small—bedroom big enough for a bureau and bed, living room no wider than a couch—but it was home forever.

"I'm not blind," Lydia said, after telling Zeyde about her new roommate. "I just find that my priorities have changed. Things that used to mean a lot to me don't mean as much since I met Kramer."

Priorities were things like privacy, habits that had grown and been nurtured and unchallenged for the eight years Lydia had lived alone in New York. While the arrangements to merge were made, Lydia didn't worry. Moving day was a disaster, though. The apartment seemed smaller than they had thought. They tripped over each other and bumped into cartons and more cartons and bags and boxes she and Kramer carried up the six flights of stairs. Who knew he owned that much? It didn't occur to Lydia until Kramer's own apartment was emptied that he used an entire room for storage. She said, "Can't you leave anything behind? What about this piece of junk?"—(wires wrapped around a switchplate)—"or that?"—(plastic Pluto the dog marionette, minus one leg).

Kramer revealed a very sentimental side: Anything anyone once dear had given him was permanent. "That item—careful now, Lydia—that happens to be a present Jim Presner gave to me in 1966, when we went up to Maine. And this—" (holding up a small metal box with a bashed-in side and two red holes, like eyes in the back) "happens to be a collector's item. It's the back of one of the first Brownie cameras ever made."

They came close to fighting. Kramer, seeing Lydia survey the ruins of her once orderly apartment, sent her out to see *Sullivan's Travels* and promised things would be all cleaned up when she returned.

He was asleep when Lydia got back. The cartons were tucked into the corners, and yes, the center of the floor was clean. Lydia got into bed beside Kramer (*My* bed, she thought, lying sleepless) and two things became clear to her. One was that if it looked like junk to her, to Kramer it was valuable or memorable, and the other was that order and her ideas about it would be considerably changed. She'd made a commitment to a man who made chaos into a life-style, who used a door as a desk top and slept under a Mexican rug, whose refrigerator was empty except for twenty reels of film. Kramer bought his midnight dinner at the deli, and his clothing when there wasn't anything clean to put on. Though he brought an immense load to the Laundromat every once in a while, he often let weeks go by before he picked it up.

Lydia woke with the sun the next morning. While Kramer slept beside her, she thought that another priority had to do with waking and sleeping. She was an early riser, her best work done by 10:00 A.M., all of her creative work by noon. She taught in the afternoon two days a week and on the other weekdays worked in the lab at school. Her energy began to flag by eight or nine in the evening, about the time Kramer's eyes were open, round and ready. Kramer attended midnight concerts, ate dinner after the late show on TV. That was another thing: Kramer loved watching movies on TV, especially the old ones that began at one-fifteen and three-twenty.

The night after he moved in with Lydia, *Night Train to Munich* was being shown on "The Late Late Show." "*Night Train to Munich!*" Kramer exclaimed, as if that said it all. "You'll stay up and watch it with me, won't you?"

"I'll try, but—"

Kramer set up the TV by the foot of the bed "so I can be with my honey when I watch." He brought a bowl of grapes and two glasses of chocolate milk. Lydia fell asleep well before the movie started, and, just after it ended, she woke for the day and said good morning to Kramer, who was nodding, eyes heavy. "It was great," he said, "especially when—" There was Lydia, long argyle socks, tying up her boots. "Are you sorry I moved in? It was so nice before I came. Remember the first night, I told you how much I liked this apartment? Now I've spoiled everything, haven't I." He slid to the wall side of the bed. "Come lie here before you go."

"I love you," she said. "You haven't spoiled anything."

"You sure now?"

"Positive."

"You know what you got yourself into?"

"I do."

"Then smile for me—that's it. Hold it now, Lydie, a big one for the folks in Omaha."

He bought two six-packs of beer the first time they went grocery shopping together. He liked sliced, individually wrapped American cheese, smooth peanut butter, and Mallomars. She bought buttermilk, the sight of which made him ill, brown eggs, sweet butter, spinach noodles, a two-pound jar of superchunk peanut butter. Lydia paid the cashier, and while their bags were being packed, they kissed, sweetly acknowledging they'd never once eat the same thing for dinner.

When they returned home from this joint expedition, Kramer drew two columns on the back of the bedroom door and wrote K.O.L. and L.O.K. in red marker on top. Expenses were supposed to be entered in the appropriate column. For instance, he said, uncapping his pen, "Under K.O.L.—that's Kramer

Owes Lydia—thirty-four dollars—half of this month's rent. Okay?"

"My dad will be delighted I've found a man who's into budgets," Lydia said. "A stabilizing influence—he'll love it." Kramer knew how Lydia's dad, child of the Depression, worried about money.

She never remembered to enter the figures. Before they lived together, they had randomly split the cost of movies and meals. There had been no need for arbitration. It seemed fair; it probably was. Kramer, who worked steadily and earned union wages, tried to explain he liked knowing where his money went. It gave him a sense of order. He didn't understand why Lydia was uneasy talking about financial affairs, but every time he mentioned money, she changed the subject or agreed to do whatever he asked, without listening to what it was. Kramer wasn't even sure where Lydia's money came from, though repeatedly she said, "Don't worry, we won't starve," laughing as if it were a private joke. Lydia had a fellowship at school and earned money teaching. For large purchases, a winter coat, a visit to the dentist, she withdrew money from the account her father had left her.

But the whole neatness question turned out not to be a problem at all. Lydia, mud-puddle lover, didn't demand her kind of neatness from Kramer. As long as he kept his mountains on his own turf, things were fine. It didn't matter that his work area hadn't any work area left on it. Nor did it matter that his bureau drawers were grab bags of clean and dirty laundry, letters, film cans, an old prep school blazer stuffed in. They were his drawers. Her drawers were equally alien to him: four stacks of sweaters, folded neatly, right side out. Silently, they agreed that private space was important to survival, and the unspoken rule that your desk is yours and mine is mine, that your drawers are yours and mine are mine, was enforced. He built a work area that spanned a whole wall in the living room, and she ached a little seeing her perfect order changed, holes drilled into plaster, photographs taken off the walls to accommodate his shelves. But it was a healthy kind of ache. Before Kramer, Lydia had thought no one could enter her closed little world; no one would be allowed to penetrate. And now, here she was, sitting on the couch and watching the plaster collect in anthills on the floor. Afterward he built Lydia shelves above her desk. She said she didn't want them, but he insisted, and only a month later they were filled.

Kramer had begun revisions on his screenplay to take out to Los Angeles, and in the evenings, while Lydia read review papers or went over lab exams, he sat under his headphones, listening to classical music, writing longhand into his blue notebook. They stayed home much of the time, hardly seeing their friends. Their sole luxury (movies were a necessity) was brunch at Rosemary's every Saturday and Sunday. Homemade bran muffins, freshly squeezed orange juice, real cream with coffee, eggs exactly the way Kramer liked them—over easy, a thin white film covering the yolk—and an endless flow of actors, playwrights, singers, and comedians waiting on tables until their lucky day. But it took all of autumn learning to be comfortable as roommates. Before they lived together they never argued. Now they had to learn each other's patterns of anger. The first time Kramer spoke sharply to Lydia, she cried. The first time Lydia was sullen, Kramer crept away, confused. The fluctuations from passion to hurt to hatred were intense and violent. Lydia watched and explored; she tried to understand his nature by feel. And what did Kramer know about this woman, silent and private, who spent her day in a white jacket and came home smelling like the sea?

Lydia wasn't aware of being so cautious with Kramer, so watchful. But one day in December, when Kramer came home, she let him go through his motions undisturbed. He unlocked the front door and walked straight into the bedroom, no nod or hello. (As lovers they had run to each other and clung, everywhere.) He took off his clothes, walked into the kitchen, grabbed a beer from the refrigerator, then ran the hot water in the tub. While the bathroom—and soon the kitchen, living room, and bedroom steamed up, mist forming near the ceiling, he stood naked, his head thrown back. Lydia, sitting at her desk, leaned until her chair was on two legs and watched the action of his Adam's apple as the beer went down his throat. Look at me! she thought. I don't feel miserable and rejected. She'd learned not to tamper with his silence. This was his way when he came home. She was pleased with herself, but when Kramer remained in the kitchen, while the cloud above moved lower and lower, she thought, Why does he run the water for so long? The walls were covered with tiny cracks in the plaster and in the bedroom the paint had begun to drop in jigsaw-puzzle pieces, leaving jagged holes in the ceiling and walls. Kramer rapped himself twice on the chest and let out two loud and froglike belches. Disgusting, she thought, but only out of habit. She was used to it now.

After the shower, Kramer's temper cooled, the dirt and frustration of his job were cleansed away. He wrapped a towel around his waist and stood over Lydia. Though she had acted as if she were busy, from the moment he walked in, she found it impossible to concentrate. He waited patiently for a single kiss. "Will you come sit with me?" he asked when she looked up, pretending to notice him at last.

"Let me finish this page first."

He dressed in the meantime. She was sorry he had.

"How's my honey been today?" he said when she sat on the couch next to him.

"Pretty good. How's my honey been?"

"Six of one, dozen of the other."

"Half dozen," she said. (This was a family joke.)

Kramer nuzzled, nose to her neck, her ear, searching for a kiss. "Ants today?"

"Horseshoe crabs. Limulus. I teach Tuesdays, remember? Do you want to hear what we did?"

"Shoot."

"Okay, the limulus is used for a lot of work in vision because it has a simple eye. That means the receptor sends the axon straight back to the brain without going through a synaptic junction." Lydia watched Kramer closely when she talked. She liked explaining her work to him but had to make sure she was being comprehensible. When he fidgeted, she could tell he wasn't following her. "It's the D. W. Griffith of vision experiments."

"A classic?"

"Sí, Cisco."

Kramer moved closer, putting an arm around her. He'd shaved and smelled minty. She wanted to share the excitement of the experiment with him. Crosscuts were made with a hacksaw and the eye was lifted out of the limulus. When it was kept in a liquid that approximated the body fluid of the animal, it could live for ten hours. Lydia explained how a single cell in the eye was stimulated, and how questions about lateral inhibition were explored. She was fascinated by the limulus: hard shell, jagged at the edges. They were such rocklike, faceless creatures. They'd been on earth so long. When she sat in her room, she heard only comforting, familiar sounds, typing in the distance, the steady hum of aquarium pumps. Only at hour intervals, when the classes let out, were there voices, footsteps. The knowledge that there were people outside, the safety of the cool, green locked room —these things she never could explain.

While she was describing the preparation of the optic nerve, Kramer fidgeted. "Am I boring you?" She was still shy, even after their half-year together.

"No."

"You'd say yes, wouldn't you?"

"If you were boring me, I'd say yes." He kissed her and rested his head on her lap, a pleasant sign, but a sign that he was restless, tired of listening.

She said, "By three o'clock, the lights were out and we waited for the eye to dark-adapt."

Kramer untucked her shirt from her pants.

"The whole room was wired up. The sound of the cells firing went from the differential amplifier to the audio amplifier and the speakers. It was like static over a loudspeaker. You should've been there."

Kramer said she should save the rest of the experiment until after dinner. He liked hearing about her work, but it was difficult at times, like listening to a story told half in English, half in a foreign language.

"Was I boring you?" Lydia said.

"That particular question is boring me, but you aren't. You never bore me. Did you eat?"

They went into the kitchen. Kramer made a sandwich that went like this:

white bread
mayonnaise
American cheese
onion
mayonnaise
white bread

"Zeyde calls that poison bread," Lydia said, seeing her grandfather at the kitchen table in Brentwood, tea in a glass, trying to work a pat of half-frozen butter into his slice of rye, gently chipping off edges with a knife so the bread wouldn't tear. A very patient man. "He says, 'They'll grow up, they won't know what real bread is.'"

"Does Hankie talk with a Yiddish accent like that?" Hankie, for Hank Greenberg, was Kramer's name for Lydia's father, whose prowess on the baseball diamond was the subject of countless conversations.

"No accent, but an inflection. And he's a gesturer. Rose made me sit on my hands when I started waving my arms around. She thought she'd condition me to keep still. But you know what's funny? When I taught, I had this one little boy who was always waving his arms around. I figured I'd ignore it, but every time he got excited he did some damage to a neighbor. Broken glasses, bloody nose. I made him sit on his hands."

"You taught little kids?" Kramer said. "When did you do that?"

"I don't know, a couple of years ago, 1972 maybe."

"You taught? You really taught school? God damn, Lydia, next thing I know you're going to tell me you were married." He stopped abruptly. "You weren't married, were you?"

Lydia fussed for herself. She made a salad plate, arranging all the vegetables like a still life, cucumbers fanned out, halved radishes in a circle, a hill of cherry tomatoes, pepper rings around the sardines. They were brisling sardines and she opened the can slowly, revealing the tiny glistening silver bodies, headless top to tail, tail to top.

"I bet you wish they had heads."

She did.

Kramer rapped himself on the chest, belched, and got up for another beer.

"You stink," she said. (Now at least there was familiarity.)

"From what? I just showered."

"From onions."

"Oh." Eyes upcast, a grown man's pout.

"Quit with the hurt look. You don't care if you stink. You ate onions before our first date, remember?"

"Jesus, I wish I knew you when you were a teacher. Did you wear pantyhose and dresses? And regular shoes?"

"All of them."

He was laughing. "You really taught school."

Lydia ate the vegetables with her fingers, making mouse bites on a cucumber slice. Her classroom had had a mural on the back wall, the colored paper faded from the sun and city dirt. The Weather. The Clouds. What's under the Rock?

"You must have made good money, why did you quit?"

Disappointed he didn't know her well enough to know the answer, she said, "Two years of making kids memorize the names of planets was enough."

"You really were a teacher?"

"I swear."

"Did you wear your glasses?"

"Of course. How do you think I saw the blackboard."

Kramer opened the refrigerator and grabbed a loaf of bread from the shelf. Peeling two slices, he began again, bread, mayonnaise, etc. "Cut me some onion?" Lydia asked.

"Please."

"Please cut me some onion, sir, thank you, please?"

Kramer cut a thin slice and put it on her plate.

"More sir, please?"

"You stink," he said after she ate the first slice.

She separated the rings and eating the largest one first, worked down to the middle, crunching loudly. "So do you."

Kramer talked to Lydia about his work, too. At the studio, they were doing the sound effects for a big-budget western. Though they had been on location for months, and millions had been spent in production, the sound crew had forgotten to record the horses' hooves, and now all their trotting and galloping had to be simulated in New York with coconut shells. The director was driving everyone nuts, making them try hundreds of combinations—green coconut shells on vermiculite, old brown shells on sand, etc., etc. When a satisfactory clip-clop was found, he said, "Fine, this will be for Luke's horse." Different sounds had to be found for every other horse. Christ.

Lydia laughed, though she knew in reality the work was tedious. Still, she was forever fascinated by the little tidbits he always brought home. Studio snow was Kosher salt and vermiculite. Car-bys (the sound of cars passing) came in Slow, Medium, and Fast.

Kramer kept in contact with his friends from film school, and he also liked to talk about them. A favorite was Slick Sam the cameraman, an idol of sorts. He was more talented than James Wong Howe, did a brilliant impersonation of Erich von Stroheim, and in six months had moved out on his wife, moved in with Joan, moved out on Joan, stayed with his wife a couple of weeks, and now—Did Lydia remember Bridget O'Connell, the woman who worked for the music publisher two floors above the studio? And did she remember how they were always dragging people in to do footsteps? Well, in this western, they needed footsteps on sand. They dragged Bridget in because she was about the same size as the actress, so her footsteps would be light enough. But when she walked for them her clothes rustled, and in the movie the actress was in her underwear. So Bridget was talked into doing steps in a bikini. Anyhow, Sam came to visit Kramer, and he met Bridget who was doing footsteps in her bikini, and now they were living together. "Oh, Connell," said Kramer. "The most beautiful tits I ever laid my eyes on."

Lydia was glad Kramer was relaxed enough not to censor his words, but did she have to be his little brother to be loved? Usually she rallied. Tonight she said, "I thought you weren't into tits. I thought it was a spiritual union of mind and body you were after."

"That's hippie shit. I'm into tits now."

Sometimes, blue-eyed and sweet, he hurt her. "Too fucking bad, isn't it," she said.

Kramer, realizing he'd hurt her, ate his second sandwich in silence, the white bread and American cheese adhering to the roof of his mouth in a perfect palate shape. He was afraid to touch Lydia when she was sullen and unhappy, though often she was sullen and unhappy when he was insensitive and ignored her. So he relayed more sexual gossip, coupling and uncoupling, engaging, disengaging. Having never been up to the editing room, Lydia imagined it to be a machine, the workers playing sexual organs.

Lydia put up the kettle for tea, and Kramer, seeing some leftover vegetables and a couple of sardines, said, "Aren't you going to finish?"

"I'm not hungry."

"I'll take those tomatoes." He said tomatahs and it made her smile. Seeing this, he said, "Come and sit on my lap."

She straddled him, legs around the back of the chair, and held tight.

"You're not mad at me?" he asked.

"No."

"You love me?"

"To pieces."

He held her tightly and swayed. They sat together until the teakettle whistled and spat. Apart they were friends again. They flipped a coin to see who did dishes, and then took separate corners and worked until bedtime.

5

LYDIA had spent so many years with her cheek to the earth, watching ants, and Japanese beetles, grubs, tomato worms, and mantises in her yard that by the time she was grown up her powers of observation were acute, her understanding of animal behavior brilliant. Her own behavior, however, was a mystery to her. Joy, sorrow, the fears that lately had grown and begun to interfere with her happiness—these states manifested themselves physically. She had no words to describe them, and for that reason could not think about them.

They received an invitation to a party. It read: "Come dressed as your secret ambition. No one admitted without a costume." Lydia told Kramer to come as God. He didn't think it was funny. He said, "You ought to come as Gregor Samsa."

"Before or after?"

"After, of course."

"I will," she said, "if you come as God."

He still didn't think it was funny.

Later in the evening, he came into the bedroom, sat next to her on the bed, and like the perfect romantic hero, took off her glasses, tossed her book onto the floor, and said, "Do you think a sheet would do?"

"What?"

"Or do you think I'd have to grow a long white beard?"

At the party he kissed both the bag lady and a princess for much too long. "God loves all his little children," Kramer said.

Days later, Lydia said, "Did you like kissing royalty?"

"Yes," he said. "She tasted like chocolate."

Lydia went into the bedroom and got under the covers with

a book. She always got answers from Kramer. She asked him because she knew he'd tell the truth. What she really wanted from Kramer were lies, things like, "You are the only person I could possibly in my lifetime ever imagine wanting to kiss." Kramer was in his own way the most honest person she had ever met. The "in his own way" was because he couldn't answer questions about his inner life, and for details about his past life, she had to ask. He never volunteered stories about childhood traumas, his first time with a girl, his three nights in jail. But when she asked, he admitted without embarrassment that he'd been a bed wetter. Lydia thought he was the most cheerful, most patient, brightest, gentlest, and best piece of horseflesh in creation. These superlatives were truths to her, and sometimes she found them depressing. Why would such a mass of perfection love such a bruised little fruit? Lydia began making lists. One evening she wrote:

> Reasons he might like me:
> 1. I like sex.
> 2. I'm just crazy enough to come to a party wearing my secret self in the shape of a hard black shell, but not crazy enough to run naked in the streets.
> 3. I am warm.
> 4. He was lonely.

She didn't wait for him to jump onto the bed and rip off her glasses. She went into the living room where he was writing in his blue notebook, and ripped off his headphones. "You moved in with me because you were lonely," she said.

"That's true."

"You love me because I don't run around with other men."

"That's also true."

When she crawled under the covers she found her missing track shoe at the foot of the bed. Falling asleep, she had a feeling something was very wrong.

As she had during many other troubled nights, Lydia dreamt of Kramer in a wheelchair. In all these dreams she was walking up an endless path to the house her parents had owned before her father died. Though the house was always in sight and the jade plants and hibiscus changed shape to assure her she was making progress, it seemed to take forever to reach the door. Just as she drew close, Kramer bumped down the two front steps in his wheelchair. The living room stretched out before her, vast and dark and bare. It was nothing like the inside of her parents' house. The only piece of furniture was a narrow velvet couch that sagged in the middle like an old mare. In the dream, Kramer suddenly materialized on the couch and when she turned toward the wheelchair she saw that her father was in it, waving furiously the way he had when the bus took her away to summer camp.

In other dreams, old friends from different points in her life, people who couldn't know each other, were inside this house, the outside of which had once been hers. Rema was lying in a corner on her back in one dream. Her fingers made a hammock behind her head, one leg was resting on a raised knee, and smoke came from her nose and mouth. Alex once appeared in an apron, flour dust on his mustache. And Willy, in a pale green bathrobe that kept opening, much to Lydia's delight.

Each time Lydia had the dream she woke up in the middle of the night to write it down. In the morning, scribbled across the page, were the names of colors and people to remind her of the scenes. But a sick feeling stayed with her for days, no need to write cues on paper. What was wrong with Kramer? Why wouldn't anyone tell her what was happening?

They made plans in winter to rent a cottage on a little Caribbean island, to leave New York for some sun. Lydia promised to teach Kramer how to snorkel. Kramer said he'd cook the eggs. In January, Lydia was on intersession and Kramer had no jobs lined up. He said he was happy to be out of work, but he seemed anxious. Lydia suggested he get an answering machine before they left. Good idea, he said. Then a week before they were set to leave, Michael called to tell Kramer about a film being shot for the American Cancer Society. It paid very well. Kramer took the job and they never went away.

Something about the job was terrible, someone made him feel incompetent. Kramer wouldn't talk to Lydia about it, but for days he came home, drank his beer, took off his clothes and showered, and after the shower was uncommunicative except for muttering about the fucking city, the stupid shits he worked with, the idiot job he wasted his time doing. Lydia felt bad for Kramer. She knew she was keeping him in New York doing work he detested. But, after so many days of being patient, she grew to hate him for his silence. She tiptoed and skulked around, sticking close to corners, not daring to turn on the radio, make a phone call, or run the water. One night she suggested dinner and he said he wanted to be left alone. An hour later she prepared some eggs for herself and he marched into the kitchen and told her she was rude for not offering. Lydia was unprepared for these black moods of despair and rage. The first week, she cried from confusion, but in time, as soon as she saw the warning signs —chin jutting, lips tightly clenched—the anger built so quickly within her that she left the house. More than once at the peak of a silent storm, Lydia left, then Kramer left, and the night would be spent in a battle of who would come home first. Kramer had always hated being home alone, but for Lydia the terror was new. She'd never had anything to lose before; the awful descent from being loved to being unloved hadn't been possible before she met Kramer.

The only time she felt peace was when she ran, watching Kramer, frozen in midair, back arched, arms above his head, tipping the ball in. When she ran it was never just Kramer at the moment, but Kramer at every moment she'd ever seen him; Kramer through the months. All the Kramers in her imagination played basketball below her, wearing boxer shorts with a stitched-up fly, Converse All-Stars, black hair damp with sweat, the muscles of his bare back gleaming.

One Sunday Kramer stubbed his toe on her five-gallon jug of brine shrimp. With a savage kick, he knocked the jug over, soaking the floor, killing thousands of tiny animals. "Murderer!" Lydia cried, ripping her coat off the hanger. "I can't stand it anymore!" She ran out of the apartment and sat in the chair in the downstairs lobby, wondering what to do. She wasn't an eater, and she no longer could bury herself in work. There wasn't a shoulder (besides Kramer's) she cared to cry on. Often she ran but her running shoes were in a locker at the Y and the Y was closed on Sundays. When she first met Kramer he said that a fast-paced double bill and a box of Raisinets were the best cure for depression. He said *Bringing Up Baby, His Gal Friday,* movies by Howard Hawks or Preston Sturges were the best. The Marx Brothers were bad. You had to be in a good mood to begin with in order to like the Marx Brothers. If you felt rotten, there were too many bad puns and wretched musical interludes to cure you. "A movie has to suck you in."

A line had formed outside the Waverly theater. The marquee announced the last days of a special Agatha Christie–Margaret Rutherford double bill. Lydia bought a ticket and took a seat in the second row. *Murder at the Gallop* sucked her in. She didn't think of Kramer once during the whole picture. Between features, she got up to see if she could buy a box of Raisinets.

Kramer saw the black ringlets, the back of Lydia's lavender lamb's wool sweater. He tiptoed behind her and extended an arm over her shoulder, so that his box of candy was below her nose. "Have a sweet, my sweet?" It was hard for Kramer to be charming when he knew he'd been difficult, but to Lydia it was a gratuitous act. The ease of his words, the cheapness of the gesture made her angrier. She turned around, and when he repeated a toneless, "Have a sweet, my sweet," she pushed her way down a crowded aisle and took her seat back. She hoped he wouldn't catch up. Then, seated, she hoped he would. She waited for him but he didn't look for her. The second picture didn't absorb her at all. Having Kramer in the same theater, probably enjoying the movie, the shit, was too much. Whenever there was a rustle, a shadow, someone standing, leaning over, changing seats, her heart beat—maybe it was Kramer; she'd forgive him. But Kramer didn't look for her, her seat grew hard and narrow, and Lydia decided to leave the theater.

She walked up the aisle, and nearly at the top she felt someone grab her wrist. She couldn't see a thing, but she heard her name. Kramer took his jacket off the seat he'd saved for her, and she stepped over his feet and sat in it, trying not to cry. Kramer put an arm around her and rested the other one between her legs. They watched the picture in silence—Kramer never talked during a movie, and the only time she'd seen him be rude was shutting up chatterers.

They didn't talk after the movie either. They went home and were loving and she didn't remember why she'd gotten angry or what they had fought about. They got into bed, made love, and she felt healed.

In the middle of the night, she woke Kramer, just to hold him. She'd dreamt she was sitting in a wheelchair in the middle of a strange room, paralyzed from the neck down and too ashamed to ask for help from the people who lined its perimeter. She wanted to talk about the dream in the morning. Kramer said he didn't want to hear about it. She said, "There I was in this strange room," and he said, "Would you kindly drop the subject?" Then he said he'd kill himself if he were a quadriplegic, or, lacking the ability, at least hope he'd die quickly. And now could she change the subject?

Lydia knew what it was to be a quadriplegic because in the dream she had been a quadriplegic, just as awake she was Lydia, wiggling her toes. Having experienced both, she knew that Kramer couldn't imagine anything except being confined to a wheelchair. In the dream Lydia had wanted a suction cup on a stick so she could use her mouth to turn the pages in her book. She had felt so strongly that the suction cup was the only thing she wanted, and not having the suction cup was all that stood in the way of her happiness right then. Her misery, the anguish that had made her wake up crying, was not due to her paralyzed body or her inability to do the thousands of things she could do awake. All she had lacked was the ability to ask, When are you leaving, please stay, will you take me?—something Lydia knew she lacked awake, too.

Kramer said, "Life for its own sake, even my life, is worthless. It's the quality of life that counts, Lydia. I could live without a leg or maybe even without an arm, but I couldn't survive paralyzed like that."

"Rema says you ought to see all her kids are able to do."

"You have to be cleaned up and fed and changed and wheeled around. It's the humiliation, not the inability to play basketball. You have to beg other people to care for you. You have to be at the mercy of others. Now will you change the subject please?"

Lydia thought of many things to say to Kramer. It wasn't begging to ask. Maybe he'd be happier if he trusted her or learned to say when he was hurting. Kramer ripped off the sheets and steamed up the bathroom for a shower.

With a heaviness in her belly, Lydia remembered that they'd fought the night before, though as usual, the particulars were elusive. She lay on her back in bed, all tucked in under the covers, the way she had lain while Kramer once nursed her back from a wicked flu. He had brought her juice, ice cream, magazines, records. He took her temperature hourly. He stayed home from work and read detective stories to her. "Well, Watson, what do you make of it?" he read in his best chin-in-the-neck English voice. But she couldn't soothe or care for him. She couldn't nurse him back from depression. When something went wrong inside him, the black cloud descended, the storm lasted until it passed, no saying how long. Lydia could never recall what their quarrels were about, what words of anger were used, how they made up. All she knew was that when she was upset at school or hurt by a friend, when the gas man pinched her or she got gypped on onions, Kramer was there to root for her and hiss at the bad guys. He probed gently, encouraging her to open up. But when he was hurting, and Lydia asked him what it was, he told her he felt it was weakness to complain.

6

By THE TIME spring arrived, the bad times seemed so long past, Lydia could hardly remember them. As a gift, Kramer bought her a little jar of brine-shrimp eggs and had to remind her of what he'd done, all those weeks before.

They spent a lot of time together, working in separate corners, meeting for coffee breaks or just to hold each other. The niceness of their lives came not from the ecstatic moments but from the pleasure they took in brunch at Rosemary's or walking to the gym together, Lydia to run, Kramer for basketball, each watching the other from a distance, as if they were strangers again, each admiring the grace of the other, desiring the other the way a stranger is desired. After showering, they met in the lobby. If Lydia was the first one down, when she first saw Kramer, he was a tall and handsome man. She watched with excitement as he crossed the room, coming closer. Not until they kissed was he again familiar. They walked home holding hands. In the winter, they'd stayed home much of the time. In the spring they went out. Kramer had work friends, drinking friends, old friends from Philly, friends for basketball, for black-market movie prints, from film school. He had friends from every area of his life, from places Lydia didn't know friends existed. Most of these people Kramer saw at their appropriate places, and his relationships with the others depended on chance meetings. But New York can be small and countless meals at Rosemary's began with Kramer and Lydia at a round table for two and ended with chairs borrowed from surrounding tables, friends joining them for a drink or some food. When old girl friends or girl friends of old friends stopped by, Kramer kept his arm around Lydia, warming her, making her feel relaxed, secure. Of all these people the closest to Kramer were Michael and Beth. Michael was a friend from work and a friend from Cheltenham, and Beth, a partner in a film distribution company, knew Kramer professionally and, personally, through Michael. Often things Kramer and Lydia couldn't say directly to each other were said across the table to Michael or Beth.

In April, Kramer knew his time in New York was ending and he couldn't talk about Los Angeles at home anymore. One night, over drinks at Rosemary's, Michael said, "Take a last look, Kramer, you may never see this place again."

"So soon?" Beth said. "When are you leaving?"

"I should've left a month ago. I got as far as making a list and balling my socks up in pairs."

"You're going too, I assume," Beth said to Lydia.

"She's a brilliant scientist." Kramer said. "They love her at school. I met her adviser, you know what he said? 'She'll make a major contribution before she's thirty.'" Kramer dropped a dollar on the table and said, "*The Harder They Come* is at the Elgin in seven minutes. That gives us eight and a half, since they start a little late. If we get up now, we'll make it on time."

"I'll get a cab," Michael said, half out the door.

Kramer paid the bill, and Beth, standing on the sidewalk outside, said to Lydia, "You really aren't going to L.A.?"

"I can't. I have a t.a. in biology."

"A t.a.? What on earth is a t.a.?"

"Teaching assistantship, sorry. And I've already done a good deal of work on my dissertation. I couldn't just abandon it." When Kramer joined them, Lydia said, "I'd never be happy if I gave up biology."

Would he have taken her if she wanted to go? Had he ever given her the chance to consider the possibility?

They were late to the movie and neither Michael nor Kramer would go in since it had started. They waited at the Tropical Tavern until the next show. Beth got drunk, and leaned against Lydia. "You're so brave, not me, I'm not. I'd go and to hell with science."

"I'm not brave," Lydia said.

"Isn't she brave?" Beth nudged the strange man sitting to her left.

"Yeah, yeah, she brave."

"I mean, they like each other. They actually like each other. Always holding hands, kissing when your back is turned. How many couples do you know who like each other?"

The man didn't answer, so Beth turned away. In an angry voice she said, "You're a fool is what you are, Lydia. You deserve what you get."

The next day it poured. The reds of the buildings deepened, the leaves on the trees were greener, the bark nearly black. For hours the rain splattered on the windowpanes, knocking to get into the apartment. Lydia was sitting on the couch, trying to read an article in *Nature*. She read the same line ten times or more, and then giving up, took off her glasses and listened to the rain, and the painful plodding efforts of a beginning pianist, who doggedly tried every Sunday, rain or not, to master "The Spinning Song." The piano had that loud plunking sound. Lydia imagined a little girl, dive-bombing in to get the right finger on the right key. With her glasses off, Lydia could focus all her senses on the rain. Her father had only been able to hear with his glasses on. In the morning, when the rest of the family woke first, he had had to grope for his glasses before he could hear them calling. She felt a dull ache. Had she been six? Eight? Before thirteen, when she was too embarrassed to come into his room in pajamas. She had stood in the doorway, watching him grope at the night table. He knocked the tissue box off the table, then the alarm clock. She tiptoed to the bed, picked up his glasses, climbed onto the bed and put them on his face. They were crooked, one earpiece below his ear, and the glasses hung limply. They laughed, he held her. They bounced. Lydia felt cold, chilled by the rain.

Kramer was wearing his headphones, doing a soundless drumbeat against his work area, sometimes punctuating it with a nod. Unable to concentrate, Lydia watched him instead. She saw him take off the headphones and slump over his desk, cheek against his papers, and she thought, He's tired. He works hard.

The phone rang twice before either of them stirred. The third ring sounded and Kramer turned his head toward Lydia, expecting, since she was closer, she'd pick it up. His glance meant to Lydia that he was picking it up. By the fourth ring, both had moved. Neither noticed the other; the persistent ring was the focal point for both. Kramer hunched over the end table as Lydia reached from her seat on the couch. When she stood, Kramer stumbled over her and grabbed her roughly, to keep from falling onto her. The phone rang and rang. Lydia tried to break free from Kramer's hold. His grip was tight and hurt her. She was about to make a joke when she felt a dampness around her neck. There was no sound from Kramer, only the splattering of the rain all around, the creaking of the ceiling. Lydia lifted her arms and brushed the hair away from his face. The ends of his hair were damp. He hid his face. He would not let her see his face. She kissed his neck and shoulders and she heard the sob, deep and tearing, a strange unknown sound. He wouldn't loosen his grip. He wouldn't let go of her at all, but holding tightly, put one hand under her sweater and tried to pull it off. She tried to help, but he held on too tightly, and after a struggle, the rip of a seam, pulled it off. Still holding, nearly choking the air out of her, he unzipped her pants and slid them down. They stayed around her ankles while he impatiently undid his own. He's afraid, she thought. I'm afraid too. Kramer pushed her halfway onto the couch. It was violent and hurried sex and he called her name again and again as if to assure himself she was Lydia. He came quickly and then was ashamed. "I love you so fucking much. I don't know how I'm going to—" she kissed him to make him stop talking. She wanted his warmth, his body against hers. He stroked her gently, again and again saying, "I love you."

They dressed silently and went back to their corners. The rain had stopped, the rich colors dried up. Lydia finished her article. Kramer was lost again under his headphones. He held her hand all through dinner that night, but neither of them said a word.

On one of those rare afternoons when Kramer was in the apartment alone, Lydia's mother called, and instead of waiting to relay the news to her daughter, she blurted out to Kramer that she was getting married. He hardly knew what to say. He didn't know she'd gotten divorced.

Lydia came home from school and he met her on the stairs outside their apartment door. As she dropped her books, took off her shoes, and went into the bedroom to change, he followed her. "Your mother called. She says she's getting married."

"Oh," Lydia said. "To Harold, I guess."

"Very cute. When did she divorce your father?" Kramer's voice was loud and he stood so close no matter how she side-stepped, she had Kramer the Wall to negotiate.

"Do you mind if I take my clothes off? I just got home—"

"Lydia, God damn it, when did she divorce your father? You never told me she divorced your father."

"What difference does it make? Kramer, please, you're frightening me."

"Being close-mouthed is one thing, Lydia." He backed her through the bedroom into the living room and onto the couch. There he took a seat next to her and searched for her hands to show he didn't mean to be harsh. "Every time something happens in your life, I turn out to be the last to know. Why is it you don't tell me anything?"

"He's dead."

"What are you talking about?"

"Don't make me say it again, Kramer. I don't want to say it."

"Your father is dead? When did he die?"

"Before I met you."

"But you talk about him all the time. His baseball team, his eating habits, his accent—Lydie, I don't understand you."

"Sometimes I forget," Lydia said. "He lived so far away and I hardly got to see him even before."

"You forget? You mean you think if you don't talk about it the situation will change? He'll un-die or something, is that it?"

Lydia laughed. Then she stood up and walked into the bedroom. Kramer bellowed, "Lydia, God damn it, sit down."

She turned around and he saw that she was crying. The other times she'd cried he'd hushed and soothed her and did everything he could to make her forget what had made her cry. This time he said, "Come and sit with me, baby."

She sat down and cried some more. When she was able to talk she said, "I'm not crying about him, don't you understand?"

"Then what is it?"

"You. I'm crying about you."

Kramer was silent. He couldn't talk about that either.

An hour later, Kramer went to the studio, promising to hurry home as soon as possible. Lydia called her grandfather. His voice was faint, as if he were fading away. She asked if it was a bad connection. Then she tried to cheer him up. She said, "Zeyde, how's the garden?"

"Don't ask."

"A lot of Japanese beetles, huh? How's Mr. Zimmer?"

"Don't ask."

"How's Mommy?"

"Don't ask."

"What's the matter? Is she marrying a creep? An *oysvorf*?" Lydia didn't remember what an *oysvorf* was, but usually her complete misuse of Yiddish made Zeyde laugh.

"Feh," he said.

"You better come out and visit me," Lydia said. "You sound terrible."

"You don't want no old man, Lydie."

"Don't say that to me. I've been asking you for eight years. You keep promising to surprise me with a call from the airport."

"I don't care no more. I never tink about you, Lydie. One day after another day after another day, Lydie, I don't care, I don't tink about you. Let them pass, one day after another day. I'm an old man, Lydie, I don't tink about it at all."

"Why are you saying these things to me?" To keep from crying, Lydia whined. Zeyde used to make like an Old-World violin when she whined, *ya-de-ya-da*. In the old days it had made her cry harder, but now it would make her laugh.

Instead, Zeyde said, "I don't tink about you no more, Lydie. Go to your baker, Lydie, he's a young man."

"Stop," she said, crying.

"Don't call me no more! I don't tink about you."

Alone in the apartment, Lydia went into the bedroom and closed her eyes. She saw a purple party dress shared with her sister Jill, her mother's plum-colored robe with satin lapels. She remembered sitting at the foot of the bed watching Rose put mascara on. Nearsighted, Rose smears the mirror with nose grease. Later, dressed and perfumed, she kisses Lydia good-bye. When the key turns in the lock, Lydia enters her parents' bedroom and opens a bureau drawer. She counts his neat stack of alligator T-shirts, blue, red, white, white, blue. Zeyde wore pleated pants and a felt hat, even in Los Angeles. She was ashamed of him, but invited her friends over and said, "Zeyde, please make a nickel cry." Now it is a lost art. "Zeyde, make a nickel cry."

Zeyde stands in the center of the living room, a circle of children surrounding him, Jill, Lydia, and three neighborhood kids. Zeyde holds the nickel by its edge, showing them both the buffalo and the Indian head. He begins a long story about how all the buffalo have been killed by the cruel and heartless white man, and the once proud Indian tribes decimated by disease and white man's liquor. The story changes each time. Sometimes the buffalo gets more notice. This time it's the Indian. Sometimes Zeyde talks about reservations. This time it's the woman with her papoose, waiting for her husband, a warrior. Zeyde is restless when he tells the story. He scratches a very naked head. (Once he said he was scalped.) He scratches behind his ear. Sometimes he blows his nose and hitches up his pleated pants. The children are all spellbound, even Lydia, who this time is confused. Papoose is the last car of a railroad train. How can an Indian woman hold a papoose? "Lydie," Zeyde says. "Lydie, you're catching flies." He continues with the story. When it draws to an end, Lydia bounces up and down, waiting for the best part. Zeyde shows the Indian. Then he squeezes the nickel as hard as he can. His whole bald head turns bright red. He clamps his teeth together and squeezes his eyes tightly shut. His knees buckle. His fingernails turn white. His upper lip recedes. His ears turn crimson. His nose turns crimson. Big fat tears drip from the Indian's eye. Why do we laugh so? It's such a sad story, why does it make the children laugh?

Lydia got up to make another phone call. She figured her mother would still be home. When Rose answered, Lydia said congratulations. As usual, her mother had someone in the kitchen and the conversation was a three-way one between the person in the kitchen, Rose, and Lydia, with Lydia, as always, answering at the wrong time.

"How's Zeyde," Lydia said, not mentioning her call fifteen minutes ago.

Lydia's mother said Zeyde was being a pain in the ass.

It hurt Lydia hearing that. "He's despondent. Everyone is dying." She couldn't say Daddy. Daddy died.

"What's he despondent for? It was my husband that died. Hold on a second. What?"

Her mother said, "In about an hour."

Lydia said, "What? Are you talking to me, Rose?"

"Just a second, Cookie. What?"

The mumbling went on.

"This is long distance calling," Lydia said.

Her mother said, "What?"

"You have friends at least. He's all alone."

"It's not my fault he doesn't have friends. I took him to the Golden Age Club. He says, 'I don't want to be with no old-timers.' Did you ever hear such a thing? What is he, I ask?"

"Why can't you be nice to him?"

That got her mother's attention. Rose said, directly into the receiver, "What do you know, three thousand miles away? You don't know a damned thing, Lydia. I give him bed and board, don't I? I let him live here. I have a new husband and I didn't push the old man into a home, did I?"

"Good-bye," Lydia said. "I have to go."

7

IN MAY there was a series of mysterious phone calls that meant to Lydia the end was here. She didn't know who the calls were from or what they were about, but when one came, Kramer would take the phone into the bedroom, shutting the door behind him. After the call he would be irritable and pick fights with her, the way he had in the beginning, telling her she was rude to bother him when he was working and rude to eat dinner alone. Their months of peace were over. They compromised less on hours, Lydia going to bed earlier, Kramer later. Chores they'd shared went undone. There were still moments when they were friends, but mostly their time together was divided between fighting and frightened passion. They never spoke about what they felt. Lydia never put her own fear into words, but often she ached all over. Once she came home and noticed fewer books on Kramer's shelves. Another time she saw that his tapes were not very well hidden in a carton below his work area.

Classes had let out at school, freeing Lydia from her teaching responsibilities, but it seemed to her everyone was going away. Brian had already left for his summer semester in Woods Hole and Harriet was off to Indiana to visit her folks. A week after finals, Lydia found Dr. Cantoni in the final throes of office cleaning. His books were in cartons, ready to be shipped off to the university in Boulder. When he saw Lydia standing dumbfounded outside his room, he said his plans had changed somewhat. He'd decided to take a leisurely drive out to Colorado with his family, leaving a good deal sooner than he'd originally anticipated. He clapped her on the shoulder and laughed ho ho, telling her he was eager to read the first draft of her dissertation. She took down his address for the third time.

The lab was empty. Not merely unpeopled, as it was when Lydia had worked overnight during the school year, but desolate, barren. Lately Kramer had begun working until midnight or one at the studio, so Lydia took her blanket from the file cabinet and planned to work late, too. But instead of concentrating, she could only wonder if she'd stayed long enough, if it was possible Kramer was on the subway heading home. She held off for as long as possible before she left school. Then she would walk slowly toward her building, climb up to the sixth floor, hoping the footsteps above were his, and that he'd hug her and light up the apartment when she got there. But Kramer was rarely home first anymore, so after unlocking the door onto a black apartment, she stood in the hallway wondering what to do. Pipes hissed, windowpanes rattled, voices and wicked laughter drew close. She was afraid if she switched on the lights she'd find Kramer sprawled out on the living-room carpet twisted, bloody, black-tongued, dead. The image changed each evening, one as grotesque as the next. Eventually Lydia had to enter, and she stumbled through the kitchen into the living room, feeling for her rocking chair, sitting in it, rocking in the dark. To get her mind off the darkness and prowlers, Lydia began making imaginary analysts' reports, playing the part of both doctor and patient:

> Lydia M. suffered from severe anxiety complexes. When she was referred to me by Dr. Haselkorn, she was living a life where no movement was possible without a ritualistic action to precede it. . . .

Kramer asked why she waited with the lights out, and after the first few times Lydia failed to pass it off as another joke. He knew Lydia well enough to imagine her reasons for sitting in the dark and said, "Why can't you be like other women and imagine I'm out with a floozy? I could come home and tell you it wasn't true. I can't reassure you now, Lydia. I can't tell you it isn't dark in the house when it is. I can't tell you I'm here beside you when I'm not."

Once strange gurgling noises began at eleven-thirty. At midnight, Kramer still wasn't home. Lydia was too shaken to determine if it was the rain, the neighbors, or Kramer's death rattle, so she grabbed her yellow slicker, pulled her stocking cap down to her eyebrows, and ran out of the house. She decided never to go back until Kramer was home. She circled twice around the block, then stopped in the all-night delicatessen to warm up. Hailstones pricked her cheeks. She felt as if she'd been wandering forever, abandoned, homeless, holes in her socks and gloves. "What do you want, sonny?" the man behind the counter asked. "You can't just stand there." Lydia said she wanted macadamia nuts, sure they wouldn't have them. But they did, she hadn't the $2.50, so she was back in the wind again, up Seventh Avenue to begin another lap. Her breath came in short gasps; melted ice was streaming down her nose. On the tenth round she saw Kramer in the same phone booth she'd been using. Just as she was running across the avenue, between bright lights and horns, he walked out of the phone booth and down the block. By the time she caught up to him, she was unable to speak. Kramer saw her painfully wide-eyed, shoulders rising and falling, and he put his arms around her to steady them. "I just called to see if you were home," he said. "I didn't want to go back to an empty house."

By the time they were in the building and four flights up, Lydia was smiling again. Kramer threw open their front door and dashed from room to room, switching on the overhead lights and table lamps and swinging naked light bulbs, and then dashed back into the kitchen, stood belly to belly with Lydia, placed his hands gently on her head and said softly, "You're short, but you're cute."

"Lydia, I love you," he said that night in bed. "Tell me you'll be okay. Stop clowning and look at me. I love you, don't cry, I love you. Smile for me—that's it, a big one. A big one for the family in Duluth."

Though Lydia could do nothing but wait for his return the nights Kramer worked late, whenever they were both in the apartment for more than three hours, she got the urge to run away. If they were home together and not in bed, chances were Kramer was at his desk, eyes closed, swaying, mouthing an occasional refrain, obscene plastic earmuffs bulging from each side of his head. He looked to Lydia like a giant insect, quivering antennae, all-seeing compound eyes. And she was another insect, flailing her arms in front of him, buzzing around to get his attention. She knew he saw her mouth move, but could never hear a word. She made broad and furious movements, throwing his clothes around to get at hers, kicking his shoes and then lacing up her own, hoping at some point he'd take off his headphones and talk her into staying. She was sorry as soon as she was dressed and out the front door. Once, determined beforehand not to be sorry, she managed to get all the way to Abingdon Square with no regrets. Then she sat on the cold park bench in her thin pants and realized she should have battled it out with him.

"What am I doing here? This is insane, it's unhealthy, I want to go home."

A presence, sensed by his warm liquor smell before he spoke, said, "Go home, darlin'. A young woman's place is in the home."

Lydia was much too curious hearing his soft voice to take offense at the platitude. She said, "I just walked out. It would be humiliating to go back already."

"Pride goeth before a fall, young woman. If he's your man, go to him." The man rapped himself on the chest, spat on the ground and said, "Go to him. Go with wings."

"That's just about the only way I could go."

The man smelled as old and musty as a subway tunnel, but he had the gentlest voice. "Is it your young man?"

"It is."

"Cutting out on you all the time?"

"I wouldn't doubt it."

"Then I take back my first words to you. A pretty young thing like you'll never get any peace with that kind. Mark my words: He'll cheat on you, then beat up on you, again and again. Young men, they just got to go waving the magic wand around. Soon as they see something in skirts, they got to stick it in. Mark my words." He cleared his throat, sounding like a stalled car, then spat up again. "Women is different. Take you. You're a pretty young thing, just wanting to have a home and a family, whilst he—"

"How do you know," Lydia said irritably. "What makes you think I don't want to live it up?"

"Hurt's making you speak like that. I can tell by your voice you've been hurt to the soul. Now my name's Ken Hall and I bet my mama's gold ring I'm right."

Lydia felt him nudge her and extended her hand to shake. His hand was as rough as rhinoceros hide, but his grip wasn't mean at all.

"You're right. He's not a bad person, but lately he has trouble talking to me. Especially when I need words."

"A little flattery to tell you you're a fine, fine woman?"

"Something like that."

"Mark my words, young woman: If he can't tell you now, he sure as hell won't be able to tell you any better in a year."

"I'm not thinking about a year from now, or at least I'm trying not to. Anyhow, a lot of the time, it's so good between us."

"You mean the loving, don't you?"

"Not just that. I mean we share a lot. We see things the same way. Do you know what I mean?"

"I know there's more to marriage than sex, young woman."

"Oh, we're not married," Lydia said.

Ken Hall breathed with difficulty. A couple walked past the park, heels scraping the pavement, conversation lost in the wind. Six grown-ups linked arms and spanned Bleecker Street singing, "We're off to see the wizard." A car speeding down the street stopped to let them finish their chorus. Ken Hall said, "Are you coming home with me?"

"No."

"I got a room, plumbing, and a nice old boy-dog named Eppie to keep you company. It's clean and neat. I got a rug and a bedspread and I work steady. Are you coming home with me or are you not?"

"I guess I'm not."

"You best remember Ken Hall's words then: It's better to be an old man's darlin' than a young man's slave. You hear?"

He got up and walked away. When Lydia got home, Kramer was asleep.

She became superstitious. She studied in the old upholstered lounge at the Interchurch Center uptown and at various Christian Science reading rooms. She found a church on Fifth Avenue that was open day and night. She was trying out all the denominations.

Friends of Kramer's had just returned from Paris and were now living in Connecticut. Kramer took Lydia to meet them.

The man's pipe seemed to serve as a pacifier and the woman, pretty and secure with seven advanced degrees tucked away, baked bread and raised babies. Lydia was introduced. Neither person took her hand. The woman asked if she were also in film. Lydia said, "No, but—" The woman turned to her cutting board, asking no more questions. Lydia's chance to tell who she was never came up again.

The woman smiled a lot during dinner. The babies smiled a lot. The man sucked on his pipe and kept his back to Lydia. There was chilled avocado soup first. It had the consistency of latex wall paint. Lydia was shaking so badly the soup wouldn't stay on the spoon long enough to reach her mouth. The others conversed in what seemed to be a foreign tongue. She discovered that when she balanced the stem of her spoon on the rim of her bowl, the spoon floated on top of the soup. She knew by allowing the soup to seep onto the spoon she would discover the maximum weight it could achieve before sinking.

When the woman cleared the table after dinner, the beige linen tablecloth was spotless except at Lydia's place, where it was a Pollock-style painting of green and brown splotches, accented with a crescent-shaped wedge of raw cabbage. When the attention was focused on the woman at the sink, Lydia picked up the cabbage and, since it was a dogless family, ate it. "Bring Lydia more salad, love," the man said. "It looks like she's still hungry."

Kramer and Lydia walked a few blocks to pick up the car. Lydia hunched over, eyes to the ground, searching for a four-leaf clover as they walked.

"Okay, Lydia, what is it?" Kramer asked.

She couldn't take her eyes off the ground. As Kramer went faster, she stooped lower, until she was walking like his pet chimpanzee.

Kramer said, "You certainly were a dynamic dinner guest."

The car was in front of them, borrowed and blue.

"Can we walk around the block once more? For exercise? Kramer, I can't help it. You didn't used to mind that I was quiet."

"That's just it, Lydia. You used to be quiet. Now you're not even conscious."

She never found the four-leaf clover, but she was still with Kramer when her mother called to give the news about her grandfather. Ninety-one and as lucid as ever, he was refusing to go through the operation to have his pacemaker replaced. He said he wanted to let the batteries run down so he could die peacefully. Lydia, at seven, had said, "Zeyde, why are you so fat?"

"I don't know. I don't eat no bread."

Her mother said, "Lydia, call him. You were his favorite. He always listened to you. Tell him not to act this way."

"What am I supposed to say?"

"That he'll die if he doesn't have the surgery."

"But Rose, he wants to die."

"That's crazy!" Then off the phone, to someone in her kitchen, "You know, maybe the old man's finally losing his marbles."

Lydia's mother told her not to talk to Zeyde if she was going to tell him to kill himself. So she didn't call. He died the next week. A week after that, Lydia walked Kramer to a taxi, thinking how he'd come into her life at the time of a death and was leaving at the time of another. She wanted to say good-bye the right way, but suddenly she was standing on the corner alone.

She went to Rosemary's, but no one recognized her. She was a stranger sitting at the table, asking for cream with her coffee instead of milk. A heavy breather sat next to her. "Candy is dandy but sex doesn't rot your teeth," his T-shirt said. He was about fifty and had a bad cough. Lydia put her elbows on the table and smiled to show the waitress she was in good shape. The heavy breather nudged her elbow, so she took her arms off the table. He kicked her, so she wrapped her legs around the stool. He leaned over, pushing her coffee cup to the next person's place. "Good-bye, Nancy," he bellowed. Lydia looked up to reply, but the man had gotten out of his seat. With bowlegged, dancing steps, he walked to the center of the restaurant and in a foghorn voice called, "Good-bye, John! Good-bye, Hank! Good-bye, Lou!" He gave his check to the cashier and saluted. "Good-bye, Sam! Good-bye, Mary!"

At the door he turned toward the tables. The customers were eating eggs or spinach salads, drinking coffee or beer. Not a single person looked up. No one acknowledged the man, though from the pizza parlor next door a scuffle and shout was heard. "Good-bye, Irma! Good-bye, Max! Good-bye, Kramer!"

Lydia turned around, but he was gone.

8

A WEEK LATER Lydia realized Kramer was dead. He couldn't answer her last questions. She couldn't call him back to redo the past, erase angry words, treat him better, make the farewell perfect, the memory pure. He was dead.

Mail still came for Kramer, a friend phoned to ask them both by for Sunday dinner. Footprints, shaving cream, dirty undershirts, there were signs Kramer had existed, but nothing to show that Lydia had existed with him. There was no longer any tangible evidence that they'd shared lives, beds, magazines, pints of ice cream. What was so puzzling was the way people appeared in Lydia's life, dominated it, then disappeared forever. With her father, there'd only been a brief cross-country phone call to inform her of the facts. "We didn't tell you in time for the funeral because you were in the middle of exams," Rose had said.

You didn't tell me you really meant to leave.

"It was a car accident, Cookie."

What did I do? How could I have known?

"The police said he died instantly, thank God."

How did she know? How was she supposed to believe he was dead? She never saw him die. He had gone from her life the day she moved to New York. He had gone much before Rose told her he died, but she could summon him up on Christmas holidays or on business trips to New York. She could call, "Daddy?" And he'd say, "Hi, sweetheart," just like that. Was she a magician?

After her mother called to tell Lydia of her father's death, Lydia kept seeing him in the street. Spying the familiar heart-shaped bald spot, the stooped left shoulder, she'd weave between people, pushing, calling, "Daddy!" Once it was someone's daddy, because he stopped when he heard his name. Lydia imagined all the fathers in midtown, from Forty-second to Fifty-ninth streets, opening their windows and looking down from thirty-six. twenty-five, or nineteen flights when her cry echoed. But no daddy answered, "Hi, sweetheart."

That was when she had an eerie feeling about her father. It was the first time she stopped to consider that it might not have been a dream. Maybe he was gone forever. But there wasn't any pain. She'd be sad if he was gone. She loved him. Wasn't she his favorite? How could he be dead? Had she seen it? *A Los Angeles man, 62, was killed today when his car skidded into the southbound lane* . . .

No.

And Kramer? Michael had called up and said, "Lydia, hi, how's it going. Look, Kramer says to tell you—"

"I know. He had to go. He left."

"We all do what we got to do," Michael said.

After Michael's call, Lydia wandered in her little apartment. She heard the phone ring but was unable to pick it up. It seemed to ring all day long. When she was growing up people hadn't been so irrational. Her mother was especially predictable and easy to read. Once when Lydia was little, her mother shouted at her for no reason, but when the tears came, her mother said, "I'm sorry, Lydia. I'm unwell and feeling cranky today."

Outside a woman was rocking a baby, trying to soothe it, to make it stop wailing. Lydia decided if she had a child, she'd prepare her for the outside world. She'd teach her about irrational acts by slapping her arbitrarily and yelling for no apparent reason. Sometimes if the child was very naughty, Lydia would hug her, and other times she'd reprimand her for doing the same thing. When a dog is disciplined that way, he'll run in circles. He'll come when he's called, but he'll come whimpering, tail between his legs, not knowing whether he'll get a rolled-up newspaper or a pat on the head. But when it happens to children they learn survival. Lydia's daughter goes into the world and finds that a teacher doesn't like her because she has brown hair, not blond. She does poorly in art because this teacher gives her crayons with the ends already chewed off by another child. She makes a friend and the friend promises to be true but proceeds to tell all the other children Lydia's daughter has stolen from their desks and said horrid things about them. Lydia's daughter can accept it gracefully. She'll grow and be healthy. And when she meets a man who says he loves her more than he's ever loved a woman, who makes her believe she's truly special, then one day leaves without warning, her girl, grown and educated in the rites of irrationality, will understand.

She snapped the earpieces off her glasses, one at a time, then tried to break the frame across the bridge. She struggled, finally succeeding when she pounded them with the heel of her boot. The lenses, though scratched, were unbroken, and she shoved them in a drawer. She thought she was safe now, but after a half-hour the phone rang. Then it rang again. Again. It made Lydia feel invaded. In time she could tell friends from strangers. Friends, knowing it was a small apartment, let it ring three, maybe four times. Rema, conscious of her own fallibility, would call twice in a row, letting it ring four times the first try and six times the second. Rema called so often that whenever the phone rang, Lydia thought of those heavy-lidded immigrant's eyes, the kind of eyes seen staring out from barbed wire in old brown photographs, and decided she could have none of it. The thought of Rema's pity made her livid, and Lydia always paced restlessly until the second call was completed, unanswered. From wall to wall the living room was twelve paces, sixteen paces if she started at the window, walked straight across the room, stepped onto the seat of the sofa, and stood on the back against the stark white wall, as if waiting to be nailed to it.

One day the phone rang four times. Then it began on the six, meaning Rema. This time Lydia picked it up, having had all morning to compose her obscenities *mother-fucking lead your fucking own life voyeur, keep that fucking long pink nose in your own fucking window.*

"Hello, Mrs. Kramer?" the voice said.

Lydia thought her heart would stop.

"Mrs. Kramer?" the voice repeated unsurely. "This is—"

"Mrs. Kramer is dead." Lydia buried her head between her legs to relieve the dizziness. Now all she had to do was reach over to the phone on the table, two paces to the left.

"Perhaps I can talk to you, then. I'm from Saint Francis of Assisi Church—"

Then pray for me, Lydia thought.

"And I represent an order that does charitable work in a remote African country, once the Belgian Congo, now called Zaire. Leprosy is not a disease of the past. It is a scourge of the present that ruins the lives of thousands of our countrymen—"

The lady was having difficulty with pronunciation. She sounded fat. "You should see the joy on a leper's face when he gets his new basket shoes."

Lydia covered the mouthpiece, laughed, and then said, "Excuse me, the baby was crying."

"You should see the joy on a leper's face when he gets his new basket shoes," the woman repeated.

When the phone rang immediately afterward, Lydia answered it. Rema was on the other end, warm and chipper. "Where have you been, Lydia?" she asked.

"A remote African country, once the Belgian Congo and now Zaire. You should see the joy on a leper's face when he gets his new basket shoes."

"Are you doing anything for dinner tonight?"

Rema's house. Rema's immigrant eyes, Ken's Solzhenitsyn beard. Soyburgers for supper. The young modern American's new midweek special. "Can't."

"Lyd—" Rema's voice had that pleading quality to it. "I know you're busy with the thesis and all, but I haven't seen you in ages? So tell me when you're free, okay? Kenny wants to see you—"

Hanging by her toes. "I don't want to come over."

To fill the silence, block out her own regrets, apologies, or explanations, Lydia said, "What's today, Tuesday? I'll come over next Tuesday."

Rema agreed, and having nothing more to say, got off the phone.

What happened was that Lydia went over the next night because it felt like it was about time to go. She decided to walk up to Eighty-seventh Street. She plotted out a sensible course beginning at Sheridan Square and continuing up Broadway to Forty-second where the avenues crossed. It was a freak June night, unseasonably cold the radio said, and her breath, a small patch of fog, preceded Lydia, protecting her as she walked. She imagined herself to be veiled in fog and since she could see no one, she imagined no one could see her. All that appeared in the night were patches of neon color floating two or three stories above the buildings on either side, bands of green or red across the width of the street at each block, directing the traffic in spurts. In the Village, she came fog to face with many pairs of skinny men, short hair, pink noses, all hands tucked safely in peacoat pockets. Farther uptown were folks with dogs that peed clouds of smoke.

Rema's apartment was in the middle of a block of old brownstones, some with heavy concrete pots for geraniums in the summer, one with small public library lions. But Rema's building, maybe because Ken had picked it out, was the least interesting on the block. It was small, fronted with glossy beige bricks, and the aluminum building number was spotlighted by a fluorescent light. The doorman had no teeth. The one before him had had no teeth. The mural behind the doorman showed a canal with neckless gondoliers who wore striped shirts and mustaches that twisted up at the ends.

Rema watched Lydia through the peephole, then inch by inch appeared, smiling, her eyes tragic and heavy-lidded, Ken behind her, a head taller, chocolate on his left cheek. The apartment was warm and a steady hiss came from the radiator. There were Navajo rugs on the floor. Lydia knew from the times before not to look at the face masks Ken had brought back from his Peace Corps days, each wearing an expression no one should live with. Hate, greed, gristle in the back teeth. Ken and Rema didn't eat meat. They didn't smoke cigarettes. They didn't stay up late. They didn't sleep with other people. They never argued. They shared chores and pleasures. They had written a ten-page wedding contract guaranteeing certain unalienable rights to each. Rema said Ken always put the toilet seat down.

Lydia did an about-face on her heels and was out the front door before Rema could lift her arms and trap her in a hug. She was a convict as she ran down the halls. She felt the shackles around her ankle. She heard Rema say, "Get her, Kenny!"

The stairway exit happened to be in the same direction Lydia ran. Luckily it didn't have a peephole and a name on it like the rest. Luckily it opened and she was able to run down and down the spiraling gray stairs, limping from the weight of the iron ball around her ankle. The dogs were barking hoarsely. One fell dead from heat and exhaustion. The air of freedom was in the street.

How good it would feel to go home and never again answer the phone; no more lepers and basket shoes. She'd give them money. *Say God bless you, Lydia, please.*

The door on the second floor was locked. Lydia kicked it, pulled the knob, threw her body against it. Though she refused to cry, her eyes grew wet, her face hot. It wasn't until she felt Ken's arms gently around her that she fell dead into a faint.

The first time she had tried to stay awake when the new year came in, she woke up wrapped in a blanket in her daddy's arms, and heard his tender voice. "It's ten-oh-two, sweetheart." Lydia was on the cold cement floor of an alien building and Ken was standing, waiting for her to focus. He held out his hand, but it had no significance for Lydia, so he withdrew it. A helping hand. She stood, unaided.

"Come on, let's take the elevator." Ken punched the button in a nervous staccato until the elevator rumbled and squeaked to the second floor. It threw its doors back, revealing a spotty mirror on the back wall, "Mario has no dick" emblazoned across it. "I won't tell Rema," he said.

Lydia hummed loudly to wipe away the image of herself, racing down and down, not even getting away, dumb ass. "Won't tell Rema what?"

"The other thing, Lydia," he said when the elevator hit the fifth floor, "I'm sure Rema will ask you to stay the night, but it would be better if you didn't. She's had this bladder infection and she ought to get a decent night's sleep. If you're short on cash, I'll give you five dollars for a cab home."

"I don't understand you," Lydia said.

Rema opened the door, wearing the same sweet expression she'd worn when she opened it earlier, the same sad brown eyes.

"I wanted to bring you a bottle of wine from around the corner."

"That's really sweet, Lydie, but it's ten o'clock. Nothing's open."

"Christ," Ken said.

Darting eyes, wife to husband.

"Right," Lydia said, sidestepping. "I was in the neighborhood so I thought I'd say hi. I didn't realize how late it was."

"Stay," Rema said, sad eyes in a pleading glance three-quarters to Ken and one-quarter to Lydia. "Kenny and I had our co-op meeting and just got in ourselves. Have you eaten?" Another pleading glance to Ken. "There's a portion of bean soup left over? And Kenny made this super banana bread? I'll put tea up, Lydie, don't say no. I can tell you haven't eaten in I don't know how long."

Rema helped Lydia take off her jacket, and handed it to Ken. When Ken walked into the bedroom, she took Lydia's hands and warmed them between her own. "Is something wrong, Lydie? You can tell me."

Getting no reply, Rema went into the bedroom and in a loud voice asked Ken to put up the tea and in a soft voice said something else. Rema at sixteen had said, "I caught Marc making out with Maryann, and I tried to break up with him, but I can't let him go. I'd die without him."

Lydia turned and stubbed her toe against a large plant pot, sending an avocado tree quivering. When she recovered her equilibrium, she tripped over a low box filled with twenty-five pounds of soybeans. Rema watched from the doorway. "You can't see a thing without your glasses," she said. "Lydie, that's so dangerous."

"Safe, Rema. I do it because it's safe."

The living room was green from plants and brown from the rugs and pillows pitched into each corner. Lydia lay on the couch, burying her face in a cushion.

"Do you notice anything different, Lyd?"

Lydia turned her head to face Rema, careful to keep her cheek against the cushion.

"Kenny and I just got the couch last week? Isn't it nice?"

Lydia rubbed her cheek against the pillow. "Mmm. Soft, velvety."

"Make room." Rema sat next to her, but faced the kitchen, listening as the water was turned on. "It's been so long? First I was busy with my class? I have older kids this year?" Rema's statements always sounded like questions. "Then I decided I wasn't going to call you because you haven't called me in an age and a half? But I figured don't let an old friendship die at the drop of a hat. Lyd? Are you going to say something? How's teaching this year?"

"How's what?"

"My mother told me your mother married Harold Wolfe. You're not upset about that, are you? You look a mess."

Lydia could picture Harold Wolfe, but she couldn't remember what her father looked like. He was a blank, featureless. She used to play a game with Rema, Mr. Potatohead. An assortment of plastic eyes, noses, mustaches, and mouths came ready to be tacked onto a styrofoam form or a vegetable. They spent many afternoons making outlandish combinations. Her father had small eyes and a long nose.

"Is it you and Kramer? Did something happen?"

"He died is what happened."

"You're kidding—Lydia, no!"

Lydia threw an arm casually across the back of the couch to show she took these things staunchly, the way you're supposed to take the inevitable death of a ninety-one-year-old grandfather.

"Lydie, was he sick? When did it happen?" Rema edged closer with each question, her mouth quivering with nervous laughter. Inappropriate response—Lydia understood. She suffered from it frequently herself. "When was the funeral, Lydia, my God!"

The water switched off in the kitchen and was replaced with the dull metal clanking of pots and pans. Rema got up and ran to her husband. "The most horrible thing—oh, Kenny!" In a moment, the two of them left the kitchen clinging, grateful, concerned for themselves, their own mortality, for Lydia. Would she be a burden on them?

"What happened?" Ken asked, taking a chair near Rema. "Tell us, Lydia."

"Please," Rema said. "You have to tell us, we're your friends. Was he sick?"

"Maybe a car accident. Just nod if I'm right. Rema, remember Kramer told you if he drove cross-country he'd take your parents' anniversary gift?"

"We would've heard if it was a plane crash," Rema said.

They waited silently, if not for the revelation then at least for tears. Ken sat tall and straight, his beard outlining the side of his face and chin. To Lydia, he looked like a man in a medical illustration, everything screwed on right. His eyes were brown and even, his nose straight, his lips pink, an okay square chin, and a forehead with a respectable thinker's ridge. Detached earlobes, not too meaty. She could sidle up to him and gently chew on a lobe. Soft and fuzzy, she knew the type, no hair on the edges, the insides sweet, not too waxy. Kramer's ears were bitter, his lobes detached. Ken would grow rigid if she took a nibble. An eye would twitch, just as it twitched when Lydia merely thought about it.

Rema sighed deeply, then lined up three cups. "Tea, Lydia? Red Zinger?" She poured; Ken cut his banana bread into thin slices. Its sweet smell reminded Lydia of how long it had been since she'd eaten. Her piece was gone in two swallows, and she asked for more. Rema reached for Ken's hand. "She may not want to talk about it."

"Marc took me to a party and then danced all night with Sheila," Rema at sixteen had said. "I want to break up with him, but I can't let him go, I'd die without him. . . ."

"It's unbelievable, absolutely unbelievable," Ken said. "And I'm sure it's painful, but you came here, so I imagine some part of you wants to tell us about it. Otherwise I wouldn't push so hard."

"May I have another piece of bread?" Lydia asked.

"Kenny's a terrific baker, isn't he," Rema said, animated, her mind far from Lydia's problems. "Last month at the block fair this man came over? He kept telling Kenny he ought to go into business? That Kenny's Swedish rye was by far the best he'd ever tasted?"

"I guess I can assume it wasn't an illness," Kenny said. "Because when I saw him a couple of weeks ago, he looked fine. It's unbelievable, when did he actually—when did it happen?"

Lydia asked to be excused, and went into the kitchen for butter. She opened the refrigerator and sat on the floor in front of it. Just like in Rose's refrigerator, there were wrapped portions of everything. She lifted a lid off a round casserole, scooped out fruit salad with her fingers, and heard Rose saying, "Don't stand with the door open like that." Foil square unwrapped, she ate a cheese and noodle something. Turning into Kramer, she rapped herself soundly on the chest and belched twice, smiling, remembering his look of innocence. Shifting focus, panicking, she called out, "Aha, I've found it," grabbed the butter, dumped the foil ball from the noodle something out the kitchen window, and coughed as she entered the living room, cleaning her teeth with her tongue as she did.

Ken had moved to the couch and had his hand up Rema's sweater. Lydia felt a sudden urge to go home. She yawned ostentatiously. No one noticed. Ken brushed the hair off Rema's cheek and said something sweet, making her slide a little lower, closer. Lydia crossed in front of them, setting the butter on the hot radiator. Rema looked up. "We were just talking about Muriel? She's this speech therapist at my school? She's got four kids and her husband just died of cancer? Everyone wanted to be nice, but she got vicious? She called Claire a nigger in front of everyone?"

Lydia crossed in front of Rema and Ken a second time, retrieved her plate, cut a four-inch slice of bread, and took a seat on the floor near the radiator. She hummed her latest atonal tune, "Keeping the Demons Away."

"She's a victim," Ken said. "The kind of woman who gets raped."

Lydia touched the bottom of her plate.

"There are limits to how much a person can be helped, Rema."

Small voice. "But I want to be there."

Large voice. "She's beyond your help."

Small voice. "I can't desert a friend, Kenny."

Large voice. "She's sick and needs professional help."

The butter had collapsed. Lydia said, "Insanity is a disease of the soul, not the psyche," then wondered whose voice that had been.

Small voice. "We were talking about Muriel? This woman at work?"

Lydia cut off a hunk of butter and touched the top of it carefully with the flat end of her knife. Spreading it like icing, she thought about Zeyde's attempts to work frozen butter onto his rye. It was late, and she'd waited long enough. Kramer would be home by now. A dark apartment meant he was fast asleep, his mouth soft and wet, little pushed-in teeth. Getting into bed beside him, she'd feel his smooth skin. He'd wake to put his arm around her, curling closer.

Lydia stood. "I must go home."

"Wait, Lydie. Finish your bread. Then tell us what we can do."

Thick yellow butter. "I didn't realize it was so late. He'll worry."

"Who, Lyd?"

"Really—"

Lydia walked into the bedroom to get her jacket. Slipping it on, she ran from the apartment calling, "Thank you, Rema, good-bye, Ken."

She raced down the stairs and on the third floor took the elevator. Once in the street, she skipped down the block to Broadway, laughing. How clean and dry the air felt. It wouldn't take long to run home. She was a runner and when she felt like this, distances were traveled in an instant. She ran a block, stopping for the red. On the second block, she felt the wind race through her nostrils. So bright in the street, streaks of yellow taxis, people, dogs. A pain in her side. No pain, no. It feels good *I need you* it feels good. Baskin-Robbins, silly armed schoolchairs with fuchsia tops, old men and ice cream *how I feel you can't imagine how.* She couldn't stop running. She'd never stop. Pain in her side *come home, I need, you can't imagine.* No money, gasping for air, she had to go home, she had to go home, she ran alone, no one below, no one beside. She ran alone, no one at home *come home come home* deep breath, deep breath, breathless sob, painful gasp. Air, needing air *come home come home* gasps that shook her body, blinding her, pain in her side. At Seventy-first Street she knelt on the ground *I need you can't imagine how come home come home.*

9

OUTSIDE, the morning came, the day passed, the night fell. Lydia was as unchanging and immovable as a mountain. She'd wrapped herself in her warm, soft quilt and sat rigid on the living-room floor. Though unable to stir, her body gave off enough heat to assure her she was alive, so she was content to sit this way forever, knees up to her chin, hands tucked into her armpits like little broken wings, quilt folded in at her feet and under her wings to keep her warm. She was alive but dormant: No sustenance was needed during diapause. "I'll prove I am alive," she said, and felt hundreds of pulse beats all over her body. Once, before she'd gotten warm, she moved her hand between her legs and touched herself. She remembered how good it used to feel. It didn't feel good anymore.

The tops of the trees were visible from where Lydia sat. She knew when it was windy. The trees bent and swayed as if waving to her. Leaves rustled. During a violent gust, the windowpanes rattled in the rotten old frames, threatening to break free. Sharp bursts of air seeped in. The windows whistled. Pigeons clucked. From an unknown room in an unknown building, as they did every night, a chorus sang "Happy Birthday" and cheered. Lydia grew cold and rocked herself. Tired from the effort, she dropped her head and breathed in the odor of her own body. She knew the smell. She knew she was alive.

Hours later, she sat with her knees up to her chin, her chin on her knees, quilt tightly wrapped. Kramer was all over the place. Clamped on the outer edge of his desk were two reels, a crank screwed into one. He was rewinding one of his films. The whirring was comforting to Lydia and she fell asleep. When she woke up next, he was in the rocker, wearing overalls and T-shirt. Newspapers were spread all over the floor. He unscrewed the paint roller from the long pole. The ceiling was done now, the walls were white. Halfway between the ceiling and the floor, all around the room, were two blue stripes, a broad one and a thin one. Kramer walked across the floor and using the pole as a pointer said, "The stripes symbolize stripes. The color's for the blood in my granddaddy's veins." Daddy, granddaddy.

"I run in my dreams." "Do you kick your legs around?" "I don't know, do I?"

Lydia burrowed her chin between her knees, trying not to sleep. She used to climb into bed for the pleasure of feeling herself drift, knowing if she lay still she'd quickly be off. Now sleep was far worse than wakefulness. When she sat on the floor, guarding the living room, scenes came and went. She could see them coming and though she couldn't stop them from coming she could make them go away. Asleep, they burrowed under her skin. Dreams ate into her brain. She never knew they were upon her until she felt herself sweat, heard her own scream. Often in dreams she was running. On and on, aching, exhausted, achieving incredible speed though her body was cramped and doubled over.

"I had a dog that ran in his dreams. He kicked his legs and whimpered if it was a chase. He salivated if he was the pursuer. Come and kiss me, honey."

Awake now, she was running. It didn't hurt. Her breath came easily, her pace was swift and light. She could feel herself breathing and it was pleasurable, as effortless as breathing had once been at night. She wore blue shorts, a white T-shirt, and in her right hand she had a lap counter. Sixty laps already run, forty more to go. When she ran, no one could catch her, no one tried. She ran alone, even if others ran with her. She was happiest when she ran and she was flushed and ecstatic now. The track was smooth blond wood, a perfect oval. Below were echoes, grown men yelling like kids, the little cries of sneakers on the polished wood floor. The basketball bouncing hard across the gym. Lydia ran. In forty minutes she'd run five miles. She hoped that time would warp and stretch, that forty minutes would never come.

Something slid under the front door—a notice of eviction? Another *Watchtower* pamphlet from the Jehovah's Witnesses?

Who else could die? Lydia never looked. She dropped her chin to her knees and saw herself two weeks ago, walking down Bleecker Street in her new raincoat, charged and never paid for. At last she liked her body as it grew dank and fetid like a log, slowly rotting.

Apricot, banana, cantaloupe, damson plum . . . *Albany, Binghampton, Canandaigua* . . . Difficult letters made her sleepy, Q, K, X, Y, Z. *Alderfly, bark beetle, chigger, Daddy, Granddaddy, daddy longlegs. Earwig, fruit fly, gypsy moth, hornet, inchworm, June bug, kah kac kad kaf kag kam.* She grew sleepy from the motion of the train. Out the window, the telephone poles smudged one into another, one into another with the rhythm of the wheels on rails. The posts at the edge of a farmland melt into a wall. She sees the tall dark-haired basketball player for the first time, for every time.

One foot, another foot, you feel good, you feel good, you feel good. With Kramer below, an hour could pass by unnoticed. She holds him at the waist, where he's lean but his flesh is soft. His back, too, smooth, soft. His face rubs against hers and they move, together, slow now, easy. He says, Oh Lydia. He's with her even through the last selfish moments, Oh Lydia. She says, It feels good, then with her hands cupped over her ears she is back in the living room, wrapped in her quilt, crying, Stop please go away *apricot, banana, cantaloupe* she shakes her head and begs him to leave. She pleads with him to go as she wanted to plead with him to stay. Kramer won't go away. He stays with her. He wraps his arms around her throat. She hears him come. She hears his special cry. No matter how tightly she plugs her ears she cries along with him.

10

W<small>HEN THE KNOCKING</small> first sounded on her front door, Lydia
was running with the Breather, Sport Shirt, Wheezer, Machine
Man, Bum Knee, and Speed King; she passed the Walker, Red
Headband, Baldy, the Talker, Bump, Grunt, and the Stud. *Hey,
nice pacing, baby.*
Huh huh huh huh.
"Don't stop! Don't stop! You're my inspiration, don't stop!"
Huh huh huh huh.
A cat was crying for love. The knocking on the door grew
louder. Lydia's pulse quieted, heartbeat slowing: In diapause the
metabolic rate is low, biochemical changes occur to allow for
survival in adverse conditions. A key turned in her lock. Footsteps sounded across the kitchen, softening as they hit the living-
room rug. The visitor had no shadow. There was no way he
could see Lydia spread-eagled under the quilt. There was nothing to be heard but the cat, gurgling and crying. She heard the
cat and the visitor's rapid breathing growing closer, lower, fast
and steady, a wheeze, a toe in her side, a voice filled with controlled hysteria whisper, "Oh Jesus. Oh my God. Oh Jesus." It
was human, not a ghost, and it fell on its knees before her,
murmuring rapid Catholic prayers.

Lydia's pulses lit up one by one along the pulse points of her
body. The shock had roused her, and though she was disappointed being back on the floor, she was curious and wondered,
as if she were reading a good mystery: Will he touch the body?
Will the police be notified? Will the perpetrator be caught?

A light switched on, and the whispering resumed: "Jesus,
mother of Mary." Lights off again, as if he'd stumbled upon a

naked corpse. Alive, eyes wide open, she knew who he was, and when he kneeled, clutching the quilt in his hand, trying to rip it off, she grabbed onto the edges in a very live show of modesty. John, the super, had already seen too much. His eye had shown through the peephole the night Lydia and Kramer were drunk and bawdy on the steps. Kramer made banshee love sounds and she moaned dramatically, twisting her head over a shoulder, seeing the glittering eye in the center of John's door. She knew he was breathing heavily, hand rubbing his crotch, hating her for it. Didn't he sneer at her for days after?

"Lydia, my God, my God. Do you mind if I switch your lamp on?"

An answer was unnecessary. John was already bouncing off the walls, patting and feeling for a switch, bumping into furniture and saying *oof!* like a player in a slapstick comedy. Light on, he crouched in front of Lydia, a dark, intense little man, face all eyes and Groucho mustache. "How long have you been like this?"

He got up and paced around the body, then, short of space, around the kitchen. She heard the soft yawn of the refrigerator door and a moment later saw him standing between the rooms, a palm flat on each doorjamb.

"Look, babe, I don't know what to say. You haven't picked up your mail all week and you haven't left out any garbage, but your friend Michael came by a couple of times asking for you, and when I tell him you aren't in he tells me—look, babe. I heard about Kramer and all. The bastard." John squeezed his nostrils together, inhaling sharply, then leaned over, chin in her ear. "I'll be back in a minute. I'll lock the door behind me, right? Then I'll knock three times to tell you it's me, got it?"

John shut off the light and left. Lydia, lying there, followed him up to his apartment, lumpy and crumbling as the rest, the smell of roach spray partly masked by strawberry incense. He had a cobalt-blue shag rug and a small L-shaped couch in the corner. One day she had sat on that couch and turned down offers of tea, coffee, and soda, as she impatiently waited for her package. A stained-glass lamp had swung above her on a fierce chain, scattering its colors around the room, making her nauseous.

The knocking began again, and Lydia slid farther under the

quilt. The same scenario unfolded: the bumping, the patting, a kick in her side. She wished John would go away but it was a waste of valuable time doing anything stronger than wishing. She'd already tried dressing and going outside. She'd already circled the block, sat in Rosemary's, circled the block, watched a movie. She was tired and all the running was silly when her quilt was so warm, its smell rich and familiar.

"Look, I'm turning on a light, okay?"

He did, then crouched in front of her, hairy, bug-eyed, one arm extended straight out and in his hand a sandwich on a white paper plate. Lydia remembered a Moroccan afternoon, when the manager of a tiny hotel had come to her room and held his arm straight out. Unable to communicate in English, he handed her a mossy crab and a hammer on a white plate. The muscles in John's arm were being strained, and the plate quivered. His voice, too. "Turkey. White meat, mayo, lettuce. Okay?"

Cars went south on Seventh Avenue. One truck carrying a heavy load shook as it rattled down the streets. A car hit the loose manhole cover and the echo rang.

"Lydia, babe, if you don't move, I'm going to figure you're a catatonic." John set the sandwich down. "If you're a catatonic, I'll have to call Saint Vincent's. They'll cart you off, babe, and this is no threat." He stood and circled around Lydia. She was the precious jewel, guarded night and day in this museum. After a few laps he strayed, exploring the shelves above her desk. He picked up the mosquito in Lucite, *Happy 26th b-day, Rema* was engraved on the bottom. "It's not a threat, babe, it's my duty. You're a nice girl. Even if you weren't a nice girl, I couldn't let you rot, now could I?" The wooden Indian was flipped upside down, an attempt made to decipher the print on its base. "You remember Mr. Marconi, 5-C?" He stopped eating too, babe. He stopped caring for himself altogether. I wouldn't want to tell you—" A tweak of the nose, meaning filth, disgust. "His daughter called me—hysterical. If she cared about the old man she would've noticed a lot sooner. See what I mean?"

Mr. Marconi had been a tiny, stoop-shouldered man who'd lived alone in the building for twenty-six years. He'd put flower boxes on the ledge of every hallway window. Because of him there'd been marigolds and coleus, portulacas with wonderful poppylike seeds. Lydia imagined Mr. Marconi lying on the floor in a fetal position, dressed in a dusty-looking suit and an old broad-brimmed hat, just the things he'd worn each time she saw him painfully climb the stairs. His face was rotted away. It was white and pitted like a wormy apple; cheeks sunken, eyes swallowed by their sockets.

Lydia touched her face. "I take care of myself. I'm all right."

John, short, dark, covered with wiry brown hair, crouched in front of Lydia and pulled gently on an arm, tugging, hoping for a hand. "Atta girl," he whispered excitedly.

She smiled. Anyone who'd won a spelling bee smiled at the victory. You couldn't exactly applaud yourself.

"Look babe, take a bite, okay? I made this sandwich myself. I bet you didn't know Old John the super was such a dynamite chef, did you?"

Lydia gritted her teeth.

"I mean, if you'd seen Mr. Marconi, you'd know—"

She didn't want to be dead, eyes open, numb to all pain, a fish on ice. So she shook her head. Mr. Marconi's face, eaten away, would not leave. Still, in diapause, nutrients are stored, metabolic rate is low. "I need no turkey to sustain me, thank you," she said, trying through words to be rid of Mr. Marconi. "I need no bread, no human companionship, farewell."

John stood, poised for a suitable retort. But his look softened and said he pitied her. Hating him fiercely for this, she closed her eyes until he left the room.

As soon as John was out, Lydia liked him. He was a good super, very hairy but compulsively clean. She could never remember a morning when she was up and John wasn't either collecting trash or cleaning the halls. Late at night he was busy, too. When she first got her apartment, she imagined there were two Johns, a day John and a night John. Twenty-four hours a day he was the eyes of the building, the ears, the mop. No matter how late or how quiet, John would be on an upper flight, standing cross-legged, leaning on his mop, watching. "Yes, I drink tea, but I'm in a rush," she'd said, the day she sat in his living room. "Is it a big package?" "The package, right. Hey, you like the Stones? I got *Exile on Main Street* and *Goat's Head Soup*. One cut, okay? 'Sister Morphine'—" "The package, John?" "Right, hang on a sec." The rug looked like blue crabgrass. "Hey, Lydia, you know about that package? I blew it, sorry, it's for Durst, 6-D, not you, I could've sworn ..."

In the morning, Lydia took John's turkey sandwich from the refrigerator. Telling herself she only wanted to look at it, to see how much meat he'd put in, she held it up and took a large bite from one half. Startled by the contrasts—sweet mayonnaise, the crunch of iceberg lettuce—she brought the rest of it into the living room and sat down to finish it off. After a shower, Kramer sometimes ate in the living room, dressed only in Jockey shorts, stark white like diapers.

Lydia got up for a glass of water and said, as if to Kramer, "The mere idea of John in my house gives me the creeps."

The kitchen window was open a crack. Holding the quilt against her chest, she pushed it closed. She could hear footsteps, the jangling of keys. A telephone, far off, is ringing. Her mother says, "Time is money ..." and her voice trails off. Her father is pointing across a sunny Brentwood kitchen to show Lydia an imaginary birdie on a bush. While she squints and strains to find it, he dips his spoon into her dish and steals a big taste of ice cream. Her mother and sister, noticing first, laugh. "I hate you," she cries. "I hate you, Daddy, I hope you die!"

"Two are dead now," Lydia said. "The other is gone, is dead, same thing."

Immediately after two dainty little raps, John rammed his key in and flung open the door. His knock said he was unsure whether he wanted her to be home, but he marched straight in, the conquering force. He didn't circle around her this time as if she were *Grief,* by some Renaissance sculptor, steeped in the righteousness of misery, but sat on the couch instead, hands clasped anxiously between his legs. "I know what it is," he said at last. "Contact lenses." He leaned forward. "No, it's your hair. You washed your hair, didn't you, babe."

Lydia lifted an arm and took in the clean smell of baby powder. "I take good care of myself," she said.

"And it's a good thing, too! If you take care of yourself, you feel confident when you face the world out there, right?"

Lydia nodded.

"Because the world out there is tough and you have to be tough to make it."

"Street sense," said Lydia, wishing she had some.

"Speaking of which, did I ever tell you about this chick on Spring and Thompson? Katherine. Kitty we called her because when you got her going, she purred like a little cat. When Kitty first got knocked up, no one knew who it was. Carmen says, It ain't me, man, so we're sure it was. Anthony says, I don't know who else, but I tell you I got some action, so we know it's not Tone. And me? I ain't bragging. Anyways, five years, five kids. Ten years, seven kids. It didn't make a difference anymore. You go into the Laundromat on Thompson, you'll see her there. She's still pretty foxy, considering all that wear and tear. Still sweet, a whole lot softer, the little ones under her feet. You know what my nephews call them? Kitty's litter. I swear it."

John liked the story. Lydia liked the story, too. She could see the old tenements in Little Italy, fire escapes decorated with plants, Tony's mamma calling Ant-nee! Lydia had never been on Thompson Street when she hadn't heard some mother call Ant-nee! And a chorus of kids, suddenly appearing from behind garbage cans and cars, Hey Ant-nee, ya muddah's calling ya. Was it ever the same Anthony twice? Had she ever stumbled unknowingly on John's nephews?

The phone rang. Lydia got up and walked around the bedroom until the ringing stopped. On her way back to her seat on the floor, she saw John, in a crouch. He was an ape trying out for the catcher's slot on the home team.

More stories. His friends from Little Italy all had adjectives in front of their names: Big Louie, Fat Mario, Sharp Charlie. His energy, his joy in telling tales about them made Lydia want to join in and talk about her friends. Her sister Jill was a good friend. Once, though, Jill had said Lydia had to make other friends. This instant, Jill said. Lydia went inside and pestered her grandfather, who'd been reading quietly in his chair. She jumped on his lap, pulled his earlobes, wiggled her fingers under his arms. "Jill says to play with me!" she demanded, until exhausted he took out his Bicycle playing cards and taught her a new game. Her grandfather was a friend but he was dead. That left Jill.

"I have a sister," Lydia said, accidentally interrupting John in the middle of his Joey the Runt story.

He was very polite. "Older or younger?" he asked.

"Older. Thirty-five."

"A little old for me. She married?"

"Peter and two kids. I never met the kids."

John bounced on his heels, then rested his palms on the ground, a sprinter on the mark. "Too bad she's married. I always wanted a sister—a kid sister, to protect. I had this older sister, still do as a matter of fact. She's a big fucking mother, four years older than me and outweighs me by about a hundred. Shit, she pulled me out of I don't know how many fights. I never wanted her to. I would've rather got my teeth knocked in. But what would happen is Marie sees me in a scuffle, right? I see her and get scared shitless. I start screaming and hollering but not from the fight. It's from her. To myself I'm crying, Get this fucking amazon out of here. She steps in and grabs me by the back of the collar and shakes so hard the fillings come loose in my teeth. Are you hungry?"

"No."

"You could use some meat on your bones so I did a little grocery shopping for you. I could bring the stuff up now, or if you want a little later. You want me to bring it now?"

"Some other time."

"Okay, no hard feelings." John said bye-bye and exited backward.

When she heard the door lock, Lydia began pacing the room. "I have a mother, too," she said, remembering how at eighteen, as a kind of graduation present, her mother had said, "Call me Rose now, not Mommy." A year later when she left for New York, it was like leaving a father, a grandfather, and a good friend. Rose lived in Brentwood, in the same house Lydia had lived in for eighteen years. Not long ago, inviting Lydia out west, Rose said Lydie's room had been turned into a guest room, though if she visited, she could still sleep there. Rose was married to Harold Wolfe now, another lawyer. Lydia's father was a lawyer. When she was little, and an ardent Perry Mason fan, she told all her friends Daddy solved hundreds of murders. She told Kramer he was the star of the baseball diamond. These things were true to her.

Lydia got herself a banana. That morning she'd called up the Jefferson Market, and persuaded them to send a crate of bananas. "Bad stomach," she told the curious delivery boy. "I get the runs." Bananas, once the skin was peeled, were sweet. They didn't need to be cut, cooked, or chewed. They didn't drip, smell suspicious, spoil easily, or need refrigeration. Her insects ate them.

"He grew up in Brooklyn," Lydia said, compiling all the biographical information she knew, trying to get an image of her father. He was a graduate of City College. His name was Maurice. Grandma Lena got fancy naming him. Jill got fancy naming her daughter—Tara, girl of dreams. Rose called up to say Lydia's father died. Kramer grabbed her by the shoulders and shook her, shouting, "He's dead." I'm sorry, she should have said. I'm not convinced he is. Where was the body? How did her life change? Why didn't she feel sad? Suppose he had really died. Did it mean because she hadn't been sad that she didn't love him? She hadn't cried when Zeyde died and Zeyde wouldn't have died if she'd called and said go through with it. But he hated going under the knife. She stood at the corner and waved to Kramer when he got into a taxi. Then she had a cup of coffee.

"It was all wrong," said Lydia. "I did it wrong."

I hate you! I hope you die!

11

SHE WOULD get better if the elements of her environment were predictable, Lydia reasoned. If like the coming of dawn and dusk all physical occurrences came on schedule, she would be well again. She knew that the walls wouldn't crumble, she trusted the ceiling not to cave in, and it was reassuring to see that there was no sign of poltergeists, no indication that the furniture would move of its own accord. Still, there were capricious events, ominous sounds. The screaming, for instance. People screamed all night long all over New York. Maybe they screamed all night long all over the world, but in New York Lydia heard them from the moment darkness set in until morning. Like the cars that skidded violently but never seemed to crash, the screams would stop suddenly and silence, just as eerie, would prevail. Was it murder? Rape? A child?

Then there was John, opening her door at all hours. He always knocked twice, but let himself in so quickly that had she wanted to surprise him and answer, or surprise him and hide under the bed (would he peek in the drawers?), she wouldn't have had time. In the beginning the visits were a shock (a dream, she sometimes thought, an imaginary visitation), and she froze when he walked in, remaining frozen and invulnerable for the duration of his stay. Lydia didn't notice the change, but after a while, she began to anticipate the knock, the key, the visit, and when John came in with her mail, a new story, a smile on his face, she was all at once angry, grateful, aware of her need. Hating especially this need, she thought of mean things to say to him: I am repelled by men with hairy shoulders. The moment he locked himself out of the apartment, she turned into the charming eight-year-old she'd never been, raspberries, Bronx cheer: Nyahhh, you jerk. It's ivy that crawls up the walls outside, not ivory. James Joyce will never be considered a great American writer. James Dean was not really a woman.

He brought her a scrambled egg sandwich, bloody with ketchup, chicken that looked like human flesh, homemade pasta. "Al dente, you know what that means, babe? It means the pasta's just a wee bit chewy. Nothing as bad as mushy pasta, right?" She wouldn't eat in front of John, but he didn't seem to care. He unwrapped his goods, gave her instructions for reheating, then crouched on the floor beside her for story time. He told her about his mother, four foot nine, "littler" than Lydia, who lived on Thompson Street, and his three brothers, also of that block. Most of all he loved building gossip. Mr. Marconi lying on the floor. The macabre was of greatest interest, which made Lydia suspicious. She didn't like being in Mr. Marconi's league. Another favorite was Rae Ann Fanella's baby Sue, whom he greeted with a tickle under the chin and, "It's John, Baby Sue! It's John!" (Lydia had seen this act a few times herself.) There were also the fighting Zilboorgs and Calabrese, the masochist— what a racket on that side of the building. Lydia learned that Panzevecchio was a one-eyed drummer and Cohen a one-legged math teacher. John was very proud of all the educated people in the building.

A week after he first barged in, John began bringing record albums. After setting the food in front of Lydia or above her on the table, he took an album from the jacket, put it on the turntable and played D.J. for her, fist for a microphone, held at his chin. "A great new group from England," or "Remember the drummer from King Crimson? He started his own band, pya da da, pya da da, *boom!* what a great drum solo, let me play a couple of cuts for you."

She never touched the albums once he left, so he brought different ones, favorites from his high school days. The Lettermen, Dion, the Shirelles. He took a Johnny Mathis album from the jacket to play "Chances Are" and "The Twelfth of Never," but his eyes grew so moist he packed up the slow-dance oldies, admitting that their ability to trigger tragic memories of broken romances and days of innocence were irrelevant to Lydia's life on the floor. "These l.p.'s won't help you get better," he said,

"What you need is something that'll shake you, wake you, get you moving. Am I wrong or am I right?"

But the new albums went unplayed too, so John gave up on records and brought magazines. *Vogue, Seventeen, American Legion, Road and Track,* whatever the neighbors discarded, Lydia got. She skimmed through a couple, but didn't read any articles.

One day, John, in his usual crouch, turned to put a bacon and tuna sandwich on the floor and Lydia noticed a paperback squeezed into his pants pocket. She pulled it out and read the title aloud. *The Deathly Enchantment.* Then the blurb, "Her dream of love became a nightmare of terror and death." On the cover was a maiden in a spaghetti-strap nightgown, fleeing down a flight of stairs, flushed cheeks, what a cleavage. John was embarrassed and said he found the book lying on the stairs, no name in it or anything. But after Lydia convinced him her eyesight wouldn't worsen from reading, he returned with ten more books, more flushed and bosomy women in nightgowns. Lydia picked up the top one and said, "I give up. Why was her name on a slab in the family mausoleum?"

"Read it and find out."

"Which face, which dear, familiar face was the mask of the killer, John?"

"Hey, hey! Don't look at the last page like that."

The advice from the albums was: Get up and boogie, have fun, live for today. The advice from the magazines was: Lose ten pounds and feel more confident, test yourself on a new compatibility quiz, find the new you. The books, fat and silly, each curled at the edges from repeated readings, didn't suggest anything. They had no relation to her life and didn't remind her of anything, past or present. It was a world of twin sisters, stepmothers, fatal beauty, cursed virgins, handsome saviors, castles, dungeons, happy endings.

Twenty-two days after Kramer left New York, Lydia decided no more sitting and waiting like a high school girl who suspects the star quarterback may call. She was going to surprise John by answering the front door and inviting him in. The only way she could do this was by stationing herself at the door so she'd be faster than his key, and, upon hearing footsteps, looking through the peephole.

The sun was pouring through the western window, making her kitchen golden with light. That meant it was just after five when she heard keys jangling. She unlocked the door. It was only His Brother, opening the front door next to Lydia's. His Brother had maybe been a neighbor for the six years Lydia had lived here. His Brother may even have been the man who caught Lydia necking on the roof with a pharmacologist named Ralph. His Brother's door whined when it was opened and hit the metal plate on the floor when it shut, screeching. A week before Kramer left, Lydia thought she saw this next-door neighbor in Gristede's, unmistakable farting schnauzer by his side. She said, "Hi." He said, "I'm not him, I'm his brother." He looked the same as her next-door neighbor. The dog looked and smelled the same. Lydia didn't know if her neighbor was him or his brother, but His Brother, she felt, had been a harbinger of bad news in Gristede's.

John didn't show up. Lydia decided she didn't care; she didn't like him anyway. But her stomach ached so badly she would've diagnosed it as acute appendicitis, had she not already lost her appendix.

At eight the next evening, John strode into Lydia's living room, announced that Baby Sue had just spoken her first sentence ("Gotta wee-wee, Unka John"), and that he was in a terrific rush. "Big date with Rae Ann Fanella, 3-B," he said, running his hands down his chest, showing off a shiny new shirt with Modigliani-type ladies dripping down to his waist. "You read *Legacy of Loneliness* yet?"

Lydia walked into the kitchen, looking for a plate or a bowl. Nothing. He hadn't brought her any food. It didn't matter. He was a fool, a jerk. She hoped he called on Rae Ann just as he was now, with his fly half down.

John was inspecting the equipment on Kramer's desk in the meantime. He read the label on a cassette, then reached for the headphones. Lydia thought of Kramer tapping on the terrarium glass. "You know Rae Ann, don't you? Blond and cute, has a kid about two?"

"Leave them alone, John. Leave me alone, for that matter."

He put the headphones down carefully. "Anybody been up here, babe?"

"Yeah, Golda Meir."

"So you don't see anybody or talk to anybody else."

"Right," said Lydia. There were only strangers now, people who didn't know it was a small apartment and let the phone ring ten or twelve times.

"Don't you get lonely, babe?"

"In the first place, you have nothing to do with lonely. In the second place, no. I'm not an ant, I'm a person. An ant alone is nothing, but Lydia alone is happy. I was happy for years without people."

"People need people, babe—"

"Good-bye, Unka John. Baby Sue gotta wee-wee. I'll see you in the next incarnation."

"Hey hey, I like you, babe, can't you see?"

Lydia backed John through the kitchen, and at the door leaned over him to unsnap the lock. "I'm warning you, John, to get out. I don't want to see you again. Ever."

John backed out the door, slamming it from outside. Lydia hadn't the chance to decide whether she was relieved or upset because the key turned in the lock a half-minute later. John slouched into the living room. "I'll tell you one last thing, doll," he said, shaking his finger at her. "I used to like you, you want to know why? I used to think there's a chick with guts. The way you used to walk was like you owned the world. You don't remember, but I used to watch you and think there's a chick who's got her shit together."

"*Out!*" she screamed. "I was happy, you creep. I was happy alone." She put her hands over her ears and screamed, "Out, get out," until long after he was gone. When the noise in the apartment ceased, she unclasped her hands from her ears, slowly refocused her eyes and looked around, as if inspecting the ruins after an air raid. She'd dressed for John. Two days in a row she'd put on clean clothing and combed her hair. She laughed, or rather said ha ha ha, but was devastated, remembering the days when she had had the world by the balls. She stood and shouted, "Elephant, ferret, gorilla!" Louder still: "Hyena, iguana, jaguar, koala!" And more, voice straining: "Lemur, marmoset, nightingale." The downstairs neighbor stabbed at her ceiling with a broom. Bang! Bang! "Nightingale," bang! "Ocelot, puma, quail." A *Q*! A *Q*! Victory!

She sat at Kramer's work area running a hand over the smooth surface. She was stupid to have trusted John, but she wouldn't let him up anymore, she'd be all right now. She picked up a reel of film, a book, the old headphones. A white handkerchief was stuck behind some old tapes. Holding it up to her face (it smelled the way Kramer had after work) she went into the bedroom and opened all his bureau drawers. In one she found a pair of boxer shorts with the fly sewn up, smelling freshly laundered. Next she searched through his side of the closet. He had a guitar looped over the head of a hanger with a string and a bathrobe half on the floor. A sweater had a misshapen point on each shoulder where the hanger had stretched it. A T-shirt was hanging, too. She pushed the other hangers away and took it, his blue shirt, the one she'd pictured him wearing when he left. The shirt smelled as if he'd worn it the day before. Heart beating, as if he'd catch her and be angry, she took off her own sweater and pants and put it on.

As soon as she lay on the couch, Lydia began to laugh. We're so nice, she thought. We're so wonderful! She and Kramer were always congratulating themselves. No one could quite match their standards, no duo was as impressive or as well matched as they were. Squeezing together like this on the narrow couch, they watched *A Night to Remember* on TV one night, smooching during station identification. Lydia saw Kramer's eyes fill up with tears not when the *Titanic* went down, not during the chaos and fire, but when Mrs. Strauss refused to take her place on the lifeboat, preferring to die with her beloved husband. "We're so lucky," he said when the movie was over.

The happy birthday people, whoever and wherever they were, sang "Happy birthday, dear Mar-tha" loudly, festively. "We *are* lucky," said Lydia. "We're the happiest people I know." Then: "Does oo wuv me?"

It had started as a joke, her imitating someone else's baby talk, but it became part of their private language. "Does oo or does oo not?"

He does! He loves me! Lydia remembered running through the streets, racing through the halls at school, unable to contain her energy. He loves me, he does! Who could have predicted she would love someone when for the longest time she had clung to what she'd considered a realistic view of romantic love, namely that it was the invention of priests and gothic novelists, and those who suffered from it (like those who had mystical experiences) were deluded. Lying on the couch, this same person was saying, "Does oo wuv me, Kwamer?" And she was feeling his kisses, hearing him tell her yes, he did, then each saying how nice, how beautiful the other was.

Remember, Lydie? I didn't mean to make you walk so fast, but it was funny, you have to admit. A duck walk, fast as you could go.

As she had many other nights, she accused him of having lain in wait for her outside the McBurney Y. Not lying in wait, he said. Merely waiting, a big difference. Seeing his gym bag, she'd thought: Very jocklike, a perfect disguise for a weirdo, and walked as fast as possible to escape. He caught up in a few broad steps, and asked for her name. Hearing it, he sang "Lydia, the Tatooed Lady" and made her laugh. He told her he was seeing another woman but his eyes said anyone willing would do. She saw the woman in his apartment, crying . She became the woman in his apartment, crying.

Why did she need him so badly? Why did just his warmth soothe her? How odd never to leave infancy, to need a man the same way one needed a mother. He could always bring her out of her gloom and make her laugh, but she had to sit out his storms. That was bad. She tried to keep a straight face and remember she was upset, but as usual he brought her out of it. He asked if she remembered that inn upstate, the one with nylon sheets. To bed with sweaty feet and awake with sweaty feet.

She smiled despite herself. She'd been so happy she thought she'd die.

And all those places we made love? In the back seat of a rented Gremlin? In the bathroom?

They lay together, talking until they fell asleep. Through the window was a lovely picture, ailanthus trees, red and green neon over the delicatessen on Bleecker Street, knuckled black pipes on the rooftops. Lights were on in the windows of their neighbors' homes, giving life to the city that was close enough to feel but distant enough to be safe. There were good smells: fresh yeast from the bread bakeries, rich garlic from a nearby restaurant. The night sounds were as regular as a heartbeat. Cars sped down Seventh Avenue, the manhole cover rattled, people laughed, when drunk they sang. Glasses clinked, lusty singing. When Lydia was happy, as she was now, it was funny. When she was alone, it upset her: All that singing. All those people.

It wasn't until she felt herself shivering that Lydia realized she was cold. She tucked her hands under her arms. She and Kramer fit so well together. They always slept in each other's arms. "Tell me you love me," she said, startled by her own voice. "Tell me with feeling. Oh, that's nice, isn't it. You can leave your hand there. Right there. That's nice."

She fell asleep on the couch, but it wasn't a sweet-dreaming sleep. Once she woke and gulped down glass after glass of water, as if she were parched from too much drinking. Another time she woke to go to the bathroom. There, dazed and groggy, she lowered her head between her knees, too dizzy to move. She covered her eyes as if the lights were on and waited until she was steady enough to stand. When she was a little girl, she called for her father at night. He made a great show of wrestling with her dream demons, grabbing their tusks or tails, dragging them out of her bedroom.

That's all it was, she thought in the morning. A dream, just a dream.

12

THE FOOTSTEPS in the hall meant two things to Lydia: one, that they'd stop at her door, and two, that they were John's. She braced herself for Kramer. She felt him put his arms around her. She pushed him away, but he held her so tightly she grew dizzy and saw the two of them in bed; Kramer knocking over the table at Rosemary's the time he leaned over to kiss her; the night he was under the headphones so long that with a violent motion she had used her forearm to sweep everything off his work area. She struggled with him, caught up in the struggle, no longer able to remember why he had left or what it felt like being alone for so long.

John peeked into the living room, doing a pantomime of surprise, raised eyebrows, mouth in an "O." "Didn't expect to find you home."

"Very funny."

"Got a complaint about you yesterday. The lady says a wild party was going on here."

"Even funnier."

"Well, what do you say? Is summer here or is it not? It's time for all God's creatures to yawn and stretch and come out of hibernation."

Lydia walked into the bedroom. The bright afternoon sun spread across the blankets and she lay in the heat of it, putting her palms out to get a handful for her pockets. In summer, conditions were favorable. Cocoons split, nymphs grew, during storms the undersides of leaves provided shelter.

"How about a weekend in the country?"

When Lydia turned around she saw John, sitting on the end of her bed. It was improper, like eating in front of him.

"We could go upstate. I got this cousin who has a house right on the Hudson."

"I can't. Really."

"Look, babe, you know how I hate to be pushy, but it sure don't look like you got something more pressing to do. Now if you don't want to go because it's me asking, come out and say it. But if it's because you think you're going to miss something if you leave this fucking apartment for a day, you got to be kidding."

... Because it's me asking. Saying that was so brave, Lydia almost liked John for it. Of course it was because it was John asking. Why in God's name would she want to spend a day with *him*? On the other hand, John had seen her lying on the floor, caught her wrapped in her quilt, tried to end her diapause. There was nothing left to hide, not that she cared what he thought. "Who else is going to be there?"

"You and me, Lydia, babe. You and me."

"And your cousins?"

"They're staying at my place, you know, like a life-swap?"

"So it's just you and me?"

"Listen, babe, it's been just you and me for a fucking lot of days and nights already, hasn't it?"

"True, but—"

"But me no buts. You didn't see your other friends, right? You didn't answer the phone, right? Right? You didn't open your letters. Am I right or aren't I?" This time he waited long and hard for an answer.

"All right, already. You're right."

"You didn't let other people come over because you didn't trust them enough. But you let old John into your house, did you not?"

"I did not."

"Come on, man."

"You've been letting yourself into my house, asshole."

"Hey hey hey! Did I once take advantage of you? Every time I come in I say, 'Do you want me to go?' And you say, No, stay. So I stay."

"You didn't ask me this time, buster."

"Look, babe. You and me don't have to play games, right? I mean I'm the kind of dude who knows when to go. I know when a chick really wants me to get lost and when she says, Hey go, buddy, and really means Hey, stay."

"The most encouraging thing I ever said to you was Well, now that you're here, stay. Get out, John. I already told you I didn't want to see your face anymore."

"Look," he said, softly now. "You were rotting in this house. You were stinking as bad as week-old trash. I've helped you, haven't I? You talk. Finally you talk. And what do you say? Get lost! Jesus."

Back turned, she heard him squeeze his nostrils together and snort. Revulsion tempered her apology. "You want a payoff because you were nice, is that it? I try not to take favors because of that. Nothing comes for free."

"No, babe, you got it all wrong. I like you, you don't owe me anything. I'm just trying to tell you that it's me, John! Me, the one you do talk to. I know you're afraid to go out, babe, and I'm sitting here telling you that I'm the one you don't have to be afraid of."

"Okay. If you can put up with me, I'll go along."

"Atta girl," he said, belting her arm. "Atta girl, right on, yeah."

She dressed in mourning colors, black turtleneck shirt, black corduroy pants. She laced up her old black boots and pulled her stocking cap down to her eyebrows for that Neanderthal look. It was cool and windy, real fickle, this June.

"My breath! My breath!" she cried, circling around once, twice, not even bumping into him. "Just think of all I missed."

John smiled tolerantly, the good nurse, taking the crazy out for a walk, first time without a leash.

"For example, I never knew you walked so slow."

They went down the street until they were by the river. It smelled like the sea, dead as it was. This was an island, after all, and she lived not too far from the coast. Quieter, she said, "I never knew you had a car. I've never been on the sidewalk with you any farther than the front door. I've never seen you with red cheeks. I'm surprised you have shopping bags from Saks. I'm very surprised you have a cousin upstate. I'm surprised you have cousins period. The fact that people have relatives always surprises me. I never knew you liked the country. . . ."

Now they were at the trucks. Lydia remembered how shaken Kramer had been the night he went down to the trucks alone. A friend had a loft on Greenwich Street and Kramer walked there one Friday night. Out of the dark a hand reached out and cupped his balls. Down by the trucks was the only place where nighttime was no threat to women, but made straight men nervous. John had his car in a little lot between the detached cabs of semitrailers.

"Is this your car?" It was a beige Valiant with a blue door, too recent to be considered antique. "I hate cars. I hate driving more than any other thing I hate. In L.A., the only way to get around is by car, not counting motorcycles, which really scare me."

John gave Lydia the two bags, and then opened the door on her side. When he crossed to the other side, she pushed the front seat forward and placed their packages in the back. The bags began to topple over, and she stepped onto a piece of cardboard in the car. Her foot went through the floor, onto the asphalt. "I forgot to tell you," John said.

They drove east on Houston Street. It felt new to Lydia, as though she'd never noticed the changes before, Italian to university to light industrial. "Jefferson Screw," she said. "Superior Printing Ink. Top-grade nuts and bolts. Are you sorry you invited me along, John? Don't you wish I'd shut up?" He said no, but was unnaturally silent, tenser than usual. It looked as if the steering wheel would snap in two from his grip. The street changed from light industrial to restaurant supplies when it intersected the Bowery. Their windshield was wiped by a resident. Lydia had no desire to look the other way.

Once out of the city, when the car was on a highway, she patted the seat in a last-minute search for a seat belt. The seat didn't sprout one, so she wrapped her arms around herself, straitjacket style. "Cars are unpredictable. They can blow up at any given minute."

John switched on the radio. Cars were made by people and people were even less predictable. He listened to the music, bouncing sometimes, too often turning to Lydia to flash a smile. What if the car in the left lane suddenly swerved into their lane? What if the car in front screeched to a halt? What then? The low cement divider was meant to keep southbound traffic from head-ons with the northbound. But a car on the other side of the divider with no trouble at all could jump the barrier and crash into them. The car behind could speed up and send them into the car ahead. Lydia held her breath. She managed to release one arm from around her waist so she could hide her eyes. You never knew. *A Los Angeles man, 62, was driving*... You really just never knew. A car from nowhere could fly into their lane and knock them off the road. Splat. John and Lydia stew. John stepped on the accelerator, the needle on the speedometer quivered and advanced, the car ahead was suddenly before them. Lydia heard the screech of brakes. She felt the violent skid, the crash, and waited for her whole life to flash before her eyes. Winning the spelling bee (a-n-t-i-s-e-p-t-i-c), under the steps with the caterpillars. If she could have raised her hand and asked, it would have been for an instant replay of the sex (the violent skid, the crash).

"Are we almost there?"

"Jesus, you sound like my ten-year-old niece." In a mimicky little-girl voice, "Are we almost there? When are we going to get there, Uncle John? When, Uncle John?"

"Fuck yourself, Uncle John."

John speeded up and passed three cars.

"Now don't go and get spiteful just because I told you to fuck yourself."

Driving at least a hundred and ten miles an hour, John turned to face Lydia. "What are you talking about, babe?"

"Help," Lydia whispered, sinking her head into her shoulders. "Please."

John pinched her knee. "We sound just like a married couple," he said.

Lydia wondered why some men always went for the knees.

An hour later they drove up to an old frame house, olive paint peeling in curlicues near the roof. There was the most elaborate F she'd ever seen on a screen door. John yawned some lion breath and searched for the keys. Inhaling deeply, Lydia was glad to be alive.

As soon as their bags were tucked in corners and separate sleeping arrangements guaranteed to Lydia, John rubbed his hands together like a raccoon before dinner, marched into the kitchen and said, "Chow time, babe." The thought of eating in front of John would've ruined her appetite if it wasn't for the fact that it was only eleven and she wasn't hungry. She pointed out the time, swearing she'd eaten a full breakfast at seven-thirty. John said, "If you were starving you wouldn't tell me, would you."

"I would."

"If I wait, will you have lunch with me?"

"I will."

"Promise?"

"I promise, already. I promise."

"Swear?"

"All right already," she heard herself say, then and nineteen years before.

John circled around the big oak table and halted in front of the refrigerator. He pulled out a can of beer, drank half of it without surfacing, then said, "What do you want to do?"

Lydia wasn't going to get into the I-don't-know-what-do-*you*-want-to-do game, so despite the fact that nothing appealed to her, she said, "We could take a walk. You could show me the area."

"There's nothing much around these parts. This is the sticks, babe."

"John, we're out in nature, for Christ's sake. God's country. Remember? We've come to yawn and stretch. Does your cousin have bicycles in the garage? We can ride up to that park we passed."

"Good idea." John reached across the table for the car keys. "Bikes."

There were birds chirping outside the window. Real birds, not fat, clucking rats on wings.

"Bikes? Who says they got bikes out here. A car, maybe."

"Bikes."

There was an impasse. John finished his beer and bent the can in two, gnashing his teeth. "We could at least look," Lydia said. "The garage isn't all that far away."

"You look."

She looked. Sure enough, on a shelf that spanned the width of the garage, under a layer of watering cans, gas jugs, rakes, shovels, garden tools, lawn stakes, and peach baskets; behind the twenty-five-pound sack of lime and fertilizer and protected by

the garden hose, coiled and ready to strike, were two fat-tired old
bicycles, one bright pink and mottled with rust, the other metallic green with streamers in the hand grips and an *awoogah* horn.
She climbed over the mess and tossed things aside. By the time
the bikes were uncovered, oil and a tire pump had been found,
too. A lawnmower buzzed far off on someone else's property.
Lydia greased the chain, the pedals, the joints on the handlebars.
The smell of mowed grass made her think of Brentwood. It had
been years since she had thought of Brentwood as home, but
now, pumping air into the tires, she did, and the whole family
was there in the yard. Her father was at the barbecue grille,
cooking hamburgers. Zeyde was serving the cole slaw, sliced by
Jill, homemade by Rose, who was calling, "Sit *down*, Maurie," in
another futile attempt to pry her husband away from the fire.
"Everything is getting cold." His face was hidden by the smoke,
beyond recall. Was he the reason she lived at home her first year
of college, driving to her classes in an old black Volvo that
looked like an eggplant? Why had Zeyde encouraged her to go
so far away? Hadn't he known that once she left, she'd never
really return? For so many years she had hardly missed them.
Now, as if paying for her years of inattention, she missed them
sevenfold; her love held back during that time was seven times
stronger. What if she flew to Los Angeles, and ran up the steps
of her childhood home, and showered them with hugs and kisses?
What if her father had been hiding there all along? I will be a
better daughter, I promise, Lydia thought.

John was in the kitchen, behind a mountain of peanut shells.
"What were you doing out there, building them?"

"Just about. Ready?"

"Lunch first."

Lydia gritted her teeth, as if to keep the spoonful of medicine
from going down. "I'm not hungry."

"Lydia, you swore. You promised. What am I supposed to do
now with the sausage and pepper already going?" He opened the
broiler, red-faced from the blast of heat.

Lydia swore on her mother's life she'd eat if John first looked
at the bicycles. All he had to do was look. He slammed the broiler
shut and followed her out to the garage. She described in minute
detail all she'd done to restore the bicycles. John circled them,

kicking the tires as if they were used cars up for sale. Lydia showed John where they needed to be greased. She thought of Kramer underneath the headphones and stopped talking. Why was it sometimes she didn't talk for days and other times she couldn't stop? Neither was comfortable.

"The sausages will get overdone. Move your ass, babe."

John approached the table carrying a plateful of sausage and peppers, a loaf of bread tucked under his arm. In his silver mitts, he looked dangerous. He tipped the platter, and fat sausages dropped onto Lydia's dish. Grease splattered onto her shirt and was sucked up and lost in the fiber. "Dig in, babe. Isn't it good? Aren't you going to say something?"

Lydia had no more words so she ate. The food was good. John tried to dump a second helping in her plate, but she stood up and went back into the garage. While John cleaned up the kitchen, scrubbed, polished, and dried the dishes, Lydia rummaged on the garage shelf, as if her fortune could be found between the watering cans. She wasn't liking John, but she wasn't wanting to be back in her apartment either. Mimicking him, she said, "Were you the one who wanted me to get fresh air, or were you not?"

John came out, looked around and aimed a wicked kick at the green bike's tires, sending it over on its side. "I fucked that bike up but good," he said with great gusto.

Lydia was pretending to be the sweetest thing alive. "Nonsense!"

He straddled the bicycle seat. It was so low his legs bent deeply when his feet hit the ground. "You look like Paul Bunyan on a mule," she said.

"It's too small, huh?"

"Yeah, it's too small. Big deal. You're closer to the ground this way, Big John. I wouldn't worry."

"Ready?"

Lydia kicked the kickstand up and coasted down the driveway, but John remained in the garage. At the bottom she circled, waiting. At last he sat on the bicycle, using his feet to walk it down the driveway. When he saw her watching, he planted his feet firmly on the ground, lifted his hands and said, "Don't shoot, G-men."

What was she doing with this person?

"Why did the little moron—Lydia, look! Why did the little moron—Lydia! Lydia?" John pressed the bulb of the horn: *awoogah! awoogah!*

How had she gotten this far? Why was she here?

"Lydia?" *Awoogah!* "Lydia, why did the little moron jump off his—Lydia, look! Why did the little moron jump off his bicycle? Lydia—"

She started to cry, and so he wouldn't see, she coasted farther down the hill, escaping the house and John. Before she reached the corner, she heard a crash, then his voice in a fury. "God damn you, bitch. I don't know how to ride this fucking thing!"

The next morning, after a huge breakfast, Lydia and John drove to the park area by the Hudson. John, age thirty-two and hairy as a tarantula, kicked tin cans and pebbles on his way into the woods, acorns and pebbles once they were inside. The air was piny and cool and they seemed to be the only people around. Lydia assured John she didn't need her hand held, and to prove her familiarity in places that he felt least at home, she ran ahead, letting spiders crawl between her fingers and calling out the names of trees. John had never heard of sassafras. With the proof in front of him, he refused to believe that leaves of different shapes could come from one tree. "It's a freak," he said, "a geek, a spaz." She dreamt up her own house on the riverbank, bark sides, cool dirt floor. John could hardly keep up with her, she walked so quickly. Traveling on, feeling the doubts and displeasures of having company, she thought how easy it had once been to live alone. Once she had thought paradise would be an old Victorian house with towers, turrets, and a winding staircase; a goat or two, edible mushrooms in the basement, an herb garden. It wasn't worth the effort saving string, but banana peels, yes, so her little red-eyed drosophila could have a fruitful existence all the week of their lives. Then Kramer came. Then being alone was being lonely.

"Jesus, bitch," John said, climbing over rotten logs and pointed rocks. (*Bitch* was his new term of endearment.) "Wait up."

She swung uprooted plants above her mouth, and pointed out edible herbs and roots. She ate familiar berries and invented recipes for those that were untried. She hid behind an oak, and believing she was alone, rested. John crept up behind her and threw twigs down her back. "Cut it out," she said, trying not to get testy. She walked faster, but acorns came next, a few stones, a pinecone. She broke into a short sprint, too out of shape to sustain the effort. But aha! he was gone. Gone too, unfortunately, was her pleasure. Now whenever she heard a rustle in the woods, she started shaking as though she had Saint Vitus' dance, yelling "Knock it off" or "Drop dead" whether he was there or not.

All this effort was tiring, and Lydia sat on a log, and had begun to drift off, when John walked over to point out a spider spinning its web. He tapped her on the shoulder and she jumped up, told him he was a fool, his I.Q. smaller than his shoe size. She felt bad for yelling at him, but minutes later he threw mushrooms at her and she felt justified.

Later that day, Lydia heard, "Save that stump for me, babe!" Trees rustled. Then John bounded over to where she sat, blew away the webs on the pine stump next to hers, covered it neatly with fern fronds, and sat down to sing, "Dawn, go away I'm no good for you," in falsetto. When he finished his chorus, Lydia asked him to move his legs. She peeled off a piece of bark from the stump and showed it to him. The underside was a maze of tunnels and galleries excavated by bark beetles. "When the larvae hatch, each one starts its own tunnel," she said. "Look."

"Put that down."

"You know something, John? There are thousands of kinds of bark beetles, but if you showed this piece to an entomologist whose major field of studies is beetles, she'd probably be able to tell you which species did the digging. Incredible."

"Okay, so what kind did that?"

"Streptococcus."

Lydia would have started feeling guilty about her lie if she hadn't noticed that John was already absorbed in other matters. He was trying to edge closer to her, but since the log was narrow, he was having a great deal of difficulty. She watched his progress and was able to dodge well before his arm was extended. Sitting in the woods reminded her of her first and only summer at camp, and the junior counselor who had a lower lip like a slab of raw meat and a hardness in his pants that scared her into total silence. She had vowed never to mix with boys, which in those days was easy enough. John clasped her by the shoulders and shook the daydreams from her. "Come on, babe. It's John! It's John!"

"You say that to all the girls."

"Don't spend your life all locked up inside because of one bad experience. Snap out of it, bitch."

"If you call me bitch once more, I'll cripple you, John, I swear."

"Atta girl," he said, socking her. "Atta girl, yeah."

A blond-haired family walked by, toting their lunch to one of the picnic tables a few yards away. The father lifted the youngest, a little girl about two, and put her on his shoulders. She slapped his cheeks and pulled his hair, happy to be up there, giggling in her violence.

"Everyone has bad times," John said, a few minutes later. Lydia let John keep his arm across her shoulders. "The cause of my greatest unhappiness was a chick named Nancy Gerardi. Fifteen and was she built."

"That about says it all."

"I know, I know, how soon we forget, right? You say to me, 'You were seventeen and she was fifteen, what did you know?' But man, we loved each other, you don't know, it was real deep, real solid."

"What happened?"

"You won't believe it."

"Try me."

"She went away to her grandmother's place on Houston Street. What did I know. Visiting her every day after school, really hurting for her. That little girl was kicked out of her parents' house. She said they didn't want her there, the place was too small. I swore I'd take care of her. Anyhow, I visit her every day after school. Grandma's this old half-deaf lady who walks with a cane. All right, that's good. Grandma sits in the kitchen watching some soapbox opera, the volume is blasting—really blasting. Nance and I are in the bedroom. Man, the minute I walk in the house, I get a hard-on. Is this embarrassing you?"

"Not yet."

"I always come in with a newspaper over my crotch. You know what the old lady says about me? I'll make good. I'm a good boy. I always got a newspaper with me. I never bother her like Freddy, the one before me, coming into the kitchen, heading right for the icebox, never even says hello or may I to the lady. Jesus, what a crude son of a bitch he was. Anyhow, the TV is blaring and Nance and I close the bedroom door and in two seconds I get her blouse off. I unhook her bra—in those days girls wore bras. Anyhow, the minute I get hot, she starts getting antsy and worrying about the old lady. One year I'm with this chick and never past the tits. I'm just a kid, you know? I'm afraid my insides will turn to charcoal if I beat off. One time and one time only I get it on with Kitty Litter. Nance finds out. She breaks up with me. I can't get in the house anymore. No explanations, nothing. Next thing I hear she's knocked up and gets married. And who do you think to? Felix Gizzi, biggest asshole on the block."

"And that's your taste of tragedy?"

"I should've known you were too wrapped up in yourself to care about anyone else."

Lydia told him to stick it in his ear, and John suggested she blow it out her nose. She walked back to the car, laughing. John followed. He was ridiculous, she decided, hurt nonetheless. John sat in the driver's seat. The family had finished their lunch and now were all pitching in to leave the place clean. The air smelled like charcoal and hamburgers, and again the urge to be home sneaked up on her, hitting her in the lower back. Her real home, the one with Mom, Dad, Zeyde, and Jill. John started the car and they drove back to his cousin's house.

He told her to rest or watch TV—anything she wanted, he wouldn't bother her at all. And he was true to his word, happy being able to prepare still another meal. Relaxed now, feeling peaceful, Lydia thought about the pathetic souls she knew in her younger days—Fat Boy Who Stripped, Salami Belcher, and the dozen or so bra-strap twangers—boys who did anything for a laugh, who said every dumb, offensive, irrelevant, or absurd statement that came into their heads, apparently believing that any reaction, even a negative one, was better than no reaction at all.

It was time to eat, and John called "Surprise!" holding up the grape jam he had bought, having remembered when Lydia had come home from the store with a quart jar. She was touched, and cleaned her plate to please him. Maybe it wasn't so crazy being here. John had problems, but he was okay.

She said, "Thanks for dinner, John, you've really been great. I'm sorry if I've insulted—"

John rose from his seat, and leaned across the table, one palm landing on his plate, the other midtable. His lips were distended grotesquely, puckered for a kiss.

"No, stop, just *stop*, I tell you—"

He straightened, a hurt look on his face. To excuse the fact that she'd flinched halfway across the room, Lydia said, "You probably don't remember, but I wasn't always like this. I used to be a nice, easygoing, real laid-back California girl. Was I or was I not?"

"You was," he said. "You still is."

She locked the door of the bedroom and tried to sleep, but the strange bed was inhabited by dream demons, shapeless fears that might have belonged to someone else, but latched on to her. Like hyperparasites, they fed off her own parasites, her terrors. She couldn't stay in bed.

John was lying across the living-room couch, watching TV. He turned and waved when Lydia walked into the room. His face was unshaven, his eyes so deep-set that from where she stood all she saw was black hollows. Still, he was familiar; he was beautiful. He lifted his leg and patted the seat next to him. "Bad dream?"

"I'll say. What are you watching?"

"*Seconds*. It's about this banker who arranges with some guy to have another life. But there's a catch, right? First he has to go through this operation—man, you wouldn't believe. Hold on, it's almost over."

John was quiet, but breathing heavily. Leaning on his lap, Lydia felt as if she were on a rubber raft in the sea. The blue haze from the TV seeped into her eyes. She felt keyed up, the way she'd once felt after not running for a few days. But though the energy pounded through her body, her arms and legs felt as though they'd be useless forever. She pushed herself as she had in the old days when she ran not five miles but six or seven, after every nerve and muscle signaled for an end. This time she made herself say (though it was whispered into the seam of the couch), "They're gone. Dead." But John was right. Everyone had bad times. Zeyde was a widower at sixty, Rose a widow at fifty-seven, Lydia at twenty-seven. Zeyde lived without Grandma Lena for thirty years and she never saw him mope around. Memories of

Grandma Lena made him laugh, brought him happiness. The music hit a flourish. John leaned forward. Lydia wondered why her father seemed so unclear to her. Maybe he was missing and not dead. Maybe Kramer would come back.

When the movie ended, John turned down the volume and said, "I got just the thing to help you sleep. Vino, how's that?" He got up, rummaged in the kitchen for a while, and returned with a bottle of burgundy, dark green with a pale label. "It's good stuff. Frog wine. Nineteen seventy-three—that was a great year. Hey, no kidding, it was. That was the year I met Anna Maria Palmatessa, pubeless wonder. Let me get some glasses."

Lydia, glad to be spared the details of Anna Maria, took a huge swallow from the bottle. Tart and vinegary, but it was fine. When John came back she took a small glass from him and felt its angular edges. It was a glass from a yortzeit candle. She felt a burst of extreme curiosity: What was John's cousin doing with yortzeit candles? Could they be for John's father? Or didn't he have a father. Or if he did, how come he never mentioned him? John poured some wine in her glass and then took it to her. He made small circular motions with the glass so the wine coated the sides but didn't spill over.

"You want to know why I do that? It releases the wine's bouquet."

"Not bow-kay. It's frog wine, n'est-ce pas? Boo-kay. And tell me, do you always entertain your women with fine vintage wine in yortzeit glasses?"

"What women?"

Was Kramer right? "You mean they are small boys?"

"What are you driving at, Lydia, babe?"

"You talk about the building a lot. And your mother. What about your father? Do you have a father?" Her heart pounded. Maybe his father had died in a car accident and he could tell her how he had acted.

John shifted around. "What do you mean, are they small boys?"

"Did he die or something? Was it an accident?"

"Rae Ann Fanella is not a small boy, let me tell you, babe. A weird chicky is what she is. Rae Ann liked to go out nice, you know? She'd pay Calabrese to take care of Baby Sue when she wanted to step out."

"Calabrese?" Lydia was drawn in now. "Calabrese, who hollers beat me, beat me? A baby-sitter?"

"You ought to see him with Baby Sue. Terrific. Anyhow, Rae Ann gets all dolled up, makeup two inches thick, eyelashes made of mink—no kidding, she told me herself. We go out to Ballato's, this dynamite Italian restaurant on the Bowery. You ever been there? Osso Buco like you wouldn't believe, and when I come in, Mr. Ballato personally comes to the table. Anyhow, me and Rae Ann are eating, and she's making with the eyes, bat bat with the mink lashes. She sits close, rubs my knee, the usual. We drink a few, then we walk down Mulberry, and sit in that little park. It's pretty quiet there, you know? Rae Ann, before my butt hits the bench has my pants undone. I swear it. She's ready to go. Then she hears laughing. It's just these two queens prancing down the street."

"Have you ever had sex with a man?"

"What kind of crazy question is that? You asked me about Rae Ann, did you not? Anyhow, we go home, she goes into the bedroom and changes her clothes. Just like in the movies she says, 'Let me get into something more comfortable, darling.' Darling. I swear to baby Jesus. I come up behind her and kind of lead her to the bed. She's shocked, man." In a Betty Boop falsetto, 'How can you do that crude, crude thing?' She says good-night and pushes me out. But when she comes by the next week, I ask her out. I'm a student of human nature, you know? I want to know what's with this chick. One minute she's giving me head and parading around the house half-naked and the next minute I touch her and it's like I tried to fuck a nun."

Lydia took a nice long drink from the bottle and waved it above her head. "Punch line! I hereby call for a punch line!"

"The week after that we go to this crappo place on MacDougal that she says is better than Ballato's. I should've made her pay. We finish dinner and I figure what the hell, we can go to the No Name, have a few drinks, maybe she'll loosen up."

"Three weeks later—"

"I got so mad, I grabbed her before she got into something more comfortable in her bedroom. Her knees buckled. Jesus I got scared. Then we were on the ground. She ripped my shirt off, tore it from the shoulder straight down."

"Afterward we lay together, smoking a shared cigarette—"

"Something like that. It turns out this chick thinks beds are for sleeping. Floors, tables, walls are for sex."

"I couldn't agree more," Lydia said.

In one smooth move, John rolled them onto the floor. Lydia managed to raise her arm to keep the wine from spilling but was so angry she nearly brought the bottle down on his head. She was laughing because she was unnerved, but she fought to gain composure. "I mean it," she said. "I mean it. I really mean it. It's not funny." She got back on the couch, hugging the opposite end from John this time.

By the time the bottle had been finished, John was on his fourth tale about the fourth woman who pretended she didn't want sex but was really dying for it. This was the major theme in his life, starting with Nancy Gerardi, who would have stuck with him if he'd mauled her instead of being respectful. It made Lydia angry, but when she protested against his belief that women falsely protest, she became another protesting woman. The wine made her feel distant, aloof. Here she was drunk, out of her apartment, and in splendid control of herself, having decided that Kramer had left her because he carried a rare and highly contagious disease, too repugnant to mention. Suppose, she thought, he came back today. She was a mess, and there wasn't a single disease she could conjure up that could disfigure Kramer. Okay: She was gorgeous and desirable. In a husky voice, she said, "Kramer really lost out. He blew it; he really did."

"No," said John. "I congratulate the man."

All Lydia's doubts flooded back. John was right; he was to be congratulated. If only she had asked. If only she had been romantic, thrown everything away, followed him—

"If Kramer was still around, we wouldn't be here together."

Relieved, Lydia laughed. "You'd still be humping Rae Ann Fanella against the bedroom wall."

"Nah, I only started seeing Rae Ann a couple of weeks ago."

"Then why didn't you bring her instead, you pig."

John was too involved in his next story to hear. "Ollie Mae, did you ever hear such a name? She only liked it with her clothes on. She'd be hot and raring to go and the minute you got her panties off, she'd dry up like a prune."

How could she care who he was with, when he was a throwback, a primitive. Only by his opposable thumbs did he manage to swing into the Homo sapiens family. He had sick attitudes toward women. He had a shag rug, for God's sake. He wore nylon shirts. He was a jerk. She said, "I don't want to hear about your women. It's sick. Tell me about your father."

"You tell me about your father if you want to hear about fathers so bad."

John said fadduh. Being able to laugh at him again cheered her up. "What's this about fathers all of a sudden. You got a thing about fathers?"

"Yeah, yours."

"Watch what you're saying, bitch." He was tense and spat the words out slowly.

"Come on, John. You always talk about your mother and her famous meatballs. What about your father? Why don't you talk about him?"

"Why don't you talk about your mother?" he said, in the same spirit as fadduh.

"Because she's far away, I guess."

"Oh yeah? And why don't you say something about your father?"

"Because he's even farther away."

"They don't live together, is that right?"

"You're supposed to be telling me about your father," Lydia said. Was it an accident or disease? Did old age claim him peacefully in his sleep? Did John visit the cemetery? Did he cry? Were the dead leading characters in his dreams? In what part of his body was the pain located? "Is he dead, John? Please tell me."

"I wish he was."

"Come on, John, please."

He leaned across the couch and grabbed Lydia at the waist, pinching at both sides. He caught her most sensitive spot. Some people call this tickling, but being grabbed at the waist didn't tickle Lydia, it sent her into howls and screams of laughter. She kicked, wiggled, and hated the way it felt. "Come on, John," she said, barely managing the words.

"Shut up, bitch," John said, pinching again.

"Tell me!"

"Shut up, bitch." Another pinch.

"God damn you, stop."

"Shut up, bitch."

She used all her strength to roll onto the floor, but the sense had been knocked out of her. Hysterical, she yelled, "Tell me about your father, bastard."

John dove on top of Lydia before she was able to get away. He pinned her arms down with his knees so she couldn't move, and nipped at her waist, again and again. She was frightened and hurt and she begged him to stop, swearing she wouldn't say another word. She pleaded, between gasps and tears, to please get off, stop, you'll kill me, I can't breathe, I can't breathe. But he pinched her with fury, and each time her body jerked, he pinched again. His face in the blue light from the TV had a demonic look, the result of her dreams and predictions. I have to lie still, she thought, I have to be quiet, but waiting for the pinch made her squirm and plead and curse, and when he grabbed her and tickled, she cried until all that existed were her sounds. I must lie still, she thought, then let out the loudest scream she'd ever uttered. John sat back, freeing her arms. Wondering who'd made such a racket, she thought: It's a good thing it's not me.

Quickly she stood up, unable to catch her breath. She circled past the bedroom, but afraid of the darkness there, ended back in the living room, in front of John. He grabbed her wrists, twisted them, shook her whole body, whispering, "Are you going to be nice now, Lydia?" There was a haunted look on his face and, when she pulled back, he grabbed tighter, twisting her wrists again. "I said are you going to be nice?"

"Stop." She shook her head.

"Be nice, Lydia."

It was Lydia and she was frightened. Please, Daddy, help, she thought.

John let go of one of her wrists and still holding on to the other pushed her hand into his pants and walked her backward into the couch. She pulled her hand free and he grabbed her wrist again. "Be nice, Lydia," he said, just as soft and crazy-sounding.

She didn't care, as long as she didn't have to kiss him. That was it. He guided her hand down the fly of his pants and made her unzip them. She wouldn't kiss him no matter what. He put her hand around his cock. It was hard and wide. She didn't care as long as he didn't make her kiss him.

"Be nice to me, Lydia," he said, using her hand to stroke himself. "Be nice." His voice got harder as he pressed her hand tighter. "Be nice," he said, moving it faster and faster.

He came quickly, and as soon as it was over, took a tissue from his back pocket and wiped her hand clean.

Lydia stood up. "I'm tired. I have to go to sleep."

She slept the night, but in the morning the first thing she heard was, "Be nice, Lydia." She sat up in bed, heart pounding, but no one was in the room. Mornings were hard. Everything was in such clear focus. She was alone in a massive brass bed, owned by Italians who kept yortzeit candles. She touched her arms, her face, remembered calling for her father. "I'm okay," she said. "I really am." On the bureau was a photograph of John's cousin and her husband. Lydia turned it toward the wall and got dressed.

As she was tiptoeing to the bathroom, she smelled the coffee. She gasped when she heard John call, "Hi, babe."

"Fine," she said defiantly. "And you?"

On the drive home, she shut her eyes to the traffic. Most of her thoughts were airborne and floated like bubbles to the top of her head, bursting, disappearing unformed. The few she remembered she was sure to say aloud, to prove to herself and John that she was intact. John told long stories. She felt him grinning at her but never opened her eyes to check. He squeezed her knee once. He was in good spirits from the weekend. Lydia felt she should spit at him and feel furious and unforgiving, and plot to make him suffer. But she felt unviolated. John hadn't made her feel a fraction of the pain that Kramer had after one wordless, sullen night. She felt as if she were watching John thinking he had hurt Lydia, while Lydia herself sat in the other corner of the room, laughing.

She got home and switched on all the lights, immediately seeing why she'd left them off all these days. The apartment was like the dead child's room bereaved parents can't bear to disassemble. Everything of Kramer's remained as he had left it, roach in the ashtray on his work area, T-shirt in a corner. There was a fine coat of dust, and she expected there were spider webs. When she sat in the rocking chair, she felt like Miss Havisham. Leaving home on Friday had broken the spell. It wasn't the same anymore. She couldn't live among the ruins.

13

L YDIA LOCKED the door to keep out thieves and snoops, to protect good people tempted by an open door, turned vandals at the sight of a TV, stereo, clock radio, untapped treasures in drawers, some slightly parted as if the objects inside needed air and now waited to crawl out. She didn't like the idea of strangers in her room, jumping on her bed. If she never returned, what she left behind was still part of her. She believed with a strangely prescientific logic that her name, her footsteps, her sneeze, her clothes, washcloths, sheets, socks, and toothbrush were all part of her. There was no hiding, even across the continent, if someone found a hair or possession of Lydia and recited the special incantation. And because she didn't want anyone hurting her anymore, she snapped the first lock to keep strangers, good and evil, from coming inside, and the second one, the one she rarely used, to keep out John. Kramer had installed the second lock the day he brought his cameras and tape deck and recording equipment to Lydia's. It was a dead-bolt lock, the kind that wouldn't open with just a credit card jimmied in the seam. John didn't have a key, so he'd have to break and enter if he wanted to get in.

She had no friends to inform of her departure, but she took the time to write a letter to Dr. Cantoni. Something about a death in the family, a leave of absence from school. Lydia said she wouldn't be back in the fall. She couldn't imagine ever returning, but extrapolating from a broken arm to a mended one, from flu to health, she decided to try believing someday she would be well. Dr. Cantoni, as projected on the sheet of paper, was a friend. "Kramer is gone, too," she wrote, "he passed away last month." She thought of Kramer as a heaven-bound Chagall fig-ure, perhaps floating over the apartment that moment. She stuck her head out the window on the landing between the fifth and sixth floors: on the clothesline, the colored sheets, striped towels, and aprons all waved to her. There was no safety in the room, the familiarity of neighbors, building, street, shopkeepers, school. There was no safety where there was coincidence, where old lovers, friends from every corner of Kramer's life, the telephone existed. In the midst of a black mood he could pick up the phone and make exquisite small talk, sprinkling an essentially meaning-less conversation with compliments, stories, gossip, local color. The day he left she had vacuumed the rug. She took the larger English muffin. Later, around noon, she teased him for writing "emerggancy" on a little wallet card telling the world about his penicillin allergies. "Let's see you spell that again," she said, though he was sensitive about his spelling and these were, after all, their last hours.

On the third landing, she took her wallet from her pack, and put two fingers in the secret hiding place to make sure she had the extra twenty. For years her father had tried to get her to tuck away a bill "just in case," but he'd been unsuccessful until today. Once he was in the city and they met for lunch. No coq au vin on Madison Avenue for Dad. He took the Seventh Avenue local down to the Village, proud that he could recite all the local stops, 59, 50, 42, 34, 28, 23, 18, 14, Sheridan Square, where his daughter lived. "I thought this was really way out when I was a kid," he said. "Uncle Sherman's pal Maxie took me to Greenwich Village. I was about fourteen."

After they kissed, Lydia took him to a bagel bakery on Sixth Avenue. A counter, a line, good luck if you got a table without a stranger sharing your conversation. He planned to have cream cheese and lox on a bagel, but the sign on the wall listed eight varieties. "Lydie, you get a poppy seed and I'll get an onion and we'll go halvsies, how's that?" When he lived in town there had been bagels period. "No, Lydie, I have a better idea. You get a sesame and I'll get an onion. Or a garlic. A garlic bagel, imagine that. Which would you rather have, onion or garlic?"

Lydia beat out a party of three to an empty table. Her father was saying he could bring a couple dozen bagels home, Rose could freeze what they didn't eat. He took his bagel and coffee off the plastic tray and said, "I put aside money for you, Lydie, so don't worry, you'll never go hungry."

Lydia tried not to laugh. His fears were real enough, though "going hungry" had always been something of a joke to her.

"The stocks haven't done so well."

"It doesn't matter, Daddy."

"It matters. Of course it matters. But if you mean, don't worry, all right, I won't. I have Harold Wolfe working with me. You remember Harold, don't you? He's investing some of your money in real estate. Real estate is always good, Lydie. Land is finite, remember that."

Lydia had trouble deciding which half to eat first. She liked to save the best for last. "Not bad," her father said. Then leaning over, "A Chinese waiter in a bagel bakery?"

"Bagels are cosmopolitan, Dad."

"Bagels are the only good thing in this whole lousy city."

He got seconds on coffee, carrying each cup at the rim, gritting his teeth, rolling his eyes to make his baby laugh, though the coffee, sloshing over the edges, was burning his fingers.

"You'll be able to finish your studies, get a good position. You'll have time to get on your feet financially."

"Daddy, I don't care about the money."

"You ought to. It's about time you cared about money. I'm not a rich man, Lydie. I put away what I could manage, a few thousand is all. But you've got to care about it, you're grown up now. A grown-up single woman, living alone in New York—"

Lydia walked down the stairs, underwear, sweater, nylon windbreaker, all packed in her orange knapsack. Had that ever happened? If, as in a film, she could have had a second take, she'd have said, "I'm pleased you put the money aside for me, and I love you no matter what." She'd tried to say thanks (for the twenty in her palm) and he had said, "What is this thank you? Why so formal all of a sudden?"

At the second floor she slid a note under John's door: "Rent all paid. Do not enter my apartment."

Six letters were dumped into the mail bin: one to Dr. Cantoni, the second a check for a year's rent. Money was sent to the phone company to cover the basic monthly charge until next summer. Three other bills were paid.

Lydia left the building with one regret. She hadn't said good-bye the right way. She'd walked Kramer to the corner that night, carrying one of his bags, laughing about its weight, though she felt it might tear her arm from its socket. She dropped the bag on the corner and dusted off the smudge of dirt on the sundress she'd worn for the occasion. Then he was standing by the cab, the door open. He waved, she waved back. The streetlights were dim; she couldn't see the features on his face, just its shape, his body. He couldn't see her and she was glad, because she was smiling. No tears; waving, waving. He slid in the cab and closed the door. She wiped her eyes so he might think she was crying. The cab pulled into traffic, its brake lights blinking red. She ran down Bleecker Street, turned right instead of left and stopped at Rosemary's for a cup of coffee.

14

Twice she sat up in bed, momentarily aware of coffee smells, voices, her eyes hurting. Then sleep again. The room was a stark and shocking white: a hospital. West-Coast early light flooding through broad windows. Home. She'd come home to search. Home to Mama. For eight years she'd been no one's daughter, had connection with no kin, as if she'd appeared on the earth (as she'd appeared in New York) full grown. She denied genes, parents, a past life. All the way across the country she had told herself this was a business trip, the search. But asleep and awake she practiced saying "Mama." She didn't want to call her Rose. On the airplane, lips moving: Mama. The stewardess had approached with food on a tray: Mama. Pillow behind Lydia's head, blanket across her lap: surrogate woolen Mama. Then on the front steps of the house she grew up in had stood Harold and Mama, his arm around her slender waist. Uncle Harold, father of Melissa and Larold, forever eight and ten. "Well, what do you think of Rosie and me? Pretty terrific, no? It's a miracle we found each other."

She sat up in bed, drenched, as if the night had been a feverish one. The room was overexposed, completely a blur. She thought of her father, groping on the night table for his glasses, knocking over the alarm clock. She groped on the night table for her own, a rimless pair from her freshman days, the only familiar object in a stranger's drawers. Last night, two fingers like forceps withdrew a doughnut from the box, tore it in two. Red jelly bled from it. "Larry has your old room, Cookie, so you'll sleep in the guest room. It's nice and bright—freshly painted."

Glasses on, the whiteness was no illusion. Walls, blinds, French provincial furniture, the legs of each piece gnarled arthritically and stenciled with gold. And Lydia in front of the mirror in white baby-doll pajamas, short ruffly jammies. A newly hatched chick. *Mama, where are my clothes?* She'd flown clear across the country and stood on their doorstep dressed in New York black (with pumpkin-colored pack) hoping to be a dream come true. "My God, what a surprise! Harold, look. Lydie's come to visit. Imagine that, just walked on a plane and bingo she's here."

It was a surprise, Harold's arm around Rose's waist. She thought her father would be here, but it's Harold's arm, covered with curly white hair. Uncle Harold for twenty years, father of Melissa and Larold—she'd named him that, thinking Larry/-Larold, Harry/Harold. Uncle Harold, husband of Norma. Red jelly bleeding from the gash. They were downstairs. All she had to do was walk into the kitchen and the evidence would be in front of her eyes: Harold's arm, a boa, wound around her how many times? "Your father was a truly great guy. He would've wanted someone to love and cherish Rosie like I do." Lydia couldn't remember her father's qualities well enough to agree or disagree, but soon she'd know. She smiled at Harold. In '62 he'd brought her two red-banded leafhoppers.

Mama? She peeked through a crack in the door. Harold's Larry was in the hall in a red kimono, waving. "Hi, sis. I'll tell the folks you're up."

Mama? "I'm no psychic but I had a feeling you'd come west to be with your boyfriend. Ask Harold if you don't believe me."

Mama, where are my clothes? Harold's arm, a boa. Mama brushing the hair from her girl's face, as if when the hair was parted, the sweet baby would be revealed. "She was always so sensitive, remember, Harold? All you had to do was look at her cross-eyed and she'd cry."

Hot pink fifty-seven-year-old ass, wife of Uncle Harold.

Suppose John told Michael and Michael told Kramer. Kramer knew Rose's address. "They're shooting in Arizona," Lydia said. She was sitting in a swivel chair between Rose and Harold, inspecting the shirt Rose had left on the bed. Clingy yellow, no stains, no sign from that party in Santa Monica eight years ago when she'd vomited Southern Comfort all over it. Her own clothes had disappeared in the night. Mama, digging into a slice of cantaloupe, was waiting to find out why her boyfriend wasn't sleeping here. Punishment for the bomb Lydia set off six years before when she'd said, "I sleep with my boyfriend in New York, why can't we sleep together here?" Now Mama insisted upon knowing why they weren't living together. Lydia wanted to tell her Kramer had died but instead said, "He's on location. They're shooting in Arizona."

She heard a thump thump thump, then Larry came in, dressed in tennis whites, behind him a little poodle, jumping and twirling, long nails clacking on the linoleum. "Come to Mommy," Rose said.

The dog jumped on Lydia's lap, cold nails on her bare thighs. She pushed it firmly to the ground. *She* hadn't been allowed to have a dog in the house. Once she had won a turtle at a school lottery. It came in a clear snail-shaped pool with a fake Miami palm. The turtle's shell had softened and Rose had flushed it while Lydia slept.

"You used to love dogs, Lydie. Back when we lived on Rodgers Road the Schneiders had Whitey, do you remember? You were just a baby and so adorable." Rose turned from Lydia to Harold. "She loved that dog so. He would growl and bite at adults but she could do anything. She'd climb on him and pull his hair and ride him like a pony. She even used to blow his nose. It bothered her that his nose was wet. She was always trying to blot it with Kleenex."

Once there was an adorable black-haired baby, and now there's me, Lydia thought.

"Are you sure you won't come?" Larry asked.

"Go on," Harold said. "Lar can introduce you to all the guys. Al, Mark—my new sister Lydia."

"Then take a nap while we're gone, Cookie. You'll feel better when you've gotten sleep."

The empty house was what she wanted and as they lined up to kiss her good-bye an old feeling was revitalized. Lydia is ten. Daddy, Mama, and Jill go out for the day. A sandwich is made up for Lydie, strict instructions not to use the oven. They shut the windows, lock the back door, the garage door, and leave through the front, double-locking themselves out of the house. "Don't let anyone in, Lydie. If someone calls on the phone say Mommy's indisposed. Don't tell anyone you're home alone." A car starts up and they're gone. A beam in the house creaks, frightening her in an intensely pleasurable way.

Lydia waited in the kitchen, letting five full minutes pass. Sometimes people returned, having forgotten an address or a gift. If they were already on the freeway, they called instead. Once the phone rang and a man with a Japanese accent said, "Rittle girl? Are you by yourself, rittle girl?" Her father. He had also called as a Russian, a Mexican, a deep-throated Hungarian. "Mommy's on the potty and Daddy's asleep," she said to men with foreign accents.

First her parents' room, the forbidden one, the only one that could yield any worthwhile results. Her toes sank into the new white carpet as she crossed the room. New bed. A bureau covered with framed photographs of four babies—Lydia and Jill as bald-headed infants; Lydia and Jill as toddlers. She had flown to L.A. to search, but now, after begging the family to leave, she was unable to touch anything. She stood rigidly for minutes before being able to persuade herself to run her hand along the bureau top and get accustomed to the feel of things here. Suddenly her fingers reached for the picture of the laughing baby. She couldn't believe she had been that fat-cheeked child, though the others, faced with the emaciated grown-up, seemed only to remember her that way. It was as if their Lydia had died at five. Harold, for instance, didn't know exactly what she did in New York, though like Rose, he had a storehouse of Baby Lydia stories. "Your mother always talks about how you could read at four. And that time you were on TV—" An apple-green organdy dress, fiercely bright lights, recognizing her mother's cough out of twenty other coughs backstage. She got down on her knees and lifted the dust ruffle. "And how you could recite all the names of the bones?" She had to look, she had to get up the nerve to search. Back in the Baby Lydia days she searched for prophylactics and love letters, proof of sex, or self, and her reluctance now, she preferred thinking, was a streak of morality lacking at ten, not a fear of finding those things. "I was good at phalanges, Harold. *Flexor digitorum pro-fundus, flexor digitorum superficialis, flexor pollicis brevis, flexor pollicis longus ...*"

Still on her knees she swept her arm between the legs of the furniture. When she used to play hide and seek with her father she called, "Come out, come out!" She knew this time she wouldn't find him behind the chair, under the couch, rolled up in the sofa bed just to make her laugh. But if she found his slipper and touched the soft fragrant leather, sights and smells would well up. Adventures would be relived. Intellectually she knew she had a father (love letters, prophylactics), that he was five foot eight inches tall, and had wiry black hair. But the feel of him, the sound of his voice, his smell, the fact of his love? What did he look like? The remembered features (heart-shaped bald spot, stooped shoulder) stood alone, as if on a dressmaker's dummy. He was without character, flesh, warmth, humanity. What did they share? Lydia bounced on her mother's bed. The remaining scenes were those she had told so many times they ceased being real and were stories. Once upon a time there was a father (Hankie, Daddy) named Maurice, and his father, Aaron, called Zeyde, meaning grandpa. A little history, cold as in a schoolbook. Some life had to remain. She was dead herself without it. No tears seeing Rose. Her arms automatically went around her mother, and instead of feeling love, as she'd planned, she felt the soft wedges of flesh below the band of her mother's bra. Lydia wanted them back. Daddy. Zeyde in his madras yarmulke with a buckle in the back, Ivy League style from a bar mitzvah in the sixties.

She pulled open a bureau drawer, rifling through laundered shirts and boxer shorts. (Kramer's fly sewn up. Socks around his ankles.) In the closet, mummified clothing, lavender blouses, lemon slacks, white shoes. Harold's bottled ships on tabletops. Rose's baroque needlepoint scenes on the walls. Zeyde's friend, Mr. Zimmer, was blind. When he came to the house, he nodded at Lydia and held his hand out, perfect aim, to shake with her. In a bowl of fruit he knew the golden delicious from the red, as if the color were absorbed by his fingertips. That was what Lydia wanted. To touch something familiar and absorb memories.

She walked into Larry's room and sat at the desk that had once been hers. Plastic-wrapped gloves were in the top drawer, a satin box of rolled-up stockings in the second. Kramer had wanted to see Lydia in stockings and a teacher's dress. In the deep drawer meant for term papers were evening bags. Was this how Larry studied for law? Lydia got up and pushed a folding closet door. It rumbled aside and she froze, listening. Was anyone home? Maybe she should check downstairs one more time. Someone could be hiding, waiting to catch her. She called, "Harold? Rose? Larry?" feeling silly, laughing at herself. Nothing. She parted the curtains. No cars were on the driveway. Lydia crawled into the closet and flipped through more clothes. On the back wall, "I hate you, I hate you" had been etched into the plaster with a bobby pin. "This is *my* room," she said, feeling the same as twenty years ago when in fury she'd carved those words. Not "This was my room." "This *is* my room," as if she still had dibs on it. Ilie Nastase on her walls. Ilie Nastase, cursing and sweating above her bedboard. Ilie Nastase leaning over to tie his laces. Ilie Nastase and Jimmy Connors, matching bands around their wrists like laboratory animals. When she was a teacher, a little boy had dropped a note on her desk: "You are very b~~ewty~~ petty." What would Kramer think if he saw her now?

Her father's study had been turned into a grown-up recreation room. His books were gone, skeins of yarn on shelves instead. Tennis rackets, cans of balls, Adidas bags. Death, death, marriage. How could she believe any of this, getting only phone calls. "You were busy with your schoolwork and I know how hard it is for you to get away. Besides, it was only your old ma's wedding." Punished for deserting the family, doomed to search in closets for her father, to look for Zeyde's presence in drawers and on shelves. She couldn't believe, with the living evidence, the two of them on the front steps. "Oh my God! What a surprise!" Her mother and Harold Wolfe, Jewish gentleman extraordinaire, father of Larold and Melissa.

Exhausted and disappointed, Lydia sat on an old wing chair and extended her legs, feeling for the footrest. An image stirred, a snapshot in poor focus. Zeyde, asleep, his chin burrowed into his chest, wearing as usual a white shirt and a gray suit jacket. He had a button imprint on his chin when she kissed him to wake him up. Where was the footrest?

Everyone was home and the noise level was above the threshold of pain. Rose was in the kitchen kneading chopped meat, squeezing it through her fingers. She pursed her lips for a kiss when Lydia walked in, then told her daughter she *knew* thin was in, but Lydia carried it too far. She should eat a good dinner, so her boyfriend wouldn't get bruises when he slept with her.

Lydia said, "Hey Rose, what happened to the footrest?"

Rose threw pea-sized bits of chopped meat to the dog twirling at her feet.

"You wouldn't by any chance know what happened to the footrest, would you, Rose? You know—" This old pair of glasses wasn't very good. Lydia closed one eye to get her mother in clearer focus. "—The footrest?"

"I have no idea what you're talking about."

"Zeyde's footrest?"

"Lydia," Rose said. "Could you crack an egg over this? I've got glop all over my hands."

Lydia got an egg. She lifted it high and cracked it across the middle with a bread knife. The yolk whizzed by, a speedy setting sun. Deciding to show some laid-back, L.A. cool, she put an elbow on the counter and in a soft voice said, "Zeyde's footstool?"

"*That* old thing? I threw it out."

It was a joke. Lydia laughed. "You didn't."

"Come to think of it, you're right. I didn't throw it out, I gave it to the cleaning girl." She was working egg into the meat. It made awful slurping noises. Babies gumming bananas.

"You threw everything out?"

Rose was humming now, cheerfully washing the meat off her hands. Lydia followed her to the sink. "All of Zeyde's things?"

"Just the crap, Cookie. Your gramps was a big saver of crap."

"Oh Mama, how could you do that. His books? His clothes? You dumped *everything*?"

"I can't hear a word you're saying."

"*Everything*? His books? His clothes? My God, you didn't—"

Rose turned to Lydia, and looked at her in silence for a while. "You expected to find gold in his pockets?" she said. "Is that it? Let me tell you, Cookie, you're a little old to get away with this. I had to listen to those phone calls of yours, complaining about my treatment of him. I wasn't kind enough. I didn't speak nicely to him. You don't know about reality, Cookie. You live in a dreamworld. Well, let me clue you in: Taking care of some ninety-one-year-old man is not pretty. Especially some ninety-one-year-old man who's not even your own father, to boot."

"Not some ninety-one-year-old man. Our Zeyde."

"Our Zeyde bullshit."

15

THEY ASKED her to sit with them in the TV room (her father's study). Seven nights running she said no. She couldn't watch TV, *bowl of grapes, two glasses of chocolate milk,* Night Train to Munich, *so I can be with my honey.* Harold took Lydia aside on the eighth night and said he wanted to show her his rock garden. He put a long arm around her, led her out back and pointed out three varieties of Kalanchoe. Then he said, "You're not mad at me, are you?"

Harold was tall, easily six-two, and had sad and sleepy brown eyes with eyebrows that sloped in the same direction. He looked, as always, as though he were ready to weep. "Oh Harold, no, really," Lydia said.

"I didn't think so. I told Rose, me and Lydie have been pals ever since that time I let her feed peanuts to the giraffe. Remember, Lydie? He leaned way over and got his sticky tongue on your cheek. Melissa screamed and carried on when she saw it, but you closed your eyes as if you were in heaven." He touched the leathery leaf of a jade plant, like the one in her dreams. "She's a great girl, your mother, and she worries maybe you don't like me."

Lydia said she liked him a lot (the truth) and did he by any chance know where she could find her dad's baseball glove?

Harold showed Lydia a croton, its leaves mottled and twisted like corkscrews. He laughed uncomfortably. "You could do no wrong in his eyes. Once you smeared applesauce all over the wall and he said you showed artistic talent."

What about his toothbrushes?

"Everyone's entitled to their happiness, Lydia, and don't you forget that." He squeezed her shoulder to soften the words and asked, as a personal favor, if she'd sit with them that night. She didn't have to watch the set.

Lydia said she was a great fan of TV, but her eyes had been bothering her. "Don't tell Rose, she'll worry. It's just eyestrain from reading in bad light. Doctor says absolutely no TV."

Harold mussed up her hair and said she smelled peachy. Rose's shampoo. Every morning she washed her hair in case Kramer rang the bell. Kramer loved broken shells and bits of glass. He said the most beautiful things were imperfect. He would find her. He would love her as she was. He would forgive her.

Mistake number one: Not sitting with the family at night. They talked about her when she was gone, each revealing that she'd pressed for clues. Rose called a family powwow, cautioning the men against using certain words in front of Lydia: *father, pa, daddy, dad, he died, passed away, left us, is gone.* Don't mention cars, New York, grandfathers, accidents. Don't say *pacemaker.* Don't use the word *death, memory, marriage,* or *remarriage.* Don't say Maurice, for God's sake. Speak about Norma and Melissa in private. Pretend this is how it always was and she's being crazy not to understand. Lydia was oversensitive. Remember how all you had to do was sneeze and she'd be *spritzing* from the eyes? Lydia knew this because new words replaced the banned ones and were ill fitting. The rooms showed changes, too: the old map of czarist Russia was replaced by Larry's undergraduate diploma, which was smaller. The discoloration surrounded it like a storm cloud. The wing chair was replaced by a canvas sling chair, completely out of place among the low plush couches and ginger jar lamps.

"I'm not crazy, I sat in that chair, I did. I remember distinctly—"

What chair? Don't be silly.

"And the globe. Wasn't there a globe up there? A relief globe? You could feel the mountains, you could scratch bug bites with the Andes?"

What globe?

Lydia tried being subtle, asking questions in a gentle voice.

"Do you still have that apple corer?"

That's not even an apple you're holding.

"I know, but it's also good with pears. You know, the small round gadget shaped like a wheel? The spokes section the fruit?"

I can't hear a word you're saying.

"Uh—you remember Daddy, don't you? The man who used to wear alligator T-shirts?"

What alligator T-shirts, I can't hear a word you're saying, I have no idea what you're talking about. . . .

"The man who said, "How are ya, Jackson,' who sang like Vaughn Monroe?"

Vaughn who? What man? Stop torturing yourself.

She bit the insides of her cheeks until they were raw and blistered, but questions burst out against her will. His pipes, his penknife, his gyroscope. What had become of his toothbrush collection? Her father had bought brushes constantly. He was interested in the aesthetics of color and style the way a stamp or coin collector is, but effectiveness delighted him most. He had flicked bristles for Lydia, showing the advantages of a rubber-tipped brush or one that had hard inner bristles and soft outer ones. He became interested in irregularly tufted brushes, boar-bristle brushes, and soft nylon ones for bedtime. When electric toothbrushes were introduced, he bought one of the earliest models. It had an up-and-down motion and was taken off the market for reasons he could have explained, and replaced with a model that vibrated properly, from side to side.

His Artur Rubinstein records had disappeared and so had their copy of *Charlotte's Web*. His City College beer mug had been taken from the kitchen and his baseball glove from the garage. She missed the glove terribly. It was brown and satiny because her father kept it well oiled. He liked to tell Lydia exciting stories about the Brooklyn Badgers, his sandlot team. The stories all starred a burly lantern-jawed man named K.O. who was dangerous but fair. Lydia had forgotten about the Badgers until coming to L.A., but without the glove, the stories themselves would remain lost. Her father never used the glove. He just put his hand in it, pushing it with the other hand. Baseball was socially unacceptable and the others snickered when he told Badgers stories. Uncle Harold tried to reform him. Rose bought him a tennis racket. Only then was he embarrassed.

Lydia felt trapped. She couldn't leave without the memories, but the search was a failure. She grew quiet and evasive, going to sleep each evening earlier than the evening before, trying to sleep through the afternoon. One morning Rose sat on the edge of the bed, stroking Lydia's forehead until she woke. "A mother always knows her daughter no matter how many years they've been apart and I have a pretty good idea what's eating you. Are you awake?" Her voice was low and soothing. Hearing the concern in her voice, Lydia struggled not to cry. "Stop torturing yourself, Cookie, you didn't kill your grandfather. He was ninety-one, how much longer do you think he could've lasted? Now why don't you put on something clean and come keep your old ma company shopping. Come on, we can get you a nice dress and sandals." Lydia was wearing a dress when she'd waved good-bye to Kramer. "You look nice," he'd said. "Did you wear dresses like that when you taught?" Lydia didn't want a dress.

The next day her mother shook her awake, saying, "Just because I don't have a Ph.D. doesn't mean I'm stupid. You feel disdain for us. You think we're beneath you. We sit together in the evenings like a real family while you go upstairs to your room and lock the door."

Lydia wanted to tell her mother she didn't feel disdain, but she couldn't think of how to say it without mentioning Kramer's death. But if she told Rose Kramer died, it would get terribly complicated when he rang the front doorbell.

Rose stood up, stretching like a cat. "I feel like a youngster. I have a new life, a new husband, and we're very much in love, Lydia."

New life . . . husband . . . very much in . . . Wasn't she even . . . Didn't she feel . . .

"When your father died it was a terrible shock. Terrible. But it doesn't help dwelling on it. You can't bring him back. You have to go out and live no matter how much it hurts. Look at me! Everyone says I never looked better and you want to know why? My friends made me run around and meet people. I took tennis lessons, pottery lessons, yoga lessons—you want to see me do a full lotus or a yoga mudra? Fifty-seven years old and I've never been happier."

But if you're not convinced they're dead? Lydia thought. If you still think they may come back?

"Lydia, for once in your life listen to me. No more talk about your father. It doesn't do you any good, it's unfair to me and it hurts Larry and Harold—both of whom like you so much. This business with your father is a closed book. It's over."

Just like that?

Rose snapped her fingers. "Just like that. Not a word more. Not a single word, I warn you." There was a harshness in the set of her mouth. "Now why don't you put on something clean and come shopping with your old ma."

Your old ma.... Lydia's throat tightened. Her mother could die. By morning she could be gone, and with her all of Lydia's remembrances. She could die and be buried with her voice, her jokes, her footsteps. Lydia said she'd go wherever Rose liked— shopping, tennis. Rose held out her hand and squeezed Lydia's. Soft skin, thick veins, a new wedding band. Her chest rose and fell. Rose had cleavage. Lydia had waited until she was eighteen, hoping at least she'd have breasts like her mother.

She trailed behind her mother through department after department (wearing borrowed white thong sandals, circa 1960) while Rose tried on straw hats, shoes, and low-cut blouses, laughed into mirrors, winked at herself. She stroked cottons, rubbed double-knits between her fingers, gauze against her cheek. She dabbed perfume on her wrists and then behind Lydia's ears. She was tireless, her color high, her eyes bright and excited. Lydia trudged up to the china department, then to leather gooods. She begged her mother for a rest so they stopped for lunch. Only then did Rose come out of her trance. "You have to buy something for your boyfriend, even if it's just a thought," she said. "What's his sleeve size?" In New York Lydia once gave a salesman Kramer's sleeve length and the man said, "What's your boyfriend, an orangutan?" "How about you, Lydie," Rose said. "Don't you want anything?"

Answers. Did Daddy go shopping with you? Did he get upset when you ran the red lights? Did he say I wuv oo, Rose?

"Lydie, your boyfriend will come all hot and tired from Arizona, you think he'll want to see that long face?"

Smile, Lydia, hold it, that's right, a big one . . .

On to sheets and linens, up to the closet shop. Did he carry Lydia on his shoulders? Was he sad she was a girl? Did he buy you presents? (This last, accidentally said aloud as Rose was signing for some shoe trees.) "For Christ's sake, Lydia, drop it."

They left that store an hour later, but Rose still had to stop at the supermarket to pick up a few items for dinner.

It had been years since Lydia had been to a supermarket outside of New York. A family of six could ride in one of the carts. Rose showed her expertise here too. She pitched the heavy stuff into the bottom simultaneously planning complete meals for the upcoming week, multiplying ounces by the number of people, minus the anticipated guests or absentees (Larry has a late game Wednesday, Kristin comes on Friday). At the checkout counter, she turned to Lydia and said, "When I die my epitaph should read: She Shopped." She smiled, wry and self-deprecating. At that moment, Lydia loved her very much.

16

Soon after Lydia began regularly accompanying Rose shopping and to tennis games, she became a daughter. She began whining, nagging, pouting, refusing to answer when called to meals, daydreaming, and shirking chores. She never knew from what age a reaction would spring, but reacting from history, she was infuriated by small things. The family embraced her. They said she was like her old self again.

To Lydia's great surprise, memories came without those precious objects. Tearing lettuce for a salad, stripping her bed, asking for pretzels in the supermarket, reverting to a cry of Ma-ah, brought up and down the scale and stretched into five syllables, triggered her memory. There was a catch, though. She remembered the wrong things. She didn't remember Zeyde or her father the way she wanted, but in a fleeting instant, an image so quick she was unable to prepare for it or amend it in any way: Biting Zeyde. The look of amazement on his face. Ignoring him for days after, holding back her love out of shame. Meanness on top of meanness because she knew he'd never forgive her. Or another. At twelve, the year she wanted to be popular, not bringing friends home because her parents (translated as her father and grandfather) were not American enough, did not look and speak like others' parents. And hollered no matter who was around. *(So? Where do you live, Judi Ann?)* All of these showed a rotten Lydia.

At night she began dreaming of her father and Zeyde. The dreams were pleasant and sleep became more important. They were usually about domestic situations when everyone was alive. Sometimes they were confusing, with Lydia being an adult or her father being balder than she remembered upon awakening. Harold sat at the table once. In another dream her father was very small except for a mammoth left index finger. In real life this finger had been broken in a Badgers game and improperly set. The last joint remained permanently on the diagonal. When Lydia was young she loved asking how it had happened. "It got stuck in a bowling ball and I tried to shake it off," he told her once. "I bent down to pick up a dime, forgot that I was stepping on my own finger and then tried to stand up," he told her in the dream. When she woke she remembered her favorite story, the one about how he was picking his nose, his mind wandered and it got caught when he inhaled. That one had a moral.

The dreams were never ominous or upsetting and when Lydia woke she had a warm, false feeling that all was well, that all she had to do was sleep to spend more time with them, to enjoy their company more than she had, perhaps, when they were alive.

For a week it was hot, dry, and over 100 degrees Fahrenheit. Rose called it perfect summer weather. Lydia was suffocating.

"If you don't like it here, imagine how you'll feel in Arizona," Rose said.

Lydia thought she'd better sleep that one off. On her way to bed, however, she was seduced by the mirror. She tried to view her reflection in a detached, scientific manner, but confronted with her gauntness she wondered why she'd ever hoped to run into Kramer. Even in her fantasies the best she could do upon seeing him was cover her face. She decided from then on to travel incognito.

At dinner Lydia found out Harold had squealed about her eyes. She pretended to be dismayed, disappointed at his betrayal. Rose offered to buy her a new pair of glasses, and Lydia resisted —because it was expected of her. The next morning, she picked out huge frames and had photogray lenses put in. Very chic, the optician said. Rose agreed, though she was worried Lydia's boyfriend would fail to recognize her at the airport. That meant to Lydia she'd passed the test.

A mysterious woman hidden behind dark glasses sat on a bench at the Greenleaf Country Club every day cheering on Rose, then Larry, and so he wouldn't be disappointed, Harold. A never-ending cycle. Lydia's penance. On the tennis courts, lithe, golden women, reminders of her own inactivity. Kramer in paradise. Stucco houses, rock and roll on car radios, blue-eyed blonds. Accompanying Larry was the least upsetting. He was such a wholesome, clean-cut, good-natured kid. Next to him, Lydia was the underworld, the dark side of human nature: black-haired, small, brown, shifty, smoke-gray glasses obscuring her face. They revealed small secrets to each other, pretending they were part of a conspiracy, youth against the adults. Larry gave Lydia a joint whenever they were together. He asked questions about women as he drove. Was it dumb to open doors these days? Was it uncool to date his buddy's ex-girl friend? Should he play as hard as usual against a girl? Lydia said yes to the last. She liked watching Larry play. He was perseverant on the courts, unwilling to let a ball go without trying for it, sullen when he lost, and exuberant when he won.

One day after a close game, a most satisfying victory, he sat next to Lydia and said, "Why do you call your Mom Rose?"

"She told me to—as a graduation present of sorts."

"Start calling her Mom. It'll make her feel, you know, more like a mother. Needed." He was rolling his head from side to side, then in small circles to ease a kink. Lydia had her face turned up to the sun so the lenses would blacken. Someone she knew from high school could show up. Rose said a lot of young marrieds were joining because it was the in thing. What if a film was being shot here and they needed some second-unit footage?

"First Jill left and then you. And your father was kind of— he was a weird guy if you don't mind my saying so. Independent. Rose had no one to fuss over. That's how she got tight with my dad. Mom was busy with this committee and that committee and Dad was just about going to work with his pants on backwards."

"Tight, Larry?"

"What?"

"Could you define tight?"

Larry gave a playful push, nearly sending her off the bench. "We gotta go, Lydio. Kristin's waiting."

Rose had her head in a giant, smoking freezer, digging up frozen bricks of food and some Baby Lydia story. Baby Lydie who said broccoli looked like trees. Who called bananas nabanas.

Lydia had promised to grate carrots, but she was sitting at the kitchen table, rigid. Really tight? Just-friends tight or really tight for real? Both families toured the Grand Canyon in the Wolfes' station wagon. Rose took care of Melissa and Larry whenever Norma had an attack. Larry forced himself to laugh until he turned purple. Melissa was a biter. "If there's one thing I cannot excuse it's biting people," Rose told her. How tight was tight? When Jill and Lydia ate at the Wolfes' they had ravioli. Doughy squares, she loved it. Fritos, Cheez Doodles, potato chips. Pretzels from a can. At nine Lydia jumped rope to the refrain of Norma nure manure manure. Norma had attacks. She had a mustache and tiny doll's hands. She was very fat and wore muumuus day and night. Very tight or just-friends tight?

"As long as you're on vacation you should visit your sister. You have the money, Cookie, and she'd be so thrilled. I may not have been the perfect mother, but you two loved each other. There was no jealousy at all. Will you eat chicken, Lydie?"

Chicken felt like human flesh. Her mother and Uncle Harold before Daddy died?

"She used to say, 'Mommy, let me take Lydia.' I never got a sitter. We gave Jilly a dime an hour to sit for you and you got a nickel so you wouldn't feel left out. Not even dark meat? Remember how you always fought with me for the pupik?"

The object she called a chicken was shaped like a football and just as appetizing. The phone rang. It wasn't Kramer. Rose said, "You won't eat any of this nice, beautiful chicken?"

Lydia said yes, she'd eat some chicken, and walked away.

Later Lydia realized her mother had lied. It was her father she fought for the pupik. She was angry and felt deceived. During dinner she kept wondering how tight Rose and Harold were when her father was alive. When the gizzard was placed on Lydia's naked plate, she said, "You take it, Rose, I don't like it."

"No, Lydie, it's for you. You're our guest."

Lydia stood up, grabbed her dinner plate and slid the pupik onto Rose's plate. Before Rose could tip it onto Harold's plate, Lydia, still standing, said, "It wasn't you who liked the pupik. It was Daddy. Daddy liked the pupik. Don't you remember, Harold? Daddy liked the pupik. Rose only saved it when she made soup. Otherwise she dumped it before he got home from work. Harold, don't you remember? Christ, we had enough meals together, the nine of us."

"Have a seat, Lydia." Larry dusted off her chair like a ballpark attendant. "I have a terrific idea. I know everyone is in training here, but a little wine would be just the thing. As the French say, a bit of wine aids in zee digestion. Then we can all get to bed an hour early to make up for the transgression."

"I ate the pupik," Rose snarled.

"No! You threw it out if I didn't catch you. You said it was garbage and we didn't need to eat garbage anymore. Garbage. That was the word you used." Lydia grabbed Rose's plate and slid the pupik onto Harold's. It was cold and black. It looked like an egg case. Very ugly.

Larry sat down, forgetting the wine. Harold clapped a hand on his shoulder and said, "Pipik. That's what we Galizianers call it, right, Lar?"

"Right, Dad."

"Do you like it?" Lydia said.

"Do I like it? Do birds fly?"

"This one doesn't."

"Don't be so literal, Cookie," Rose said, laughing. "She's always been like that. When she was just a tiny thing at nursery school she came home with one of those plaster of paris casts they do. This one was a face, and she'd used stones for the eyes and shells for the smile and so on. I said, 'Lydie, what a wonderful face. Who is it supposed to be?' She looked at me, very blank. Very serious—like she's looking at me now"— (they all laugh, except for Lydia)—"and she says, 'That's not a face, Mommy. That's plaster of paris, and these are cowrie shells and that's elbow macaroni . . .' You were always like that," Rose said tenderly, taking hold of Lydia's hand. "Always."

Through Rose's persistence, they were able to get through dinner without further incident. Harold helped by eating the pupik, finishing a drumstick, both wings, and when the meat was carved away, taking the carcass apart bone by bone and leaving that bare. There was a program Harold wanted to watch on TV, so he suggested they all retire into the TV room. When it was over, he'd serve coffee and his special dessert. Larry asked Lydia to please come, too.

Lydia sat on the rocker. Maybe they were poor. Maybe the pupik was garbage. She could respect that. Why did Rose have to say Lydia shared it with her?

Larry sat cross-legged on the floor, very intensely practicing knots. Harold was leaning forward, intensely watching the set and next to him sat Rose, cotton stuffed between her toes. She shook a bottle of frosted polish, rattling the little ball inside. A police siren was wailing on TV. It reminded her of New York. Here she never heard sirens, she wasn't as conscious of the fragility of her own life. Daddy loved chicken. Kramer didn't eat chicken. He didn't like getting his hands greasy. Kramer ate watermelon with a fork, knife, and salt. Daddy salted his beer. Daddy never burped. Gurgles formed in his throat instead. Kramer loved to burp. Harold and Rose cheated on her father. Maybe they didn't. Something was wrong. Everything was wrong. What was wrong with this picture?

A woman screamed, loudly and persistently, enjoying herself, Lydia decided. Harold said, "Idiot. Damned fool. Why did she run off with him when she knew he had a rotten past?"

The screaming changed into hiccuping, an attempt at explanation. Harold asked, "Lydie, did you ever hear of Murder, Inc.? I knew, personally, two of those characters. Two!"

Rose hunched over, aiming the little brush at her big toe. Kramer's toes were bent from bad shoes. He ripped off his toenails when they grew too long. This was her father's study. His law books were on the shelves. The TV replaced ... "Where's Daddy's rolltop desk?"

Rose looked up and frowned.

"You gave that to Rikki, didn't you, Rose?" Harold said. Then to Lydia, "Larry's girl friend."

"Ex-girl friend," Larry snapped.

"The kid didn't have a desk. She told us she studied on her bed, which was why her grades were poor."

"Huh," from Larry.

"You liked her at the time," Harold said. "So we did, too."

"You were in New York," Rose said.

Lydia got up. Rose pulled the cotton from between her toes and followed her. "I want to talk to you. I'll meet you in my car."

Lydia put on her borrowed white sandals and sat in Rose's car. It felt like a long time before Rose showed up. Lydia was sorry she was missing the end of the program.

Rose drove for about fifteen minutes, running the reds, doing sixty on residential streets. She pulled into the parking lot of an unfamiliar supermarket. It was nearly nine and the sky was dusky. Inside, it was painfully bright and the air felt frosted. Rose grabbed a shopping cart and weaved up and down each aisle, throwing a few things into the cart with neither her usual speed nor decision.

At aisle nine, canned fruit and juices, Rose stopped sharply and in a controlled but angry whisper said, "Lydia, I'm warning you for the last time. No more about your father. Not a single goddamn word. Have you got that straight? Not another word. He's dead and I don't want to hear about it."

"But why?"

"What are you, thick? I've given you enough chances. Now no more, so shut up."

Lydia caught up to Rose. She knew she had to keep quiet, that the best thing to do was walk beside her mother and not make a sound. Just calm down and give Rose time to calm down and the next day or a day later when they were alone and relaxed, she could try again. This would work. As a child she'd seen that look on Rose's face, and it was, as Rose said, a final warning, the last bit of control that came after normal hollering and before total hysteria. Lydia's heart was racing. Only once or twice in her life had she pushed past this point. She walked beside Rose. Seconds passed and instead of calming down, soothing herself with her own warnings, the urge to scream grew powerful. She thought of John. The urge to grab Rose got so fervent that Lydia could only calm herself by stepping back and in a soft voice, hoping it would help (knowing it wouldn't), saying, "I know you don't want to talk about it but I need to know. I won't mention him again. Larry said you'd been tight with Harold for years. What does that mean?"

Rose wheeled the cart sideways, blocking the aisle. Still whispering, she said, "Listen, you little bitch, I didn't wish for that man to die, do you have that straight? But I wasn't sad when he did. He died quickly, they told me that. And I thanked God it was quick. But let me tell you something, Cookie. I was glad. You hear that? I was glad. I was pleased, baby. I was happy." She was screaming now. Lydia had her finger to her lips in a desperate pantomime to calm Rose. But it was too late. Rose backed her against the aisle. She felt the ripple of cans across her back. She heard the lights and freezers hum, the lush piped-in music. Rose was whispering now, but it was fierce, more frightening than her shout. Her hands were clenched on the grocery cart. White knuckles. Frosted nail polish. Frosty air. "I was happy the son of a bitch was gone. You got that. You dig that, Cookie? I detested him. He made me sick. He made me want to die. I stayed with him for your sake, for you, you little bitch. I should've left. Look at you—you're just like him. Disgusting. Look at you. Look at the way you've turned out. I could've left him twenty years ago and I would've had a chance to live. Look at you, you're an ugly, skinny street rat. No one could love you. You're an ugly, skinny street rat, you're disgusting." Rose grabbed a cart and turned sharply down the next aisle.

"I needed to know," Lydia said. "It was important I find out."

That night she dreamt she was at an intersection. The light was green and the traffic was lined up at the crossings. Brian, her lab partner (though he was taller here), tapped her on the shoulder and said, "Your father's in the phone booth there."

"Impossible. My father's dead."

"You better hurry up because when the light turns red he has to go."

The light turned red and Lydia, recognizing his face, ran into the street. Cars honked. People shouted at her. Brakes screeched. She got to the other side and called, "Daddy, Daddy!"

Her father got out of the phone booth. She put her arms around him. She hugged him and kissed him on the neck, the cheeks, the lips. It wasn't the right way to kiss him, but she was so happy to see him. She was crying. Her chest hurt. "Daddy, where have you been?"

He shook her off, stepping back. "Away."

"Why didn't you call? Why didn't you tell me where you were?"

"I was away. I couldn't call."

He was so cold. Why was he so cold?

The voice woke her up. She touched her face, felt the wetness on her cheeks. Everything came to her at once: Daddy, Kramer, Zeyde, school, home, nowhere to go.

"It's okay, Lydia," the voice said.

Had she been crying? Was she still?

"Ssh. It's okay." It was Larry, sitting on her bed, holding her hands. "It was only a dream."

It wasn't a dream and it wasn't okay. They were his shoulders, the broadness of them. The stubble on his face when she kissed him. The roughness, the smell of tobacco. His voice that she couldn't summon up before. It was real. It wasn't okay.

"Go away," she said to Larry.

17

IN THE new city she was not only blind, she was dumb, unable
to ask for a cup of tea in a sticky little cafeteria off Piccadilly
Circus. She gestured and pointed because her own voice was too
strident compared to the voices of the women with pink and
swollen steam-table faces. Peter was in the phone book. She left
her pack on her seat to mark her place, let her tea steep, and went
to the phone. Pip pip pip, coin in, the woman said, "Hello?
Hello?" soft and breathless, showing no concern when Lydia
didn't answer. Not yet. She gulped down a cup of cold tea, then
pointed to the lady for another. The last time, the sisters had met
in Rosemary's for hamburgers and a shared beer. Jill had two
babies, but she still cared for Lydia. She asked if her neighborhood was safe; she stressed the importance of protein. At Los
Angeles airport Lydia had thought about this as she lay across
a row of molded chairs, trying to sleep. The edge of each seat
cut into her spine, and when she rose she felt in her arms and legs,
by her lightheadedness, the need for love, a tangible aching need.
New York was impossible, Los Angeles had been a mess. They
tried to smooth things over when they drove her to the airport.
She begged them not to wait; she pleaded, hugging and kissing
Harold and Larry. Her mother held her too tightly in her arms,
weeping. "Please. Mama, please, it's all right," Lydia said, knowing at that moment she couldn't take the plane to New York as
she had planned. When a colony of ants was attacked by a
slave-making species, the survivors knew better than to return
home. No matter if there weren't other nesting sites, if food was
scarce—they knew collectively there was no safety in a besieged
home. Enemies could attack again. For Lydia, the enemy wasn't

John, who could easily be fended off, but something far more fierce that she couldn't fight with fists or double locks.

How do you get someone to love you? "Don't bribe them, Lydia," Rose would tell her. "Act like yourself." Knowing how to love wasn't like swimming or bicycle riding—or screwing for that matter—where you never forgot once you'd mastered the skills. How odd, in fact, to know how to make love but forget how to love. It was more like running, where you grew weak when you didn't practice, your muscles atrophied, lungs became inelastic, unable to take in enough air. But Jill had taught her how to dance, how to wear her hair, to be polite, to brush her teeth. There was a chance here; there had to be.

The customers got quite an elaborate setup for tea, a little metal pot with boiled water, a cup and saucer, a pitcher for milk. Despite the production, in the teacup was a bag, not real leaves. She tied the string around the handle and poured. Then she remembered the photographs she'd packed in the front pocket of her knapsack. Zeyde, felt hat, pleated pants, suspenders, a pout on his face, lips slightly distended. And Kramer, number twenty-two, sewn-up boxer shorts, socks around his ankles, one foot resting on the basketball. There was no photograph of her father. Like a character in a novel, she visualized him according to her needs and mood at the time. In the cafeteria he was Alan Ladd, short but incredibly handsome, and when the people at the other tables stared, it was out of admiration. The woman facing Lydia had no teeth. The man at the side table had a deep and croupy-sounding cough. Kramer was right. Her formative years had been spent under the steps with caterpillars. She'd been absent while other children were socialized, learned manners, through trial and error found out how to deal with the world. In London she expected dapper men in bowlers and ladies with their Pekingese. What she got was a sticky Formica table, ketchup in a plastic squeeze container and under both her elbows.

Why, for instance, had she hailed a taxi from the airport? Why had she said, "Piccadilly Circus, please." Because she'd ambled stupidly out toward the cabs, and when a black door swung open, she'd gotten in the car and said the first name that came to mind. Then terrified that the driver could see her mental state, she composed herself and said, "The right side."

The money was strange, so she tipped too much, then on the

street adjusted the straps of the knapsack so the load was high and tight, and walked purposefully down Regent Street as if she knew where she was going. It was nearly two o'clock, the second Friday in August. The buildings were old, as she'd expected, and wonderfully gaudy. They reminded her of the seventyish actress in her building in New York, who wore a layer of makeup and a piece of jewelry for each year past youth. Decades of grime and coal dust had been sandblasted from only half the buildings, so that one section of the street was lined with black buildings, the other white. But what disturbed Lydia were the plastic signs that hung like necklaces on all the buildings, below cupids, Niobes, oval windows, and sculpted trim, advertising the same fast-food restaurants as in America. LAX to Heathrow. "Today I arrived," she wrote in the notebook she purchased in an airport shop, unable to think of anything else to say.

At 5:45, after three hours and seven cups of tea in the cafeteria, Lydia went back to the phone, waited for the pip pip and dared to say hello.

At 5:46, Jill invited her to dine with the family.

In the underground it was rush hour and civilized. Both the standing and the seated swayed in unison with the gentle motion of the car. America had the tired and hungry, Lydia thought as she looked at the faces. America also had the beggars, accordion players, terrorists in sneakers, masturbators, operatic drunks, and dwarves. No one placed onions at her feet on the ride up to Hampstead. And though there were five stations before hers, no one sat in her lap. Everyone in the car had two eyes, a nose, a mouth, four limbs. The mouths were small and tight. The train didn't whistle and scream and neither did the passengers. Jill had said, "Where are you? It's noisy, I can't hear." She said cahn't, she was a stranger, it was a mistake. "You're at Lyons, you say?" Jill covered the receiver and said, "Peter, the poor girl's at Lyons. Oh my Lord." The laughter was familiar—big-sister laughter. Her eyes would fill up. "All you have to do is look at Lydie cross-eyed and she cries," said Rose, laughing, too.

At Rosemary's Jill said, "When I was your age I was a wife and a mother. I had responsibilities. I had to think of my family before I made a move."

"Are you sorry you had a baby?" Lydia asked.

"Tara's alive, she's a person. I can't wish she wasn't here when I can't even imagine life without her."

"And when does a baby become a person?"

"The moment it's born, maybe before."

"I'll never have a baby. I couldn't imagine life so dominated by anyone."

That was when Jill laughed her big-sister laugh. "And all the tenderness you give to caterpillars and snakes, bugs and spiders and many-legged things? Oh, Lydie, sweet, life won't always be so easy."

Feeling her appendix scar to remember directions, she climbed hills, left, right, right and right, and too soon was on their street. It was getting dark and the sky was pink from the streetlamps. They lived in a square brick house, white trim, gables, a brick wall enclosing the yard, cement globes on the ends of the wall. The garden was out back. Jill once wrote she was terribly fond of roses.

She sat on a wet wooden bench in the alcove and listened to the footsteps inside. The mailbox said Sanderson. Jill had met Peter at a tea her sorority gave. Eta something something. Kramer pledged for a fraternity his freshman year. He'd never find her now. Noisy cars, motorcycles struggling to climb the hill. Peter used to bribe her with money for the movies. Lydia let the polished brass knocker go. She didn't want Jill's dinner to burn.

Peter, trim red beard, balder than before, answered the door. He shook her hand, then stood back to let her enter. Inside the air smelled of long-stewing lamb. It was a home and she was going to be good. No more messes. Peter walked Lydia into a large living room and went upstairs. She remembered he was shy. A rug was on the wall and the floor was bare. On the far side of the room, hunched over her crocheting on an old brocade couch was her sister. Pale hair, pulled away from her face with a tortoiseshell hairband. Still beautiful but older. Lydia imagined she'd look the same as in L.A. at eighteen.

"Come and give me a kiss, Lydia." Jill sat with her cheek extended, fingers working a crochet hook. Lydia leaned over and kissed her lightly, delighted by her sister's soft and perfumed skin. "Look at you," Jill said. "All grown up and I still call you my baby sister. Do you hate that the way you used to?"

Lydia shook her head, then put out her arms to smother Jill in a hug. The look on Jill's face told her this was the wrong way. She felt the cans against her back in the supermarket and put her arms at her side. "I'm so happy, I don't know what to say," she managed, remembering at last that when she'd reached for Jill's hand in Rosemary's, Jill had been uncomfortable and pulled away that time, too.

"I thought you were ringing me from California. Just last week Mother wrote you were in Brentwood. She said Harold adored you and was hoping you'd stay."

"Did she tell you she was hoping I wouldn't?"

"Of course not, Lydia." A stitch. Another, another, as if the crocheting were automatic, independent from the rest of Jill. "Mother is a newlywed though."

She had a high forehead, and her skin, pale and yellowish, was strangely attractive, addding to her fifteenth-century look. Her eyes were unnaturally green from contact lenses. Lydia heard footsteps and turned away from Jill. It was Peter, a child attached to his hand.

Tara, twelve, blond and delicate, approached Lydia with the confidence of a beautiful child, and Lydia became Tara's little sister as she'd been Jill's: sloppy, careless, bending unsteadily for the kiss. "Hello, Aunt Lydia. I've seen your photograph." There were red marks on the bridge of Tara's nose, suggesting that bad eyesight had carried down through this branch of the family as well.

"Yeah?" Lydia said. "*My* photograph?"

"Isn't my big girl beautiful?" Jill said, patting the cushion next to her. Tara sat down and was encircled by her mother's arms.

There was a roar just then and the second child came bareling down the stairs, through the living room, swaying from side to side like an A-train express, halting with a screech and a somersault in front of Lydia, where he lay on his back and kicked vigorously. None of his family paid him any mind, but Lydia was speechless and horrified. She wasn't prepared for this; no one had told her it was this bad. She forced herself to smile, thinking, Look at him—his face. Look at his face. Then she panicked—did it seem that she was staring? The child stood up, and Lydia's smile, meant for him, quivered at the corners. She pretended to have food caught behind a wisdom tooth and explored with her tongue in an effort to appear unconcerned. Panning the room she saw Jill and Tara huddled—whispering about this tension? Peter had eased into a chair against the wall, looking calm—pretending? The last image was Jacob's arm, the terrible one, which ended below the shoulder with four fingerlike pieces of flesh. There were nails on the fingers. She looked long enough to see the nails—was that staring? His shirt had a long sleeve for his left arm and was specially tailored for the deformed one. Why hadn't they warned her? Why didn't they cover it up? It was so quiet, she heard the stew bubbling in the kitchen. *Everyone can read my mind.*

"Go wash up now, children," Jill said. "I'm sure Aunt Lydia is starving."

"I'm starving too, Mum," Peter said.

For all their talk about marriage and babies, Lydia never imagined Jill as a mother, much less a Mum.

Tara and Jacob stood at the foot of the stairs, transfixed, fascinated by the new visitor, the aunt. Two mouths, gaping, curious. Lydia felt like exhibition A.

"She'll tell us all about it at dinner," Jill said. "Go on upstairs. Tara, see Jacob washes up."

They filed into the dining area and sat inches below a thousand-jeweled chandelier on a dimmer system. Jilly went from plate to plate, ladling green peas, potatoes, chunks of lamb. The stew steamed up Lydia's glasses and when she looked up, a family in fog exchanged a few words, clinked knives and forks against dinner plates. Chairs scraped the bare wood floor as they came closer to the table. In unison. This was a real family, Jill at the foot of the table, Peter at the head. Jacob sat next to Lydia. He had a head of thick lamb's wool, deep brown eyes, and when he opened his mouth the ragged edges of two very new front teeth showed. As he ate, quite neatly, Lydia noticed, staring out of the corner of her eye, he knocked his shoes against the chair legs and hummed a strange primeval tune.

I am going to be perfect, Lydia thought, a joy to each one, a delight to have around. Auntie Lydia, Mummy's maiden sister.

Peter said, "This certainly has been our month for American

guests. The Wrights on their way to Brussels. My brother's friend Simon. And that lovely girl, what was her name?"

"Peter can never remember names. It's infuriating." Jill made a stern face to show she should be angry.

"I'll remember. She was from San Francisco. Barbary Coast, that's the mnemonic I used to remember her name. Barbary. Bar ... bar ... Barbara. That's it. Costello. Barbara Costello. From San Francisco."

"Oh Daddy, you're so clever," Tara said.

Peter picked up his knife and fork and began eating again. "Yes, Barbara Costello. Lips as red as cherry wine."

"Cherry wine? To me it looked like she'd been drinking blood," Jill said.

"I didn't like her either, Aunt Lydia," Tara said. "She blew her nose on our dinner napkins."

"Did she? I missed that," Peter said. Then: "Let's find out what Lydia's doing on these distant shores."

"She's involved in a research project." Lydia tried to catch Peter's eye, but it was impossible. No wonder her father had found him evasive.

"Did she say how long she'll remain in Mother London?"

"Until her project is completed," Lydia said.

"When I was in school—God, years ago—we started back in mid-September. That gives you about a month, am I right?" Jill asked. "Are you going to tour the Continent or just England?"

Lydia said she was playing it by ear.

"May I have seconds, darling?"

More stew, lamb steam on Peter's plate. He praised the food, finished the second helping and praised that. Then he tipped his chair back and massaged his stomach, a fat man's gesture, though Peter was still quite lean. Did Jill know the subject of Lydia's dissertation, he asked.

"Ants," said Lydia.

"Oh my," Tara said. "I hope you didn't bring any with you."

Lydia folded her hands on her lap, signaling, it seemed, the end of dinner. Tara cleared the silverware, Jill the dishes, Jacob slid under the table, Peter up the stairs! How well orchestrated. Lydia rubbed her eyes, and when she focused again, the table was freshly set, and Tara was standing in front of her with a teapot covered in what looked to be a brown crocheted sweater. "Mummy," she said, "don't they have tea cozies in America?" Then, after Lydia's attention was fully on her: "I made this myself, Aunt Lydia. It keeps the tea hot. Nothing's more horrid than cold tea."

While Jacob was rubbing his face against Lydia's ankle, Tara went into the kitchen and returned with a saucer, which she held in front of Lydia, just above her sight. "You've never had this either, Aunt Lydia, and perhaps you won't like it at all. But we love it"— seeing Peter descend the stairs —"don't we, Daddy?"

"Mmm," said Peter, "trifle."

Jacob, sniffing dessert, was up in a flash.

"Mummy's certainly being English tonight, isn't she?" Daddy said.

"Mummy's always English. Mrs. Cloudsley-Brain says Mummy is more English than the queen."

"Did she now?"

Everyone was seated again when Jill said, "While we're speaking of the English, Lydia, perhaps I ought to warn you that London isn't a night city. Things close down quite early here."

Lydia swallowed a big mouthful of trifle. Nothing had ever tasted as sweet or delicious.

"Mother said you were like a ghost. She said you wandered through the house at night, opening closets, flushing the toilet at three A.M."

"We go to bed early," Tara said. "And we get up with the birds. Isn't that right, Daddy?"

Look at the birdie, Lydia. Over there, in the orange tree. . . . "I go to bed early. That must have been Larry up at night."

"Larry Wolfe, my God, I forgot all about him. Does he still bite?"

"That was Melissa."

"Melissa, right. What's the little beast up to these days?"

"She lives in Van Nuys—"

"Predictable!"

The two sisters shared old family stories and laughed. Norma's ravioli, Larry faking the measles with Merthiolate, Melissa peeing on the kitchen floor. Lydia asked for seconds on the trifle, and when she got it, she separated the layers, taking a mouthful of custard, a taste of pound cake, some berries and brandy. Tara reminded Mummy to tell Aunt Lydia when the pubs closed and the tubes stopped running.

"My sister," Jill said, laughing, "used to stay up all night long, lying flat on her back under the covers with a flashlight between her knees, reading until morning. She was always the ambitious one—from the time she was a little girl she planned to be a great scientist. Madame Curie number two. Mother was worried, Lydie, she said you wouldn't see any of your old friends. She said you dropped out of everything."

"Terribly old-fashioned," Peter said. "The last time I heard of anyone dropping out it was 1967."

"It's not at all funny, Peter."

Tara covered her mouth and let out a forced laugh. Jacob watched Tara and followed the act with identical movements and sounds. Lydia separated her last bit of trifle, ate the cake, least favorite, first, then the custard.

"Where are you staying tonight, Aunt Lydia?" Tara asked.

"A student hostel."

"Then you have a place to stay," Jill said.

Swallowing, Lydia summoned up an old memory. Kramer in London. On Gayfere Street. "A friend told me about this hostel near Westminster Abbey."

"A hostel? Is it clean?"

"I guess."

"But you have a reservation?"

"A reservation? No problem."

"You need a reservation, Lydie, London's packed with tourists in August." She stood up, scraping the chair across the floor. "Come on, the phone is in the kitchen. Let's get you set up and Peter can drive you there later."

Lydia remained in her seat.

"Do you think she knows of such a place?" Peter asked after a few moments of silence in the dining room.

"You've made it up! Lydie, tell me, is that true?" Softly, no accusation. Then big-sister laughter.

Lydia said no, there really was such a place. She felt light-headed and though the words came out without a pause, she couldn't look up. She never saw Jill reach out for Peter's hand, and hardly heard them ask in unison for her to stay the night.

At the end of a long hallway upstairs were two doors. Behind one was a toilet—an honest-to-goodness crapper, its black tank floating overhead. Behind the other was a bathtub. She found her room on the fourth try. It had oak trim from ceiling to floor, outlining the windows and doors just as Lydia once outlined the pictures in coloring books. There was a single bed (that hurt, the narrowness of it), a small desk by a window, and a Victorian double-doored wardrobe with an inset mirror on the doors, each showing a completely different image. In one mirror, Lydia's body rippled as if she were swaying. In the other she was squat. She loomed closer, horrified to see how much she looked like Jacob on this side; pudgy cheeks, black curly hair. She knew he "wasn't quite right" when he was born, she'd heard one arm was bad. No one had said anything further. Lydia stuck her arm inside her sweater, tucking her elbow against her side, then adjusted the sleeve so that four fingers dangled loosely at her shoulder. Would she ever get used to him? There was a knock at the door. Fumbling quickly, Lydia barely managed to have her arm out the sleeve when Jill came in.

"I just wanted to make sure everything was in order," Jill said. One foot had slipped from its shoe and was creeping up her other calf. "Kiss good-night?"

Lydia took her sister's hand and began to cry. "It's—" Relief and fear, distressed by the damaged son, aching to be part of the family, to be loved. "Nothing. Really, it's nothing more than exhaustion, jet lag. I'm so happy to see you."

"We're happy to see you too, Lydie."

Although the "we" was puzzling, the "happy to see you" was a strong sedative that made sleep less frightening for her. The pillow was stuffed with feathers, and her cheek sunk deeply into it. She listened, trying to familiarize herself with the house's night noises, but there were none.

18

WHEN Lydia woke the next morning, her head was clear. She didn't hide under the covers or go back to sleep or pretend to be sleeping for hours. Getting out of bed she realized—and this was the brightest of all her thoughts—that it had been months since she'd looked forward to a whole day ahead. She splashed cold water on her face and dressed, aware of other voices, of water running in a sink somewhere. And this, too, was an omen: waking with the rest of the family, sitting down to breakfast on time. Less than a week before, Rose had ripped off Lydia's covers, shaking her until she pleaded, "I'm up, I swear," only to cover her head the moment Rose left, trying to avoid the thousand unpleasant frames that presented themselves as soon as her head cleared. The search, the scene she made at dinner, the last bit of milk knocked over in the refrigerator, hanging in droplets on all the shelves, lying in a pool among the vegetables on the bottom. In this house in Hampstead, among the warmth and love of this family her mind was clear. She could set out her photographs of Kramer and Zeyde because this was already her room (in L.A. it remained the guest room and Lydia the guest) and no one would enter without knocking. Her room. She pulled at her hair, loosening the curls which had coiled up and tightened while she slept, like flowers closing at night. Then she walked downstairs.

Peter and Jill were sitting close together at the table, their knees touching, their voices low in conversation. How gracious and lovely they looked with washed faces and combed hair, fully dressed for the day. There were no eyebags or morning breath here. Hello, they said, then asked in turn about her evening, the mattress, the breeze, the heat. Lydia was about to say how extraordinary the night was (no dreams of death, disease, or loss of love), how nothing clouded her mind, when Tara whirled by, a pastel blur, and curtseyed in front of Jill like a debutante. "Does it match, Mummy?" she said. "I chose the socks because they're yellow and there's yellow in the blouse."

Arm in arm, Jill and Tara went into the kitchen, and moments later, the smell of breakfast wafted out. Lydia sat across from Peter, content to gaze in silence at the china with its lovely pastoral scenes: Gainsborough trees, hounds, ladies in full skirts, fluted coffee cups that made the ladies in the scene look like Lydia in the left half of her wardrobe mirror.

Egg, bacon, and tomato was served. Toast was going clockwise around the table in a chrome rack just as Jacob appeared. He was buttoned up all wrong. Half his shirt collar hit him in the chest and half rested midchin. His fly was unzipped. No fuss was made. Tara called him over, grabbed him by the throat, slapped his hand when it flapped, pinned it behind his back, and zipped, buttoned, tucked, tied, and combed him. Seeing herself in Jacob, Lydia looked away. She stopped herself from blaming him for the disruption by emulating the Sandersons, by feeling nothing, making no fuss.

Morning conversation concerned what clothing to wash, buy, or mend for the children, which car had to be garaged, what niece, nephew, or friend was having a birthday. Daily functions were of the utmost importance here. Lydia cleaned her plate, ate three slices of toast, and was still ravenous. She couldn't get enough. Her priorities in New York had been upside down; that was the problem. How could she think about food or clean clothing when she was so busy watching for death to come creeping around the corners. All that believing and denying; all the nights she spent waiting to find Kramer bloodied on the carpet, all the days bracing herself for Zeyde's death. Jill held her cup out while Peter poured coffee, and when Lydia saw the loving look they exchanged, the tenderness, the joy they got from simple things, she realized the key to happiness was domesticity, not searching, seeking, pondering the unanswerable. In New York she paced, pulling at her hair, clucking like Chicken Little, "Oh my, oh my, what's going to happen to me?" "You'll get old and die," Kramer had said. "That's what'll happen." Then let it be this way: peacefully.

After breakfast, Jill and Peter brought out maps, brochures, Barbara Costello's *Blue Guide* to London, and a photocopy of the Wrights' two-day city tour. Sights could easily be divided into must-see, should-see, and optional. Lydia remembered Kramer's Yes, No, and Maybe piles and wondered how she'd explain that all she wanted to tour was the house. The farthest she wanted to explore was where there were cold spots and where it was warm. To earn a chair, perhaps, to become one with the Sandersons.

They spent all day describing favorite museums and parks, fortifying her with food and hot drinks, trying with their enthusiasm to cure her of what looked like a particularly severe case of jet lag, to help speed her recovery. Jill had always been an Anglophile, which was why her sorority sisters brought Peter around all those years ago. And though it was Peter's decision to move back to London, Jill had been thrilled. "Do you remember, Peter?" "She hurried off to a museum every day except when the baby was sick," Peter said. The British Museum, the National Gallery, and the Tate were must-sees. The Turner sunsets—one couldn't help being stirred.

Lydia thought their love for London was admirable, their faith and allegiance in difficult times inspiring. It made her hopeful, yet presented her with her first conflict: how to be the perfect houseguest and at the same time remain in the safety of their rooms awhile longer. She remembered when she was eight, about Jacob's age, her parents left her with the Wolfes for the weekend. Norma Wolfe grilled calves liver, the most detestable food Lydia could imagine at that age. Melissa let out a scream when Norma put a square inch of liver on her plate. Larry covered his piece in ketchup, gobbled it down in long doglike gulps, then forcing himself to laugh, spat the whole mess back onto his plate. Lydia ate in silence, excused herself from the dinner table when the meal was over and vomited in the bathroom. The next day, hearing Norma describe what a perfect little girl Lydia had been, how they hardly heard a peep from her all night, how she was a joy to have around, Lydia decided it was worthwhile, vomiting and all. Twenty years later, Lydia realized if she wanted to stay with the Sandersons she still had to be a joy to have around. So she agreed with all their suggestions. Yes she was going to travel through Cornwall and Devon, yes she was only staying a week, she planned to visit Paris, she'd give Amsterdam at least three days.

After dinner on Sunday Jill and Lydia sat together, hardly exchanging a word. Jill was crocheting, her fingers animated, moving in circles, independent of the rest of her. Lydia was thinking about Kramer. A year ago they had walked out of the Museum of Modern Art together, laughing about *Bluebeard's Eighth Wife*. He kissed her on the corner of Fifty-third and Fifth while they were waiting for the downtown bus, then asked if she'd move in with him, though it was only for a while. She didn't follow him to L.A. because she thought it was impossible to love him without her work. But since he left she'd been unable to work or love. It had to change. In the mirror, she hardly recognized herself.

Tara came in to kiss her mother good-night, and when she left, Jill said, "You realize I won't be able to take you around now that the weekend's over. But you couldn't be afraid to go by yourself —not a girl who's lived alone in New York all these years."

"I'm not afraid," Lydia said.

"Last week Dorothea Cloudsley-Brain and I walked to Tenton House to see their collection of fifteenth-century harpsichords and spinets. It was really quite marvelous, Lydia, and so much of London is like that. Every stone in every old building tells a long and noble story."

Lydia opened her mouth, wanting to tell the truth this time, but her throat constricted, no words would come out.

"And there's a science museum in South Kensington," Jill said after a while. "You may not be interested in art, but you have to admit that a science museum would be right up your alley."

Lydia had to explain but the only words that formed were those that described their childhood. A big sister's devotion. Jill teaching her the jitterbug; Jill explaining the difference between a nice girl and a good girl. She held her hands out but quickly folded them on her lap when she remembered Jill didn't like that kind of contact. So she smiled instead, the happy moron. She strained to say something, but the harder she tried, the more she remembered what she couldn't say, what Los Angeles had taught her: Don't argue. Don't touch. Don't ask questions. Finally, see-ing the expression on Jill's face change from confusion to annoyance, she said, "I *am* afraid," and took a deep breath. "Would it bother you if I stayed home? Just for a while?"

"Would it bother me?" The fingers stopped moving. "Well, I don't suppose so, though I'm awfully busy and—Lydia, it's ridiculous. How can you travel all the way to London and stay indoors? Your vacation is almost over and when you get home and all your friends ask how you liked London, what will you tell them?"

"That I loved it. How happy I was here."

Jill looked up, an eyebrow raised, and Lydia, meeting her gaze, saw a slender, fair-haired woman in her thirties, an Englishwoman, no one familiar.

She went upstairs to her room where her father, Albert Einstein, brilliant and affectionate, wrapped his arms around her and gave her a kiss, his mustache coarse and itchy against her cheek. "You're my favorite daughter," he said, then warned her about the apocalypse. Change was the essence.

"Oh go on, Pop," she said, sure that life would remain static in this household, the Sandersons unaffected by the world, forever caught up in the mechanics of living. Geniuses can be wrong, she knew, explaining to Papa that this household was not set in time.

It looked to Lydia as if her wish to bask in the love of this family was being fulfilled, and alone at night, she went upstairs and whispered, "Papa, look!" Didn't they rush at her each evening with questions about her day? Weren't they concerned in the morning with the quality of her night, asking if she slept well, if the bed was too soft? It was true Peter didn't talk to her, but he was shy, he'd forgotten their long history of playing pishapaysha deep into the night, after Jill had gone to sleep. Pishapaysha, learned from Zeyde, meant "peace" and "patience." So when Peter said to Jill, "She must be stifling up there, that room's a furnace," Lydia understood. "She's fine, don't worry," Lydia said.

The rules were straightforward, determined long before Lydia set foot on English soil.

"Papa," she whispered, "do you see?"

"No, Lydia," he said. "Change is the essence, and you will be the agent of change."

19

A WEEK PASSED. Or was it two? It had to be two because Jacob and Tara had started back to school. When Lydia first found out she'd be left in the house with her sister, she was elated. The family was nice enough, but as of yet they were strangers, not of her blood. Now that she'd finally found the appropriate words, she wanted to be alone with Jill in order to make herself clear. Animals communicate by chemical means, by smell and taste, but people use words and gestures. She had made the mistake of trying to know Kramer by feel, but this time she would do better. He died, I miss him, I can't get over it, she yearned to say.

The first morning the children left for school, Lydia followed Jill into the kitchen chattering, trying for a human response. "Do you mind that I'm here?" she asked. "Is it okay if I stay?" Jill went about her household chores. "Mm?" she said, or "Mm-hm." Panicking, Lydia raced up to her room. She sat on her bed until her heart quieted, her pulse returned to normal. We're sisters, she thought, the same species. If time had frayed the bond between them, time would help repair it. Everything would work out. Perhaps the years apart had made Jill uneasy, and to be sure Lydia's own vocabulary was rough.

She went downstairs and experimented with easier questions: Could she help out? Did Jill like being a mother? Did she hear about her old friend Amy Levinson who was a Jesus freak and had a child called Gift of God? Did she miss her friends back home? All that came from Jill was a simple yes or no. She volunteered nothing. She never smiled.

Lydia tried for three days, hoping for a shared laugh ("Melissa! What a little beast!"), a confession, some tears, an opening so she could tell someone how she felt. Because her efforts failed, she recorded the failure in her notebooks, analyzing the data, as she'd done with experimental evidence in the years past. Exactly what was the difference between uh-huh and yah? Was the first a stronger affirmative than the latter? Did mm mean much the same as hm or was it closer to yes? And when Jill said yes, stretching it out as she often did, adding a few extra esses, did that mean she agreed or was it just to register that she heard? Lydia's wrist hurt after recording her observations. And her joints ached when she got up. The inactivity, intellectual and physical, was crippling her.

One Saturday when Lydia went down to breakfast, she noticed that the maps had been refolded and put away in their proper drawers, the tour books were back on shelves. They knew she wasn't taking that trip through Cornwall or Devon; they suspected she'd never get to France. Toothbrush in the empty slot? Unpacked knapsack? Pictures on the desk in her room? She wasn't sure what signs revealed her permanence but together the family asked the same polite questions, and alone with Jill the silence still prevailed. Her father that evening said, "Stop worrying, Lydia! You have nothing to fear but fear itself!" But though she knew he was right, she couldn't stop.

She lapsed into silence when the new week rolled in. She began to watch instead, hoping close observation would help her to locate her sister somewhere within the shell of this English housewife who wore green contact lenses and had on pantyhose and lipstick by 7:00 A.M., who stayed home and crocheted, dressed in a suit. So when Jill piled dishes into the sink to save for the cleaning woman, Lydia followed behind, picking up a forgotten spoon or a sugar bowl, silent as a stone. Jill went upstairs and Lydia trailed behind, pretending she had things to attend to as well. She practiced meaningful gestures and phrases in the mirror (Mm? with an eyebrow raised; a long yesss while she lowered her chin). Hearing Jill's footsteps, she waited a discreet (she hoped) minute or two, then descended to try again.

The questions had become interminable; the silence was ponderous and felt unfriendly. Lydia decided on a take-charge approach, and the next day, when she came upon her sister peeling apples at the sink, she said, "Here, let me," taking the peeler from Jill's hand.

Jill grabbed the peeler back. "*No*, darling," she said.

There was a bowl, a canister of flour, a rolling pin. "Okay," said Lydia. "I'll roll the crust, I know how."

"That's Tara's job, and she'll feel terribly hurt if she comes home from school and finds you've taken it away."

Lydia was momentarily stunned to find out how late it was. Though time dragged, with the routine of the last few years gone, the hours and days of the week had lost all meaning. "I'll set the table."

She went about opening all the kitchen cabinets, looking for the china. Jill was behind her, shutting each of the doors in turn. "I know!" she said when Lydia found the plates. "Why don't you keep Jacob company? He'd love that."

"Jacob?" Lydia asked, as if she couldn't quite remember who Jill meant. The truth was that their son had obviously taken to her, if she was correctly interpreting the ankle-nuzzling at mealtimes. "Isn't there anything else I can do?"

But there wasn't.

Profoundly disappointed, Lydia picked up the newspaper and sat in the living room planning to circle flats to let. As much as she wanted a family life, she couldn't stay here under these conditions. The only solution was to flee again. She circled the cheapest two flats listed, one in Brixton, the other in Notting Hill. Jill sat down to crochet and when Lydia looked up to ask for her advice, she saw the sister who long ago came back from a date, sat on the edge of Lydia's bed, and told her where she'd gone, what kind of car the boy had, what they ate for dinner. If she had flowers, she held them close to Lydia, and in the dark she could imagine how beautiful Jill looked dancing. Once she said, "I had an awful time and when we kissed, I could feel his teeth." Lydia, who was nine, thought this was curious. I could feel his teeth? But the story, like all of them, ended with "Don't say a word to Mother," or "This is just between you and me."

Was Jill silent because being married her allegiance was to Peter? Why then had Jill told her sister private things in Rosemary's, saying, "This is just between you and me?" Lydia was wise enough not to ask if Jill knew about Rose's affair with

Harold (though she ached to know). But what about tender, innocuous memories? "Remember when Rose caught me shoving handfuls of dirt into my mouth?" Lydia said. Her eyes were brimming with tears.

Jill shook her head. She didn't.

"Or when you sang 'Good Night, Irene' at Cousin Louis's bar mitzvah?"

Uh-uh.

If nothing else, Lydia understood why Rose kept only baby pictures on her bureau. She knew the babies. The adults were strangers. High school Jill *was* a completely different creature from grown-up Jill and no matter how long Lydia searched for the old Jill, she'd never find her, just as Rose was never able to understand Lydia simply because she knew the adorable baby Lydia had once been.

Toward the end of September, Jill began to disappear. Not always, but the disturbing thing was that when she did, she never announced her destination nor the expected time of her return. The only clue Lydia had to her departure was when Jill said, "Make yourself some lunch, please. I don't want to have to worry about you when I'm gone."

One day it was pouring outside. The rain was clattering on the drainpipes, making an unhappy metallic sound, and Lydia, instead of giving her thesis defense as she should have done on this day, sat rigidly in the Sandersons' living room listening to the rain, and to an assortment of unearthly voices and one earthly one belonging to Mrs. Bannon, the cleaning woman. Mrs. Bannon had "been with Jill" since Jill first moved to Hampstead eight years ago, yet every morning she had to be formally invited inside, and every morning after taking two timid steps, she gazed with wonder around the room as if it were all new to her. In a meek voice she said, "Fine morning today," as she followed Jill into the laundry room, dressed in a gray coat and scuffed pumps. Reappearing in smock and slippers, her arms around her bucket, she humbly asked, "Have you got a bit of cleaning up for old Mrs. Bannon?" Jill ticked off finger by finger ten chores to be done, and the woman spent the day cleaning things Lydia never knew could be cleaned—walls, ceilings, undersides of furniture. She, too, has demons, Lydia thought when she watched the woman attack invisible cobwebs or wipe up imaginary dust. Mrs. Bannon nodded each time a finger was raised and an order given. Then: "My Johnny received first communion today" or "Poor Uncle Morris passed on last night." Mrs. Bannon had a seemingly infinite number of fertile children and grandchildren who in turn were baptized, received First Communion, and were confirmed, who got into trouble, looked for trouble, or had been born unlucky. Jill, on the other hand, had only two responses: "Oh how lovely" and "I'm terribly sorry to hear that."

Lydia was thinking about this when Jacob came home from school and plowed straight into Mrs. Bannon on his way across the room. At that moment, Lydia understood exactly what had happened to her. Like Mrs. Bannon, she, too, had become a ghost, a nonentity. If a new rug were laid on the floor, the family would notice for a few days, but once they were accustomed to softer footfalls, they'd never regard it again. So, too, with the new table, a new chair, with Lydia herself. At dinner they asked how her day was, if the rain had dampened her spirits. She couldn't believe how stupid she'd been not to see that the depth and nature of their inquiries had never changed. They were merely a formality, a cultural tic. It was up to Lydia to be the catalyst.

The next day, when Lydia heard Jill's footsteps in the living room, she rushed to meet her. Breathless, her words spilled out, her voice was hardly audible. "I had a boyfriend and he left me," she said, grateful she could speak, yet aware how silly it must have sounded, how incomplete.

To her surprise, Jill said, "So he's left you."

She was dressed to go out to a mysterious Wednesday appointment, raincoat in the crook of her arm, collapsible umbrella dangling from her wrist, swaying slightly. Psychoanalyst? Secret lover? Lydia thought of Catherine Deneuve in *Belle de Jour* and was disturbed, imagining her sister in bed with a sadist who had scars across his cheeks.

"Then why did you tell Harold's son he died when he really left you and went to Arizona? Mother wrote and said—"

"Don't tell me, I know, I blew it. But don't worry, I won't ask you a lot of questions about them. I've learned my lesson."

"You can't just go around saying your boyfriend died, Lydia. That's horrible. It's just awful, really."

It *was* awful. Lydia remembered how Larry had slid halfway

down the bench when she told him her boyfriend died. And then the silence, the same one she'd tried avoiding when she first met Kramer. Then: "Kristin had a sister who died. She was only two when it happened and the sister was just born." And on the way home an hour later: "I don't really know anyone who died. There was your dad, but I never got to know him too well. And your granddad, but he was old and everyone knew he'd die. And—" Fidgeting, rubbing his face, "my friend Matthew Kanin. His mother felt lousy one day and said she had a headache. The next day she was dead. Aneurism. Just like that." And every other case he knew over the next three weeks, dogs, friends of friends, actors, politicians. Heart attacks, cancer, suicide, accidents, overdose, worms (that was the dog).

Lydia said, "To me he died. It feels the same."

"The same as what?"

"Neither answers your call."

"You mean you tried to get in touch with him and he didn't respond? Is that it?"

"No, he's dead, they're both dead." Or was that a lie? Lydia remembered Kramer shaking her, hollering, "What do you think, he'll un-die or something?"

"That's a strange definition of death you have, Lydia. I wouldn't go around telling his friends about it." Jill looked at her watch and said, "I can't stand around all day. I have an appointment at noon."

She was seeing a doctor, she was deathly ill, she would die and be buried with her bad feelings toward Lydia.

"You aren't sick, are you? Please, Jilly, be honest, tell me."

"There's nothing wrong with *me*," said Jill.

"Look, I know better than to ask you a million questions. In fact, I won't ask you anything at all about them—"

"Ask me what? Why do you keep saying that?"

"I don't know what she wrote you, and I'm not sure I care to find out," Lydia said. "But she must have mentioned how upset she got when I asked questions about Daddy."

"I don't understand what kinds of questions could possibly have upset Rose."

"You know, what he was like. Things like that."

"Lydia, he was your father. You ought to know what he was like as well as anyone."

"But I didn't think about him for a long time."

Jill sat on the brocade couch and patted the cushion next to hers. When Tara sat there the first night, Jill had put her arm around her and said, "Isn't my girl beautiful?" Now she said, "I didn't think very much about him, either, but when you first came here, I took one look at you and immediately thought of Daddy. Do you remember how upset Mother used to get with him for wearing those black suits of his? She called them his undertaker suits. Well, when you stood at the door all dressed in black like that, I was so surprised. I thought, My God, how she resembles him."

Lydia said, "Oh?"

"Don't you remember how he always wore those suits no matter what the weather? And short knitted ties with his Phi Beta Kappa tie tack?" Jill covered her mouth with her palm just as she used to when she wore braces long ago. She was giggling, and although the sound was one that Lydia remembered, Mrs. Bannon turned and stared as if she'd never heard Jill laugh. "Poor Rose, always trying to dress him up. Did she ever tell you why she fell in love with him? Because he was driven. She said he was a fiery youth. I can hardly imagine."

There was a buzzing in her ears, soft at first, then more intense, until it seemed to fill her brain. She spoke loudly to hear her voice over the awful noise in her head. "Okay," she said, "he was a fiery youth and he had a lot of toothbrushes and he liked baseball and all that. But what *else*? You don't mind my asking, do you? What was he like as a father? I mean his personality. What did he teach us? Why can't I remember anything else?"

"Maybe there isn't anything else to remember, Lydia. He was so wrapped up in his work, he wasn't around all that much."

"*No!*" Lydia shouted. "That's not true. He was wonderful, he was beautiful, he was *everything.*"

By the sound of her own voice she recognized the lie. "No," she said again. Then hurriedly: "I was only kidding. He was an ugly skinny street rat and no one could love him." She sat back. She had touched the wound and found that it wasn't quite as painful as she'd imagined.

"I wouldn't go *that* far," said Jill, laughing uncomfortably.

"Wait—before you go away, tell me one thing, okay? Just tell me if it bothers you that I'm here. I can leave, you know. I'm remarkably strong." Lydia made a muscle, pulled her hair, tapped her front teeth. She grinned, hoping to convey optimism, but what her sister saw was only a bizarre expression, a kind of leer.

Jill stood up, umbrella swinging. "You were the one who wanted to be famous, Lydia. You were going to be a world-famous scientist. All I ever wanted was a good marriage and a family. People laugh at that, it's not enough to want anymore. They think it's a simple life, the easiest thing in the world. Well, it's not, you know. My life is full of things I can't control. Illness, for example. Mothers count their baby's fingers and toes, did you know that, Lydia? Well, I can't do anything about that. I can't will my family into good health. You want me to be honest with you? All right, I will. You can stay here as long as you like, but I don't want to have to think about you. I have Peter and the children, and honestly, I haven't got all that much more to give."

She walked toward the door and with her back turned, said, "What does one do about a sister who comes to visit and sits around the house all day? You don't want her to leave, because you're worried about what might happen to her."

"How about letting her be useful?"

"I'm not going to have my own sister clean house."

Mrs. Bannon beat a couch cushion three feet away.

"I can baby-sit," Lydia said. "You and Peter should go out more often."

"How do you like that? She's telling me to get out more often. You ought to follow your own advice, young lady. Mrs. Clouds-ley-Brain lost her first husband a year after they were married, and she said one has to keep busy and active if one wants to forget one's sadness. Introspection is morbid. It doesn't get you anyplace."

The front door shut and Lydia felt alone. Though she was annoyed that Mrs. Cloudsley-Brain's advice was identical to Rose's, she decided to leave the house.

The air outside was cool and dry. Lydia was stunned. It had been stuffy inside; no one ever opened any windows. She walked out back toward the garden, and pretended, in case Mrs. Bannon was peeping through the kitchen curtains, to be interested in roses, their color, the fragrant smell. Touching velvety petals she saw aphids, the same aphids as at home. The roses got nourishment from the soil, the aphids got nourishment from the roses, and the ants got nourishment from the aphids' honeydew. It was perfect, it really was. She ran upstairs and searched through her pack for her loupe, hurrying into the garden again, dropping to her knees to comb through the grass. She dug her nails into the dirt, scraping clots loose, like a dog searching for bones. Why bugs? Because she was born myopic and they were closest to her when she was little; they were in focus when she played outdoors. That wasn't why, though. Insects adapted. In millions of years, through changes in climate, through droughts, hurricanes, blizzards, earthquakes, pesticides, and urbanization, they did better than survive, they prospered. They adapted to life everywhere, taking the color of the land, the tasty ones fooling the birds by mimicking their poisonous relatives. Why bugs? Because they're little, they eat less, they fly. Why this? Why anything? What is too much?

She dug into the earth, feeling the cool soil under her fingernails. She dug deeper, tearing clumps of grass and weeds, laying her face on the earth, feeling the mud against her cheeks. Their life made sense. Her life made no sense. She crawled into the corner of the yard and combed through the rich decayed matter near the walls. Flesh, bones, sinew, hair; those physical remains existed in the ground somewhere, but there was nothing for her. She'd dreamt him up, a character at home with the rest of the night creatures. Goblins, witches, fairies, leprechauns, fathers who loved their little girls. Why was she mourning for a man whose only gift to her was bad genes? Rotten leaves, flower petals, bits of orange rind, webs, ants. An ant's life made sense. The queen stayed home and laid her eggs, small workers fed the larval broods, medium ones went on raids, the biggest fought, they ran along the flanks of warriors. Every member had its place, every member worked, mated, procreated, communicated. The misfits died. She squeezed wet soil between her fingers like Rose kneading chopped meat. Damp rich earth smell on her arms, her face, and neck. Mothers counted their baby's fingers. A daddy longlegs crawled onto the back of her hand, tap-tapping like a blind man. Granddaddy, daddy, for what? A worker, a drone, a place in the household? She couldn't love without her work, she couldn't work without love. The daddy longlegs crawled onto her wrist and she crushed it between two fingers. In an instant it was liquid, it was nothing.

Lydia got off the ground and went back into the house. Her face was streaked with mud; leaves and twigs clung to her sweater. She passed Mrs. Bannon and went upstairs to run the water for a bath.

At night, she did not dream about her father, and upon awakening she felt a moment's relief knowing that her unconscious had not played tricks on her while she'd been defenseless, asleep. Laughter came from downstairs, and her mood changed abruptly. Though she dreaded joining the Sandersons this morning, she dressed quickly so they wouldn't worry about her.

She took the steps one at a time: He wasn't Albert Einstein. He wasn't F.D.R. He was dead and she'd made it up. She was tired of all the feinting and dodging and inventing. It took up all her energy, it prevented her from feeling well. This is the worst, Lydia thought, facing the family in the dining room. This is the bottom, the pits, I couldn't sink lower. But her eyes were bright, and when Peter saw her, he turned to Jill and said, "She looks good this morning."

"You can do something for us today," Jill said when Lydia sat down. "Mr. Cousins, the man who picks Jacob up from football camp, is ill. Do you think you could meet Jacob this afternoon? It's not far."

Football camp? Like the sports camps advertised in the back pages of *The New York Times Magazine*? Your boy on the courts with Jo-Jo White. A photo of Jo-Jo one-on-one with a chubby ten-year-old in Keds. She said, "Football camp?" and was in the midst of asking Jacob the name of his team when there was an enormous clatter of dishes followed by Jill quite loudly demanding to know why Jacob didn't tell Mummy he hadn't any socks.

"Got socks on my feet," he said. Then to Lydia: "Don't got no *team*," as if she were stupid. "I pick things up with my fingers and I kick bags and I play football. Miss Peters says I'm as good as Georgie Best but not spoilt like Georgie is spoilt."

"You mean you've been wearing the same pair of socks all week?" Jill asked.

Lydia laughed. "Oh, it's physical therapy."

"He has, Mummy," Tara said. "He's a filthy boy, I smelt it yesterday."

"What else do you do?" Lydia asked, curious now.

Peter leaned across the table and said, "Confess, my son, have you devoured all your little stockings?"

"TYING AND BOWS AND BUTTONS AND FASTER THAN HER—" Jacob said, jumping out of his seat and pointing at Tara. "AND I DO MY SHOES AND MISS PETERS SAYS IF YOU DON'T USE BOTH HANDS, JACOB, YOU'LL NEVER LEARN TO JIGGLE."

"Juggle, idiot," Tara said. "And stop shouting."

20

Jacob's room was sparsely furnished: bed, bureau, desk, no sign of human habitation. Lydia sat on the bare floor while he built motels with red and white snap-together bricks. She was no longer horrified that he didn't hide his deformed arm, and watched now, interested. He didn't have a thumb on the fingers that hung from his shoulder, and so was incapable of any fine-tuning. But he grasped things between his fingers and was able to tuck things tightly under the little shoulder stump. When he used two hands, he brought the left arm across his chest to the right side, and Lydia understood in time that he purposely used the bad arm when the good alone could do. She'd seen him kneel and twist his body to the right side to pick up a football, when with half the effort he could bend and pick it up with the left. Now to build walls, he picked up pieces in his left hand and fed them one by one to the right, where he snapped them together between his fingers. He sat with his legs bowed, the soles of his feet flat together. For attaching larger pieces of architecture, he spread his feet apart and used them as a vice.

This particular motel, which like the other would be demolished in a day or two, had a long white unit with four red doorways, so far, and red-framed spaces for windows. There were chimneys over each door. It could very easily fit up in the Adirondacks except for the chimneys, which to Lydia were very English.

"Don't you ever get tired of building motels?" she asked, a little tired of watching.

"I build swimming pools."

"Are you building one for this motel?"

"Can't. Pools use all the whites. Can't have a red pool. No one wants to swim in a red pool, you know."

The calendar in Lydia's notebook marked this day as Columbus Day, but it seemed to Lydia that she and Jacob had begun this habit of sitting together on his bare wood floor a very long time ago. These days no form of bribery would stop Jacob, upon returning home from school, to "leave Aunt Lydia alone."

Sometimes Lydia was a little embarrassed, and when he pulled on her sleeve she pretended for Peter or Jill's benefit that she was resisting, that she had better things to do than follow Jacob upstairs and listen to his interminable questions while he built motels. So she made a face for the adults while he tugged persistently. When Jill said, "Leave her alone, for God's sake," Lydia, half pretending, replied, "It's all right, I don't mind." During these exhibitions, torn between what she wanted to do and feeling odd enjoying it, she was reminded of Rema's disapproval fifteen years ago, when Lydia mentioned someone she hoped would be a friend. Marilyn Tannenbaum, a new girl, carried a pet grasshopper in a metal Band-Aid box with holes punched in the lid. Rema said, "She's only in seventh grade," quite disgusted. They were in eighth. "Everyone will think you're a creep if you hang around with younger kids."

So Lydia shrugged, and sighing went upstairs to sit with Jacob until dinner.

"I can imagine," Lydia said, still thinking about swimming in a blood-red pool. "What else do you play? Have you ever heard of Monopoly?"

Jacob shook his head, not really listening.

"My Zeyde was a great player of Monopoly. Land is finite, he used to say. Hotels are finite. Railroads link the nation."

Jacob hinged a narrow west wall to a long north wall, ignoring her. In the silence she felt silly, and knew she'd lied again. True, her Zeyde was a great lover of Monopoly, but it was her father who said land was finite, and she was through glorifying her father. She wasn't going to sit and tell Jacob fairy tales about him, deceiving him as she'd deceived herself, by creating the ultimate Daddy. It was different with Zedye. She hadn't nourished a fantasy about him, so although she missed him, she didn't feel cheated by his death, only saddened. It was no lie that they'd been close, that she was the favorite grandchild. His last words had been "I don't tink about you no more," but she understood that he was tired and wanted to be released from his love for her, his responsibilities. He was old and ready to die. Of all the deaths —Kramer's, Zeyde's, and her father's—this last one was the hardest one because it was the death before the real death, the end of a dream. She missed Zeyde, she still hurt knowing Kramer was gone, but when she thought about her father she was furious with herself for having presumed she was godlike, for attempting to resurrect the dead in order to be comforted. Humiliated remembering herself on hands and knees, searching under beds and bureaus in Brentwood, she thought: Daddy, you brought me this low. Still, angry as she was, she felt relieved of the chore of keeping the lie of him alive. Now that she was at liberty to think what she pleased, she was able to listen, too. The moment she stopped fearing someone would speak the unmentionable, her perceptions sharpened. No longer afraid of the impertinence of a child, she could sit with Jacob.

When she picked him up at the clinic the first time, her quadriceps ached from the climb up the steep hill, her breath was labored, her flabbiness so distressing she vowed never to leave the house again. At the same time she felt a certain pride in having been given a responsibility. She followed the orange lines Peter had marked on the street guide, her chest thrust out. As she sucked in the warm moist air, she became convinced that humidity was as healthful for her as it was for greenery.

The teachers and therapists didn't wear football pads on their shoulders. They didn't have greased eyes or mouth bits as she half expected. (When Lydia was lacing her shoes preparing for this voyage, Jill had crouched beside her to say, "It's so much nicer to call it football camp, don't you think?")

Heels clicked sharply on the linoleum. Jacob broke into a run, his cry of "She's my aunt!" echoing in the hall.

Yes, an aunt. That's exactly what she was. She took his hand, but by the time she left the building, her pride had wavered a bit, replaced by the old need to be something. She remembered how Kramer boasted of her brilliance to everyone they met, telling friends how important her work was.

A baby-sitter. Her spirits flagged. She didn't notice Jacob yanking on her arm until he ran off and wrapped himself around a signpost. Looking up, she realized he was trying to catch her attention. "I'll show you the fast way, Auntie," he said.

She agreed, so they walked in silence. Lydia thought it would be nice to say something to him, but children were not in her repertoire of known creatures. Besides, he seemed quite content to hold her hand. After a few moments he began to hum, and Lydia was reminded how she, too, sang to herself while she examined injured flies or watched female mantises eat their mates. She, too, had spent most of her childhood alone, humming while she went about bandaging broken branches of trees with masking tape, cheerfully singing when she stuck a stolen hypodermic needle into an orange to see if it would explode, a soft hum sending smoke up her nose when she tried out her father's pipe.

Jacob dragged her through a backyard, where they had to wind their way through a flower garden and jump over a cement wall. She did this, following Jacob next down a tree-lined path and up a hill. Suspecting this was a longer way, she stopped and glared at him to see if he'd confess.

Jacob sucked his lips in and said not, "You're right, Aunt Lydia, we're halfway to Dover," but, "You don't like me."

"Of course I do," said Lydia.

"Don't," he said.

"Do too," she insisted.

And she did. She was just uncomfortable, she had no experience with kids.

That night, as he hinged west walls onto north walls, and built chimneys so high the structures toppled, she decided it wasn't her problem if he was oversensitive. She was sitting here, wasn't she? Just because she didn't do tricks was no reason for him to think she disliked him. Lydia was mulling over this problem, trying to free herself from responsibility, when Peter sat on the floor between them. "Thank you," he said to Lydia, looking directly at her. Then in his broadest midwestern American accent, "Soup's on, kids." Jacob didn't respond, so Peter picked him up by his ankles, and swung him around until he screamed, joyfully pleading for more. Lydia's father had done that to her. He had carried her on his shoulders and swung her by the ankles while she cried, loving it. But she got older, too big to be tickled and swung around, to have her nose stolen and later revealed between her father's fingers. Then he was uncomfortable, not knowing what to do with the older little girl who was growing into a young woman. Not in his repertoire, he might have thought. The words between them became scarce. She was supposed to believe, to remember his affection. Rose said, "Of course he loves you. He brags about you to everyone." But on the phone, when she called long-distance from New York, he said, "Hi, sweetheart, let me get your mother."

When she came to visit and said, "Where's Dad?" Rose said, "He's finishing up some last-minute work."

When she went up to his room he said, "One minute, sweetheart," and continued working.

When she joined the family in the TV room, he fell asleep on his back, he couldn't think of things to say.

It hadn't been enough. She was left with nothing.

Recognizing his love for her, Lydia swore she wouldn't do this to Jacob, and to keep her promise she talked, often saying foolish things. And it wasn't easy. It hadn't been easy for Peter either, but he sat with her now, he talked to her on an adult level. If the conversation wasn't interesting, Jacob ignored her. He was devoid of manners, apt to say "Shut up" or decide not to hear. Sometimes when he did this, she got furious with him, and stooping to an eight-year-old's level, called him names or stomped out. Although these incidents seemed to have no effect on Jacob, Lydia always felt miserable after one of them. If she couldn't do better with him, how would she ever succeed in the over-twelve world? I'm hopeless, she thought, when she was back in her room. I'll never change.

21

THE SANDERSONS had begun to act upon Lydia's suggestion that they get out more often, and by the time October ended, they were spending many evenings away from home. One weekend they drove out to Kent to visit friends, and though Tara slept at a friend's house, Lydia was left in charge of Jacob. She greeted them at the door in Jill's apron when they returned, and despite seeming surprised that nothing had burned, broken, or exploded in their absence, they began to plan for another weekend jaunt.

Her days filled with chores, with added responsibilities, and most often by the time Lydia got to bed, she was exhausted. Knowing sedentary people tired easily, she blamed her fatigue on inactivity. Without the satisfaction of a paper written, a review completed, a problem solved, it seemed she was immobile; it felt to Lydia she did nothing all day long. But one evening she sat up in bed and listened: The voices were gone. There was no more echo in her head. That was when she suspected the voices had been gone for a while, but she'd been too occupied to notice.

Monday evenings, Lydia felt rewarded for her labors. Jill went to her life-drawing class after dinner, and as soon as Lydia was through amusing Jacob, she joined Peter in his study. Until Jill returned, they sat upstairs talking, sometimes drinking brandy. They were reserved with one another; neither dreamt of revealing any dark secrets. But the limits in this case suited Lydia. Peter never asked why she stayed in the house all day, why she hadn't returned to school. She felt these things went not only unmentioned by Peter, but perhaps unnoticed, and so in the magic of his room she was a grown and responsible adult again. He gave her books to read; they talked about their work.

Trying hard not to think of her future, she let the days continue in this manner.

One evening, after Jacob was asleep, Lydia went into the living room and sat across from her sister. "I hardly see you anymore," Jill said. "What do you and Jacob do upstairs all night?"

"Tell stories."

"Wouldn't you like to meet some adults?"

(Everyone will think you're a creep, Rema said.)

"I was thinking of having a party. I used to have parties quite often, you know, but I haven't entertained at all since you've been here. My friends accuse me of hiding you away." Jill's fingers moved in circles, needles clicking. A vest for Jacob.

Parties meant meeting people, first fights, waiting for phone calls, waiting for history, adjusting to his body, his smell, his leaving. It was too much. "Actually," Lydia said, quickly reaching for a newspaper, "I've been looking at flats in the paper. Is twelve pounds a week expensive for a furnished flat in—let's see —Earl's Court?"

"You can't live in Earl's Court," Jill said, close to laughing. "You have to be Australian."

"How about Hammersmith?"

"How about if we make it a going-away party?"

Lydia went to sleep thinking of ways to dissuade Jill. The house would be messed up. People would burn cigarette holes in the furniture. She was busy as it was and preparing food for sixteen people was time-consuming. And expensive! Besides, the neighbors would complain. The friends she left out would be offended. Her expensive ceramic figures would get broken or ripped off. Even in Hampstead strangers always crashed parties.

But time was different here, and when at last, on the Saturday evening Jill and Peter had tickets to see the Monteverdi Choir, Lydia had concocted the perfect reason not to have guests (germs), Jill said, "But Lydia, the party is tomorrow."

They locked themselves out with their own key and Lydia went to her bedroom and lay down on her narrow bed. After all this time, Saturday evenings were still hard. It was as if she expected to walk with Kramer to Chinatown, wearing something a little nicer than she wore the other nights of the week. Her blue-green plush corduroy jeans. Were they still in New York? Lydia went into the bathroom and rummaged through the medicine chest until she found what were either sleeping pills or antibiotics.

Hours later, still wide awake, she found Tara in front of the TV, her head resting on one shoulder, a thin stream of saliva dampening her cheek. From Jacob's room came a rumbling and humming, but Lydia decided she didn't give a damn what he was up to.

The clock hit six and six-thirty before her eyes. At 7:00 A.M. she went downstairs to fix breakfast for the family. She was sitting on a counter stool, half dozing, half watching the water boil when she heard above, like thunder from the skies, the closet door open, a scrape against the floor, the clop-clop of Dr. Scholl sandals on the stairs.

Jill stood in front of her, dressed in a floor-length robe, surveying the kitchen with a possessive eye—the bowl of eggs, the double dishes of jam. "What are you up to?" she asked.

"Helping out so you could sleep late."

"Sleep late? You couldn't have chosen a worse morning. Your party is tonight and I should've been up an hour ago."

Clop-clop she walked to the foot of the stairs and called up to Peter. Lydia was shocked. She thought Jill's volume had been deposited in L.A. Then on the way into the kitchen, Jill stopped at the dining-room table to turn the knife blades inward. "It's sweet. It's really very sweet of you. Did you use the open loaf of bread?" Before getting an answer she opened the refrigerator, pulled out a half-loaf of bread and held it by the tie, letting it swing like a pendulum in front of Lydia.

Lydia went upstairs and lay crosswise on her bed, grumbling to herself about Jill. Jesus, she thought, an anal retentive like her fucking dad, everything just so. She was dozing, feet on the ground, when she heard a knock, then Tara's proper little voice demanding that Aunt Lydia come downstairs.

The eggs spluttered in the kitchen, and in the dining room Jacob was kicking the chair legs, chanting, "Watermelon, watermelon, where's me watermelon," remembering Lydia's story about Kramer's all-watermelon diet (he thought he was getting a paunch). Lydia took her place, the lower half of her face sunk between her palms. "You didn't put up me cereal. You forgot me food," Jacob said.

Lydia hooked an arm around his neck and brought his head

upon the plate as if she planned to dine on him. "Cut it, baby-cakes," she said.

"DON'T CALL ME BABY ANYTHING."

Clop-clop, breakfast was served. Guests were coming at seven that evening and everyone was to be cooperative. The kitchen was off limits for the day. The Bannons would arrive to serve and clean up, but there was much to be done before then. And: "Jacob, how did your furniture get into the middle of the room?"

"Pushed it."

"You pushed it, did you? When was this?"

"Last night."

Jill to Lydia, an eyebrow raised. "He could've walked out of the house and you wouldn't have noticed."

"Hire someone else," Lydia mumbled.

"Haw haw caw caw," from Jacob, who lacking his morning cereal was mashing a banana onto a piece of toast, trying to get it level so the jam wouldn't wiggle off.

"Anyone for more toast?"

"Me, Mummy, me," Peter said.

Tara clicked her tongue like a disapproving aunt.

"I'm going to town in an hour or so. Maybe Lydia would like to come along," Peter said. "After we do our chores we can go to the heath. Lydia hasn't been to the heath yet, has she?"

"She hasn't been anywhere, Daddy," Tara said.

Lydia said, "I'd like to go."

"Would you now?" Peter threw his napkin on the table, ready to start out.

"Make it another day, won't you, darling?" Jill said. "You promised to take Jacob with you today. Jacob, you want to go shopping with your daddy, don't you?"

Daddy said he thought he could handle Lydia and Jacob at once.

Lydia laughed. Jacob followed in style. Over the tumult, Jill said, "You can't carry all those packages into the park, Peter, it's ridiculous."

"Then we'll just go shopping and save the heath for another day."

"That won't be very interesting to Lydia."

The teakettle screamed.

"Does anyone want more tea?" Tara asked.

"I'll get it, Tara, darling."

As soon as Mummy was out of the room, Tara sidled up to Lydia. "Which would you rather do, Aunt Lydia? Be with Mummy or with Daddy?"

The choice seemed simple enough before it was phrased that way.

"Tell us quick before Mummy comes back!"

Mummy was back on cue, hands out for teacups. When she got to Lydia, there was only enough water for a half-cup. Lydia was pleased. Everything had significance this morning. She reached across Jacob's plate to get the sugar.

"You really shouldn't," Jill said. "I've been trying to teach Jacob manners, and that doesn't set an example."

Jacob reached across Jill's plate for the jam, which he didn't really want. His arm knocked into his glass of milk. Peter saved it from toppling.

"It's such a beautiful day," Lydia said. "And I really would like to see Hampstead before I move."

Jacob crawled under the table during Jill's little biographies of who was coming that night. A Mr. and Mrs. something. A Mr. and Mrs. something hyphen else. A Mr. alone and a Miss who came with much praise. Jill hoped the charming Miss would like the Mr. "I met Cecily in last year's drawing class. She's a graphic designer, but her interests lean more toward the human figure. She says the woman's body is the ultimate organic form."

"Sounds like Cecily, all right," said Peter.

"She's marvelous, really Peter, and she'd make some man a perfect wife. She's thoughtful and level-headed and good-spirited. And beautiful—even you have to admit that. I'm not the type who pushes marriage on everyone. I couldn't for instance see you married, Lydia, though when I was your age Tara was just beginning school and guess where you were, Jacob?" She peeped under the table. "Jacob was in Mummy's belly."

"Aunt Lydia can't be married, Mummy. She goes to school."

"Aunt Lydia quit school. If Aunt Lydia was in school she'd be home by now."

"Have you really quit school, Aunt Lydia?"

"I've taken a leave of absence, like a vacation. In America they call it getting your shit together. When your father was teaching school he took a leave of absence to get his shit together."

"*Must* you?" said Tara, sighing.

Peter reached across the table for Jill's arm. "I never went back after my leave of absence."

"I mean before that. You took a leave before you quit."

"Of course, darling, Lydia's right. I took a leave of absence when we were married."

"But Aunt Lydia can't get married, she's in school," Tara said. Then satisfied she'd made her point, she excused herself from the table and put a Mozart flute concerto on the stereo. Darling this and darling that, Lydia thought. Darling that said, "She's nervous because of the party."

Lydia went upstairs and weighed herself. She was ninety-six, up three pounds since moving to London, hefty enough to join the public world.

"You always wear black," Jacob said, adding with each step, "black, black, black."

They were climbing Frognal, three across the sidewalk, Lydia in the middle. Peter and Lydia took long strides, leaning, plodding, almost in slow motion, arms loose and swinging to help in the upward push. Jacob watched to imitate, but he teetered when he walked, the rhythm of his steps was unbalanced. Realizing he'd never be able to take steps as broad he began to hop, and was gradually far ahead of the other two. Peter and Lydia climbed slowly. No one else was on the sidewalk, but there were people in the front yards, mostly older women, pruning bushes, planting, wearing canvas gloves and cobblers' aprons. The air was perfumed with roses and the sun was strong. It seemed a world of women.

"Why do you wear black?" Jacob asked when they met him at the top of the hill.

"I don't know. Does it bother you?" Lydia asked.

"Witches wear black," he said. "Ugly witches. Nasty ugly bad wicked ugly witches. With nasty black ugly dresses. Witches that fly in your room. Witches that steal your toys!" He was screaming and stamping as they crossed the street and walked down a narrow dirt path. "Ugly witches with nasty ugly faces, they steal your toys, they eat your custard. Ugly black nasty witches they give you cancer, they eat your insides."

Lydia said she was sorry she asked.

"That's enough, Jacob," Peter said.

In moments they were in daylight again, standing on Hampstead High Street across from the butcher shop. Quail and duck hung by their feet on a rack; white and brown rabbits were dead but unshorn. Jacob took her arm and said, "Don't dawdle, Auntie" and laughed.

The streets were old, the brick buildings crooked. There were mostly women here, too, but young fresh-faced ones. Maybe the gardeners had to shop at a different time. Lydia followed behind Peter and Jacob, plodding in her heavy boots. The woman approaching had orange hair and oranges in a string shopping bag. Behind her was a girl in clogs, sandy hair cut in bangs across her face. Lydia thought: I am a nasty, ugly witch.

At the greengrocers were giant, torpedo-shaped cucumbers, round Canary Island tomatoes, carrots that were pale and fingerlong. As they passed, Jacob reached for a large mushroom and Peter took his hand so he'd release it, skipping the rebuke. "Did you know," he said to Lydia, "that Jacob and I were both born and bred in Hampstead? And we love our village, don't we, my son?"

"How long were you in the States?" Lydia asked.

"Hm. Is Lydia trying to find out how old I am?"

"Lydia's just making conversation," she said, looking at the faces again. They were different, a tight-lipped race. As one who'd swallowed a Japanese beetle at nine, a moth and countless gnats, Lydia noticed there were no gaping mouths here.

"Seven years," Peter said. "You were just a baby when I first came around, do you remember?"

"I wasn't a baby, I was fourteen."

"And the wariest little thing I ever saw." Then to Jacob, who was making circles around them: "She wasn't happy about having someone steal her big sister away."

"She stopped giving me French lessons. I never got beyond vingt-trois because of you," Lydia said. From the start, she'd known Jill was serious about Peter because she became secretive. "Did he kiss you?" Lydia had asked. "None of your business," said Jill. "Could you feel his teeth?" "Lydia, be quiet."

"I was very idealistic in those days," Peter said. "And naïve enough to think my time would be spent on scholarly matters, not in departmental warfare. I received tenure by the time Tara

· 175 ·

was born, but I was only an assistant professor, and Jill was anxious for a change of scene."

"Do you feel like you've given up, Peter? Do you ever think you made a mistake?"

Jacob was weaving between them, bored with the talk.

"There's no such thing as leaving a part of one's life behind without moments of regret. We live well, though. These are hard times to be in England, but we hold our heads above water."

"Don't dawdle, Daddy. Auntie, don't dawdle," Jacob said.

"Do you like the liquor business? You don't feel an emptiness?"

"I'm too busy to feel empty or unhappy, and by six I'm home with my wife and little ones, Hawthorne in my library."

"Behind glass doors—"

"But always available, Lydia. Always in reach. I've been working on a critical study of *The Marble Faun*, you know, a new angle. *The Faun* has never been properly understood."

"Auntie, don't dawdle. You don't know your way. You'll get lost. Who will find you if you get lost? No one will find you. It'll get dark outside and you haven't a jacket and you'll get chilled to the bone and your Zeyde can't find you and you'll die."

"That's enough, Jacob," Peter said.

The bell jangled when they entered the cheese store. It stank of sour milk inside. A fat man, all freckle-covered scalp, was arranging a pyramid of cheese on top of the counter. He brightened when he saw Peter, turning red with pleasure. His greetings tumbled out, rapid gestures orchestrating the words. Good morning, Mr. Sanderson, how nice the weather, how warm for this time of year. Dry, it was true (he hoped Mrs. Sanderson's roses hadn't suffered), but wasn't it delightful, the sun? Perhaps it should rain at night. That was it—between the hours of midnight and four? Peter nodded and yessed back and at the first opportunity pointed to a round of Stilton, then asked if there was a second. He took three pounds of the second piece, which Mr. Lewis assured him was a superior cheese. Would the children like a taste? The children? Lydia wasn't too happy about that. A nudge from Jacob assured her he wasn't either. Peter's wedge was cut away and the walls around the edge of the cheese crumbled. Jacob and Lydia each got two clots that fell.

Peter turned down the Brie, saying it wasn't ripe enough and chose instead some Bel Paese. And a piece of Cheshire. Would the children like a taste of that? A hand loomed over the counter, red fur on the knuckles. Lydia was hating the man. She took the cheese and then the empty sour-smelling fingers searched out a cheek and grabbed hold of it, a pound of flesh in return. I am on the verge, Lydia thought.

"Who is this lovely child?" Mr. Lewis asked.

"This is Lydia, my wife's sister."

"Here for a visit, are you?"

Lydia nodded, furious. She didn't come outside to be called a lovely child. So what if she was short? He was fat and she didn't call him a lovely fat man, did she?

"Where are you from?"

"New York, New York, U.S.A."

"New York, is it? Nasty place. People getting mashed all the time. Knocked off, you Americans say. Just yesterday I read in the paper about this bloke, goes off on a holiday, comes back to his flat, finds his best friend with his wife. Goes off his head and shoots them all. Splatters their brains all over the walls. Goes out into the street and splatters some more brains. Then his own—square between the eyes, he gets himself. Did you read it?"

"Afraid not." Lydia elbowed Peter, wanting terribly to leave. Peter told Mr. Lewis he was all set, and the man wrapped the wedges in waxed paper, wrote the price of each item on an unfolded bag, then counted the wrapped pieces of cheese, the prices on the bag, and mouth moving rapidly, computed the costs. Five minutes later, he looked up, eyes bright and liquid.

"Murder City, *The Observer* calls it. The paper said that considering the propensity for murder in New York, it seems a crime—"

"You have it memorized?" Lydia said.

"Not the whole thing. It was quite a lengthy piece."

The bell jangled and a giant-sized blond came straight up to the counter. She kneeled to get nose level and said, "What a gorgeous piece of fontina. Is it Italian, I hope?" The voice was distinctly American. Lydia wanted to jump on her and cling for protection. In an instant she saw a friend in town, another exile, her confidante. Her new friend had tree-trunk arms and legs and a short, blunt nose. Midwest maybe. Chicago? Peter got his change back, time was running low. Lydia said, "You're an American! Where are you from?" It wasn't a particularly inspiring opening, still Lydia was surprised when her friend went on sniffing cheese, ignoring her. "I'm from New York," Lydia said. "Murder City, as they call it here."

The friend turned around and in an irritated voice said, "I'm Canadian, not American."

"Well, same—" Continent, Lydia would've said, given a second more.

"To you Americans it may be the same thing but to a Canadian it's a damned insu!t being confused with an American. A damned insult."

"Jesus, save me," said Lydia, more bored than angry. Was this why the travelers plastered tremendous Canadian flags on their packs and wore maple leaf pins and patches?

The Canadian leaned over the counter, the tip of her nose against a piece of Morbier. Disgusting, Lydia thought, turning toward her.

"Stay away," the woman said. "Just stay away." She stood up tall and crossed her arms.

Lydia walked up to the woman. She felt dwarfish and inadequate. In her closed palm, the cheese was gooey. "I want you to tell me what's so great about Canada," she said, stepping so close she could smell the Canadian's perfume. "Tell me. Ice hockey? Margaret Trudeau?"

"Oh my," said the cheese man.

"Lydia—" from Peter.

"Shut up," she said to both of them. "Lay off."

"They won't let me stay up. I get to stick me head through the banister and wave is all," said Jacob.

"You're mad, you know that? You're a bloody maniac," the Canadian said.

"What's. So. Great. About. Canada," Lydia said.

The bell jangled and everyone inside the store froze. An old man entered and stood at the door, mystified by these strange figures frozen in awkward poses.

The cheese stuck to the inside of Lydia's hand. She walked up to the counter and deposited the damp lump.

"Mr. Lewis—" Peter began nervously.

The old man at the door gurgled with joy.

"Mr. Corliss," the cheese man said. "Do come in. Lovely Cheshire today. Good-bye, Mr. Sanderson, warm regards to the wife, I hope your niece has a pleasant stay—"

Outside the shop, Lydia caught up to Peter and said, "Do you believe he said that? Tell your niece to have a pleasant stay? Ha ha ha."

Peter watched his feet as he turned the corner. Before entering the grocery store, he asked Jacob to wait outside with Lydia. A bulldog was parked outside too, tied to a signpost in the sun, licking its chops and blinking. They kneeled to rub his ears and pet his squashed and wrinkly face. People were much more loving toward ugly animals than ugly people, Lydia thought, half listening to Jacob's song, this one with words. Something about Daddy putting Auntie in a box? To ship her off where?

"What for," Lydia said.

"Nasty Auntie Witch," Jacob said, his fingers exploring between the folds of the dog's snout.

"I didn't think he was angry." The tip of the animal's pink tongue darted out, licking Jacob, making him giggly and distracted.

When Peter returned, he was grim-faced, sure enough.

"Let's stop for chocolate, Daddy, please, Daddy, let's," Jacob said, pulling on Lydia's sleeve, smiling up at his aunt.

22

THE PASTRY SHOP was filled with women too, gardeners on a tea break. Older women. Peter sat at the only available table in the back, and sounding very tired said to Jacob, "Go up front with Aunt Lydia."

The pastries were lined up in neat rows, tiny tarts, the fruit red and shining; cookies shaped like stars and crescent moons; gingerbread boys; marbled brown and yellow cakes. Jacob leaned against the counter, finger tracing from one row to the next, down again, to the right, the pointer on a Ouija board, drawn by magic force to the chocolate squares. The waitress said she'd bring one to his table, so Lydia and Jacob dodged handbags and packages, a woman's voice, quite loudly saying, "—can't bear seeing deformed—" Peter was waiting with his chin held high and proud, a portrait of dignity. Jacob had heard, Lydia was sure, because she kept hearing the words repeated, the murmuring and laughter.

The aisle was blocked by a waitress, trayful of pastries and coffee perched on stiff fingers above her head. Lydia sat down and said, "Look, I'm sorry if I blew it in the cheese store," not meaning to sound flippant.

Peter was unresponsive, and by the time the waitress brought Jacob's chocolate square and took the rest of the order, Lydia was trembling so badly her knees shook. "I said I was sorry, Peter," she said, her voice sounding brusque this time.

"I accept your apology."

"Is that all? Could you say something else?"

"Oh forgive Auntie the witch, Daddy. Do forgive her."

Peter coughed and looked away.

Jacob plucked a cherry out of his chocolate square. Reminded by Peter of his fork, he clutched it in his hand and held it tightly as he hunched over the pastry to nibble at the edge. People are staring, Lydia thought, unable to eat her strudel. They're staring at us. She peeled the layers and scattered them on her plate.

"Eat with a fork like a human being, for God's sake," Peter said, glaring at his son, all black curls and deep brown eyes.

"A rope belt and tennis shoes is what he wears. I do admit he's kind to animals, but I still don't know what my Rosalind sees in him," said the woman at the next table.

At their table, a laugh was shared. Peter smiled, maybe it would be all right. "I'll bet you're glad I'm moving out," Lydia said.

"Stop being a child, for God's sake. I have a right to be angry with you. You were rude. You humiliated me."

"You're right. I agree with you." Lydia nodded and kept nodding. "That's why it's good I'm leaving."

"What's wrong with you? I didn't say you should pack up your marbles and go home. I said I was angry with you. I get angry with Jacob and Jill and they don't pack up and leave. You can be furious with someone and still care about them, you know."

Lydia was afraid she'd cry. She didn't want Peter to excuse her and pretend everything was as it used to be. She wanted him to catalogue her shortcomings and save her from wondering why he disliked her. She didn't want blanket forgiveness. She didn't trust it. She ate a little dessert to show she was functioning, but there was such a terrible silence at their table, such loud buzzing all around. Jacob leaned over and kissed her and she started to cry, then to prove it was a lie, laughed, choking a little, wanting more then ever to look normal. She thought how Zeyde loved her even after she called him a fatty and pinched him, after a month of being rude. She thought of Zeyde and tried to believe Peter. Lydia wiped the strudel flakes off her face and smiled. There was a deep collective sigh at the table.

Peter extended an arm, and got a waitress to bring a half-cup of coffee. Jacob asked loudly where the loo was and left.

" 'Like the angel whom Jacob wrested with, she's ready to bless you when once overcome . . .' "

"Hepzibah," Lydia said. *"The House of the Seven Gables."*

"I've never seen anything like it in my life. Your parents must have given up when you were born."

"What do you mean?"

"You *are* a bloody maniac. How can you be my gentle wife's sister?

"Didn't they tell you? I'm not, really."

"I'd believe that if it wasn't for our other crazy maniac. Whatever it is, it skipped a generation in our line. I hope at least he grows up to be as scrappy as you. He'll need it, you know."

The coffee arrived. Peter dropped four heaps of brown crystals in, holding the spoon high, plinkety-plink, then filled the cup to the top with cream. It was wonderfully childish, the way Lydia drank her coffee when she was first allowed.

"Have you got anything to wear tonight?"

Lydia stared dumbly, blinking like that bulldog.

"You haven't, have you."

"She comes in black," said Jacob, surprising them with a quick return. "She is evil. The good people of Frognal will not sleep easy in their beds tonight. A mad killer murderer has been seen in the streets dressed in black."

"Let me buy you something," Peter said.

Lydia shook her head, but he gulped down his coffee, stuck out a finger for the check, and was set to go.

They stood inside the little shop. Gifts frightened Lydia, but Peter was delighted by his idea, and she realized she was giving him a chance to forgive her. She couldn't say no. She'd look around and not find anything suitable. The store was tiny, four racks of clothing, a wicker basket with crocheted vests and hats thrown in, a narrow counter with scarves. It was one of those stores that bought from independent designers. Cottage industries. Expensive, she thought, noting how few items there were, how nothing appeared more than twice. Peter said, "The girls are wearing long skirts. They're awfully nice, Lydia, don't you think?"

The only saleswoman sat in a wicker chair, stroking a white Persian cat. Lydia felt shy, unable to speak until Jacob said, "She wants black!"

"I do not!" she said.

Peter pushed a skirt aside, then the next, the hangers screeching down the rack. Lydia started to ask if he bought things for Jill, when he held a skirt up to her waist. She raised her arms automatically, forgetting her reservations. It was a long calico skirt, red flowers in a field of yellow. She hid behind the curtain of the dressing area, slid out of her black pants and thought, Let it fit, let it fit. It did. She looked in the mirror, doubtful, but when she walked out to show Peter and saw the smile on his face, she felt differently. The saleswoman, still stroking the cat, said, "Perfect."

They were out in five minutes. A simple thing like a new skirt changed Lydia's step. The sun was brilliant and she walked home with her eyes half-closed, her arm around Jacob. Peter was two steps behind with the packages. She was sorry she had embarrassed him with her attack of I.R., the same affliction Kramer used to tease her about. He had stolen a coin box from the Mental Health Association and repapered it, so it read: "Help Cure Lydia of I.R.—Inappropriate Response." When friends came over he solicited dimes. Everyone laughed, including Lydia, glad to be freed from the responsibilities of a social gaffe. Now she really wanted to be cured. She wished not so much for manners, but that her behavior would be appropriate at all times, the same as other people's. Just as her happy baby years hadn't prepared her for the shock of adolescence, her solitary adult years had failed to train her for a life in the public world. For years she had hoped she was unique, her only dream was to make a contribution. Now she wanted to fit in.

Lydia looked up and found she was walking alone. Jacob was a few yards back, digging in his pocket. She stopped to wait and Peter caught up. He put his arm around her and squeezed her shoulder. He forgave her, and she was happy again.

Jill met them in the foyer in her rose-colored bathrobe, freshly showered, pink and smooth-skinned, the way Lydia remembered her at countless dinners in Los Angeles. "Are you sure we have enough wine? What about Mr. Cloudsley-Brain's rosé?" She fussed with a bud vase, moving it to cover a white water stain, then arranged the dried statice to make the bouquet fuller. "You bought plenty of Brie, I hope . . ."

Jill went on, talking in a clipped voice, fretting about the party. She's upset, Lydia thought, seeing how rigidly she stood, her hands in fists at each side. Her skin, which hadn't a single freckle or line on it, looked tightly drawn. Under Lydia's hair, her forehead was marked with three horizontal lines, each sloping downward on the right. While Jill was peeking through Peter's packages, Lydia held her hair up and talked to herself in the mirror. It happened, yes, she said. It didn't, no. It happened, yes, but she was forgiven. It happened, yes, and Peter said, "I forgive you." No matter what expression Lydia made, her forehead creased in exactly the same pattern. She hoped her behavior was not as beyond her control nor as indelible as the lines on her face.

They tramped into the kitchen, Jacob grabbing on to Lydia's sweater, following her like a caboose, chugging, blowing off steam. She dropped her bag on the floor and sat on a stool next to him.

"Daddy bought me a chocolate cake with a cherry on it," Jacob said to Jill.

"Chucklit," Lydia repeated.

Peter kneeled in front of the refrigerator and tried to squeeze his packages onto the shelves. It was packed already; plastic-covered trays, baking dishes, mixing bowls. He shuffled the jars on the inside of the door and tried to wedge the cheese between them. Jill watched, arms closed, her dominion disturbed. "And you're not going to want to eat your lunch now, are you, Jacob? Mummy's gone and made you a sandwich."

"I ain't hungry."

"Aren't. Peter, you are horrid. I'm not going to have time to fuss when he gets hungry at three, you know."

"Jacob, listen my son: This kitchen is off limits at three—out of bounds, verboten. Entry forbidden. Do you read me?" Peter took a bowl of olives from the refrigerator and was about to pop a giant one in his mouth when Jill slapped his hand. The olive rolled zigzag on the floor.

"Daddy bought Auntie the witch a strudel. Strudel, got it right, don't I, aye?"

"Daddy bought who?"

"Auntie the witch a strudel a strudel. Auntie the witch a strudel. It's what we calls her, Auntie the witch, don't we?"

"We most certainly do not. Her name is Aunt Lydia, and I

don't believe she wants to be bothered by you. Now come on, are you going to eat your sandwich?"

"Auntie the witch, you'll eat half, won't you?"

"I haven't made Aunt Lydia a sandwich." Flustered, turning from Peter to Lydia, "How can you let him call you that? It's awful."

"She said I could call her Auntie the witch, didn't you, Auntie?"

Lydia had no intention of squealing on Jacob, but she suspected now was a bad time to contradict Jill. "Well," she said, never attempting to complete the sentence. "Actually, I—"

"Don't encourage that, Lydia."

"—don't." There! A successful maneuver.

"Auntie the witch, come upstairs." Jacob tugged on Lydia's sweater, pulling both his aunt and the chair across the kitchen floor.

"Jacob, Mrs. Bannon just waxed this floor and I'd like it to look nice for at least this one evening. Now you go upstairs and wash. Aunt Lydia doesn't want to come with you."

"Does too! We don't want the old sammy. We et."

"Don't give it to him," Peter said, putting his arm around Jill's waist. "He'll fidget around, undo the sandwich, drop a piece jam-side down and spill his milk. Give it to me instead."

Jill peeled his fingers back one by one. "And you're going to eat a banana and jam sandwich, darling? I suppose you'll be asking for chocolate milk next."

"Mm," Peter said. "Chucklit."

"Come on, Auntie the witch!"

"Now stop that. Just stop calling her that. I'm your mummy, not Lydia, and if you say that one more time, I'll smack your fresh little bottom."

"Jacob, go upstairs." Peter had one deep furrow in his forehead when he made an angry face.

Jacob bowed. "Yes, Father. Yes, Mummy, Come on, Auntie the strudel."

Auntie the strudel followed Jacob as far as his bedroom door, then seeing he was back in the motel business, begged off, claiming she had better things to do. She wanted to show Jill the skirt, to hear her sister say, "Try it on, go ahead," then smile the way

Peter had when she saw Lydia dressed in it. "It's lovely, you look marvelous." It was Jill, after all, who'd spent years trying to get Lydia to be attentive to her clothing, to wear matching colors. Jill was the one who had taken Lydia for a training bra (though by that definition, Lydia thought, she'd forever be in training).

In the kitchen, Jill was on her hands and knees hunting for something—a lost contact lens? Peter was sitting on a stool with his long legs splayed out, crooning, "Please, my love, I'm calling for you." A smile for Lydia.

Jill stood, holding an olive. Plunk into the can.

"I would've et it meself, such a clean floor our Mrs. Bannon left you. Come and sit on me lap a moment, duckie." Peter clapped his legs together and pat-pat-patted them, eyes cast upward.

"I don't know why he should be able to come home like this —the white knight—and make me laugh," Jill said to Lydia, laughing. Lydia joined in, relaxing a little, feeling less like she'd intruded on something extremely private.

"Come on, American bay-bee, the old lap cries out for you," Peter said.

Jill edged closer. "You are a beast."

"Come on now." Little coaxing voice. "Come on, duckie."

"Promise first you'll clean up after yourself today. How will your son ever learn if you don't?"

"I'll make all the promises you want if you come here first."

Jill turned to the sink and Peter leaned over, grabbed her around the waist and brought her gently onto his lap. "Mmm. You smell like a forest. You are delicious."

She wrapped an arm around Peter's neck to balance herself, and in a soft voice said, "I don't mean to go hysterical on you."

"I know you've been working hard, darling. But haven't I been a good boy? I took your most troublesome child—"

Me? Lydia thought.

"—and bought him sweets and then got cheese for my true love. Pat me naked pate, duckie."

She kissed it instead, surprising Lydia with her tenderness and affection. Jill's eyes were closed; she was so steadied by Peter's arms she failed to hear the racket on the stairs, and picked her head up only when her son was in front of her, outraged.

"Mummy," he said. "Yuch."

She tried to stand, but Peter held on. "Do you mind? This

woman happens to be my wife, and I'm allowed to hug her."

Jacob looked disgusted. "Auntie, where's my sandwich?" he asked as if by her actions his mother had become invisible, his nonmother.

"It got et," said Peter, his head peeping out from under Jill's arm.

"That was mine. Mummy made it for me."

"Peter—" said Jill, relenting.

"No," he said. Then: "What would you like instead, Jacob?"

"Nothing." He stomped back upstairs.

Jill saw the package under the counter and bent to pick it up. "My present," Lydia said. "Should I try it on for you?"

Jill opened the bag and shook the skirt out. "Rather bright," she said, blinking.

"I think it's quite nice, certainly a change from the old basic black, black, black, as our Jacob says," Peter said.

Jill looked at the seams that had been so carefully matched, then the waistband, the hem. "Expensive, isn't it?"

"My treat," said Peter. "She didn't bring anything to wear to the party."

Lydia suddenly felt foolish and was sorry she had let Peter talk her into the skirt. It was so out of character. On her it would be a costume, she'd be ridiculous. She closed her eyes, hating it.

"You bought that for Lydia?" Jill asked.

"I did."

"I sit home making flowers out of radishes, and you go out for cakes and tea and buy her presents? When was the last time you bought *me* something?"

Peter stood to get himself a glass of milk. "Now, love," he said.

"Don't now love me, Peter. Just—why don't you get out of my sight. Both of you."

Peter stayed. Lydia left, wishing she'd left the week before.

She heard a tinkle she thought was shattered glass. Walking into Jacob's room, she saw him kicking a cluster of half-built motels, scattering red and white plastic bricks under the bed, between shoes and socks and hidden tangerines. When he saw Lydia, he walked over, and bringing his leg way back like Georgie Best, kicked her squarely in the hip, the same place she'd hurt her leg when she fell on the truck such a long time ago. Voices were raised downstairs. Hurting more from the memory than from his well-aimed kick, she tackled him, threw him fireman style over her shoulder, and dumped him on his bed.

Was her presence causing tantrums on every floor or did all these upsets have a meteorological origin? Or maybe—most likely, the more she thought about it—this was an aspect of family life she'd forgotten. Lydia bathed and washed her hair; she looked at herself in the medicine-cabinet mirror and with a hand mirror to see her profile, the back of her head. She hadn't scrutinized herself in a long time, but there was a party tonight, and before all parties it was important to see what others would see.

Later in the day, Jill was beating something white and foamy in a mixing bowl, and despite the buzz of the mixer, she heard Lydia come into the room. "If you need a blouse, look on the left side of my closet," she said.

Lydia stepped tentatively forward (To say what? she thought, I'm sorry for being alive?). "Are you okay?"

"What do you mean—because Peter and I had words? Didn't you ever get annoyed at the fellow you lived with?"

"I guess," Lydia said.

"Then stop being so shocked. If you're part of this family, we don't have to hide our feelings, do we?"

Peter had said, "I get angry with Jill and she doesn't pack up and leave."

"Besides," Jill said, laughing, "that was nothing."

Lydia sat down. Of course she and Kramer had been annoyed with each other, but they never had words or verbal fights. They never called each other names, argued about opposing views, tempers flaring. There were only black moods and hurt feelings. "He was a slob and he never called me to tell me he'd be out late and he ignored me when I was upset," Lydia said.

"And you?"

"I could've been nicer to his friends."

"That was your biggest sin?"

"I'm secretive, I guess," said Lydia. "And I'm kind of odd about money."

"Just like your father."

"Will you *please* stop saying that?"

"But Lydia, you were always Daddy's favorite."

Jacob was walking on his toes, his footsteps softly carrying him across the kitchen. He was trying not to be noticed, but the effort of being quiet made him sniffle loudly.

"It's a myth," Lydia said. "You tell me what makes you think I was his favorite."

When he was behind Jill, he drew a finger like a six-shooter, ready to dip into the bowl. Jill said, "You just were," as she pushed Jacob away with her free hand. He poised to kick his mother, but she turned and met his eyes. He saw her anger and knowing better skulked off.

"Come on," Lydia said, rising from her chair. "Naptime for Auntie."

"Take Aunt Lydia's skirt," Jill said to Jacob.

She went to her room, muttering about her father. A lot of good it did her now, hearing she was his favorite. Jacob followed, skirt dragging like a train.

When she lay on the bed, one arm tucked under her pillow, he dropped the skirt on the floor and climbed beside her. He rolled close, then squirmed around until he was comfortable. His breathing became deep and even. Then he settled in. Half-asleep, Lydia thought: It's the weather, the time of the month, the witching hour, a full moon, not me. She untucked her arm and put it around Jacob, and in a moment, she, too, was asleep.

23

While Lydia lingered in her room, the guests began to arrive. The highs and lows of their enthusiastic greetings drifted upstairs. Before tonight, she could only count four kinds of parties. There were family parties that she attended with puckered lips and left with red and pink kiss imprints on her cheeks and forehead, smears where an aunt, seeing the mark of the aunt before, said, "Ooh, honey, you have lipstick on you," and with handkerchief and spit tried to wipe it off. At departmental parties, she dressed in jeans and got the chance to talk to people about her work and theirs. She heard rumors of similar research at other universities, of complementary work and helpful technique. Two kinds of parties were held in huge Upper West Side apartments: the ones before Kramer, which Lydia attended alone, hoping to meet someone nice enough to leave with, and the ones with Kramer. This last kind was the worst. Just because they didn't go in order to find people, didn't stop women from finding Kramer. Lydia had the unhappy opportunity of watching the tactics which even the least self-conscious woman used to make herself attractive. Rapt attention, eyes wide, easy laughter, suggestive remarks, sexual stance. She dreaded these parties, but the thought of having Kramer go alone to be with twenty other women, each lovelier and more relaxed, was worse. Kramer was not one to say, "You were the most beautiful of them all," though on countless cab rides back downtown, he put his arm around her and said what a fool a certain woman was, what an emptyhead, how dumb. Though she didn't always agree, she appreciated his effort to demystify the unavailable.

But this was an entirely new species of party, made up of

relatives mixed with strangers, not in her field. Its purpose was unclear. Why were people she'd never met invited to a party to see her off? Off to *where*? Though Lydia had announced her departure, she didn't know where she was going and they'd neglected to ask, hoping, she supposed, not to delay her. "Do you have reservations? Is there really such a place?" they'd asked the first night, and she'd stayed for over two months.

Jill knocked on her door, so Lydia left her room. She walked to the top of the stairs, thinking how she'd gone from solitude to a family to the streets of Hampstead to a party in such a short time. And now, tripping on the hem of her skirt, lying helpless on the floor. . . . It wouldn't do. She took each step slowly and stopped halfway down. The guests had all arrived. Tara had curtseyed and Jacob, it was true, got to stick his head through the banister and wave, was all. An old gentleman at the foot of the stairs had a face like Mark Twain, and a belly the size of a basketball, neatly tucked below his belt. His hand was extended, palm up.

"Everybody! Everybody! The guest of honor tonight—"

A flock of pigeons flurried into the air. A toothy one, a couple of baldies, prominent hipbones in a black knit dress. An interesting collection of shared characteristics (Caucasian, under six feet, over twenty-five) and individual oddities. Roman nose, capped teeth, knock-knees. Long flamingo legs like L.A. Harold. More detached lobes than attached, three with glasses, a blond (that had to be Cecily). Lydia took hold of the gentleman's hand and became Scarlett O'Hara, skirt and petticoats lifted for the last stairs. She thought she heard Jill murmur, "Lydia," disparagingly, so she dropped the hem of her skirt. The blouse problem had been solved easily, and the silky borrowed one felt nice against her skin, but she hadn't had the heart to bring up the footwear dilemma—namely that all she owned were construction boots and running shoes and Jill's feet were four sizes larger than hers. She had scrubbed her toenails and hoped for smooth floors.

"So you see, I do indeed have a sister," she heard Jill say. Relieved, she smiled at the gentleman.

"My daughter," he was saying, "tells me formalities like 'Mister' are terribly old-fashioned nowadays. I said, 'Dorothea, the old pussies can keep calling me Mr. Cloudsley-Brain since I haven't anything better to offer.' But for lovely young ladies like you, my dear, I'd be delighted to hear you call me Harrison."

"How dja do, Harrison."

Over the heads of the taller guests, a voice called, "I've heard so much about you! From your lovely sister!" Tips of fingers waving. She waved back. The flock moved closer, calling out introductions, a name, a name they preferred being called. She was dizzy, her air stolen, the oxygen used by someone else. She lifted her hand to her throat, nodding, smiling. Suddenly she caught her breath. The crowd was gone and she was alone at the foot of the stairs, breathing deeply.

Mrs. Bannon, looking professional in a rented black uniform zigzagged through clusters of people, carrying a silver doily-lined tray. Morsels of food on toothpicks disappeared into polite yawns. Bacon-wrapped pineapple, cheese puffs, mushrooms. Mrs. Bannon said, "Surrey," bumping into guests to get their attention. Lydia resolved to smile and wander for the evening. Sitting in a corner drew attention from evangelical types and good Samaritans. She ate a mushroom and headed diagonally across the room to where Mrs. Bannon's Johnny was stationed behind a cloth-covered table, pouring drinks. She was just ordering a gin and tonic when she felt an arm link through hers, the distinct pressure of being pulled backward, away from the table. It was Mr. Cloudsley-Brain, escorting her to his circle, jamming her not too gracefully between his middle-aged daughter Dorothea and Richard the art teacher. Dorothea was saying in a voice etched with passion, "Why didn't they just eat snow? I was always under the impression that one could sustain oneself for the longest time eating snow."

"—The Magellans, the Cabots, the Hudsons. Didn't they eat leather when their provisions were used up? I'm quite certain I read somewhere they ate their belts and shoes," said Mr. Cloudsley-Brain. White tufts of hair sprouted from his ears like cotton plugs. They were talking about those football players who ate each other, he whispered to Lydia, to bring her up to date. Terribly strong material, didn't she think?

Lydia nodded, but she was absorbed watching Cecily cross the room to meet the art teacher. She was anxious for this moment to happen, having hoped there'd be important clues in other lovers' beginnings, guidelines she could follow. And there—yes!

Cecily squeezed into the circle. She turned her back on Richard and jabbed Lydia with dangerous hipbones. She patted Lydia's hair, then pulled a curl. Twisting her head toward Richard she said who *was* her stylist. (Her first words.) Where *did* she get that perm?

"They didn't eat them alive, my dear. They waited until someone died before they ate him," Mr. Cloudsley-Brain said to his daughter.

"Cooked or raw?" said Richard. Cecily cocked her head and smiled at him.

"Cooked, cooked, young man."

"Perhaps they simply went barmy, Daddy," Dorothea Cloudsley-Brain said in a whisper. "Perhaps it wasn't the will of God at all but weakness, Daddy, weakness and fear that drove them mad."

"Human meat is like venison, on the sweet side, tends to toughen at a young age. After eight or so the flesh, as a culinary delicacy, loses it succulence."

Cecily looped an arm through Richard's. "My dear," she said, "the only one I find even *vaguely* edible is you."

Mr. Cloudsley-Brain was behind her when she speared her tenth mushroom. She heard his slow and heavy footsteps following her toward Mrs. Bannon's Lisa, who had a tray of champagne and long curtains for hair, parted by the tip of her nose. Lisa Apso. Lydia took a glass, and as the first sip was swallowed, she felt the light carbonation sting her nostrils. She also felt the ubiquitous arm of Mr. Cloudsley-Brain across her back. At that point she stopped running and asked herself instead why she was afraid. He was at least seventy and his daughter was only ten feet away. She willed herself to relax and smiled at him. Mr. Cloudsley-Brain asked if she'd oblige a silly old man and take them off. Just once for a silly old man. He did a jig to keep her from passing, and she started to say there was nothing to see, her eyes weren't beautiful. But he was as polite as he was persistent, and besides, it was only for a moment. Lydia took off her glasses. Her pheromones were on, she guessed, and he thought she had beautiful eyes. If that's what it was about, why switch on a light and see an image different from the one she was given? Why not feel lovely? Across the room stood Cecily and the edible art teacher.

He was small and thin, definitely tender-looking though a good quarter-century past the age of succulence, and he was nodding sagely. She made birdlike movements with her head, pecking as she spoke, her hands in constant motion. Mr. Cloudsley-Brain asked Lydia if she could dance. "Not really," she said. Well, good, he replied, since neither did he, or so he was told.

They went into the dining room, closer to the source of the music. The moment Mr. Cloudsley-Brain put his arm around Lydia, she stepped on his foot. She prayed he wouldn't reciprocate, thereby blackening her toes. They moved vaguely with the music, Mr. Cloudsley-Brain turning left, and Lydia leftward, too. Each tried to correct the error, and they bumped into each other, mashing shoulders. "We are *terrible*," Lydia said, laughing. She asked him for a second dance.

Mr. Cloudsley-Brain told Lydia he was retired, but remained quite busy with guitar lessons and Spanish class. He didn't feel he was biding his days doing useless things, hobbies that had no meaning. People, his own daughter included, thought it was sweet that he played guitar so many hours a day, that it was adorable, though faintly ridiculous, that a man of seventy-two should spend hours at the mirror, watching his tongue properly form the vowel sounds for perfect Castillian Spanish. But in a month he was leaving for Barcelona to study with one of the greatest teachers of classical guitar. He planned to stay in Spain a year, unless, of course, he fell in love, in which case he'd stay longer, perhaps making a permanent move.

Momentarily stunned to hear these words from still another person she liked, Lydia said, "Oh, you're leaving?"

"You can lead if you want. Either that or follow me, one or the other, but you mustn't skirt the issue."

Lydia began to laugh, weak with happiness. "Mr. Cloudsley-Brain, you're wonderful."

"Harrison, dear," he said, squeezing her so tightly only his protruding stomach saved her from broken ribs.

She took off her glasses and blinked. Mr. Cloudsley-Brain sighed, he laughed at himself. She put her arm around him and he hugged her again, taking her breath away. "Now mind you," he said, "I'm quite serious. I go around doing as I please and everyone assumes I'm a bit dotty, a harmless old thing."

"Does that make you sad?"

"Not at all. I only regret things weren't easier when I was" pointing to the art teacher — "his age."

"What do you think?" Lydia asked. "Will it work out between those two? Suppose he likes her and she likes him."

"They'll go home together. Isn't that right?" Mr. Cloudsley-Brain beamed like a schoolboy with the right answer.

"Probably."

"Do you like him?"

"I don't know. I haven't talked to him."

"Talk! What has it to do with talk?" He released her hand **and** said, "I think we've danced enough. Why don't you go over and see if you like him."

"Me? Nah."

"Go on, go on, go ahead," he said in a coaxing voice. "Maybe you'll like him."

Lydia hesitated. She felt an arm around her shoulder, her feet distinctly walking her toward the art teacher.

"Harrison Cloudsley-Brain," he said, extending a hand to shake.

Lydia was giggling and felt ridiculous.

"Richard Robertson," the art teacher said.

Mr. Cloudsley-Brain raised his arm. "Sorry, you'll have to excuse me. My daughter seems to— One moment, Dorothea!"

"You're an art teacher," Lydia said, left in a corner with the edible man.

He frowned. He said he didn't like instant categorization.

Why not? she thought, saying, "Shortcuts are necessary sometimes. You'd learn a lot about me if I told you I was a myrmecologist and ants were my whole life."

He obviously thought she was kidding, but his face was stiff and expressionless.

"You never laugh," she said.

"Neither did Voltaire."

"Ah, his mistake."

In the meantime, she was perfectly happy directing her energy toward figuring out how to get Mrs. Bannon and the cheese puffs without losing Richard's attention. Jill was right. Introspection was morbid. Sitting in her room she worried about quadriplegia and Kramer, about Rose dying before they were reconciled, about getting old and making no contributions, about the quarter of the world's population that went to bed hungry. Alone she tried to resurrect the dead, she missed her father and the father that she'd never had. Yes, she'd get old and die, but at this moment, it was nice listening to edible Richard, eyes on his chin with its off-center cleft, half imagining what he'd look like naked. She raised a finger, madame to garçon, the check, s'il vous plait, and Mrs. Bannon bustled over. Richard was talking, gesturing in broad strokes. Ah, he was a painter, not an art teacher. It wasn't the categorization that disturbed him, it was the reminder of his inactivity. He hadn't used oils in two years, though he sketched quite reflexively, finding scribbles on everything. Kramer always drew on restaurant napkins; diagrams, flow charts, K.O.L. and L.O.K. for finances. She began to ask why he'd stopped painting when he slipped three fingers between the buttons of his shirt and scratched, eyes narrowed, enjoying it. Smelling flesh, Cecily appeared. Lydia laughed again. The apocrine glands most certainly existed for a sexual purpose, producing, as they did the musky odor of passion. What other function could they possibly have? Cecily wrapped her arms around Richard, and to prove she was more intimate with Jill than Lydia was (and thus, Lydia supposed, more intimate with Richard) she went on about the grand old days when Jill threw the most marvelous dinner parties, and now, the pity, only hors d'oeuvres and drinks and *not* because everyone was trying to slim. Ah, food was so dear these days.

The pheromones were saved for Richard, and the talk successful in getting rid of Lydia. She said good-bye, pleased to see how easy a leave-taking could be.

She roamed a little. Jill was in the kitchen, kneeling in front of the refrigerator. Mrs. Kolodney was smiling and nodding at Mrs. MacAffee, though her eye was on her husband, who was demonstrating yoga excercises to Cecily, whose hand was on Richard's ass. She talked for a few moments to Dorothea Cloudsley-Brain, and then searched for Lisa Apso. Throughout her life it had been all or nothing. All her love for Zeyde and Kramer, nothing for the rest of the world. Before tonight at a party she either ignored a man or took him home. It wasn't necessary. Small talk was the appropriate response. Exchanging a few words, sharing a laugh. A laugh was like a sneeze; for a moment, at its peak, consciousness was lost, control, inhibitions, sense of self. She remembered the way she'd laughed at Zeyde's buffalo nickel trick no matter how sad the story. That's the trick, she thought, the magic key.

She was still laughing much later in the evening when Peter approached with a chair under each arm. After setting them both in front of Lydia, he sat in one, obstructing her view of the drunken men who were kicking high and singing football songs. His hands were folded on an imaginary desk between them; Professor Sanderson, breaking the bad news. "Sit down," he said. Lydia stopped laughing. At ten she'd been called down to the principal's office, trembling so badly she nearly peed in her pants. "Sit down," the principal had said, leaning across the desk. "I understand you know how to spell antiseptic."

"Where are you off to?" Peter asked.

"Now?" When he laughed, she remembered Rose saying, "Don't be so literal, Cookie." "Oh, Monday you mean."

He nodded.

Across the room, someone said, "Carmelita has never in her life used a toothbrush."

Lydia laughed, stalling.

"I know it's a little early for good-bye, but the MacAffees have come up from Kent and they'll be staying the night. We won't have time for a proper good-bye."

"Oh," said Lydia.

A deep breath. "We loved having you. You were a marvelous guest."

"Please don't say that. First of all, it's not true, and second of all it'll make me feel worse."

"What do I say then? I know. You were a strange houseguest, but I do believe I'll miss you."

He stood and reached for her hand, but as soon as contact was made, both were uncomfortable. They pulled apart. Lydia felt his edginess and recognizing her own, held out her hand to try again. He grasped it, pretending to practice the perfect handshake. She showed him the soul handshake, the feminist grip. He showed her the solicitor's handshake, the M.P.'s, the public schoolboy's. Contact was made. Unspoken words sealed the pact.

24

ON SUNDAY, Lydia said to Mrs. Bannon, known to come from
elsewhere, "Where do you live?"

"Finsbury Park, N4."

"Do you like it there?"

Mrs. Bannon chewed on every question sent her way, then
regurgitated it moments later. "Do I like it there?"

"Yes, in Finsbury Park."

"In Finsbury Park? It's our home, you know. We live by the
park and the ducks! Straight from your hand they eat. Biscuits.
They like biscuits best. We save the broken bits in a jar. They
like McVities, those little duckies. They know what's good."
Mrs. Bannon, engaged this extra day to clean up the party's
residue, was fluttering the back of an undershirt on tabletops,
lifting each of the ashtrays and ceramic objects, wagging the
cloth like a piece of bait. Lydia trailed behind. "Football for
Johnny," Mrs. Bannon said after a while. "He don't even have to
take the tubes." "Chewbs" is how it sounded.

Lydia would have preferred using some good English tact,
stretching the inquiry over a month's period, but she'd told the
family she was leaving Monday and today was Sunday. Each
table leg was a human calf, and starting at a knobby knee, Mrs.
Bannon wrapped the leg in the cloth and with circular motions,
as if to ease a cramp, rubbed and wiped until she reached the
floor. "Is it far?" Lydia asked.

"Is it far?"

"Finsbury Park."

"Finsbury Park?"

"Yes, Finsbury, Finsbury," Lydia said impatiently.

"I don't live in Finsbury, love. Finsbury's in the city."

"Then where do you live?"

"Where do I live?"

"Right, please, where do you *live*?"

"Finsbury Park, love."

"Is it far?"

"Finsbury Park?"

"Finsbury Park."

"It's not too far, don't you worry. Victoria is down the street and I take her to King's Cross, walk a bit and I'm on the Metropolitan. Or else I take Victoria to Euston, get on the Northern into town and pick up a few things on my way to Mrs. Sanderson's. The Northern's awfully smoky, makes me cough." Mrs. Bannon coughed for proof on her way to the closet for a vacuum. For once the place was a mess, butts in cups of wine, wine on rugs.

"Do you like it there? I mean, do you know someone in Finsbury Park who might want to rent a flat? It sounds like the kind of place I'd like to live, Mrs. Bannon. I love ducks."

Mrs. Bannon, looking like the recipient of bad news, fidgeted with the loose threads from a button, as if surprised it was missing, though it had been gone as long as Lydia had known her. Then she switched on the vacuum. Lydia sat in her chair. She became Mrs. Bannon and said, How disgusting that a lady of means, a lady of leisure at that, would ask for a flat in my neighborhood. It showed something was wrong with the girl, you know, up there. She was a little off.

Lydia waited out the lunch hour and when the vacuum was whining again, she crept close behind Mrs. Bannon and in a barely audible voice said, "I have something to tell you, but first you must swear on your life and the life of your babies never to utter a word."

Mrs. Bannon gave the machine an obligatory push-pull and switched it off. Lydia sidled up, smelling milk and scouring powder. "I'm not really Jill's sister. She calls me sister, of course, but the truth is, I was adopted, sort of. That is, never legally adopted but they fed me and clothed me and walked me to school and so on."

Mrs. Bannon tsked and turned away. "I always said, Agnes, those girls are as different as day and night, black and white, up and down."

"My father died, did you know that? My father was the one who took me in. And now my stepmother. My stepmother and I have never been close. She always favored Jill."

"Her own, of course."

"Anyhow, my stepmother lives in Los Angeles."

"I met the woman and I said to myself, Now there's a sneaky one. Wouldn't trust her in my house for a minute. I caught her doing all sorts of things, never would tell a soul."

"Like what?"

Mrs. Bannon lifted the undershirt from her pocket and dusted the slats of the Venetian blinds. The metal bent and clattered and Lydia had to strain to hear the words. "—and the day she opened that letter to Mr. Sanderson, now I wasn't spying on her, mind you, I'd come into the room for my pail. And she says to me, You ought to learn to knock, Agnes. I don't work for her, you know. I work for Mrs. Sanderson. The cheek! Says as long as I'm here, Agnes, you're to knock before you come in. Mrs. Sanderson, such a sweet little thing. Delicate, you know. *She* calls me Mrs. Bannon."

Lydia didn't need to go on about selling pencils in the street or getting secondhand gloves for Christmas. Mrs. Bannon possessed a hearty imagination and only had to look at Lydia to grow dewy-eyed. Before leaving for the day, she slipped a note to Lydia, and on it a name, address, and instructions for the tube.

Lydia woke at dawn and stuffed her photographs and clothes into her knapsack. It saddened her to see how little she'd settled in, how all evidence of her stay could be lifted in a minute. Downstairs she stood half in half out of the doorway. She imagined the family gathered around, begging her to stay. Jill said she'd given their lives a richness. Tara apologized for being prissy. Wait—was she crazy? Why was she leaving when after all that groping around, artlessly trying to be loved, she finally fit into the family, adapting to their ways. She'd become invisible for Jill, neat for Tara, a friend for Jacob, a sounding board for Peter. At a party for twenty people she didn't merely survive, she had a good time. Was she aimlessly running again? Lydia made up her mind to go back upstairs.

Jacob's room was warm and still. He didn't hear her enter, but as soon as the mattress dipped where she sat, he woke up. The night-light was on and Lydia put a finger to her lips. It was five o'clock in the morning, she whispered. Had he ever in his life been awake at that hour? He hadn't, so she held out her arms and carried him to the window, lifting him high so he could see the odd hue outside, hear the first birds cawing.

"Are we going somewhere, Auntie?"

"I am. I'm going to find a new flat today."

"Why?" He wriggled out of her arms like a puppy.

Lydia thought of a lie. But that was impossible so she told him in very adult terms that she was supposed to stay overnight, and here she'd spent two months. Jill had to feed her and worry about her as if Auntie was a third child. "If they wanted another baby, they would've had their own."

He paced the room, preparing to kick. Lydia stepped away, but kept a level tone as if she were undisturbed. "You know how Mrs. Bannon tells you about her duckies? I'll be near the ducks. As soon as I find out my exact address, I'll ring you and you'll come have a cuppa char with your Auntie. How's that?"

He glared, still pacing, not understanding that she had to leave. "Jacob, baby, please—"

Loud enough for the whole family to hear, he shouted, "I'm not a baby, I hate you ugly witch, I hope you die!" Just as she'd cried, "I hope you die," to her father years ago. Lydia shut the door and stood in the hallway. Leaving was like dying.

Walking down Frognal for the last time she thought how much harder it was to have thoughts of self-fulfillment when there were children. There was no way to explain her dreams or plans, her fears of growing old and being nowhere.

Mr. Miskyll, the name on the paper, appeared before Lydia when she rang the buzzer. His house was attached to the others, the only mustard-colored building on a short, white street. Lydia could tell Mr. Miskyll knew her story, but wasn't one to appear softhearted. This was only an interview, he brusquely informed her. He didn't need to let the flat to just anyone, and as he'd never rented to an American, an American was just anyone. He wasn't sure, though he liked Clint Eastwood. Did Lydia come from Texas? Had she ever been to Hawaii? Mr. Miskyll was a rangy man, with a face like a turkey. His cheeks were hollowed, the flesh hanging in dewlaps. His hair looked charged with electricity.

Lydia eased the pack off her shoulders and dropped it onto the sidewalk in front of his mustard house. American she claimed to be, and the way she spoke proved it. Charles Bronson she was not. Lydia, Mr. Miskyll's first in-the-flesh American, became with each response, she saw, America personified. Orphaned, waifish, underfed America. "They have black eyes," she imagined him saying at dinner that night. "They got eyes black as a Greek." And remembering the strangeness of the stranger, he could say with great authority, "Things aren't so good as they make out in America. Things are better in Finsbury Park where they come with all of their worldly possessions on their back and weighing all of what, seven stone?" But the questions: Would she be having young men knock her up all hours of the day and night? Lydia clapped a palm over her mouth and solemnly shook her head. And she wasn't, you know, in the family way or anything like that, was she? She certainly didn't look it, but early on, with all those breakfasts coming up quicker than they went down, she could be. Satisfied with her answers, Mr. Miskyll ground his heels into the bare dirt in his front yard and pointed to a window at ground level, at white curtains, parted in the middle. "My wife," he said. "My daughters, Sheila, fourteen, Maggie, six and a half."

Lydia waved, smiling.

"What are you grinning at, eh? Think you'll pull the wool over my eyes, do you? Well, listen here, miss, have you got the money? Show me you can pay up now. Do you work? Have you got a regular job?"

Lydia was too stunned to invent, so she dug into the side pocket of the pack and came up with a wad of bills. "The flat is nine pounds a week, right? Well look, Mr. Miskyll. I've got enough to pay the rent for half a year at least." She tucked the money back in the pocket and stood up straight.

"And what'll you eat, eh? You can't eat air, you know, and we won't have you by when you come knocking, hungry. There's four of us to feed and food's so bloody dear."

Lydia knelt and slid the straps of her pack onto her shoulders.

She adjusted the load by giving a little jump, wiggling, flexing, then buckling the waist strap. "Okay, then, Mr. Miskyll."

"Not at my house, miss, not at my house. Not a shilling until you go upstairs. We don't want you knocking, whining the room's too small, the chair's too big, and all of that."

Lydia didn't complain to Mr. Miskyll, but having evaluated his nature, neither did she take the risk of letting him know how much she valued the flat, how delighted she was to be settled in such a short time. It was hard being a stranger in a new city, not knowing which neighborhoods were good or what to expect for the money. The last time she'd looked for a home was when she'd arrived in New York for the first time. She stayed with Uncle Lou in the Bronx, and for the week she was there, kept thinking, This is New York? Finally she left her uncle's, and on his suggestion stayed at the Salvation Army Evangeline Residence while she apartment-hunted for the next three months. On Wednesday mornings she waited at the first delivery point for *The Village Voice*, armed with pencils and dimes, listening to the others on line talk about good and bad streets and exchange hints about how to *shmeer* landlords or rental agents, the smoothest way to bribe a super. The only reason she got the apartment in John's building, she later found out, was not because of the hundred dollars she slipped to him, but because beforehand John had decided men were slobs and he would only rent to a woman. The following year, he wouldn't rent to anyone under thirty, and the year after that, he stopped renting to women because they were fickle and broke leases. So Lydia didn't tell Mr. Miskyll how happy she was. If he knew he might reassess the dingy rooms and up the rent.

And they were dingy! Vowing not to get used to it and accustom herself to the grime, whenever Lydia came home with groceries, she pretended she was a guest, and tried to see the flat from the friend's point of view. Soon she would meet people, and she'd want to have the nice ones over for dinner or tea. She bought blue-and-white-striped dishes and a teapot for these guests, and tried to arrange the furnishings according to their standards. It was too easy, she knew, to forget how others lived. Her previous nest had been an unlit place, suitable only for those who communicated by tactile or chemical means. The first time Rema came for lunch, she stepped into the kitchen and said, "God help me —please?" when she saw the formicarium on the table. Just because Lydia enjoyed watching her ants during meals didn't mean others would. "Lydia, I love you," said Rema, trying to compose herself, "but if you don't move that thing, I think I'll be sick."

In the meantime, her only visitor was Mr. Miskyll, who stopped by at exactly 6:30 on Thursday for his nine quid and ten minutes of small talk—the weather, the economy, the state of the yard. He was as bored as she, but bound by convention. In a rare moment of openness, he told Lydia that generations ago his family left England for Poland, where the respectable Mitchell was mauled. He was first-generation English after a gap of many years, but he'd atoned for his forebear's desertion by marrying a Howard. He hoped things would be better for his children, though God knew, he had problems with his Sheila, always sneaking around. Lydia nodded. Whenever she went out at night she saw Sheila Miskyll passionately kissing a young man who was built like a walking stick.

Deciding she wanted someone else to talk to, Lydia went to the post office on Blackstock Road, and bought a stack of aerograms. She described her new attic flat to Rema, the toilet four flights down and so cold she sat on her hands when she used it. "It's a lovely little flat, with ceilings that slope so low I can only walk upright in half of each room. There's a sitting-room area with a miniature chair and a footrest by the gas fire. The bedroom has a view of the yard." Writing cheered her because the flat was ceaselessly cold. Mr. Miskyll said to his mind storm windows were frivolous, and as fast as Lydia pushed coins into the meter, cold air seeped between the panes of glass and ill-fitting sashes. The rooms were dusty, mold grew on the baseboards no matter how much she cleaned, and the walls were so spongy from years of wallpaper (roses over daisies over stripes) that no tacks stayed in, no pictures could be hung. She went to Woolworth's in Islington, bought three undershirts and a picture postcard of a Parliament she'd never seen. "New York is great, wish I were there," she wrote to Harriet and Brian at school. A new graduate student had probably taken her place at lunch, fitting in effortlessly, extending the relationship as she'd never done, with phone calls and dinner parties. It didn't matter, Lydia decided, though she hoped *someone* noticed her absence this fall. She hoped at least one person wondered where she was. Her hand shook as she addressed the card. It was too much to expect someone to miss her when as nostalgic as she herself had grown in exile she didn't grieve over Harriet's absence or anticipate a reunion with Brian. It was her work she missed. It was arriving at school in the morning to find her papers just as she'd left them on her desk, knowing by the time she pulled up a chair, she'd be oriented, a minute later completely absorbed. She didn't tack posters of Swiss vistas or mountain lakes on her walls like the others did. She knew the walls were grubby, painted institutional green ten years ago, brown and crazed from water stains. She knew because the condition of the walls was a main topic of lunchtime conversation. At her desk, Lydia went into a trance. Cracked paint didn't exist. There was no room for thoughts of success or failure or sex or men or death. Once Brian admitted he was obsessed with earning honors; working, his thoughts were half on the Nobel Prize. Lydia was astounded. Her vision was as narrow as a laser beam.

If I go back, Lydia thought. She shook her head and tried again. *When* I go back that will never change. She was a good scientist, blessed with an extraordinary ability to concentrate, to focus. But the rest of her abilities had atrophied, the other parts of her life were a mess. She wanted to learn to be a friend, to talk, to live in the public world among people.

A cup of tea would calm her. Lydia filled the kettle, then struck a match to light the stove. The burners were gummy and when at last the gas ignited, a loud foof! startled Lydia, made her jumpier than before, jolted her memory. Time didn't heal all wounds. All time had done was teach her what illusions to keep. Before Kramer left, she didn't think about her father's death. Her refusal to accept it had been easy enough since he wasn't in her everyday life. Maybe he was in California, too busy to call. Rerouting her thoughts to avoid his death, she cut him out of her life, she lost his love. Now that she was finally able to accept his death she missed him more than she had for years, but he was back again, he was vivid. She didn't need his slippers to remember his smelly feet. She didn't need his City College cup, shattered and pieced together with Elmer's Glue, to recall the man who could be short-tempered and infinitely patient in turn. He was black-haired, her dad, but no Clark Gable; a *bona fide* Badger but no Hank Greenberg. She wanted what was left now that he'd died. The memories, painful as they often were, enriched her life, gave it texture. Time, in teaching Lydia about survival, made her wise enough to seek the memories but not to dwell on the unanswerable—what will become of me? "You'll get old and die," Kramer said. And he was right, of course. But what would happen to her in a month or a year? She composed a letter to Dr. Cantoni, telling him her address, her plans to return in the summer. She mailed letters to Harold and Rose, to an assortment of people she hadn't considered friends before. Who missed her? She became obsessed with this, wishing she'd left her tracks someplace, if only a mark in someone's sand. What about the Sandersons? At breakfast, did they say, "Ah, Lydia," with affection? Had her chair been taken back upstairs or did it remain at the table, forever Lydia's chair? She'd loved the mornings at the Sandersons, the flurry of activity when she woke, each person busy dressing in front of different mirrors, each person getting ready for the day, their thoughts on their separate afternoons, yet their bodies miraculously appearing at the same time for breakfast. Here the rooms were so dark it was hard to know when the sun rose. The floors were grimy and cold, and like the walls, layer over layer, plaid linoleum over green apples over red and blue specks. The bed was held up on three legs and a block of wood. The wardrobe door creaked open whenever she lay down. The sink was in the hallway between the two rooms, and she'd searched for the refrigerator for an hour before realizing it wasn't cleverly disguised as something else: It just *wasn't.* There were no mirrors as there were at home, she thought, writing on the back of a postcard (red-faced Beefeater on the front), "Greetings from the penthouse, £9 furnished, near the tube and park." She wrote her address and the number of the pay phone downstairs and underlined *please* three times and *call* four times.

"You'd love it," she wrote to Beth, Kramer's nocturnal friend who'd told Lydia she was a fool and deserved what she got. "With winter coming the days are a blink long. Night expands to plug up the gap. Life would be long and productive for you. Come visit, you'll meet many tall, dark-haired men."

Greeks, Cypriots, and Irish lived in the houses in Finsbury

Park, but on the street there was little sign of their lives. In New York, the poverty was crueler, the streets uglier, and far more dirty, but there was always life, shown though it often was through shattered windows and spray-painted curses. Here was only an impersonal sameness. No one sat in chairs or stood on corners outside. There were no domino games, no bocci, no salsa. In the tunnel to the underground, a graffito said, "Love and sex is good for you all."

"Get some, Mum," a red-faced man said, looming overhead on a billboard, his plate of sausages aimed at the passersby.

Like a retiree, frightened by the stretches of free time each day, Lydia began a regimen of long walks, setting out immediately after breakfast each day, and often not returning home until dinnertime. Standing in front of Mr. Miskyll's mustard-colored house she saw chimney pots, row after row of them, all perched atop the same four-story house. She began to walk and found in every direction street after street, mile after mile the same. She walked for miles, and when she grew tired, she found a bench and took her sandwiches from her backpack. She lunched in Clissold Park, in Walthamstow Marshes, Hackney Marshes, Springfield Park. She watched red-cheeked boys play football in ankle-deep mud, wearing the most determined expressions. Duplicates of Mr. Miskyll, gaunt men coughing from bronchitis, passed her in each park. Sallow, lumpy women fed the pigeons or the coots. She carried with her lunch a small spade, bought in a closet-sized shop on Seven Sisters Road, and after eating, she dug patches of earth to see what was sleeping beneath. Brian had criticized her for this sort of curiosity. Ants were her life's work, not silly pets to play with. He thought that being a naturalist, watching with a nonscientific eye conflicted with her goals. She decided to write him a letter and tell him he lacked a sense of awe. If he really wanted to win prizes, he had to think larger, to consider the total, to be amazed by the incredible order and intelligence of a society of ants. Brian's major flaw was thinking he could understand everything.

She found earthworms, millipedes, sow bugs, and beetles. Whether larva, pupa, or adult, nothing was alone; there was no one of a kind. Every creature existed with others of its kind, feeding on smaller creatures, fed upon by larger ones. Sometimes she took clots of earth home in plastic bags, and spilled them onto a cookie tray. In one batch there were callows, newly emerged worker ants. She remembered then that insects didn't emerge from the pupal stage behaving like adults; they were clumsy and sluggish; it took time before they could fit into the community. Once at work she'd put a few callows straight from their nest into a column of raiding ants. The callows were disoriented and interfered with the elders. At the time she'd laughed, seeing how they were pushed aside. Now she thought: It takes time, I must be patient.

On the Wednesday of her second week, Lydia walked to Waterlow Park. It was drizzling so lightly she couldn't feel the rain, so she dug and picnicked, and in the afternoon called on Karl Marx, buried in the cemetery at the southern end of the park. There, in front of the cracked, gray stone (1818–1883) she began to sneeze. Searching for a tissue, she saw the tiny drops of rain that covered her jacket like fish scales. She didn't want to get sick; not now, not living alone. So she took the tube back to Finsbury Park, deciding to make a quick stop at the butcher's before going home.

The store was crowded when she arrived. She stood in line behind an extremely wide woman, and dipped left and right to see what was in the butcher's case. Lamb kidneys were sixteen pence a pound. She could blanch them to get rid of the urine smell and broil them for dinner. The taste was strong, but they were cheap and packed with nourishment, and besides, the perfect kidney shape and color was pleasing. Having grown up in L.A., she found it easy to forget that kidney-shaped referred to kidneys, not swimming pools.

The man in front of the fat lady had hair as blond and coarse as Carl's. Lydia stood on her toes and saw the familiar corduroy jacket, the cuffs of a freshly starched shirt peeking through. It *was* Carl, her old boyfriend. She wanted to call his name, put her hand on his shoulder, tell him she misunderstood, she was intolerant. He mumbled his order and she pushed ahead to get closer. As she was jostled from behind, she felt his arms around her, his joy at seeing her there. Kramer was the one who'd made her forget there'd been pleasant times with Carl—a trip to Montauk, mushrooming in Pennsylvania. First she was chilled to think how much life changed with each man, then she was annoyed, knowing their lives didn't change with each woman. Because of Kramer she'd forgotten she hurt Carl, she'd been mean. Forgive me, she thought, I understand.

His order was finished and paid up. Her voice, she was afraid, would be hoarse from disuse, the words a mere growl. He turned around, his face lowered as he checked the contents of his bag. "Carl?" she whispered. He looked up. His skin was pitted, his nose had been broken. There was a squint in one eye. Or was it a wink?—at Lydia.

She went home without the kidneys and drafted a letter to Carl. "I saw someone," she wrote. "He reminded me of you."

25

THE NEXT MORNING, Lydia missed Carl, and in a rotten mood, blamed Kramer for ruining her, silently harkening back to the days B.K.—Before Kramer. By lunchtime, searching for friendly faces, for someone to spend a few minutes with, she knew two things were true. Number one, she never liked Carl all that much, but spent time with him because it was easy, and number two, she hadn't really been all that independent either. She hadn't felt alone before Kramer because she believed in her father's love; she used it to keep warm at night. Had Kramer never existed, this illusion too would have failed. Now she was alone. "No family?" Mr. Miskyll said. "No mum and dad? Just you against the world?" "Just me," Lydia said, and this time it was true.

Maybe to comfort her, to give her a sense of extended family, Mr. Miskyll brought the evening paper upstairs when he came to collect the rent the following Thursday. He threw it on the table, and leafed through it, pointing out articles of interest, by which he meant whenever an American was mentioned, whether Henry Kissinger, Elvis Presley, or Jeanne Dixon. He tapped each sharply with his forefinger, as if enraged. "Here's one they put in for you," he said.

One they did indeed put in for Lydia, though Mr. Miskyll couldn't possibly have known, was a small article about the National Film Theatre on South Bank, which was ending up a retrospective of films starring Humphrey Bogart. Bogie was in a characteristic pose, cigarette smoldering between his lips, and Mr. Miskyll's finger jabbing at his nose. "Him," Mr. Miskyll said. "Yes," said Lydia, leaning over to read the small print. "He's American, all right." Ernst Lubitsch was the subject of the next retrospective. Mr. Miskyll pointed out Billy Graham, and went home.

The National Film Theatre had two screening rooms. NFT One, which was larger, showed popular retrospectives, films directed by Cukor or Hitchcock, or starring Bette Davis or Edward G. Robinson. NFT Two, the small room, had more esoteric programs; the films from Yugoslavia and Finland, the ouevre of René Clair in French. Lydia took the tube to South Bank and bought tickets to all the Lubitsch shows except *Bluebeard's Eighth Wife*, and to a few pictures at NFT Two. "Just in time, thank God," she said to the woman in the box office. The woman smiled patiently, no doubt used to dealing with hundreds of fanatics. Lydia didn't bother explaining that she was a regular person who liked movies, not a filmmaker, a film historian, an ardent auteurist, a director, a director manqué, a budding star, or an editor of any sort.

Nor am I an escapist, thought Lydia, as the nights passed and she sat arm to arm amidst an audience of over a hundred, watching a movie about men and women with children in supporting roles. It wasn't escape; it was a three-credit course entitled Intro. to People I.

When Kramer first met Lydia he said, "How was it possible to grow up in America, in Los Angeles, movie capital of the world, for God's sake, and not have seen *Snow White*? Hello? Where were you? How did you manage to miss *Gone with the Wind* or *Psycho*? What is it like to be an adult and not have seen *The Wizard of Oz*?" But the big question, in all seriousness, his voice full of awe and disbelief, "Lydia, what was childhood like without Walt Disney?"

He found out before long, of course.

You should see me now, Lydia thought, rushing off to so many movies she, too, found it hard to believe that before Kramer the only time she saw a film was on a first date. She became, in November, so experienced, she could sit through three in a row, as she did for the Apu Trilogy, bringing hard-boiled eggs to crack on the arms of her seat, choosing bananas over apples because crunching during the quiet part of a movie was a serious breach of cinema etiquette.

He should have seen her become a regular in the cafeteria at NFT, a window seat saved for her alone. Every night she sat with a carafe of wine or a cup of tea, and blocking out her schedule for the week, spread the tickets across the table like tarot cards. Would she meet a man? Would her fortune change? Outside, lights were strung across the banks of the Thames. The Houses of Parliament glittered; Big Ben was a second moon. Tired from her afternoon walk, she always enjoyed the lab section of Intro to People, the cafeteria. It didn't take long before she was exchanging pleasantries with the old man who looked like Leon Trotsky, and the frizzle-haired woman who carried her chihuahua in a shoulder bag. She always said hello to Big Foot, an average-sized American kid, who wore at least size 15-EEE shoes, and although no words were spoken, she exchanged nods with the lean, intense look-alike couple as soon as they strode arm and arm inside, both dressed in leather, their hair close-cropped, three earrings in each ear.

She felt at home, and often thought that although Kramer had gone, at least he had left his love of movies. Like Zeyde, who'd passed on his love of Russian novels, and her father his feelings about success.

She hardly attempted to fool herself into thinking it would go on like this; her days walking, her nights at the movies. By the time the brochure for the next NFT One series was mailed to her flat, she knew her course was over. The roll of bills she'd confidentially flashed at Mr. Miskyll was gone.

Trotsky cheered her up on the last evening of the Lubitsch retrospective by inviting Lydia to his table and asking if she'd "share some wine and conversation." "Sure," she said, hardly arguing when he said he'd buy the wine. While he went to wait on line, she glanced over at Big Foot, sitting at the next table. As always, he was drinking soup, and had in front of him an interesting device, a kind of bookstand that held a book open with metal clamps on either side, allowing him to read while he ate. Close up she saw the book was called *Readings in Mammalian Cell Culture.* Feeling a connection, she waited for him to look up and acknowledge her. But he was so self-sufficient, so totally absorbed, he never did. At that moment, feeling acutely single, she hated Kramer and vowed if she ever saw him, she'd never give him the satisfaction of confessing her love for movies.

Trotsky returned, and they had a pleasant discussion concerning the sexuality in Lubitsch's films. What Trotsky admired most was the artful way Lubitsch suggested intimate moments, the way he was genteel as well as skillful enough to make a closed door so significant, the audience couldn't fail to understand what went on behind it. He was sorry tonight was the last in the series. Lydia told him she wouldn't be returning for the Ford films. "But you must," said Trotsky. "Don't be deceived into thinking he's no more than a bang-bang-shoot-em-up American director."

"I know," Lydia said. "But I'm presently unemployed."

"That, too, we have in common," said Trotsky.

They said good-night, shaking hands. Trotsky had seen an earlier screening of *Design for Living*, and assured Lydia the print was good.

The lights went down just as Lydia entered the theater, and she found her seat during the titles. On the screen, Gary Cooper and Frederic March were in a train compartment, struggling to speak their awful French to Miriam Hopkins. The audience laughed. Lydia with them, though she understood that problems in communication were hardly a joke. Gary Cooper had just fallen asleep and was resting his head on Frederic March's shoulder when the picture jumped, the frame tore; under hot projection lamps it burned and curled at the edges. The audience hissed. When the lights went on, Lydia saw that Big Foot was seated next to her, his long legs draped as far as the knee over the seat ahead. "I've seen this movie four times already, so if they can't mend it, I'll tell you what happens."

The lights dimmed once again, and there was Miriam Hopkins in her perky little hat, busy sketching the two men as they dozed. And what an artist. Gary Cooper's sensual lips, sketched in a flash, his straight hair with the cowlick in the back. Big Foot couldn't have been more than twenty-five, and to sit through this movie a fifth time, no matter how good, was a sign that he was some kind of film freak. If he's a filmmaker, Lydia thought, I'm telling him I'm married and forbidden to speak to men. I'll refuse to exchange a single word with him. History will not repeat itself. Miriam Hopkins walked off the train arm in arm with Frederic March and Gary Cooper. Lydia shook her head to scatter her thoughts. She didn't know this person's name, he was too young, and besides, she'd seen him with a woman once. Lydia laughed at how ridiculous she was. "Immorality may be fun, but its not fun enough," said Edward Everett Horton on screen. Everyone else laughed.

Just as Kramer always said, nothing cleared the mind better than a good movie. Lydia forgot about Big Foot and her filmmaker phobia. When it was time to leave, she looked down the aisle in both directions, and estimated if she exited left, she had more, though distinctly shorter, people to step over. She exited left; Big Foot went right.

Outside it was cool but not as damp as usual, and Lydia decided instead of stopping at the cafeteria, she'd go straight home. Maybe she'd walk across the bridge tonight, and take the train from the north side of the river.

Someone was panting behind her, so she speeded up. A male voice said, "Boy, you walk fast." She turned and saw Big Foot, walking beside an old black bicycle. "What station are you going to?"

Lydia told him she was heading for the footbridge. Did he care to join her?

Big Foot bounced when he walked; high up on his toes, then down again, his curls flying. In his quilted jacket, he looked inflated; the Michelin man.

Lydia was a little uneasy, so before they reached the bridge, she asked exactly *why* he'd seen the movie five times. It was a pleasant romantic comedy about a woman named Gilda, who falls in love with a playwright and a painter—best friends as well as roommates. The "design" is her idea that the three live together, with Gilda playing mother of the arts. For the sake of peace and friendship, and for the betterment of art, the rule that there be no sex is supposedly enforced.

"I liked it the first three times I saw it, but the fourth time I hated it. Tonight was for the purpose of determining which opinion was right."

"And which was it?"

"I like it. The time I hated it, I saw it in New York with an audience that judged it with a contemporary sensibility. They hated Miriam Hopkins. Remember that scene where she describes what it feels like to be in love with each of them? How with Tom it starts at her feet and goes up through her head, and with George it starts in her head and tingles down to her toes? The audience went bananas booing. And the mother of the arts thing? If they had fruit they would've thrown it. I felt like such a pig for having liked it the first three times that I went home and cleaned up my girl friend's apartment."

"You saw it in New York?" Lydia asked. "Are you from New York?"

"For a couple of years. I've lived all over."

"Oh where?" she said. "What street?"

"I had a sublet on Bleecker and Charles for a few months, and then—hey, what's wrong?"

Lydia collapsed against the railing. Big Foot started; his hands flew out to catch her in case she fainted, slipping into the river. Really she was happy. She touched his orange nylon sleeve and said, "I'm home."

He laughed. When they were walking again, his bicycle clicking by his side, he told her it was nice to meet someone who was so cheerful. Lydia had lived for so long inside her own head, with only her morbid thoughts for company, it sounded as if he were talking about someone else.

The water was black below. They were nearly across the bridge, and the sound of traffic was loud again, motorcycles, car horns, the purr of finely tuned engines. "You're not a filmmaker, are you?" she asked, realizing he hadn't explained why he'd seen the movie the first four times.

"Me?"

An eternity went by. She speeded up. Behind her, he said, "I just like to go to the movies."

"It was just that I see you a lot." Relieved, she went on. "And the chihuahua lady, and Trotsky ..."

"Trotsky! Exactly! One afternoon I sat really wracking my brains, thinking Freud, Lenin, Joyce—I couldn't remember who it was he looked like. But it's Trotsky resurrected, that's exactly right."

"I've always admired your book contraption," Lydia said.

"That?"

"And how self-sufficient you are."

"Not true. I bring books with me because I hate eating alone."

"Oh no," Lydia said. "You're so complete."

"I'm complete, all right. I mean, I live alone, I cook and clean for myself, I entertain myself. If I've been extra good, and I usually am, I take myself out for a movie."

Big Foot told Lydia that after graduating from school with a liberal arts degree, he'd changed his plans and was now taking courses in organic chemistry and biology to prepare him for medical school in the fall. Lydia thought: I could help him with his studies, a (ha ha) patron of the sciences.

Would he go to medical school here or in the States? How many more courses would he take? What field would he specialize in? Though Lydia asked a lot of questions, she was unable to prevent his inevitable one: "What do *you* do?"

She said, "Nothing," so softly she had to say it twice. It made her feel naked, a zero, a garbage maker. Still, anticipating a moment like this, she'd decided it was important to fend for herself without the protective coloring of a career. She wanted to be respected before her talents were revealed.

At the tube station, it was determined they could take the same train and ride together for a few stops. He lived in Kentish Town, not too far away from Lydia. Her spirits were high again. She was pleased he liked to talk to her, though she couldn't help thinking that six months ago she'd taught two biology labs and worn a white coat with acid holes in the elbows and her name above the pocket—like a gas station attendant, Kramer had said. He probably assumes that I'm rich and spoiled, Lydia thought. So she said, "Actually, I was looking for a job, but I don't have working papers."

"Hmm," he said. "What are you looking for?"

"I don't know. Something outdoors would be nice." Lydia secretly imagined herself in a park uniform, spearing paper and trash, or at the zoo, throwing raw meat to the tigers. Big Foot thought for so long either he'd forgotten what he set out to think about, or else he really knew of some kind of job. Lydia said she was strong, loved the outdoors, and knew a lot about animals.

"A few friends of mine have gotten temporary work at this place called Adams. I'm not sure where it is, but you could probably get a listing. There's a woman there, I forget, Duncan or Munchkin or something on that order, and apparently she gets jobs for illegal aliens and ... um ... but—" He was saved from further discomfort when the train pulled in, bringing the acrid smell of hot rubber with it.

Big Foot carried his bicycle under his arm, and when the doors closed, he said, "I don't know what she'll be able to dig up, but I doubt if it'll be outdoors."

Under the harsh light in the train, she saw he was younger than she'd first imagined. His eyes were yellow-brown, the lashes straight and spiky. He bent his knees and talked into her ear to avoid telling his story to the strangers. Big Foot had moved to London in July after he'd been rejected from medical schools in the States, because his father, a neurologist, had pull here. London was familiar to him. His folks had split up when he was a kid and since that time he'd spent every summer in London with his dad. For years he swore he wouldn't become a physician, but, in a way, that was because he didn't want to blindly follow in his father's footsteps. As soon as he made up his mind to try and get into medical school, he knew what he'd always wanted was to be a G.P. in a small town. Did that sound overly romantic? Did she know that the English, per person, consumed more refined sugar than the people of any other Western country? And excluding the Germans, they drank more beer?

The train pulled into Leicester Square, which meant she had to leave. Wondering what to say in situations like these she said, "Well, I guess I can go a couple of extra stops and pick up the Victoria instead."

He smiled; he seemed happy to stand with her for a few extra moments. Why did she think of him as another lonely person in London, when he had a father, friends from his past summers, and most likely a girl friend? "Did you get the brochure for the Ford festival?" he asked.

Lydia nodded.

"So I'll see you there, I guess."

She shook her head.

His forehead creased, his mouth slipped open. Was that dismay? It was nothing compared to what she'd felt the night she checked every pocket in every garment she owned, then shook her knapsack violently, lifted dusted slabs of linoleum, crawled under her bed to find only slob's wool, dust balls as big as plums. "It's my own fault," she said to Big Foot. "I've always been careless about money."

Her father's warning that she should be attentive to her finances had not been merely his Depression-induced paranoia.

He'd been right. "A single woman living alone . . ." he'd said. She laughed, remembering. The train pulled into the next station and Big Foot joined in, apparently believing she wasn't too worried. And she wasn't anymore: She was invigorated. Her father had been right but for the wrong reasons. She didn't have to hide dollars under the mattress, waiting for hard times to roll in, but unless she expected always to be dependent, to be supported by someone, she would have to concern herself with financial affairs.

Euston, Lydia's stop. Big Foot walked to the door with her and when the train slowed down, he put his hand on her arm; he opened his mouth to say something. She said "Good—" and stepped out onto the platform. The doors shut before her "—bye." She saw his surprised expression before she turned her back. Walking away she felt awful; she couldn't watch the train leave, carrying with it a person she'd known for only an hour. Good-bye Mr. Cloudsley-Brain, good-bye edible art teacher, Good-bye Big Foot. This felt the worst. Maybe, she thought, I'm more vulnerable; more apt to cling to just anyone.

The night before the coldness inside her flat had been invigorating; she fueled herself on what she called fettucini Alfredo. Tonight she knew she was eating only spaghetti and margarine for dinner, and furthermore, that she was freezing. Were other people better equipped to accept the limits? Maybe this was why she didn't have friends, why her lovers, before Kramer, were never her confidants. She hadn't learned to have a nice talk with someone, then look him in the eye and say farewell. Peter had told her one night that it was possible to have friends that wouldn't put up the bail money for you or jump in the river to save your life, but who liked and respected you nonetheless. I'll get over it, Lydia thought.

By the time she climbed into bed that night, she knew she'd been rash; it was a mistake. It was different from what it had been with the edible art teacher. She and Big Foot had liked each other. In her effort to learn to say good-bye she'd been too quick. She remembered his puzzled look; his dismay. I can get a job. I can save money and buy more movie tickets. Sleepy, half dreaming, she thought: I can see him again if I want.

No MATTER how shabby the building or how poor the company, it was never Fat Louie's Discount Shoe or the E-Z Credit Corp., but the Royal Business Equipment Corporation or William N. Potts, Insurance. On the door to the employment agency that specialized in jobs for illegal aliens, it said Adams Appointment Agency—London's Foremost Employment Specialists. Adams wasn't exactly a high-class operation. It was a dingy place with frosted glass partitions and folding chairs, run by a champagne blond named Mrs. Duncan, who was somewhere over sixty. There was one magazine Lydia had the option of sharing with the two foreign-looking men who sat on either side of her during the hour wait, but it was nearly as aged as Mrs. Duncan and in far worse shape.

She didn't get a job throwing steaks to the tigers. In fact, the next day when she stood a half-hour early in front of an old building that housed more companies with formal names, Lydia didn't know just what she'd be doing. All she had to prepare her for this new life was a white appointment card, introducing her to someone named Mr. Hatchett, and a lucky scarf around her neck. Who expected to begin a job so soon? She'd anticipated having at least a week to gear up to it, though there was no way she could have survived the time without asking her sister for a loan. Still, she said "Tomorrow?" to Mrs. Duncan. "I'm starting on a Wednesday? Are you positive?" Yes, dear, said Mrs. Duncan.

She walked home from Adams in a daze. What would she wear? She didn't have the time or money to buy a dress or a decent pair of shoes. Panicked, she remembered one of Rose's maxims: "You don't have to be a fashion plate, Lydia, but you can always be clean and neat," and in the evening, she went out to the Laundromat and washed everything she owned. At 11:00 P.M., when she took her clothes out of the dryer, a strange challis scarf, bright red paisley, clung to her pants leg. "It followed me home," she whispered, stuffing it into her bag. The only other person was the proprietor, snoring in the corner.

Now in the morning, she was standing in front of a factory building on a cobblestone mews off Tottenham Court Road, with the card and the scarf, hoping that clean blue jeans were dressy enough. When it was impossible to delay any longer, she entered the building. She climbed up an unlit stairway, patting the cool walls. Being in graduate school was like being in the army. Both left one curiously unprepared for encounters with the outside world of job interviews and worries about proper clothing and problems with doors that wouldn't open. Lydia pulled on this particular door with both hands, but all her strength was needed to break the seal. When she succeeded, white light spilled out. She shielded her eyes, blinking, but the image from fluorescent fixtures stayed on her retina, and it seemed the longest time before people formed and voices were heard. She put her hands down and saw long tables that spanned the length of the room. Women milled around, talking softly. She stood in the doorway, thinking, I need money. A giant clock said 8:20, but it could have been any time. The windows looked out onto a brick wall; they were a wasted effort, a tease. Each time the clock made a loud tick, the women swiveled their heads sharply and checked the time, sharply facing forward again, like toys in Geppetto's workshop, their movements mechanical, forever wound. Those who, swiveling to face the clock, noticed Lydia reacted with the same amount of interest spent on the water cooler or the gray metal lockers. She counted six young, light-haired and slender women (blue eyes, brown eyes, glasses, attached lobes, detached lobes) and one tremendous redhead. Was it perhaps a *Mrs.* Hatchett? As Lydia walked forward, the redhead's upper lip curled; the tough expression of a boss. Her chin and neck were the same width, one unit, and her hair was teased and worn on top of her head like a giant flaming boil. She turned away. A moment later, just as the clock hit eight-thirty and zero seconds, the conversation came to an abrupt halt. Set on springs, the women made awkward, hurried movements toward the chairs. "Good morning," said Lydia. "Does anyone know where I can find a Mr. Hatchett?" No one spoke, so she tried again. "This is, I presume, the Malcolm S. Cage Lighter Corporation, Limited?"

That didn't work either, so she set herself down on an empty chair near a mountain of brown, wrapped packages. She'd give it another ten minutes, and then decide what to do. In the meantime, to pass the minutes she fished the circular for the John Ford retrospective from her bag. Not only did she need money, she also wanted to see Big Foot again. So what if he had a girl friend. She liked talking to him. She'd probably like talking to the girl friend too.

The women, though seated, had their hands folded on their laps, and were utterly silent. The one with the waist-long ponytail set a transistor radio on the table after a few minutes, and shortly after that, the honey-blond propped a mirror against the wall and combed her hair over her face. She made a fresh part and swept her hair over one shoulder, Veronica Lake style. Then she turned, chin to her shoulder, to get a view of her profile, and catching Lydia's eye said, "Yes, this is Cage," before combing her hair back off her face for a center part. Time clicked by loudly on the kind of clock most often seen in schools, its face so large, the spaces between the seconds so broad, time surely passed slower.

Without warning, there was another awkward hurried burst of motion, and in unison, each woman reached for a tray, pulled staples from a brown package, unfolded letters. Lips moved, forming words, then the objects—cigarette lighters—were lifted, and the wheels flicked. Little bursts of flame dotted the room like fireflies, with a silent and sporadic flow. She understood both what the lighter in the Malcolm S. Cage Lighter Corporation stood for, and why there was this second burst of activity. A little man in a long white lab coat was leaning against the doorjamb, trying very hard to look fierce. He had deep-set black eyes and hair, worn in bangs, that covered only half of a very broad forehead. Lydia searched her pockets for the white card, preparing to say something, though in all this time she hadn't thought what. Words of a friendly introduction lined up (the lucky scarf around her neck). "Hi, my name is—" she said, interrupted by a long, low scrape of wood against wood. The redhead was coming toward her, head burrowed into a massive chest, charging across the room, nostrils flared, a wheeze in the back of her throat escaping between her teeth. Lydia stood up. Unused to seeing grotesque people in London, she was more curious than disturbed. The woman clamped a hand on the back of Lydia's chair and gave it a violent pull. "That's my chair," she said. "It's got my name on it and that means it's mine." Sure enough, scratched into the top wrung was *Diane*. Laughing, Lydia said, "Are you Diane?"

"Am I Diane?" The massive chest expanded and contracted in the effort to breathe and speak at once. "She wants to know if I'm Diane. Won't someone tell her who I am?"

The crowd murmured Diane, yes, she's Diane, she is, that's her. Mr. Hatchett took the card from Lydia. "You must be Lavinia's girl, an American, aye? That's her specialty." Lydia thought of the foreign-looking men in the agency and was disturbed. "I'm Hatchett. These girls call me Bill, though I didn't much like it at first. You can call me Bill, you might as well. What's your name?"

"Lydia."

Diane pushed the chair back to her place, as slowly and gratingly as possible.

"Lydia, is it? Bill." He stuck out his hand to shake. "Well, come with me, Lydia."

He said Biw for Bill, wif for with and sounded to Lydia like Elmer Fudd.

Cage made the world's finest lighters. Table models, personal models, some that used butane, others standard lighter fluid. The company hired the best designers to craft crystal and ceramic bodies. Mr. Hatchett said Lydia would see bronze, silver, even gold bodies, though in these times, only a dozen or so gold ones were bought each year. He lit up a cigarette, offered Lydia one, and when she refused said that people all over the world smoked no matter what they said about health and such. A cigarette was an offer, the way a peace pipe had been. Nothing would change that. Anyhow, this was the business to which Bill Hatchett had given twelve of his years, and these were the lighters—he gestured to the workers in this second room: eight people, long tables, windows looking out onto a wall, a giant school clock, blinding fluorescent lights. In this second room were the men, all young, mostly blond, all with cigarettes in their mouths, as if to punctuate Mr. Hatchett's speech. This was where the lighters were fixed. The other room, where Lydia would work, was where they were checked and packed. Mr. Hatchett led Lydia between the tables picking up lighters along the way. There was a "more than adequate, in fact quite generous" warranty on the lighters. Many that came in for repair were far older than the warranty covered; had seen light much before Lydia herself, no doubt. Take this potbellied lighter. Mr. Hatchett leaned over a pink-faced boy and picked it up. The orange glass body had a blue phosphorescence, as if penetrated by an oil slick. "This one's older than me mam," he said, turning it upside down and giving it a shake. He mussed up the boy's hair and said, "Get to work, laddy. Show our new girl how hard you work around here."

The boy turned. "Hello, hello," he said, eyebrows up, voice as low as it would go. Lydia blushed. He couldn't have been more than fifteen.

They continued the tour, walking between the white-coated boys. Mr. Hatchett picked up broken lighters and explained about cracked flints, leaky bodies, busted springs. He made a strong case for the Battered Lighter Syndrome, showing pliers marks, screws with bent threads, scratches, and dents where people had forced the lighters open or jammed them shut when the parts weren't properly aligned. The repair crew was very friendly. They said hello, hello, winked, asked if she was married, where she was from, if she'd ever been to Hawaii. Hawaii was a dominant theme. The smallest boy was sent out for coffee and Lydia was led to an old wooden chair by Mr. Hatchett's desk, in the corner. The whole room was thick with cigarette smoke. Lydia kept wiping her eyes to keep the tears from dribbling. Mr. Hatchett pulled the staples from a small brown package, dumped out a pile of Styrofoam slugs, and unwound ten yards of toilet paper before finding a thin silver lighter. He sniffed the underside, shook it, flicked the flint and said, "We never try and figure out what's wrong by guesswork, you know. We use the best modern methods." He gave the lighter another sniff, then shook the package. A spring and screw rolled under the desk and when Bill Hatchett leaned over to look for them, a blue letter fluttered from the package into a heap of other letters, also folded.

By the end of her first day, Lydia was an expert at work. Bill told her when she would be paid, the bells announced breaks and cleanup time, and a cadaverous worker named Rita barked, "Marys!" when it was time for lunch. The boys in the repair room offered Lydia, by first break, more friendship than she could handle. She turned down cigarettes, but left the room with six in her hand. She was asked out to lunch and to the movies. "I have a boyfriend," she said, wondering who she meant.

Her second morning, she learned, listening to Diane's loud, asthmatic speech, that the fucking Aussie before Lydia left after a bloody week and before that the wog. Lydia didn't know what a wog was, but she had the situation assessed. She asked Leatrice, her pug-nosed neighbor, where the coffee machine was, but only much later learned its location from Margaret, the girl with the mirror, who gave curt answers when no one else would. She needs a friend, Lydia thought, asking, "How long have you been here? Where are you from?" Cage was a sorority of sorts, and she had intruded on the existing order. If she wanted to be accepted, she was going to have to prove herself.

November was gone, and with it the sun. In the morning, when Lydia left for work the buildings and people were indistinct, and by the time she pushed Cage's heavy door open at the end of the day, it was black outside. Night fell at four-thirty. Let the optimists tell her how lucky she was to be in London this time of year, as it had much more daylight than Iceland: She was still California-born and missed the sun. What a winter. It never snowed, and the temperature rarely hit freezing, yet the persistent dampness pentrated her clothes, her skin, what little fat she had, so she was never warm all the way through, never without a slight internal tremor. December was up and running, and Lydia understood the meaning of "chilled to the bone."

She wasn't unhappy despite her long hours at Cage. During lunch she nourished herself on Margaret's limited conversation, and when the bells rang, she accustomed herself to the rhythm of the work, and lost herself in the motion. She never violated the order in which things were to be done: wheel flicked, bottom checked, screws undone, insides checked with a jeweler's loupe, tank filled, letter read, packing number slipped in, package stuffed and stapled. Thematic variations were important.

Wednesday, Lydia decided to do everything left-handed (ambidexterity was a good skill to possess in case of emergency) and on Thursday she'd try guessing the sex of the lighter owner before reading the letter. No wonder Bill Hatchett avoided these notes: They contained, along with requests for repair work, chronicles of despair and hard times. Pensioners living on beans and toast, writing to say their lighter, a retirement gift from the railway department, used up too much fuel. Bedridden widows in council housing, who had to pay little Johnny 25p to take the package to the post office. Things like that. On her agenda, Lydia listed, "Reply in person," for an upcoming week.

Following her own advice, she often called Jill when she returned home in the evening, and though it seemed the moment a connection was made, the hallway traffic got heavy (one tenant rifling through the mail, one sitting on the top step while the bath filled up, a third with her head out the door, listening until the line was free), Lydia made peace with the phone.

Ten minutes into every conversation, Jill said, "Why are you *doing* this to yourself? It's so unnecessary." Yes, she understood Lydia wanted to earn her way home, and she knew a weekly paycheck was very satisfying. But there? In that manner? At that place, her sister, Madame Curie Number Two?

To Jill, that *place* was a hellhole, inhabited by psychically deformed people. Lydia in the telling could laugh. Diane, this red-haired mastodon, stood, clutching her bosom, whenever Rod Stewart was on the radio. She sang with no self-consciousness, swaying, trancelike. The three Marys rose as a single unit the moment Rita barked, "Marys!"

Other times Lydia felt compassion. She saw how too many years of the kind of factory rhythm that kept Lydia alive during the day blotted out whole parts of a person's consciousness. Margaret, the obsessive groomer, had been at Cage for five years, which made her a senior member of staff at twenty-one. Rumor had it that her fingers bled because she flicked so vehemently. She came to work on Saturdays, and though money was undoubtedly a factor, just as important was her feeling that there was nothing better to do on Saturday anyhow. For Diane, Cage was conceivably a happier home than the place she slept, but Margaret was an outsider, who came from Dublin, and the others were suspicious of her. Besides, she worked too hard for their taste.

Needing to tell someone, she told Jill about the war between the sixteen-year-olds in the repair room. Nigel, a gentle boy, told Margaret, whom he not so secretly adored, that ever since he was tiny, the only thing he wanted to be when he grew up was a hippie. Could he help it because he hadn't grown up fast enough, because times had changed? Why should Dave care if his hair was long? Dave, the enemy (hair shorn like a U.S. Marine) wore tight, cuffed Levi's, and steel-toed boots, weapons aimed at Nigel's shins as soon as Bill Hatchett slipped out. Which reminded Lydia: How was Jacob?

"He's a darling," Jill said. "Mrs. Tanis says she hardly hears a peep from him in class, now that he has Vasant." Vasant, Jacob's new friend, was an Indian boy, "from a very fine family—his father's a surgeon."

And Tara?

She'd been coming along to art class with Jill. Did Lydia remember the art teacher at the party? Well, he said Tara had a very good sense of color.

And Peter? Would she put him on?

"Peter sends his love."

"Could you please tell Peter to get his ass over to the phone," Lydia said.

"Lydia."

"It's important."

This could cause a skirmish, she knew. Jill would say to Peter, "What was so important?" and when he said, "Oh, nothing, love," she'd feel suspicious, and be angry with both of them. Lydia was sorry, but Jill was a hard person to explain things to and it was urgent she tell Peter he was in real danger of becoming still another shady father, increasingly out of practice when little daughters grew into women or little sisters became big sisters-in-law.

Peter got on, said hello, how are you, and promised to get the rest of the news from Jill.

"Come on, Peter, the call's on me," Lydia said.

But six heads peeped out of doorways, and Lydia let him go, waiting instead for a better opportunity.

December's second lesson: It was futile to wait for better opportunities. Furthermore, the Perfect Opportunity was a mythical creature that never had existed except in the minds of procrastinators. Was it possible to warm yourself sufficiently to avoid the shock of ocean water? Was there an ideal time to ask an employer for a raise or break up with a lover? No, only bad times (when the glum-faced accountant has just departed from the boss's office, when the boyfriend has just been fired). But the right time? The best opportunity? Even Jill once said, "If you wait for the right time to have children, you never have them."

Lydia thought about this issue for much too long. Then one morning she said, "Okay, this is it."

The sky was muddy. She hadn't slept as well as usual. After work, she went upstairs and changed into the appropriate clothing, thinking: These are my own rules, I can always change my mind.

First she made the phone call. She said, Peter, I feel you fade-fade-fading-ading-ading, an echo in her past. Would he talk to her when she called from now on.

He laughed, and said, "Right."

That done, she went outside and put one foot in a light step ahead, then the other foot, tentatively as if for the first time from Ma to Pa, Baby Lydia, standing upright, walking, breaking into an easy trot, the deepest breath needed to move faster. But then a sharp pain in each ankle, traveling up the calves. Oh, sore *gluteus maximus, tensor fasciae latae, rectus femoris,* hamstring, hamstring. Suggestion of diaphragm cramp. *I can do it, I can. I can't, I can't, I don't want to, go away, I don't want to. I can. Slow now, slow, it feels good, I can.* Muscle replaced by fat. How easy to deteriorate, how hard to build up strength, to heal. Her shoes, squashed in the bottom of her pack, had been easy to forget, to put off while waiting for the perfect time, the ideal Monday. It was Tuesday; she was impatient with the baby steps, the slowness, the aches in her chest, the side stitch; O, faithless lungs, miserable deceitful diaphragm, traitors to her will. *Gastrocnemius, tibialis anterior, soleus, peronei;* o, my aching calves, *huh huh.* The weather, the pavement, the time didn't matter. When, ten minutes into her first attempt, a wheeze latched on to the end of every inhale, she felt cool drops on her nose, saw the fields become spotted from the rain on her glasses it made no difference. The rain didn't cool or distract her. The effort of doing something once as easy as breathing took all her attention. Every atom of Lydia in the left foot, the right. The perimeter of Finsbury Park was under two miles and she struggled to finish, *Daddy, Kramer, Zeyde, I once could, I can,* beginning from scratch, an infant from Ma to Pa, *Daddy, Zeyde, Kramer, I can do it, I can, go away, I can.* The rain beat down heavily. She ran to the top of the park and down, three hundred pounds, ninety-one years old, and this Mount Everest. Blue gym shorts, long johns underneath, undershirt, sweatshirt, resurrected shoes, white with green stripes like warpaint on the sides, *I don't want to, go away, I can, it hurts, I can.* A figure approaching, *I can't huh I can.* A figure on the pavement, black umbrella above his head. She added a burst of speed, *it's okay, breathe deep, you can breathe.* The figure was closer, a male in a black raincoat. Lydia ran, passing him.

"Ammonia! Ammonia!" he called out. "You're crazy! Ammonia!"

27

LYDIA was lying in bed with one man and six oranges. Although the man was leaning back against the pillows at an awkward angle, he was quite adept at juggling three of the oranges. So he did just that, until Lydia shifted, causing him to slip. One orange rolled onto the floor; Lydia rescued the other two before they fell.

"I didn't expect," Lydia said, continuing their conversation. "Which isn't to say I gave up hope. Remember, that in my fantasy I walked up to you and said, 'Guess what? Today's my birthday.' And you offered to split a carafe of wine with me."

Still sore about this subject, he said, "I still don't understand why you did it. Didn't it occur to you that I didn't just carry my bike all over the city? I usually rode home. Why else would I have it? For company?"

"It could've been broken. Or maybe you'd been riding all day and were tired."

True, he said; he'd give her points on that. But it didn't make her behavior any less odd. "I'll tell you exactly what we were talking about: small towns. I told you I wanted to be a G.P. in a rural area."

"Right," said Lydia. "Like William Carlos Williams you see beauty in the lives of working people."

"You're making fun of me."

"I'm not; I swear."

"Okay. Then suddenly you say, 'Oh, by the way, I'm not going to NFT anymore.' And boom, the doors shut. Like a maniac, I stuck my fingers between them, trying to get them apart—"

"Which isn't done in England," Lydia said.

"I didn't know your name. First I was upset. Then I thought: Wow, this person's a sadist. Or else—"

"Go on," Lydia said. "You can say it."

"A fruitcake."

Lydia asked herself two questions. Number one: Where did he pick up these quaint expressions? Number two: How come she'd been lying here for eight hours, a whole day, when B.K. she ran out of a man's bed at 5:00 A.M. leaving nothing more than a cryptic message? For eight whole hours. Was it because today was Boxing Day? No. That was why she could, and nothing more. Or was it because he didn't give her time to feel nervous? As soon as he felt her drift, he talked to her or jumped on her or put music on or juggled or told a story in a foreign accent. What a funny, sweet, lonely person. If she and Kramer had been complements, two sides of a coin, attracted because of how different each was from the other (one outgoing, the other introverted, one sloppy, one neat, an artist, a scientist, an evening person, a morning person), then she and the person beside her were very much twins.

The person beside her was Andrew Wickenden, alias Big Foot. Thinking about the first time he'd bounced along beside her in his inflatable jacket warmed her, and she pushed the oranges to the end of the bed, moved closer and kissed him for the thousandth time that day. As if he were new to it, he said, "You'd think all this kissing would become boring after a while. It doesn't." Andy, Andrew Wickenden. Initials A.W. as in aw, sweet mystery, aw, you beautiful doll. Not that he was beautiful, objectively speaking. His nose was too long, his teeth protruded so his lips wouldn't quite close over them. Still, from the start Lydia had been attracted to him, and as the days passed, she often thought how beautiful he was; long-lashed eyes, fair skin, soft hair. Thinking he was beautiful made her feel beautiful, and when he told her nice things she believed what she never had before: that although objectively she wouldn't win prizes, it was possible for a man to care for her and not be insane, deluded, or half-blind. This was what it meant to be capable of love. To be able to receive love without denigrating the lover. To love back.

"I never knew a Lydia," he said when at last he found out her name. (Later he said he'd never met anyone at all like her.) This reminder of her uniqueness pleased her endlessly, and she yearned to hear it once a day. She'd never known anyone like him either, though once there'd been an Andrew in her life. "The first boy who ever liked me—let me amend that—the only boy dumb enough to like me in high school."

"Ah ah—cancel-cancel, Lydia," he said, as he did each time she said negative things about herself. The cancel-cancels drove her nuts, though they forced her to realize how laced her conversation was with self-deprecating thoughts, how much a part of her they'd become.

"Okay, cancel-cancel. This Andy was Andy Ralph Grossman—five feet tall, carried monogrammed handkerchiefs. I said, 'No Andy, I don't want to go out with you,' but he came over every night, and on the sly asked my Zeyde how one said, 'I love you' in Yiddish. 'My friend wants to know,' Andy said."

Yes, she told Andy. She'd seen the expression on his face just as the train doors closed. She'd turned her back out of habit or awkwardness. It had felt like a mistake, but she'd told herself these things happened all the time. You met someone nice and said good-bye; she'd never been very good at doing it and imagined her discomfort came from her inexperience.

She had gotten a job, and a short time later opened a bank account, proudly stashing away pound after pound, content for a while in her newfound miserliness, a reaction from her former days when she totally disregarded finances. Then one day her birthday had arrived. Dressing, she had tried convincing herself that it didn't matter, that she was too old to expect birthdays to be festive. But as the morning passed, the certainty that she'd get no cake, that no one would surprise her with something wrapped or ask her what she wanted made her increasingly sad.

Growing up she had gotten wonderful gifts. Rose had the knack of buying her something feminine and expensive that Lydia denied ever wanting yet loved once it was hers. A cashmere sweater, a gold bracelet, beautiful things she felt unworthy of owning. Her father, with his eye toward quality and utility, had spent hours reading consumers' guides and canvassing neighbors so he could get her the highest-quality item, the one with precision parts and superior workmanship. For her tenth birthday, Rose had given her an amethyst ring. From her father, her first microscope. He'd bought the boy's model, having assumed it would be better made. Rose had been furious, and said it wasn't right. But that night, they'd all examined their hair, skin, drops of blood. Zeyde, chuckling, had offered earwax, Daddy an eyelash. Rose, pretending she was annoyed had said, "Here," quite gruffly, scooping a dead fly off the windowsill.

So when "Marys'" rang out at lunch that day, Lydia took herself out for a Chinese lunch on Gerrard Street, and though it was a nice thought, it didn't make her all that happy. Maybe a night at the movies would do the trick. She still had a membership to the NFT, and she could always buy a giant-sized box of Raisinets, or the equivalent if they weren't available. It was possible she'd run into Big Foot there, and though it was out of character, she could walk over to him and say, "Guess what, it's my birthday," and they'd split a carafe of wine, clink glasses, celebrate together. It was her birthday; anything was possible. Maybe he'd be there with another girl. Lydia decided it would be easier all around to go down to the West End for a movie.

She ended up at NFT because she'd made a mark there; she'd been happier, she'd felt less alone. The dog lady was standing on the cafeteria line. Pointed ears and ratlike eyes protruded from the bag that was slung over her shoulder. The woman took her sandwich with one hand, using the other to push her pet back down. The dog gave an angry yap. Big Foot turned his head and looked first at the dog lady, then directly at Lydia, standing behind her. He lowered his eyes. He doesn't recognize me, Lydia thought, walking toward him. I refuse to make an ass of myself by saying, "Hi, remember we rode the train together?" But it was too late; the words had escaped, a blush was warming her ears.

He looked up at her and she realized she'd been wrong. He knew who she was, but he didn't like her. His eyes were a warm yellow-brown, but he cast a cool glance, took her in feetfirst. She saw his straight lashes, so unusual with curly hair. When he said, "How come you ran off like that?" she knew just what he meant.

"It was my stop."

He went back to his book. She stood there while he read about mammalian cell culture.

In bed next to him, she said, "And I thought: Tough, so what if I could help him out."

"You didn't really think that."

"You're right. What I did really think was: Easily hurt, this one. A pouter."

They had walked across the bridge again, his bicycle between them. This time he told her outright that he usually rode home. Feeling reprimanded, she became inhibited. Their silence disappointed her; the connection she'd felt at first was lost. But at the stop before Lydia's, they planned a lunch date. That evening and the next day, she found herself looking forward to the date, three days away, once again thinking how nice it would be to spend time with someone whose interests were the same, who was experienced enough in a common field so that their conversations were at the same level. She wouldn't be cast in the role of teacher.

As far as science was concerned, that is. Andy had just turned twenty-three, and though Lydia had led a somewhat sheltered life, she was far more experienced than he, and from the first he looked up to her, asked her advice, made her relay cautionary tales again and again, like a child caught up in the magic of a story. She'd said, "Don't tell me," immediately after having asked how old he was—this mischievous child, who had taken on the job of making her laugh.

He met her at Cage, and from there they walked to Gerrard Street for Chinese food. By the time their meal was served, he wanted to know if she'd meet him there the next day. Lydia said money was tight, and though it was true she let Trotsky pay for wine, she wasn't in the habit of letting men pay for her meals.

Could men invite her home for supper?

She supposed so.

Two weeks ago, three days after their lunch date, they met at NFT for a five-thirty showing of *Straight Shooting*, a silent Ford film. The archives had received the print with Hungarian subtitles, and on the train back to Andy's, they made up possible scenarios, and laughed so hard they missed their stop.

They walked a mile to his flat. Then up the rickety stairs. Inside he switched on a lamp, and when Lydia saw a bed, a nightstand, a hardback chair, she felt dulled by an inexplicable sadness and said, "Oh."

Andy took her hand (they hadn't yet kissed) and said, "Well, it's not the Ritz, but look—here's where I work." He wanted to show her where he sat ten hours a day, but when she felt the pressure of his large hands on hers, her feet got heavy; he nearly dragged her toward his desk. He worked in a windowless corner, so he wouldn't be distracted by sun or birds or children at play. Three shelves held heavy texts, and under the lowest one a fluorescent fixture was mounted to light the desk.

He worked here hour after hour, hands in his hair. Lydia washed his hair a week later, and she found little scabs in his scalp, the crusty proof of his tension. Only then did she notice how he picked at himself when he studied, how he made his head bleed.

His flat was larger, so they spent the night there more often than at Lydia's place. Andy was so proud of the home he kept, she couldn't tell him how much she hated it; how the cleanliness, the order in which he kept it reminded her of her own life. It was the home of someone who was used to living alone, who lived an overly structured existence while waiting for someone to mess it up.

The dinner Andy prepared for Lydia, like the meals he ate each night alone, was scrupulously balanced but colorless, bland, a chop, a vegetable, a salad made on Sunday evening and stored in a plastic container, a little doled out every night for a week, or until the cucumbers became sour and watery. There was something meager and controlled that disturbed her. He asked for so little, yet he needed so much, this hard-working young man who got around town on a bicycle, and did calisthenics in the morning, who never smoked, never tasted anything stronger than wine and never felt the desire to do so. At times, the older woman, she felt it was her duty to corrupt him with drugs or kinky sex. She told herself his order was unhealthy and had to be cracked. But Andy had friends and a family, and as far as she could tell, there was nothing bizarre or pathological about his behavior. He was capable of being alone for long stretches of time, but he didn't enjoy it; he didn't thrive in the dimness as she had. He used the order to protect himself, waiting all the while to cook a meal for a friend, to care for someone, to be in love. He hated his life alone.

Andrew peeled the skin off an orange perfectly, without breaking the membrane. Lydia dug her nails in too far, and got an eyeful of juice. Lifting her hands to wipe her eyes, she saw her yellow fingertips, the deeper orange under her nails. She remembered her first night with Kramer, when her blackened nails had disturbed him.

He must have seen the glimmer of something sad in her eyes because he said, "Are you tired of lying around?"

"I don't know; are you?"

He put an unbroken segment of orange into his mouth and shook his head.

She kissed him, and his breath was sweet and orangy. Pulling away, she felt the acid sting her lips.

28

HE SUGGESTED the Finnish films at NFT. She brought him to Bermondsey because Bill Hatchett grew up in Bermondsey and told her almost all his friends and cousins had ended up in jail. They shared a jellied eel, and he hated it, she could tell. They went to Epping Forest on a cold afternoon, then to a series of historic houses Jill had suggested long ago. The furniture and paintings behind the velvet ropes were dead for Lydia. She had no sense of life being lived in the houses, meals eaten, dances danced, sex in canopied beds. Andy said you needed a sense of history to enjoy them. Lydia thought it was a love for aristocracy. Not that it mattered, she always had a good time when she was with him; on a borrowed bicycle through Regents Park, or following behind a group of American tourists on a Jack the Ripper tour. Walking through Whitechapel, Lydia remembered why, when she was growing up, she'd loved being with Rema. Silly as she was, Rema had been imaginative, she made every event an adventure. When they walked to school, dirty men followed their trail, cars tried to run them down, schoolmates whispered, lunatic eyes peered through curtains. Andy was like that, too.

They held hands in the street and stole kisses in the movies. Lydia couldn't help thinking how different it had been with Kramer, when all she had to do was accidentally brush against him; all he had to do was spy her naked ankle, and they'd be tumbling. From the start, she was both shier and more friendly with Andy. They shared a lot of worldly interests: biology, the movies, a love for exploring unknown parks and neighborhoods.

Though she considered herself an urban person, her love for the outdoors resurfaced with Andy (with Kramer it had been submerged), so that they hiked through acres of woods and bicycled through miles of city streets much as she'd done before she met Kramer.

At first she saw Andy on Friday nights. Later, when they began to spend so much time going places, they spent Friday night and all of Saturday together. It wasn't long before they were spending all of Saturday night together in order to start out early for Sunday's events.

At home alone, Lydia became increasingly edgy. Just because this wasn't hot tumbling love at first sight didn't mean she was incapable of falling for him, of growing to love him, then having to leave again, making another break (breaking in the process). Yet Lydia knew this: Either a relationship was stagnant, the boundaries determined from date one, or it progressed and intensified. From the start, she'd seen Carl twice a week, and had it not been for the gonorrhea incident, it could have gone on indefinitely like that. Twice a week: never learning more about him as time passed, never giving more than she'd given at the start. Maybe that was appropriate behavior with landlords and superintendents and storekeepers, but Lydia didn't want it anymore with lovers.

If Lydia was tired of the kind of relationship she'd had with Carl, it meant she wanted to be with a man she genuinely cared for. It would be natural when they began to spend more time together, revealing more to each other, growing more involved. . . .

At first she felt safe, protected by his youth, and when things began to speed up, she calmed herself by saying: He's just a child, no harm, really. By the time they reached the all-weekend-long-and-twice-during-the-week phase, she'd begun to think: Stop! Whoa! Hold your horses, Lydia, this isn't what you want. Seeing how nervous she was after one of her nights alone, Andy accused her of performing mysterious cancel-cancel incantations on herself. And he was right, of course. The good doctor-to-be told her he had the perfect cure for what ailed her: An increased dosage of Andrew Wickenden. Five times a week to start. . . .

One night, anticipating her solitude, Lydia sat down to a nice garlicky dinner, a book for her companion, when there was a knock on her door, a tenant announcing a phone call for her downstairs. Who could it be?

By the time Mr. Pomme Frite on the other end announced she'd been elected Flicker of the Month by the National Association for Lighter Repairers, she had no doubt. Andy a.k.a. Dr. Doalot and Harvey Glowworm, trying to fool her as her father had (*Rittle girl? Rittle girl?*). Could she pop down to Ball Street to have her photos snapped for the tubes? Ms. Flicker collects arthropods, hopes one day to have a toilet. Modeling's on her mind, too.

As soon as he finished his spiel, he said, "Hello, Andrew Wickenden here. What time do you want to get together?"

"How about eight," Lydia said. "Tomorrow."

"Oh." Hurt silence. Her refusals stung like an angry slap. She felt apologetic.

"I'm a mess, really."

"Is that what it is? You're never a mess. I'll see you in—"

"*Andy*—" sternly, wanting to skip details. She'd eaten a plate of garlic au gratin for dinner, her hair was greasy, and on the tip of her nose was an underground pimple, a red stoplight—disgusting. "Take my word for it, I'm revolting."

"Ah ah cancel-cancel, Lydia."

"*I am disgusting disgusting,*" she said, wanting to say it, reveling in it.

"Cancel-*fucking*-cancel, Lydia," he said, about as angry as he got.

Fifteen minutes later, bicycle carried under his arm, he arrived. She opened the door, and saw him in his newsboy cap, a shy smile on his face. Awfully presumptuous, she thought, vowing to be sour for at least ten minutes.

She watched the clock, her mouth thin with anger. Andy made an awful joke, a reference to Rita as Lady Cadaver. Lydia laughed, then remembering her resolve, she checked the time again. It had taken him less than five minutes to cheer her up.

Later in the evening, he said, "You don't have to go to work tomorrow, Lydia. You can be sick, you haven't missed a single day—you haven't missed fifteen minutes since you started."

"No," Lydia said.

"Trying to break Margaret's record, is that it?"

"I don't get paid when I stay home."

"Oh." Mouth pouty.

In the middle of the night, he shut off her alarm clock, hoping when she overslept she'd change her mind. But out of habit, Lydia woke at six, and when she found out what he'd done, she held her breath and slipped out of bed, deciding to sneak out of the flat and leave him stranded in Finsbury Park. Let him disguise himself as an Andrea and set out midday without being nabbed by Mr. Miskyll. It would serve him right.

But Andy was a light sleeper and woke before both her feet were on the ground. Arms extended, arms around her waist, he tried to pull her back down, wanting to make love.

He would pack sandwiches and meet her at Cage for lunch.

Tired from a day's work, she'd push the heavy factory door open and find Andy there again, asking if she'd go home with him. Yes, she knew she could bathe at his house as well, but she wanted to bathe at her own. She knew he had aerograms, she believed it was possible to run in his streets, she was not Greta Garbo, but she wanted to be alone.

Oh.

One Saturday morning, after making scrambled eggs while she lay naked in bed, playing Camille, practicing a gorgeous death, he came in with breakfast on a tray, and ended up putting it on the bureau, diving into the covers and saying, "Let's screw instead," in his matter-of-fact way.

Dreaming of angels in the snow, rainstorms, blue Caribbean water, she'd wake to find him kissing her back, under her arms. She'd feel his downy chest hair, hear a soft growl.

This controlled person had become so extravagant with his love he was driving her crazy.

"Here's what I'm doing," she told him Sunday. "I'm going running and then I'm going home to read and then I'm planning to get to bed early."

Lips downturned. "If that's the way you want it," he said.

That was the way the miserable spoilsport wanted it.

When she heard the cry, "Andrew for Lydia!" the following night, she knew something was amiss. No jokes? No disguises? No alias? She took the phone downstairs.

He said, "Listen . . . uh . . . could we meet for lunch tomorrow? I have to talk to you about something."

A draft blew through the unlatched door, chilling her. "What is it?" she asked, worried.

He . . . uh . . . wasn't at liberty to say.

The next day at work, Lydia thought: I deserved it, I have no one to blame but myself, it's all my own fault.

On the way to meet Andrew, she nearly ran over a bent old woman with matchstick legs, who was standing in the middle of the sidewalk, cooing. When Lydia turned back to apologize, she saw the veiled hat that had been fashionable in the thirties, and the feathered crowd that had gathered around her. Only the nodders and peckers understood the woman's language.

"What's wrong?" Andrew said, after kissing her.

She said, "Nothing," still expecting to get a sock in the jaw.

"Did I ever tell you my mother had been married four times?"

He had.

"Well, the fourth one just fell apart, and she's come to town for a few days. I don't know why yet, but I'm not going to be a go-between and harass my father for her."

"Which one was he?"

"Two *and* three—fourteen years the first time and two the second. Anyhow, she's pretty upset. *I'm* pretty upset. I mean, she needs someone and I can't turn her down, but number one, she's a nonstopper, did I tell you that? A nice lady, but an incredible mouth. I can't get any work done when she's around. I say, 'Mom, can you read a magazine, take a walk—something?' This morning, she finally did that—she took a walk. An hour later she brought a guest home for tea—a woman from downstairs."

"And number two?"

"You know."

"I don't." (She did.)

"I won't be able to see you until she's gone. At first I thought the three of us could at least have dinner again, but she's pretty miserable and she doesn't look too good. I don't think she'd be up for meeting friends. Strangers she'd bring home, but not friends."

Lydia asked what happened.

"I don't know, but I think this one left her. I didn't like him.

He was this gross, cigar-smoking businessman from Cleveland, of all places."

"Of all places? I thought you were born in Cleveland?"

"Cincinnati, Lyd. And as my mother says to out-of-staters who make the same mistake: Don't confuse culture with crass."

He walked her back to Cage, and in the dark stairway, kissed her good-bye.

Late in the afternoon, she had an eerie feeling that he was still standing in the darkness downstairs, frowning, silent, unhappy. She was so convinced of this, she excused herself from her table, and went to check. "Andrew?" she called softly, expecting a reply.

He wasn't there, but his sadness lingered, tempering her relief.

With Andrew's mother in town, Lydia was alone again. But secure in the knowledge that someone out there cared for her, she was perfectly happy alone. Though she wanted to love and be loved, to have contact with the public world, it was equally important she have time alone. Her need for space would never change; she saw no reason why it should.

There were also practical reasons why her separation from Andy was good. When she and Andy used to meet for lunch, she found on returning to Cage that something at her place was missing, something was always wrong. Margaret could be persuaded to explain. *Diane* was etched on the side of the stapler, that's why it was exchanged for this rusted one that ate staples. The L on her staple remover stood for Leatrice not Lydia, so naturally its rightful owner took it back. Her sweater was on the floor presumably because the hanger belonged to someone else. Why not? Her jeweler's loupe, In box, tape dispenser and packing number, according to Rita, were Rita's and not Lydia's. Lydia learned to make do with the Out and not the In box, and found that the end of a metal nail file worked fine to get staples out of packages. It was a challenge finding new tools to replace the old stolen ones, new methods to do the chores. Her one tactical error, a setback in gaining admission to the Cage Ladies Club, was her handling of the packing number affair in late February. The slips with her number had disappeared, and genuinely puzzled she went into the repair room to tell Bill Hatchett. She found him peeping out of the folds of his white coat, clipboard under his arm. "Aren't we putting packing numbers in anymore?" she asked.

"No, that is, we are," he said, straightening to his official posture. "No package is allowed to leave Cage without a packing number. You didn't forget you're number seven, did you? That's like forgetting your own name, my girl."

"Maybe I've run out?"

Bill marched into the checking room, Lydia in tow. The last echoes of whispered conversation died in the air. He stopped at Rita's seat, lit a cigarette, and waited. She was a fierce-looking woman, a mane of blond hair three inches black at the roots, skin like pumice. Her eyes were pale green and unnaturally light. Lady Cadaver indeed. Rising for the occasion: "What is it, *Mr.* Hatchett?"

"Rita, have you nicked Lydia's seven?"

"That's exactly what I've done, *Mr.* Hatchett."

"Rita, you've been number ten since the twentieth of November, two years ago."

She stepped an inch closer, and growled, baring rotten teeth. An old circus lion. "Your chart don't mean fuck-all to me, *Mr.* Hatchett."

"Look, I mean I don't care what number I have," Lydia said.

"I get seven or I quit." Finger jabbed in her own chest like a knife. "Got that, sister?"

Rita circled Bill, drawing closer, ready to lock arms in combat. Bill, the ever-cool captain as the ship hits an iceberg, said personally he thought ten was one of your better numbers.

"Seven, *Mr.* Hatchett, is the number I get. It's Derek's birthday, seventh day of the seventh month and I get it or you know—"

"Yes, yes, where I can stick the bloody job."

A tactical error, yes, but Lydia couldn't very well say, Look, I didn't mean to squeal. Her situation remained stable at Cage. In the morning she gave a cheerful hello, then began a little one-sided conversation, drawing on the previous day's gossip. "How's James today, Margaret, feeling any better? Send him my best, won't you? Morning, Diane, morning, Mary Three." Lydia took her seat. The work was boring, her days long with the tedium, but she didn't dread waking, dressing for the day, waiting with the others for the exact moment, eight-thirty and zero seconds, when Bill Hatchett burst through the doors, threatening to dock anyone who wasn't "at it." She was cheerful and learned after a while that her co-workers were reluctant to speak to her only when the bosses, Rita and Diane, were around. As soon as they stepped away, little kindnesses were bestowed upon her. Leatrice winked whenever backs were turned, and of the Marys, Red-haired Mary (Mary Bridie to the girls) and Mary Elizabeth were civil. Just Mary, called Mary Three by Lydia (the nickname stuck, though no one remembered the origin), smuggled in three tiny Seckel pears for her. Now that Andy had stopped coming around, Margaret ate lunch with her. Margaret was the most intense person Lydia had ever met; she groomed herself as vio-lently as she flicked, pulling the brush through her hair with rapid strokes that made loud crackles, filing her nails with a rapid scritch-scritch that drove Rita wild. After a particularly unpleas-ant episode with Rita, Margaret confided to Lydia that she didn't care how nasty Rita was. Next year or the year after Margaret was leaving Cage; she was going back to Dublin to marry her James. Lydia imagined Margaret with three babies in three years, four babies in four years, six in six, and decided it was a better fate than six years in a lighter repair factory.

She worked hard, and the proof of her labor was seen in her bankbook and in the blisters, followed by callouses, running from the tip to the base of each thumb, from flicking hour after hour. She knew the top ten tunes in England (five were American imports) and though disturbed sometimes when an hour passed and all that went through her mind was the refrain of a popular song, Lydia felt strengthened. When she ran she did multiplica-tion problems, *huh huh, 40 X 4 huh huh 160 huh huh 160—9 huh huh 9 X 4 huh huh 35 huh, no, 36 huh huh* ... trying to figure out how much money she'd spent the past week, how much she expected to spend for the upcoming week, how much earned, how much saved, the price of plane tickets, when she'd be home. Always poor at arithmetic, she rarely solved the problems. But she bud-geted herself carefully. Her father would have been proud, but then again, he was a little weird about money. He'd spend it on concrete things, gifts for Lydia, a house, a pool, but when it came to dining out or taking vacations, he was impossible. Rose had had a closetful of travel brochures and a headful of dreams, but other than the trip to Grand Canyon with the Wolfes, they never went away.

Food, heat, rent. Like Kramer, she counted movies as a necessity. "I had my greatest feelings of well-being when I was working at the lab," she told Andy. Here at her happiest, there was a hole. What kept her going was the expectation of getting back to the lab, going home. So much time had been lost already. Major breakthroughs occurred weekly. Would she go home and be outdated, her knowledge obsolete? "Leatrice, you look great today, I like your hair. Mary Elizabeth, did you find your wallet? Anyone want coffee while I'm up?"

A Mr. Coitus on the wire for worker number ten.

A Mr. *Who*? Lydia rushed to the phone.

"Andrew Wickenden here."

"No kidding," said Lydia.

"Listen, sorry to bother you, but I can never catch you home. Have you been seeing someone else? Tell me, is that true?"

"False, so stop worrying."

"Promise me the weekend," Andy said. "I think the old bird will be gone by then."

Lydia promised.

When the workday was over, she hurried home, changed into her running clothes, ran around the park, came home, sponged herself clean, packed a sandwich and fruit and walked to the library to scour through *Nature, Science,* and whatever entomological journals they carried. She read every article germane to her own work, starting six months back, taking notes on important studies, copying whole abstracts. Too many months had been lost, and in biology, time was crucial. She thought of the sign tacked over Bill Hatchett's desk: LOST TIME IS NEVER FOUND, and deciding to disprove that, rearranged her day and gained more hours. Her smart hours had to be shifted to night. It was crucial she be alert from 7:00 to 10:00 P.M., not in the morning when she was flicking wheels and calling, "Morning, Mary Bridie, hello Rita!" She went to bed later at night, and caught up on sleep during lunchtime. Like Thomas Edison, she learned to refresh herself on ten-minute catnaps, taken legally on her break. After work, she was bleary-eyed and dragging her feet, and the hardest chore was getting herself dressed to go running. She knew, though, that after she ran, she was recharged and ready for long hours at the library.

One night before closing time in the library, she found B. Wigglesworth's pioneering work, in which he reported locating the source of juvenile hormones in insects. In 1936, when his countrymen were living on government soup, and Hitler made anti-Semitism law, Dr. Wigglesworth (oblivious of political chaos and impending war? despite complaints from family and friends?) after months in the laboratory, located the minuscule glands near the insect's brain. Wigglesworth, what a name. Destined to be an entomologist, just as her years under the steps had destined her.

Dr. Shorey had been publishing a lot while she was gone. There was a review of his new book on pheromones and lobsters. Kramer thought it was a joke, her silly self-deprecating humor, but they'd find evidence of pheromones in people, too.

The librarian was clearing her throat five feet behind Lydia. It was fifteen minutes past closing time, and she'd have to return the journals. She packed up her books and papers and walked slowly out of the building, thinking of New York and Kramer. The chemistry was right, the pheromones. He trailed her, knocked her over. But it was more than pheromones. They loved each other's dreams. Back in her own neighborhood, she thought of her father's cheapness, and decided it was crazy not to stop and warm herself with a cup of coffee and a bowl of soup. She wanted noise and laughter. The pubs were closed, but in the Greek café nearby, someone was always singing or crying. The dreams that separated Kramer and Lydia were the same ones that cemented their relationship. Master plans, great ambition, the desire to conquer the world at any cost. She loved him for that. "Risk," she said the first night. She'd taken the risk and lost.

29

Wʜᴇɴ sᴘʀɪɴɢ arrived, Lydia began to mark the time not in days and weeks, but by letters or lack of letters. March, by this standard, was a cool and sparse month, without so much as Rose's opus, a bimonthly journal which featured the adventures of Harold and Rose, the remarkable recovery of Norma (the abandoned wife) Wolfe, as well as personal opinions, political commentary, and a fresh supply of maxims for Lydia to apply in appropriate situations in London. Free in the 2/12 edition was "God gave you brains, use them," which alluded to something Jill had written about Cage, hoping Rose would "speak to" Lydia about the matter; a staggering voyage, considering that Jill and Lydia lived about three miles apart. On 2/26 came "Cheap is cheap," a reply to Lydia's complaint about her inexpensive winter jacket that ripped under the arms.

By mid-March, the only word Lydia had received from the States was a postcard from Rema, announcing her pregnancy.

"My childhood friend, six months gone!" Lydia said to Andy. "If I make it home by June, I'll be just in time for the birth."

"Don't be a jerk, Lydia. They're not going to let you in the delivery room."

"Aw, don't grump at me," she said, kissing him.

He'd told her his mother's extended stay had made him fall behind on his studies; that the pressure from school was what made him irritable. But Lydia began to wonder if it was really because she'd mentioned her departure. He needed peace of mind in order to catch up with his work. Maybe this was the time to make the final split, before they became inextricably bound, before their bickering wiped out the memory of good times. And they had been bickering. Lydia, her mind half on her departure, had hidden out in the library; she'd upped her mileage to six or eight. But that made her feel worse; not only was she a coward, but she was making her pleasures, work and running, synonymous with escape again. No good. She'd have to be a grown-up and discuss this with him, tell him the way she felt.

One Saturday Andy borrowed a soft plaid blanket and a wicker hamper from his father, and while Lydia soaked in his private tub, he packed a special picnic lunch.

They were off to Richmond. Leaving the house, his mood was light. He took her arm, and rested his hand on hers, pretending to be a real country gentleman. The sun, he said, brought out the shine in her hair, and could they stop for a second so he could personally feel where she'd put on those five wonderful pounds? "In my head," Lydia said, prompting him to drop the hamper and give her a skull massage. If he were to assess character traits he wouldn't read palms or go by the shape of the skull. It was definitely hair. His hair was kind of curly, but very tame, domesticated. Hers was thick and wild, earthier, less cultured. He kissed her, and she was happy being loved.

They reached the park, and when they found a fairly dry patch of grass, they set up camp. Andy was struggling with a rotten cork, quite happy babbling to himself, pretending he was a French wine steward, when suddenly Lydia dropped flat on her stomach, as if there were an air attack above. She took off her glasses, and put her nose to the dirt. Andy abandoned his wine and his Monsieur Henri imitation and blew into a paper bag, hoping the explosion would affect Lydia in some way. It didn't. She had coaxed a trail of ants onto the earpiece of her glasses, by this time, and was saying, "Andy, look!," like her father, forever summoning her to the window to look at birds. Rose may have loved him when he was a fiery youth, but only Lydia looked at the cardinals and tits in the yard. "Look closely now, see how she touches the ground? Just slightly, enough to leave a scent spot. Lots of ants leave lots of spots and lots of spots leave a trail the whole colony can follow for food and directions. Pheromones—fantastic."

"Ants," Andy said, standing up. "Shit, where?"

Lydia looked up and saw him standing with his arms crossed, looking so unhappy. She said, "Come on, let's find somewhere else to sit." She thought of Dr. Gray telling the Junior Entomology Club (she'd joined earlier that day) that there were about thirteen million insects in an acre of "good English meadow."

He was more comfortable in the second place. They ate lunch and finished the wine, and when the wind began to blow, they wrapped the edges of the blanket around their bodies to form a cocoon.

She was feeling warm and contented, a little drowsy from the wine when he said, "How come you've been avoiding me?"

"Because I'm going away, I guess."

"So you keep reminding me. What I want to know is why you can't be here while you're here?"

Lydia said she was sorry if she pulled away; it wasn't because she didn't like him, but because she did.

"Have I told you you're the most romantic person I ever met?"

"Me? Is that a joke?"

"All I know is you're the only one I know who still believes in forever. You're so romantic you probably don't even know this, but the rest of us think six months and auf wiedersehen passion. Don't you realize that the life-span of devotion, unless it's pathological, is five years? Haven't you ever heard of the seven-year itch?"

"Sure, Billy Wilder."

"Go ahead, change the subject."

Lydia untucked his shirt and sweater, and put an icy hand on his chest. He begged for mercy. He swore he wouldn't call her romantic ever again. She stopped to think, though: Did she believe in the impossible? Yes. Though she never knew a case of forever-love, did she believe in it? Yes. Maybe it was another dream she held on to; the maximum, love's grand prize, a-million-to-one odds. "I believe," she said.

"That's sweet."

"And you—how can you be a cynic at your age? Watch out, buddy. If you've stopped believing at twenty-three, you'll be in big trouble at forty."

"That's easy for you to say. You were born and raised in one house and lived for what—twenty years with the same parents? One would tend to believe in forever under those circumstances."

"My mother *was* getting it on with Uncle Harold."

"Proof that forever is an illusion."

"No," said Lydia, upset now. "Difficult but not impossible."

"Right," he said sarcastically.

"I don't understand it—you of all people, the most possessive man I've ever met. Why do you cling so much if it's only for a short while?"

"Maybe that's why I do. I never said it would be easy when you left. My God, it took me a month to get over Judith Leslie."

A *month*? Lydia thought.

"Look," said Andy. "Suppose I moved to New York."

"And then?"

"Just suppose for the sake of argument. Would you live with me?"

"I don't know, I hadn't thought about it."

"Okay. Then suppose again for the sake of argument I didn't move back to New York, but I saw you over Christmas vacations and for summers. Suppose we wrote mad, impassioned letters and spent hundreds on phone calls. Could you keep loving me?"

"I guess I'm more cynical than you think," Lydia said, "but those things don't usually work out."

"I know," he said, and then was very quiet.

The sun had hidden behind a cloud, and cold air blew through their human cocoon, chilling her through the layers.

They cleaned up the area, stopping to kiss or hold each other. Then they walked to the train hand in hand.

Andy rested his head on her shoulder and slept for the long ride back to her flat. Lydia thought about permanence and devotion. Was it naïve to want to grow old beside someone, to live for years with the same man, in a relationship that constantly deepened? Or was that the wrong kind of illusion to keep, one that would, when it shattered, cause her terrible pain? She thought about Harold and Rose and her father.

As Uncle Harold, he was married to Norma, but it was obvious she was too busy hating herself to be interested in him. He had his work, his children; in his spare time he became a genius of home improvements, adding rooms as Norma added pounds: a back porch, a patio, a double garage; the driveway resurfaced and widened, the backyard leveled, the kitchen made totally electric

Maybe one day Harold decides to ask Rose a question about acoustical tile. As he approaches her house, she is just getting out of her station wagon. He hurries up the driveway and is close behind when she slips on a patch of oil, able to catch her in his arms and prevent her from falling. Worrying she'll misconstrue his aid, he lets go quickly. She turns around. He holds out his arms in a gesture asking forgiveness. She falls into them. Their fate is sealed.

Maybe not.

Maybe it is one of the innumerable evenings the Wolfes and her parents go out for prime ribs and end up at the Wolfes for coffee and Norma has a gall bladder attack and goes upstairs to lie down. Lydia's father puts his head against a couch cushion and says, "I just want to rest my eyes." A second later, he is snoring. Rose goes outside for some fresh air, disheartened by the fate of the evening.

Harold follows Rose, thinking it's a perfect chance to get her opinion on Melissa, who's become something of a discipline problem at school. He finds her on the back porch, shivering. Stepping behind, he undoes the buttons of his golf sweater (a birthday present from Maurice and Rose) and says, "Here, put this over your shoulders."

She turns, intending to kiss the cheek of this dear friend. Unthinking, he searches out her lips. She responds, passionately. The reserve breaks.

"I've adored you for ten years," Harold says, though until this moment he hasn't really known it.

The kiss has released the same feelings in her. "Oh, Harold, you always seemed so aloof."

They cling. He says he must have known somewhere inside if he touched her this would happen. And then there's Maurice, who he genuinely likes, though frankly ... he always thought she could do better.

And then there's Norma, who Rose pities. "I always wondered if you had a *real* life together," she says, delicately suggesting sex again.

They kiss.

Most likely it was neither of those ways. What made a difference wasn't how they got together, but that Lydia expected her mother to live out the rest of her days in memory of her father.

So what if they were tight before her father died? Her mother's loyalty was frightening. Hearing her say, "I did it for you, I was married to a man I detested for your sake," was horrible. Hearing her mother say she loved Harold was not. Lydia, lover of grand dreams, would have less respect for her mother if she lived a half-dead life, having sublimated all desires, not going after what she wanted, ending up in old age only to say: My life was nothing.

Had Norma known about Harold and Rose? Had her father? Lydia suspected her father, at least, hadn't been attentive enough to see Rose's attention waning, her interest gone. Then he died, and Norma was officially abandoned. Rose had related the uplifting tale of Normanure when Lydia was in Los Angeles, continuing it by mail while Lydia was in London. She had gained fifty-three pounds and had a heart attack shortly after Harold left. Her doctor told her she'd die if she didn't lose weight, incipient diabetes being the least of her problems. "Wire me shut!" she reportedly hollered from the hospital bed, using up all her breath for the effort. They didn't wire her shut. Instead, Harold bought her a summer at Sunnydale Farms. "The milk farm," her kids called it. "Guilt money," Norma sniffed. She stayed for months. She stayed far beyond the time it took her to lose not only the fifty-three pounds, but fifty more. When the kids finally demanded she come home, she introduced them to Marvin Blumberg, the farm's director. Marvin, a former three-fifty-pounder, five years ago near death due to obesity, was a divorced man, attractive, "though not my type," said Rose.

In Rose's latest letter, Lydia learned that Norma had become the West-Coast recruiter for Sunnydale Farms. She gave slide-illustrated lectures from Vancouver to San Diego, including her own "before" pictures. Norma at her grossest, snapped by Rose and Harold (she forgave them) and Maurice (may he rest in peace). She wasn't bitter anymore.

Melissa was bitter. Melissa would not visit her mother if she married Marvin Blumberg. As of the letter dated 2/26 Norma was going to marry Marvin Blumberg.

When Lydia got the letter relaying the news about Melissa, she thought: Melissa, you selfish pig, what difference does it make? She was glad no one was there to monitor her thoughts, because she knew that she had also been like Melissa: the Forbidder. And at her worst, spiritually in Norma's league, too self-absorbed to give. Lydia imagined Norma in the hospital, without a husband, critically ill. "I have no choice," she may have said, "I might as well forge on."

It was late when they got back to Finsbury Park, and Andy impatiently started up the stairs while Lydia stopped to rifle through the mail on the hall table. A woman said, "You silly thing" to someone on the other end of the line. Okay, so I am a foolish dreamer, Lydia thought, bypassing for a moment the one letter not addressed in a neat vertical English pen. "For me!" she said, ripping the envelope apart. "I told you!"

She skimmed the first page, and when, by the second, she caught the meaning, she began to cry. The woman on the hall phone said, "Shush, please—" but she couldn't stop. Andy had raced down the flight, and was on his toes behind her, trying to read the words. "Tell me," he said. She tried to say it was fine, she had no reason to be crying. It was a letter from Dr. Cantoni, a cheerful letter, much time spent apologizing for his delay. He hoped she was enjoying London. Personally, he found the change highly salutary. Work was going well, and the skiing was fantastic. His kids thought Boulder was a great place to live. Next sabbatical he'd take in Switzerland. In the meantime, she shouldn't worry so much about her leave of absence. True, time was crucial and developments were frequently being made. But why not think instead that when she returned to New York she'd benefit from others' work and gain new perspective on her own?

Lydia stopped sniffling by the time they reached her flat, but Andy was somber. She tried to explain her tears, but he wasn't cheering up. They went to sleep early.

Sometime toward morning, when the room had just begun to fill with a curious pink-gray light, Lydia woke, aware of a change, a hollow spot in the mattress. She got out of bed to look for Andrew, her bare feet sticky against the cold linoleum. She found him in the sitting room, bent over a book. His hands were in his hair, and he was tearing at his scalp.

She was right after all, he said. They ought to end it now. She believed in forever love, but not, it seemed, with him. He was cynical and saw only how finite love was, yet would have followed her anywhere if she'd loved him enough. She didn't. He guessed he wanted a woman who was totally devoted, who made him the most important thing in her life. That was the impossible situation, not the geography.

He remained at the table; she sat in a small chair by the gas. Neither spoke. The weight of her sadness made her feel thick-limbed and heavy, unable to move. She heard the alarm go off in the bedroom, and wanted to hold him once before she dressed for work. When she approached, he turned away.

30

SHE MISSED his phone calls, his visits at lunch, the quiet evenings when he was beside her, his enthusiasm. Fifty times she planned to phone him, but only once did she go through with it, and she was sorry afterward she had. They were silent; there wasn't really anything to say. Lydia was comforted when she remembered Andy saying he got over his last lost love in a month. That meant at any moment now he would be free of her.

Without Andy to distract her work was intolerable. The rhythms were no longer soothing but monotonous. She felt trapped by the closeness of the workers on either side, by the stale smoky air, her own clothing, her rotten boots. She wanted to go home, and her real home, she felt, was New York.

One Thursday Lydia took off her boots because the ragged edges of the linings were scratching her toes, biting into them, causing each toe to push against the next one: warfare in confined quarters. She thought of working one-handed or working with her breath held as she inspected every second lighter (good practice if she ever took up diving). She thought of working with her cheek against the table, or singing as she worked, light opera only. She thought of the fifth toe on each of Kramer's feet, chubby and nailless, like dog toes that didn't quite sit with the others. She thought of Zeyde, who wore long pants and shoes on the beach, and whose toes she most likely never saw. Tired of thinking, she took out Dr. Cantoni's letter and reread it as she'd done at least once a day for the past month.

"Something bloody awful stinks in here," said Rita.

Ignoring her, Lydia padded across the cold floor in her socks, and got the orange out of her bag in the locker. She split the peel the way Andy had taught her. The fragrance pervaded the room. Diane lumbered over and stood behind Lydia, wheezing on the back of her neck, pointing. "Coming into work like she's the bloody queen, then sitting eating her meal while we work our bloody asses off. I wonder what our Mr. Hatchett would say."

Lydia ate the sections slowly, licked her fingers, and since Diane was still behind her, turned and belched. Thank you, Kramer, for still another gift. Groans throughout the room as if this were the sickest ward in the hospital. Lydia smiled. "Sorry, Margaret," she said.

The radio was switched on and Diane stood to sing "Poor Georgie" with Rod Stewart. But the heckling started again with the next song. Lydia was tired and wanted only to be left alone this morning, so she found her book and made her way to the toilet for some peace.

The natives were quiet when she returned. Managing to get caught up in the one-handed breathless rhythm she'd established at last, she worked well until the bell reminded her she was hungry. Having overslept, Lydia had not only forfeited breakfast, but hadn't had the time to pack lunch either. Using her toes, Lydia explored under the table until she captured a boot. She leaned over to lift it, and the second one came along, too. The laces had been tied together. Cute, Lydia thought. Terrifically mature. She put them on the table and examined the laces with her loupe. It wasn't just one knot, it was a line of them, a whole tangle of tightly pulled knots. Her stomach was growling, complaining relentlessly.

Lydia set out to pick at the knots. She pretended not to notice, but the workers had migrated from the coffee machine and were swarming around the table now. Diane was so close, Lydia could feel the heat her body gave off. The knots were so tight, before she could loosen the first one, both her thumbnails ripped. The crowd buzzed. If she put her head on the table, would they all go away? Was it possible if she closed her eyes, in a few minutes the knots would miraculously untwist? No. Instead, she would walk out of here and never come back. But she couldn't do that because her boots were laced together. Lydia imagined herself barefoot on the train, and felt so pathetic, she came close to crying. Rita let out a coarse and joyful laugh just then, and Lydia forgot her tears and thought: I'll kill her. I'll knock her teeth down her throat. She grabbed hold of her boots by the laces and stood up. Now what? She'd never in her life hit anyone; not her mother or sister, not at the height of anger. She was an adult, a reasoning, reasonable person. Had she ever balled up her fist before? Where did the thumb go, outside or inside the other fingers? Rita walked over, cocked her head, and cackled, "Got a problem, little one?"

Lydia said, "I strongly advise you to get these knots out of my laces."

"She strongly advises me," said Rita, making Lydia aware of how ridiculous she sounded, how formal.

She was a grown-up. She would handle this rationally. "Okay, it was an adorable joke, I laughed myself silly. *Now* will you get them out?"

"Oh adorable, adorable," trilled Big Diane, coming closer.

"Look," said Lydia, like a mother who's lost patience.

They went big-eyed. They looked.

"What is this, monkey-see, monkey-do? Get—"

"Get—"

"Get—"

"These knots—"

"These knots—"

"These knots—"

She clicked her tongue; they clicked their tongues. "*Out!*" she roared. "*Out!*" they roared in return. She held one boot and swung the other until with a thump it hit Rita's shoulder, with a second thump her back. Suddenly she was David, armed against the giants with a slingshot; Daniel Boone, wrassling with a bear; Sheena, Queen of the Jungle as she whipped the boot around and heard it thump. She turned, expecting, hoping she'd have the whole army to fight. Diane? Leatrice? Anyone? Who cared. Lydia, big and menacing, swung the boots and waited. The women were motionless until Rita remembered she'd been hit and let out a high-pitched sea gull's cry. The crowd hurried forward to see if she was bleeding.

Lydia swung her boots, aiming the right toe at Diane's back. "Let's go, monkey-do, get the knots out."

"I had nothing to do with this," Big Di whimpered.

"I don't care, get them out. I'm starving. If this is the way to handle things around here, fine, I understand. You get one minute, Diane, not a second more."

"But I didn't—"

"Fifty-two, fifty-one, fifty—"

Diane shook her head. The flesh trembled, a current running beneath her skin. Forty-nine, forty-eight. They weren't even friends, Rita and she, Diane whined. Mouth open, she wheezed for sympathy.

"Forty," said Lydia. "Thirty-nine."

Mary Elizabeth put her hand on Lydia's shoulder and said, "Leave her alone, she's not a well woman. I'll get you new laces if that's what you want."

"It's not the laces." Lydia bit her cheeks to stop the excuses from rolling out; her nails were soft, her eyes were bad, she'd missed breakfast, she was in a grouchy mood. Roar, don't whimper, she thought, saying, "I'm hungry. Someone get these untied."

"I'll get you lunch, I'm going out as it is."

"A sandwich," said Lydia. "Any kind" was in the wrong spirit. "Cheese with mustard. A slice—no, two slices of raw onion."

"Raw onion, right," said Mary Elizabeth.

Mary Three tiptoed over. "So awfully glad you did that," she said, fingers reaching out to touch, to feel the flesh of the victor. "Awfully glad, Lydia. Awfully glad."

31

THE REWARD was continued peace at Cage, though Lydia was unable to shake the deep-seated feeling that nice girls didn't have to fight with their hands, especially nice girls who were blessed, as she was, with the ability to reason. She decided at last that the event had occurred simply because it was a Thursday, and in the Lydian scheme of things, bizarre things always happened on Thursdays.

Most scientists, Lydia knew, had a streak of the irrational somewhere within their logical minds. Some held tightly to things their mothers told them (Chinese skin street cats and serve them as pork; a midnight snack will give you nightmares; don't cross your eyes, they'll stay that way). One biologist told Lydia he caught the flu because he'd slept in cold bed sheets. Another man, an eminent biophysicist, wouldn't go into a partition of a revolving door unless his wife squeezed in behind him. He said it was bad luck for them to be separated. Lydia laughed when she heard these things. She found it hard to believe that trained minds could harbor such medieval thoughts, though she, of course, was inordinately fond of four-leaf clovers and firmly believed in the law of Thursdays. Evidence could never prove or disprove anyone's deeply loved superstition, but exactly a week after the shoe fight, Lydia fell to her knees while she was running in the park. Just dropped to her knees for no earthly reason. Boom.

On the third Thursday, Mr. Miskyll came for the rent ten minutes early, and Lydia, just back from the park and concerned about the continuing pain in her knees from the Thursday before, was less attentive than usual. While he was muttering on about the bloody Rhodesians, the bloody nasty rain after all this time, his missus with a bloody awful toothache, and some bloody cripple who'd come asking for a Lydia with a different name, her eye strayed toward the windowsill, where she kept her milk and eggs. Cheese omelette? Scrambled eggs and onions? She paid Mr. Miskyll when he'd quieted down, and after putting a mark in the rent book, he left. Locking the door behind him, she said, "Feed me, Lydia," and got the eggs. That afternoon—another strange Thursday revelation—Margaret had said she didn't drink coffee because it was too bitter and though some said milk dulled the bitterness, milk was awful stuff that dribbled from a cow's underside. "And eggs?" Lydia had asked (cracking one now). "They come from a chicken's bottom and chickens are the filthiest animals." Had Lydia ever seen a chicken? Did she know where eggs came from? "They're not from a factory, you know. Those eggs come straight from the bottoms of those filthy birds." Margaret curled her lip up to her nose, making a wizened toothless look. Lydia was sure Margaret had never seen one of those disagreeable faces in the mirror.

Omelette au fromage, for you, mademoiselle. Perfect! In deference to Margaret, no more eggs hard-boiled for lunch. Jacob didn't like eggs either. Lydia saw him sitting at the dining-room table in Hampstead, mashing a banana onto a slice of toast. When she visualized him, the image was an old one, and his arm, something she hadn't thought about in months, shocked her. She saw Jacob across the living room that first day when she'd been afraid to look and afraid to avert her eyes. Then she heard Mr. Miskyll say, "Some bloody cripple came asking for a Lydia with a different last name."

She ran down the stairs and knocked on Mr. Miskyll's door. When no one answered, she thumped on it, hammered it, kicked, and called loudly for him.

"Yes?" One eye of the missus appeared through the crack in the door, iris blue, but not really white where it should have been.

"Can I see Mr. Miskyll, please?"

The missus closed the door and called, "You're busy, aren't you, Dad?"

The eye was back. "Come tomorrow, miss."

"It's an emergency!" Lydia put her shoulder to the door, and found herself beside Mrs. Miskyll a second later. The two women exchanged long looks, each so curious about the other, neither noticed she was being closely regarded. Lydia was still wearing her sweats. Mrs. Miskyll had on a blue cotton dress, double-breasted like a uniform. Pink rollers neatly quartered her scalp, and her little mouth was an angry, glistening red. Remembering her mission, Lydia continued toward the sitting room, where Mr. Miskyll was watching a tiny screen and sipping tea out of a dainty cup, the saucer in the palm of one hand.

"Who was it who came to see me, Mr. Miskyll?" she asked.

Without turning from the screen, he said, "How am I supposed to know? Do I look like a bloody gypsy?"

"What did he look like?"

"A cripple, I told you that. Now what are you doing here? My missus told you I was busy. She told you that, didn't she? I heard her myself, so get out now, go on." He rested the cup on his knee and made shooing motions with both hands, as if Lydia were a swarm of locusts, flying close to his face.

"Could you give it to me again, Mr. Miskyll? Was it a big person or a small person? What did he say?"

"Like I told you, he came asking for a girl named Lydia. I says, And what's the last name, and he says something I never heard in my life, a different name than the one you gave us. So I says to him, well we got a Lydia, but not the one you're after so get on now, get on." He made more shooing motions. "Cheeky little bastard. Wouldn't take no for an answer."

"His mum probably spoiled him on account of his being a cripple and like I says to Dad here, if we had a cripple for a child, we'd bring him up with the others and not spoil him on account of his being a cripple. If that's God's way, that's God's way and you make the best of it." This from Mrs. Miskyll, who couldn't seem to get enough of Lydia, and was still engaged in watching her closely.

"He's not a cripple," Lydia said softly.

"Maybe that's the way they come from New York City, all filthy with the sleeves of their jackets cut off."

"Did he say where he was going?"

"I don't believe Dad asked. Why should he? What business is it of Dad's where the little boy goes off to. It's not as if it's his little boy."

"Can you tell me when the boy was asking for me? I mean, can you do that, please?"

"Let's see now, Sheila was home from school, it couldn't have been dark. She comes running and running, 'Oh Mum, the most horrid thing—' she's a sensitive one, our Sheila. And I says, what is it, Sheila?"

Mr. Miskyll's head swiveled sharply. "Where is she now," he said. "Where is our Sheila, Mum?"

"Good-bye," Lydia said. With her running shoes on, it took her less than a minute to reach the tube station. She ran through the tunnel, and when she reached the train platform, she had no trouble spotting, among the commuters, the back of a black-jacketed man, and the hands she wanted encircling the man's back, black enamel on nails so long they curved inward.

She leaned over the gate and hollered, "Sheila Miskyll, Sheila Miskyll!" until the hands let go of the leather, and the girl stalked over. Her hair was mustard-colored like her father's house, and she wore a tiny fake-fur jacket with a nipped-in waist, higher than her own. Her shoes had thick soles, four-inch heels, and cutouts, each revealing one black-nailed toe. Close behind stood her boyfriend, lean and two heads taller. It was getting dark, and Lydia wanted to look for Jacob, but she needed someone to wait outside the house in case he tried there again.

"And what do I tell my dad when he comes and says, Why are *you* sitting on the steps like a fat pigeon. He says that to me, you know. He's a nasty thing, not that Davey thinks I'm fat, do you, Dave?" Sheila whirled and flung her jacket open. She was as round and big-bosomed as a pigeon.

"Your dad won't bother you if you tell him you're waiting for my nephew," Lydia said. "He was the one who told me about Jacob in the first place."

A train pulled in and the station was filled with clatter and smoke. People climbed off the train, put their tickets in the machines, mounted the stairs wearily. Manners wouldn't help in this situation, and Lydia was in a rush. Crude as it might sound, she was ready to say: Listen, kid, I've seen you with your walking-stick boyfriend a hundred times and been mum about it. Now *you* do *me* a favor.

Sheila must have been thinking along the same lines. Before a word was spoken, she stamped a fat shoe on the ground, and was up the stairs before Lydia.

Huh huh huh. She didn't sing out for him or call his name because he'd be frightened by the echo, the disembodied voice calling Jacob! up and down streets, over row after row of chimneys. Was he dressed warmly enough? Was he frightened? She ran around the perimeter of the park, thinking of reasons he might run away. Jill had said Jacob had become quite attached to a little Indian boy from a very fine family. School was going splendidly. The lake looked frozen. "Just me," Lydia said, because it was and it frightened her. Hearing a voice was comforting.

The second time around the park, she caught the scent of food; something cooking, deep-fried, maybe. She ran farther. Out of the dusk appeared a white truck, like the ones that trailed through the streets back home, ringing bells and selling ice cream. The man inside the truck was handing out newspaper parcels to an orderly lineup of men. Lydia looked for a small figure among them but found none. Although she was worried, her stomach was empty, and the fish and chips smelled good.

No one stirred in the lineup, there was no buzz or hum, but she heard a voice, quite distinctly saying, "Auntie!" She turned. The men were all silent and serious as if this were a breadline and each was ashamed. "Here I am!" the voice said. She looked beyond the wagon, into the street, afraid she'd never find him, or worse, that she was imagining the whole thing. But again: "Here, Auntie!" Standing behind her was a figure, jumping, waving, shouting, "Auntie!"

Lydia turned and in a second had Jacob in her arms. He squirmed, complaining, but she hugged him tighter. He smelled of mud and fish. Greasy lips brushed across her neck, and in a boastful voice, "I knew you'd come, Auntie. I saved some chips for you." Then pulling away, eyeing Lydia's long johns and gym shorts. "Who dressed *you?*"

Lydia was silly from nervousness and kept laughing. "Were you at the flat again? Did you talk to a girl on the steps of my house?"

"Big fat witch, sitting on the steps?"

"Did you?"

"She called me Jackie. Your auntie's going to beat hell out of you, Jackie, she says."

The chip was cold and slick with oil, but tasted delicious anyhow. "Did you laugh?"

"Right in her face, Auntie. She's up looking for you in the park, Jackie, and she's going to beat hell out of you."

"You didn't believe her, did you?"

"I says Auntie the witch don't beat me."

"You have any money on you, Jackie? We can share another fish and chips."

In a threatening voice: "Don't call me Jackie."

"Sorry. Can you loan me a few p till we get home?"

Though reluctant, he dug a fifty-pence piece from his pocket, and Lydia went to the wagon and had her order doused with vinegar and salt. By the time she returned to Jacob, the oil had soaked through the paper. Jacob said he wasn't hungry, but when she unwrapped the package he leaned into the steam and put his fingers in. He blew on a hot chip, just as she did. The wagon backfired and took off, and they were alone.

Their fingers collided as they battled for the last chip. "I got it," he said.

"I didn't want it anyway."

"You did, you did."

She did, so she changed the subject, asking instead if he was cold. "We could head back to my flat, where it's warmer. I have snails, you know."

He didn't seem particularly interested. "I have two millipedes and some ants and a real beauty of a mantis."

"What else?"

"That's not enough?"

He was clearly disappointed, but stood anyhow, giving Lydia a warm, chubby, very childlike hand. On the way down Seven Sisters Road, Jacob said he'd tell Lydia about his day if she told who dressed her. She said she dressed herself. He played football, she ran. They were nearly on Lydia's street when Jacob said he had been very good in school and hadn't stood until he was dismissed. Then instead of walking to the front and waiting for Mr. Cousins, he went out back and ran down the path where no one could see him, and threw his narsty old books into the bushes because he was never going back to school. Then he found the tube—that was easy. He'd seen it a million times. He took the lift downstairs and it was fun, so he took it back up then down again then up. The man in the lift made an ugly face so after this ride he stayed down. He gave the ticket seller Aunt Lydia's postcard —the one with the Beefeater on the front and her address on the back. The man didn't know where the address was, but he checked in a book and when he found the right street, leaned toward Jacob, from his seat behind the glass, and said, "You sure you're not up to some mischief, are you lad?" but he laughed and laughed so Jacob didn't have to run away. On a piece of paper, the ticket seller wrote out where to go, what train to take, when to make changes. He told Jacob to look for a nice lady, an old one, to show him where to get off. Could Jacob read? He offered to prove he could and the man said, "All alone, are you? What, does your mum work?"

They were at Lydia's house. She showed him her name on the outside doorjamb. "Be very quiet," she whispered. "I'm not supposed to have boys upstairs."

"Eyeglasses are horrid," Jacob said.

They were in the sitting room. Lydia was replacing a milk bottle on her windowsill.

"You look nasty in eyeglasses. Everyone laughs at you. Freaks wear eyeglasses."

When Lydia turned around, Jacob was sitting so still she convinced herself she hadn't heard a thing. A moment later, facing her, he said, "Ugly."

Lydia thought of saying, "How would you like it if I said that to you?" but that was one of Rose's lines and a poor sort of code, based on fear of retaliation. So she said, "Don't be rude to me, you little varmint."

Jacob squirmed in his seat, picked at his nose, and made his milk slosh over the side of his glass. Then he stood up and said, "You're going to send me home."

"Sit down, I hadn't thought of sending you anywhere." Her father used to tell her he'd give her back to the Indians when she was naughty.

"You'll tell on me."

"That I will. But I'm sure when your parents know you're safe with Auntie the bespectacled witch, everything will be hunky-dory."

He ripped his coat off the back of the chair and struggled to put it on.

"They'll get nightmares if I don't tell them where you are," Lydia said.

The jacket dropped to the floor. "What kind?"

"Nightmares about you being run over or kidnapped by horrible villains or strung up by your toes by ogres."

He jumped up and hollered, "Ogres! Ogres!" until he got tired and remembered he was angry. The stern face was put back on, the coat picked up. Lydia asked Jacob to wait while she got him a hat. She went into the bedroom and found her stocking cap. Pulling it down to her eyebrows, she lumbered into the hallway, arms straight out in a pantomime of a sleepwalker. "Where are you, Jacob? I can't see."

She stumbled around, hitting against the sink, making a robot-style pivot on her heels, nearly falling down the stairs, another pivot, and while his head was thrown back in laughter, she grabbed him at the waist and carried him into the bedroom.

"Auntie can't see! Auntie can't see!" he cried, collapsing onto the bed.

He fell asleep. Then she did. Ten minutes later, she left him snoring softly and went downstairs to call the Sandersons.

They hadn't been worried about Jacob because on Thursday he went to football camp straight from school, and he wasn't due in for another fifteen minutes. They refused to believe that *their* Jacob was upstairs in Lydia's flat, and with a parental logic that escaped Lydia, they took turns on the phone proving to each other why she was wrong. There was no reason he'd be in Finsbury Park; there was no earthly way he could have gotten there; it was ludicrous to suggest he'd skip football camp. To quiet them, Lydia said maybe they were both right. She'd call back in fifteen minutes in case the real Jacob Sanderson showed up in Hampstead, proving the one upstairs to be the clone.

They believed her finally, and now took turns on the phone outdoing each other's irritation, husband grabbing the receiver from the wife and back again. There was school the next day;

he was sneaky running off; they shouldn't reward him for his mischief; he was spoiled as it was ... "Stop! Stop!" Lydia shouted, since by now the battle was between the two of them, and Jacob had been forgotten. "I'm leaving London soon. Please let me have one day with him."

"No!" said Jill.

"Just one day," said Peter, hanging up.

The last word won.

She went into the sitting room, tore off a small piece of lettuce for her snails, and dropped it into the bowl. With small sucking motions they crept from every corner, until they covered the lettuce. They weren't all that slow. Their pace was steady, constant. She imagined them breathing *huh huh huh* then heard herself breathing, running, the squeak of sneakers, Kramer below, arms arched over his head. She wondered how he remembered her and if, one day in the backyard of his stucco house, he called to his new blond girl friend and said, "Hurry, quick, wait until you see this beautiful lacewing!"

Jacob was still asleep when Lydia woke the next morning, so she dressed and went out to the Greek store on Seven Sisters. The owner was dragging his cartons of kitchenware out onto the street, just setting up shop. Bananas were strung across the window. She bought currant jam and bread and took three bananas, making a gap in the yellow curtain.

At breakfast Jacob complained about the flavor of the jam and after listening in silence, Lydia said, "This isn't a restaurant, you know." Rose again. How embarrassing.

They went to the zoo: his choice. Jacob was very interested in eating and only sporadically interested in the animals. The other people were very interested in Jacob. He liked the camels. He admired their eyelashes and called, "Here, camel, here, camel," even to the nearby llamas and vicunas. He inhaled with pleasure their sharp odors, and pointed when they chewed with great hinged jaws. After about a half-hour with the camels, the clouds parted, and when the sun appeared, it was as white and brilliant as in L.A. Remembering her trip with Harold twenty years before, Lydia suggested they trot up the hill and look at giraffes. Jacob wasn't interested until she told him they had long eyelashes. Then he waved good-bye to the camels, "Good-bye camels, good-bye camels," held on to the guardrail, and dragged his body stiff-legged up the incline.

Lydia told him giraffes ate cactus and were afraid of heights. They were friendly with gnus, ostriches, and zebra. Jacob made fun of the way Lydia said zebra, and sang "I'm a g-nu, how do you do."

The giraffes stood close to the people, the sun behind their pretty faces. Lydia stepped back and shaded her eyes to see. Jacob stepped farther back, shaded his eyes, squinted, and said, "They're stupid." It was no more animals after that. It was hot chocolate and a Kit-Kat and let go of my hand. He walked ahead of Lydia and when she caught up to him, he dawdled, pretending to care about tapirs and warthogs.

She was exhausted by the time they reached the snack bar. Jacob went to get their hot chocolate, and Lydia, finding the cleanest-looking table, collapsed in an orange plastic chair by the window. Outside a busload of children pulled up. They walked in twos, like in the Madeleine stories of long ago. She watched until Jacob's voice distracted her. He was giving his order to the counterman, hollering and articulating slowly, as if the man were deaf and foreign. The man put the order on a tray, and leaned over to watch Jacob get the tray against his chest, balancing it with his good hand and the deformed one. He turned—it was balanced beautifully—screwed up his face, and headed toward a woman who had dark hair and glasses, but otherwise looked much different from Lydia. She was fat and fiftyish, for a start.

"I'm here," Lydia said.

Jacob froze, listening. This time Lydia stood up before she called to him. She'd spent enough time trying to recognize friends by the way they walked or their general shape to figure out Jacob's problem. "Here!" she said again, waving.

When he got to the table, he dutifully placed the hot chocolate in front of Lydia, and then sat down. The foil from the Kit-Kat kept him busy for a while, but when the chocolate was gone, and the foil was as tight and small as a ballbearing, he said, "I want to go home."

"Okay," said Lydia. "But will you first tell me why you call me Auntie the witch?"

"You know, Auntie."

"Yeah, but I forget. Tell me again."

"Because black, black, black." All four upper teeth were white and perfectly square, gaps between each, reserving space for the future.

"Pretty new choppers, aren't they?"

"Eh?"

"Choppers." Lydia made animal chewing sounds. She snorted, grunted, and gnashed her teeth. When he stopped laughing she said, "So you think I'm ugly, do you?"

"No, Auntie."

"But my glasses are."

Chest thrust against the table, Jacob began kicking the hollow metal table post. "Everyone laughs at you in eyeglasses. Freaks wear eyeglasses."

"What's a freak?"

"A boy who wears eyeglasses."

"That sounds like the kind of thing you heard some idiot in school say. Some fat kid with a runny nose and rats in his pockets."

Jacob dropped his foil ball and made a face. Lydia found it near her feet. "A story for you," she said. Once upon a time whenever she was unhappy she stopped wearing her glasses. She thought if she didn't see all the dirt and shabbiness in the street, the sick and mean-looking people, she'd feel better. But the world became an obstacle course. Things jumped out at her. Bumps in the haze became taxis running the lights. Giant loping beasts were sheepdogs, quite friendly close up. The crazy person on the corner, whom she dodged to avoid, turned out to be a friend, waving and whistling, one of the few who understood that Lydia couldn't see. Most of the others thought she was a snob because she never returned their smiles and greetings, never having seen them. Now she wore her glasses.

"Mummy wrote a letter to Mrs. Tanis. Mummy wrote and spoiled everything. She tattled and spoiled everything. She told Mrs. Tanis."

The hollow metal table post was chiming from his kicks.

"Mrs. Tanis made you wear the glasses?"

"Ugly witch. She spoiled everything. Reading Mummy's letter, Jacob Sanderson come here this instant. Up to the front. Your mummy says—I hate her, Auntie. Ralph Iverson and Eugene and Martin, they laughed."

Jacob got up and marched over to Lydia. "She says, she says. I want to go home, Auntie." Then: "Your mummy says you better wear your eyeglasses. Where are your eyeglasses?"

Lydia, playing Jacob, said, "I hid them under my bed."

"*She* had them and they laughed. She had them in her drawer, and your mummy says— And she squeezed me and they laughed. And she squeezed me arm and—show the class how lovely you look in your new eyeglasses, Jacob Sanderson. I buried them, Auntie. Ralph and Martin, they laughed."

Lydia imagined Mrs. Tanis to be a large, muscular woman, who kept her hand clamped around his upper arm, shaking him until it was time for a good yank, which meant stay still. That type would lean over to put his glasses on, and her ugly grimace would make him flinch. For spite, she'd let them rest askew, the frame on a diagonal, then grasping his shoulders, turn him around to show the class. They *would* laugh. Jacob stood next to Lydia, pushing away the arms meant to go around him. What could she tell him when she had only learned three weeks before that good values aren't always effective, that reason and compassion often fail to work. Rose's credo, Even-Steven, was moral but ineffective in a child's world. The kid with the biggest mouth got the biggest bite. There were no rewards for the runt, the freak, the child who turns the other cheek. The teacher gives him crayons with the ends already chewed off by the perfect child. . . . It was awful to fight, but pure virtue wouldn't help him survive.

"No one else in your class wears eyeglasses? Or braces on their teeth—bands—what do you call them?"

"Lawrence Moody metal mouth, he got all silver on his teeth."

"You think he's a freak?"

"Lawrence Moody metal mouth *is* a freak, Auntie."

"Because he's got braces on his teeth?"

"He don't have teeth up here and his mummy walks him home from school."

"Does he have any friends?"

"Lawrence plays with Lloyd, Auntie. Lloyd is a freak, Auntie. Lloyd is an idiot." Ijit, he said.

"Was Lloyd his friend before Lawrence's teeth got messed up?"

"Lloyd *is* Lawrence's best friend. He's an idiot." Jacob was exasperated, as if his aunt were an idiot, too.

"Jacob, it doesn't make a difference if you wear eyeglasses. Do you know why?"

He jumped out of his seat and stood, tensed, ready to run. She wished she could distract him or make him laugh—most of all that there were something smart to say.

"Mummy says I'm like all the other children."

"Well, that's not really true. I bet there isn't a single boy with choppers as nice as yours. Or a temper as bad. I bet there are stupider boys—"

"Martin Seehof cannot read baby books. Martin Seehof cannot read a bloody thing."

"Did I ever tell you I was born wearing glasses? Tiny little glasses, a bright fire-engine red."

"You were *born* wearing eyeglasses?" This time when Lydia held out her arms, he went over to snuggle in a softer seat: her lap.

"Not actually born with them, but I've had them for so long it's as if I was born with them. I never minded wearing glasses until my mother told me I shouldn't feel too bad because inside I was like all the other children. The more I thought about it, the less I liked it. So I began eating dog biscuits. Everyone else ate Oreos and vanilla wafers, and I figured if I ate dog biscuits, I wouldn't be just like everyone else."

"You ate dog biscuits? That's stupider than Vasant. Vasant eats paste. Mrs. Tanis says his insides will get glued up."

"They tasted awful—very gritty. But when cookie time came, I was a big hit."

"You ate dog biscuits, Auntie? What did your dog eat?"

"We didn't have a dog."

"Where did you get dog biscuits?"

"In the supermarket."

"You ate dog biscuits? What else, Auntie?" Jacob was swinging his legs, and though he missed the center post, he got the legs of the chair and Lydia's legs. "Go on, Auntie. Tell me what else you et."

"After a while the kids stopped paying attention to the dog biscuits, so I came to school in a bright yellow baseball cap and wore it all day long. I had to stay after school because I wouldn't take it off during flag salute."

By junior high school the change was startling. Boys entered into the picture, and acceptance became paramount. She was inept. She never learned what was creepy to wear (dresses that buttoned in the back, ankle socks) or how to act. Her classmates called attention to her oddness, making her realize that the dog biscuits and the baseball cap were irrelevant because she *was* odd. Jacob said, "Tell me, Auntie," but all grown up, the names they called her still stung. He persisted, and feeling the heat from each insult, the shame, she recited, like the twelve plagues God brought down on the Egyptians, "Four-eyes, tin teeth, frizz bomb, Uncle Ben. Uncle Ben was the most hateful. They called me that because I had dark skin and curly hair. And I was flat-chested—I wasn't as grown-up-looking as the other girls. I got sick a lot in the seventh and eighth grades, and whatever I didn't catch I faked. I'd wake up in the morning and say, 'Ma, I don't *feel* good.'"

Jacob laughed at her imitation of Lydia at twelve, but she remembered lying in bed, refusing to go to school because the boys in the back (there were always boys in the back, real or imagined) taunted her about—what was it this time? When she knew an answer in class, she jumped up and down, waving both arms, blurting excitedly, "I have two things to say!" So they named her "Two Things to Say," as if she were an Indian. She hadn't known until then girls were supposed to be reticent.

"So when my mother took me shopping I asked for a dress like Judi Ann and sneakers like Rema."

Jacob jumped up, shouting, "You didn't want to be a freak!"

"Right, but it didn't matter if I wore my sweatshirt inside out or had pointy-toed sneakers."

He was hopping on one foot now, wanting more, but she had run out of stories. She said at last, "Look, Jacob, if you wear your glasses at least you'll be able to tell the mean faces from the nice ones. Because there are always going to be idiots who call you names. You have to forget about them instead of trying to copy them. That fat kid with rats in his pockets—"

"Robert, I hate him, I *hate* him!"

Jacob ran straight across the cafeteria, smack into a busboy carrying a tray. Butts and paper were knocked over; half-filled cups of chocolate spilled. He panicked, and whirled around to race the other way. Lydia couldn't stop him as he wove through tables and chairs, but when he headed for a corner, she trapped him in her arms and held tightly. People turned to watch him struggle and kick. A tsk; a tall man demanding Lydia leave the child alone. "I hate him! I hate him!" Jacob screamed, until exhausted he began to cry. Then his crying could not be soothed. Lydia didn't have answers. There weren't any answers to give.

"Jacob," she said. "Turn around and let Auntie see your face."

He tucked his head under his arm like a wounded animal. She said, "How many boys in your class can find their way to Finsbury Park all alone at night and not be scared? Aye? You tell me."

"Vasant can."

"Then where is he? Show me this Vasant who can find his way to Finsbury Park."

"He's home, Auntie."

"Is he your friend?"

A nod.

"What does he do, besides eating paste?"

"He quacks, Auntie. Vasant quacks like a duck."

"That's pretty good."

"And he's got all kinds of things his dad gave him. He's got a black bag like a real doctor and he's got a special stick and he's got a special thing that—" He took a deep breath. "I want to go home."

They left the zoo. Lydia didn't know whether home meant Hampstead or her flat, and when they were on the street, she said, "Do you know which way to go?"

He ran after a woman, stopping her before she crossed the street. "Where's the tubes?" he shouted.

Hampstead was home, and though he said quite bluntly he was old enough to go alone, Lydia followed. She let him ask for the right train and watched him squint and stand on his toes to read the signs. She hoped for a kiss when they reached Frognal, a big hug, a proper good-bye. But eyeglasses, angry parents, the laughter at school, and Auntie were all forgotten for now. He wanted to be home and ran ahead without her.

32

MINUTES after she polished off the last bit of trifle, Peter dug in his trouser pockets, jingled his keys, and told Jill he'd drive Lydia home. "YOU SHOULD'VE DRIVEN ME HOME THE FIRST NIGHT!" she shouted, but the car radio was turned up so loud she wasn't sure he heard. Outside it was pouring.

Her street was so short in the street guide only COL, the first three letters of the name, fit onto the allotted space. Peter was able to find the street and her house without asking directions. Lydia wondered if he'd been here before.

"Do you want to come up for a few minutes?"

"Thank you, no," he said, pulling the key from the ignition and plunging them into silence. He made no move, and though Lydia sensed he had something to say, his demeanor made her unsure she wanted to hear just what it was. Dinner with the Sandersons had been peaceful and familiar, interchangeable with her first dinner if Tara hadn't said, "For dessert we have trifle, Aunt Lydia. Remember how much you ate last time? Daddy couldn't believe a little person could eat so much."

"We can sit in a little café up on Seven Sisters if you like," Lydia said.

Peter said, "All right," then getting out of the car repeated "café," the way Lydia pronounced it. "Caff. You're certainly getting English, aren't you?"

"I try to make myself understood. For instance, I don't say tomahto, but I say aubergine, since who ever heard of an eggplant around here."

"That's what's easiest to learn," said Peter. "The different words—elevator, lift; eggplant, aubergine. But that hardly matters, as you well know."

She well knew. Only after months in England was she able to understand the difficulties in traveling to a foreign country where the language was the same as at home. If, she told Peter, she'd moved to France, by the time she was fluent in French, she'd be on her way to understanding nuance and gesture. But when she'd arrived at his house, she was so delighted to be sharing the same words, she took far too long to notice that the meanings and intentions were different.

Inside the café, Peter tested tables with his palms until he found one that wasn't shaky. Their centerpiece was a plastic cherub, stark naked. Peter's arm shot up; he ordered two teas.

In an instant, tea was delivered by the owner, who stood at their table, beaming at them long after Peter had said, "Thank you" and "That'll be all."

When the owner left, Lydia said, "Everyone thinks I'm Greek." Peter smiled; his mood no longer seemed so ominous. Creating a whirlpool in his teacup, he began to talk about *his* first year abroad, and all the surprises that greeted him there. No one walked—the sidewalks were absolutely barren. The first three women he dated had the habit of slapping him when they felt playful. And the Jewish families he met—everyone was always hugging and kissing and talking about their traumas.

"Not Jill," said Lydia.

"Yes, and she was the first American woman I could fathom. In so many ways she was familiar, as if we'd grown up beside each other." What a surprise then, the first time she took him home. In the bosom of her family, she was Jilly to her parents —Rosie and Maurie (How do you do, they said, introducing themselves with their diminutives). "And you, of course, were Baby Lydie."

That was true. Lydia missed their warmth, her morning kiss. She thought how the closeness she failed to have with her father was something Jill never dreamed of wanting. Their distance— Lydia's and her father's—was regarded as intimacy by Jill.

A group of dark-eyed people entered the café and pushed two tables together. The music that came from the old record player was scratched, warped, and tinny. No one seemed to mind.

"You really love him, don't you?" Peter said. Lydia went

through her litany (Daddy, Kramer, Zeyde) wondering who he meant until he added: "He pouted for a week when you left Hampstead. I kept finding him in your room, looking through the wardrobe drawers."

His bare head gleamed, as if Mrs. Bannon had lemon-oiled it that morning. "He'll be okay, don't you think?" Lydia said.

"Jill seems to think it'll be worse for him when he's a teen-ager, but then again, she's never gotten over her discomfort, so it's difficult for her to imagine that others can. She loves him, but she can't forget, the way I do. Have you ever seen a newborn, Lydia? Ugly, most of them. They're red and splotchy. Tara was like that. She was a little water rat when she was born, a wrinkled little thing. Jacob was magnificent. Perfect. Bald-headed like me but beautiful. She wouldn't nurse him because Tara, she said, would be jealous seeing Jacob at Mummy's breast. So she took those pills that made her milk dry up, and I held Jacob and fed him. I turned that upstairs room into a study when he was born, so I could stay home and be with my son. And Jill stayed with Tara so Tara wouldn't be jealous of the baby."

"But she is jealous of him."

"She is. I suppose because he gets pity and she needs none."

Peter glanced furtively at the people nearby, who were giving the waiter their order in Greek. Satisfied they weren't staring at him, he unbuttoned his jacket, and reached for something in his breast pocket. Lydia had a strange feeling that they were playing a scene in an old grade-B detective movie. The meeting in a remote café. Dark, mysterious strangers. An envelope removed from the agent's breast pocket. His hand on top of it, sliding it across the table. "It's all so delicate, you know. One builds a house for shelter. There isn't any shelter. Your father never worried about Jill because she was sheltered, she had me. But Lydia, his baby, was all alone. We assume you spent all your money—"

"Why did she hate him?" Lydia asked.

"Hate is an awfully strong word. He was, after all, her father."

There was no logic in statements like that, but she was silent, she couldn't explain. The envelope was in front of her, cream-colored, a formal invitation. Mr. and Mrs. Peter Sanderson request—

"Your plane fare. You'll starve before you get home on your salary."

"No!" said Lydia. "I told Jill I have money. I'm saving it for next year, so I can finish up my dissertation." She slid the envelope back.

It was in front of her again.

Lydia got up to leave the café. Peter followed, picking up the envelope, she supposed. She didn't turn around to check.

In the street, he turned his trench coat collar up, and buried his hands deep in his pockets. She felt safe back in the movie again.

They stood in the dim light at her door, telling each other how awful it was to say good-bye, the awkwardness of it. She took her key out, ready to leave. She wanted to kiss him, but she felt him stiffen, so she pulled back.

"You'll take care of yourself?" he said.

She promised she would.

Peter took his hand from his pocket and extended it. Lydia grasped it with her own. When he turned away, she felt the rough edges of a note.

Inside her building, under stronger lights, she saw it was a twenty.

33

WHEN Lydia returned to Cage, Mr. Hatchett's messenger requested she come into the repair room immediately. Should she fake a cough? Walk with a limp? Lydia hung up her coat and went in.

Mr. Hatchett was standing at his desk, arms held straight out, and in them a white lab coat pressed so stiffly it didn't unfurl when he shook it. "We at Cage"—in his attempt to be formal his voice rose an octave—"should be awfully pleased if you accept the position of manager—manageress, so to speak—of the repair crew."

"I couldn't."

He tossed the coat to her, all formality gone for now. "Come on, Lydia my girl. What say we sort out the details over a pint. Time cards, schedules—there's a whole lot of rubbish."

Fantastic, her rise in the organization. Lydia went back to her seat but found it hard to work. Having been proclaimed manager she felt out of place in her little wooden seat between Diane and Mary Three just as before. So at ten she interviewed herself. Yes, she said, I spotted her the day she walked in. I said, "This is a leader, this is a tough, responsible, reliable person." She'd still flick, read, and staple with the others (thinking about it made her giddy) but Bill said she was to bark. "Put a little growl in the voice, my girl."

The lunch bell rang. Bill escorted Lydia to a spare little pub down the block. It was dark inside and the bar was hardly six feet long. The barmaid called out to Bill when she saw him, and catching Lydia's eye said, "Watch out for that one, love. He's a devil, he is," and winked.

"She's just a good friend of the wife, aren't you?" Bill put his arm around Lydia and when she eased away, he did, too.

They took the booth closest to the door and when both had taken good long drafts, Bill said, "If it's Diane holding you back, I wouldn't worry. I'll tell you something no one else knows and I figure you won't let on about it, seeing as you aren't always in the corners with the lot of them, or taking off to the loo in pairs like the rest of them do. When they do that I get so bloody mad I could take them by the scruff of the neck and throw them the bloody hell out. What, does one of them pull the chain while the other one pisses? What is all this?" Bill finished half the glass in one swallow and leaned across the table. "You don't do that. You don't fancy girls very much, do you, Lydia?"

"As friends I do."

"I mean, I don't see you hurrying off to the loo with someone's nose in your bloody ear. I'll bet you don't have a lot of girl friends, you know, away from Cage."

"I don't and I'm sorry for it."

"Not me, Lydia. The way I figure it, they're only your friend when it's good times, but if you're in a bit of a jam, then where are they? Hiding under their bloody beds if you come asking for this or for that. Not me. My missus she can't learn her lesson. She's always blowing off about this one did this and that one did that and I says, 'Get rid of 'em. Get rid of the whole lot of 'em. What do you get out of it? Better to use your time to some good than spend it gossiping with them.' "

Lydia envied Bill's wife for having this one and that one to complain about. Bill was saying it was family you could count on, blood being thicker than water. "After all, Lydia, family is family. Brothers are brothers and sisters are sisters and there's not much they can do about it, is there?"

"There isn't much they can do about it. But friends have chosen you. They've picked you out from the others."

"Wrong, Lydia. You've got a bit of luck having no husband or babies, no mum to see get old and wet herself like a baby and hardly know you except once in a while. But you can't expect your friends to stick around when things get a bit rough."

"Not all of them, but the ones that do—" If you put your glasses on, you can tell the friendly faces from the mean ones, she thought.

Bill got another pint for himself, took a long swallow, wiped the foam off his mouth, and leaned across the table. Lydia was lucky being free and free was what she was. He'd fancy being alone. He'd go off to some tropical paradise, some sunny place, maybe hire some bloke to fan him off when it got hot. That's all he'd want. Maybe ... He stood up and the scowl was replaced with a smile, dimples and all. He made broad motions with his arms and waved two men over. She thought by his happiness they were long lost brothers, but in the course of the conversation, it appeared he'd seen them just the day before. Arms around shoulders, another round was ordered, then, glasses raised, they toasted to Lydia's success.

A half-hour later, she stood in a beery haze, and left them talking about a team and a bet, a missus and some money, and floated back to Cage to try on her white coat.

Ammonia! Ammonia! She ran and at night their faces merged, their bodies were one; tie tack, knitted tie, naked scalp, red ears, ball in a hoop, pleated pants, black hair, immigrant eyes, muscular shoulders, suspenders in L.A., little pushed-in teeth, alligator shirts, headphones, Daddy, Kramer, Zeyde, Daddy, Kramer, Zeyde, bent over a microscope; skin, blood, lashes, hair ...

One warm May evening after her run, she walked down Seven Sisters and thought how fortunate she was to have been loved so deeply.

At work the next day, she stood at the window, staring out at the brick wall. Of course she was sad, having lost them.

She put her hand up to her nose and saw the streaks of red. "Dust," she said. "It makes my nose bleed."

34

JUNE AGAIN, and morning. The windows didn't open and no cool air came out of the vents. Lydia plunged an arm up to the elbow, digging for keys at the bottom of her pack. When she felt them, she withdrew her empty hand, relieved. Five minutes later, she searched again, jingled them this time, counted to make sure the outside, two inside, and mailbox keys still hung on the chain.

Traffic on the Van Wyck snaked forward, chrome glinting in a mean white sun. Some of the bus passengers, glancing outside, coughed into handkerchiefs, choking from the filth. Lydia smiled. Her seatmate adjusted his tie. He was a toothless man. His hat was pulled so low his ears bent forward, overlapping the brim. His shirt, once white, was shades of yellow. Gray rivers ran down the front, sauce spots measled the fabric. The tie, which he straightened, tucked in his belt, untucked, adjusted, petted, tied and retied, was iridescent hot pink. Tightening the knot once again, he gave a quick sidelong glance at Lydia and said, "Quit the grinning, sister."

Tourist, she thought, hearing his American accent. Then she heard another voice, another American accent. Home. Sweat trickled down her back. Long ago she ran barefoot, tiptoed under lawn sprinklers and felt the same surprise of cold droplets of water.

In front of the East Side Terminal, she stuck her arm straight up and in an instant was sprawled in a back seat, the door not yet closed, the cab in midtown traffic. She squinted, looking at the faces of pedestrians and drivers, feeling she'd recognize someone soon. It was her city, after all. But there were strangers here and until Seventh Avenue she was disappointed, afraid she'd be an alien again.

Summer in the city: dog shit steaming on the sidewalk, trash lining the street, flies, spindly trees put up yearly by block associations, the people much hardier than the greenery.

The moaners, mumblers, and pinchers graced Sheridan Square. The court jester in tights, spots of rouge on his face, recited Shakespeare in front of the cigar store. Ken from Kentucky rolled by, white party dress, skates, blessing people with his magic wand. And the onion salesman on his stoop outside the supermarket, hawking his single red onion. "Fifty cents! Onion! Onion! Fifty cents, you got an onion for your loved one!"

Cars and trucks blaring horns, people talking, laughing, hawking onions. London was quiet, a city of echoes. New York was rude. Lydia wanted to walk up every street. There'd be other days, but never a time she so acutely felt the joy of home.

More sidewalk cafés than last year. Fewer plant stores. A mounted policeman, way up there on his sleek steed. Peter once had a horse named Ebony. Kramer had a clubfooted chicken named Blackie. Only Kramer could have had a pet chicken. Lydia walked south on Seventh Avenue, laughing. She turned into Rosemary's and stood in the doorway to announce her arrival. Rosemary's: where she'd sat countless times with Kramer, where she and Jill had had their last intimate talk. No one recognized Lydia. No one glanced up from eggs and coffee when she said, "Yoo-hoo, I'm home." But that night when friends were outdoing each others' crazy-people stories, she'd be remembered. "The weirdest thing happened to me this morning. I was having breakfast at Rosemary's when this lady plants herself in the doorway, cups her hands around her mouth and calls Yoo-hoo, I'm home, then doubles over cackling maniacally. Early in the morning, I swear it."

Her building stood, all the bricks in place. John, wearing black gloves and low-waisted jeans, was sweeping the sidewalk, saying hello to everyone who walked by, carrying on conversations that lasted only until they passed. The sun had darkened Lydia's glasses. She held her breath and squeezed the keys in her palm so they wouldn't jangle. She would achieve the impossible by entering the building without John noticing. She stepped into the lobby, put the key into the lock, and—"Lydia! Jesus, mother of Mary"—The key worked and she was safe inside. She heard John say, "Mr. Mazucci, nice day, yeah, yeah."

The hall was cool; no mail in her box. She climbed the stairs two at a time, then stuck both keys into the locks and pushed the door open. Foof! What a smell. A trail of *Watchtowers*, block association leaflets, and specials from the supermarket made a white pathway into the living room, one pushing the next a step forward, a year's worth. Locking the second lock had paid off: No one had been inside the apartment.

Lydia tried the faucets, flushed the toilet, and opened the cabinets as if this were an apartment for rent. The morning sun shone onto the kitchen table, lighting the glistening fuzz: dirt, asbestos, ash, misplaced matter sprinkled like December's first snow on all the tables, the chairs, and the shelves. She lay on the living-room rug and made an angel in the dust.

Andy once asked if she played Gandhi. Lydia looked at the roach-egg cases and said, as Jacob might have: Yuch. No Gandhi she. Then she saw her bed, which had been neatly made up, the pillows fluffed underneath the spread. There was something funny and pathetic—in the midst of all that chaos, she had made her bed. "Poor Lydia," she said, as if referring to someone else. Dried leaves were sprinkled on the blanket, twigs and stems in hanging pots. And in her beautiful terrarium, everything was dead. There was always regret. She wasn't nice enough, she wasn't sad enough, she should have left her lucky scarf to Margaret. There was no way to make a clean break. Look at that! Brown sludge at the bottom of the jug; an inch of dead brine shrimp. Lydia stood on her bed and took the glass globe off an upper shelf. Once her mealworms lived on an all-bran bed. Now it was powdery waste, no bran. She removed the wire mesh and lifted a chunk of withered gray potato, porous from dozens of tunnels bored through. She started to place it back in the globe when she saw a faint ripple, like a crab under sand. Searching through the powder she found two black beetles and one pale pupa, a sleepy thing lying in a half-circle. They were the most adaptable, able to metabolize starch into water. A whole year on a single chunk of potato. Not bad. At the market she'd buy them a potato, and for herself pine-scented cleaner and ammonia. *Am-*

monia! The windows, never clean, were milky now. Floor cleaner, vacuum bags, bleach. She found a sheet of paper in her desk drawer and made a list.

Wood, oven, tile, porcelain, window, dish, upholstery. Twenty dollars spent on cleansers and implements. Mop, broom, chamois, sponge. When she'd finished shopping she tied up her hair in a kerchief and changed into jeans and the same soft shirt she wore when she and Kramer painted the apartment two years ago. She was filling a bucket with suds when the phone rang. This time she answered it.

"Lydia, hi, you just get in?"

Her neat stack of memories spilled over, hopelessly disordered. She'd never be able to replace them now. "This isn't true," she said. Lion's-claw chair, John in the country, Jill's backyard, la la la. "Where are you?"

"Los Angeles. You don't sound happy to hear from me."

"Happy isn't exactly the word for it, Kramer."

"I've been trying to get you for so long if it wasn't for rent control, I would have figured you moved. Are you living with someone else? Is he there? Maybe you aren't free to talk—"

"I'm here alone, relatively."

"You have a boyfriend?"

Lydia sat in the rocking chair as she had the first night they were together. It creaked; she laughed.

"Watch, you're going to tell me you're married and have a kid. Is that true? Well, leave the bastard, I say."

He was chuckling, the old charmer. Out of her life for a whole year, and now he had popped in to make a few jokes, win her heart, then leave again. "I'm going to get off the phone and unpack," she said, still unable to admit to housecleaning.

"Unpack? Lydia, don't unpack. That's just what I've been calling to tell you. For weeks—no, *months,* it seems. I wrote you —the letter wasn't returned addressee unknown. I got this job down in the Philippines. A lot of pictures are being made down there these days because labor's cheap. We could get a house, and Michael says servants cost next to nothing. You wouldn't have to wash dishes, Lyd."

"Michael's in Los Angeles?"

"Didn't you know? He moved here in February. The last

straw, he said, came the night he was taking the IRT back from Fifty-first Street. There was this subway holdup, just like *The French Connection.* He says he tried to get in touch with you but you were always out."

"And Beth? She never answered my letter."

"Beth and Michael are co-writing the screenplay for this Philippine extravaganza."

"What about her business?"

"She sold her share, Lyd."

"What a dumb thing to do."

"Lydia, not to have an argument with you after all these months, I'd like to say that your sole flaw has always been a lack of romance. What good was the film distribution business when Michael was in L.A.? It's not like what happened to us. It was her job, not some lifelong dream. Besides, you have to admit, the Philippines is kind of exotic—and warm. You'd get some color in your cheeks, Lydie."

"A lack of *ro*mance?" said Lydia. A lack of romance? Why was it one man told her she was the most romantic woman alive and another that she lacked romance? Neither of them was talking about the Lydia she knew. Why would she want to go to the Philippines? What did that have to do with romance?

"I'd rather be in Philadelphia."

"Are you kidding? Michael says Philly's *The Asphalt Jungle.* Gangs are very big again. Knifings, the works. Lydie, look, I know this is sudden and it's been a long time, but I've missed you a lot, honest to Christ. I've never been good at saying these things but—"

"Oh God," said Lydia, rocking slowly back and forth. It took so long to learn to live without him, and now he was back on the phone saying she lacked romance.

"—say you'll come, Lyd. We were good together, you know we were. Remember how you always said we fit? This never should've happened. It was a huge, fucking blunder—"

"What are you doing in the Philippines?"

"Me? The sound man."

"You left New York to become a director."

"Lydia, you know what it's like out here? There's a recession and business is not good. The streets of Hollywood are filled with very nervous people. Twenty million resting on a picture, they're bound to be nervous. Did you know that the ad budget for *King Kong* was more money than the entire gross national product of the Philippines?"

"What about your screenplay?"

"These guys don't want original screenplays. They want a proven property like an adaptation of a novel. What Beth and Michael are doing—it's all wham, bam, nurse gets raped, goes bananas, guns down the entire male population of Sulphur Springs—I can't write that. To tell you the truth, when I first came out here, I thought if it would get me a job directing, I'd try. So I did, I don't know, twenty treatments. Then one day I sat down and said, Why am I knocking my brains out? Do I want to be like those guys? One's asthmatic, one twitches all over, one is covered with eczema—Christ, a lot of sickies."

The apartment was hot and stuffy. Lydia's throat ached. She went over the shopping list in her head and decided to add cough drops.

"I'm out of the studio, which was what I wanted, and already I've gotten some good work down here, so I can't complain. No more industrials. No more American Cancer Society or Best Foods. Lydia, I don't know, ambition is fine, but not at the expense of a good life. That's what I've learned out here. I want some balance; I don't want to spend the rest of my days hustling. What about you? I haven't seen your name in the paper and I keep looking. I get *The New York Times* every day."

"I never went back to school."

"I don't believe it. I just don't— You didn't go back to school? What happened to your dissertation?"

"It's probably dusty. I haven't touched it in a year."

"Lydia. You didn't come with me because you were working on your dissertation."

"Kramer, did you ever ask me? Did you ever say—Lydia come with me?"

"What do you mean, did I ever ask. You wouldn't have come."

"How do you know? You never asked."

"You were so wrapped up in school it would've been a waste of breath."

"Oh boy, is your memory ever slipping. You forget you had

your plans all made up a long time before we met. Every day you told me how you were leaving. It would've been a little presumptuous to pack my bags and hitch a free ride with you."

"Presumptuous? I loved you. You know that."

"Okay, I knew you loved me. But since you never said a single word about my—"

"I had respect for your career, for God's sake. I couldn't assume you'd just up and—"

"But you're doing that now."

"I thought you'd be done by now. And you could—I don't know—study some—"

"What are you doing in the Philippines anyhow? You went to Los Angeles to be a movie director."

"A major contribution before you were thirty, remember, Lydia? What happened, you gave up? Tell me, did you give up? I still love you, I don't care if you gave up. Tell me. Say *something*!"

"Stop shouting!"

"Well, if you gave it up you have to come out here now. I've been a fucking mess. This never should have happened, and anyhow, you're out of your mind to stay in that stinking apartment, rent control or not. And you can tell John he still owes me that twenty dollars."

"You tell him. And I didn't give up. I took a leave of absence, a sabbatical. I had personal problems."

"*You're* telling *me*?"

The harder she rocked, the less she felt herself shake. She put her feet on the edge of the seat to get more swing. "Johnny Guitar and Vienna, remember, Kramer? The bitterness of people who once loved each other. You shouldn't have called, it's unfair. You can't imagine what's happened."

Soft voice, the anger gone: "Tell me, Lydie. What happened?"

"I'm hanging up, it doesn't make a difference anymore. Goodbye, I've got to run—"

"I even bought a subscription to *Runner's World*. I looked for your name whenever there was a piece about an East-Coast race."

"Ha."

"Don't tell me you stopped running. You were compulsive. I thought you'd die if you stopped running."

"Every time I ran I saw you, Kramer. I had to recondition myself and run in the streets away from basketball courts."

"Are you careful of cars?"

"Yeah, I'm careful."

"What about the pollution, Lydie? The guy I run with wears a surgeon's mask."

"You run, Kramer?"

"Five miles a day. We could run together, Lydie—"

"God, I bet you're beautiful. Some poor woman—"

"Lydie, you wouldn't believe. There's a higher proportion of gigglers in L.A. than anyplace else on earth."

"Yeah, but the blonds."

"Blonds. Big deal."

"That's what you went out there for—"

"Now that's stupid, for Christ's sake. I came here because my job was a dead end. I came out here because I was making both of us miserable, remember? I mailed you my address, you never wrote. Blonds—Christ. Lydia, look. It's very warm down in the Philippines—semitropical, bugs as big as your fist. I'll buy you one of those stereo microscopes like your father promised you. Lydie, look, I'll stop asking. I'll hang up and never call again. Just tell me if you still love me. Didn't you think about me at all?"

"Oh, every once in a while," she said, tasting the salt of her own tears. She felt as if she were consuming herself: Lydia into Lydia, reborn inside out. "Of course I thought about you. I thought I couldn't live without you, I couldn't get over it. But then I did. Until a minute ago, I could think about you and feel warm and not get all worked up. You and my father and Zeyde—you were all part of my past, all memories."

"And this? Stop crying and tell me what this is?"

"This is something I've imagined. You're sweet and you sound exactly like the Kramer I loved because I've imagined it so many times."

"Lydie, please, this isn't a dream. Say it isn't a dream."

She was healthy now. She didn't have to worry she'd be swallowed up by love—that was part of the past, too. "Okay," she said. "This isn't a dream. I'll tell you what, Kramer. Why don't you come out to New York. I'm not kidding. We'll give it a try. We can find a new apartment, a fresh start."

There was static on the line. They heard another conversation, soft and indistinct. So much time passed it was as if they'd stopped talking in order to listen.

"I have a commitment," Kramer said at last. "I'm set to leave in two weeks. If I break it, I'll blow my chances out here. But look, I'm saying it now. I want you to come. I really do."

She shook her head. A year ago something might have worked out, but not now, not after she'd lost so much time. She remembered her father at the stoplight, the dream in which she could feel his shoulders, and smell his pipe tobacco. How vivid a fantasy could be. "Then it's a dream," she said. "And I'm sad because when I wake up, it'll be over, and you'll be gone again."

"Okay, forget it. I'll catch the next plane out, Lydia. I'll see you tomorrow."

Had he really said that? Had she said "Okay"? How had the call ended? She knew she hadn't said good-bye because it felt odd saying good-bye to a memory, a vision of someone running, tipping a ball into a hoop. The image ran its course and then her mind switched to something else, something more immediate. Lydia pulled a sheet of toilet paper off the roll and blew her nose. Kramer had said it was a stinking apartment.

She walked into the kitchen, smiling for the studio audience. "You're right, Kramer," she said. It was musty and smelled like an attic. It wasn't a question of most or least romantic, but merely one of bad timing, of geographical limits. Despite all the uncertainties of love, she wanted to try again, and though she knew she could live alone, she hoped she'd get to share her life with someone. But to sacrifice everything? That wasn't romantic, that was crazy. To go full circle from living in a closed, inflexible world to attempting selflessness was mad. Lydia opened the refrigerator door and was thrown across the room. The stench was unbelievable; a glimpse inside revealed black mold, a fur coat on every jar and bottle. She leaped forward and kicked it shut. It was hot in there. She tried the overhead switch and when the lights didn't shine, she remembered she hadn't paid Con Edison. Lydia laughed for the folks in Omaha. She laughed for the family in Duluth. She liked the sound of her own laughter so much—it was hearty, the tenor had changed. When she was steady on her feet, she stepped on a chair, opened a window, and aired out the place.